Praise for *The Midnight Rose*

'I finished *The Midnight Rose* on the flight back, and I loved it! What an absolutely fantastic storyteller – I was immediately immersed in the story, and absolutely compelled to keep reading to the very last page . . . A real treat'
Katherine Webb

'Irish-born Riley is quietly becoming a huge success story' *Red*

'A captivating read from Lucinda Riley. Ideal for a book club' *Daily Mail*

'Spellbinding storytelling' *Choice*

'A strong, often nostalgic offering'
*Daily Express Weekend*

'Romantic fiction at its most captivating'
*Lancashire Evening Post*

'This is a beautifully written story that captures the imagination'
*Shropshire Star*

Praise for *The Light Behind the Window*

'A fast-paced, suspenseful story flitting between the present day and World War II . . . Brilliant escapism'
*Red*

'A beautifully written book that secures Riley's authorial status and proves that her golden penmanship is no mere fluke . . . This is the perfect literary novel to move those readers who wish for something more fulfilling than chick-lit, yet just as entertaining, witty and heart-stopping. The language is dramatic yet truthful and Riley has such a delicate touch with mystery and intrigue that it's difficult to predict where the plot is going . . . Riley's descriptive nuances are so evocative, a TV drama is bound to be imminent. A literal and literary page-turner'
We Love This Book

'Just sink in and wallow'
Kate Saunders, *Saga*

'Yet again, I have been totally entertained by another great story that is well-written with an intricate plot that is multi-layered but tied together so well . . . I became really emotionally attached to these characters . . . This novel really is a joy to read, expertly woven together and mixing social history with family dramas and love and relationships – the perfect blend'
Random Things Through My Letterbox

Praise for *The Girl on the Cliff*

'[Lucinda Riley] manipulates the strands of her plot with skill'
*Independent on Sunday*

'An emotionally charged saga . . . Riley is a writer to watch' *Sunday Express*

'Lucinda Riley knows how to write a captivating novel . . . it's layered, it's intricate, it's just brilliant . . . a truly brilliant read'
Chick Lit Reviews

'[A] haunting and engrossing new novel . . . superb characterization, atmospheric locations and a well-paced narrative keep the pages turning and the imagination in thrall . . . perceptive, warm and exquisitely wrought, *The Girl on the Cliff* is another triumph for a talented author'
*Burnley Express*

'An enchanting and mysterious story of hope after loss, populated with warm characters'
*Candis*

Praise for *Hothouse Flower*

'Atmospheric, heart-rending and multi-layered'
*Grazia*

'Romantic, revealing and rich in heart-rending emotion and atmospheric detail . . . could well be the pick of Richard and Judy's spring bunch'
*Lancashire Post*

'The parallel stories have many layers, and the characters are touching and very humane, which makes this page-turner a perfect beach read'
*Elle*

'This romance novel conjures up the past in an imaginative way'
*Star*

'It's a great story, full of atmosphere'
Bookbag

# The Angel Tree

Lucinda Riley was born in Ireland and wrote her first book aged 24. Her novel *Hothouse Flower* (also called *The Orchid House*) was selected for the UK's Richard and Judy Book Club in 2011 and went on to sell two million copies worldwide. She is a multiple *New York Times* bestselling author and her books have reached number one in a number of European countries. Her stories are currently translated into 28 languages and published in 38 countries.

She lives with her husband and four children in the English countryside and in the South of France.

Also by Lucinda Riley

*Hothouse Flower*

*The Girl on the Cliff*

*The Light Behind the Window*

*The Midnight Rose*

*The Italian Girl*

The Seven Sisters Series

*The Seven Sisters*

*The Storm Sister*

# The Angel Tree

LUCINDA RILEY

*writing as*

LUCINDA EDMONDS

PAN BOOKS

First published as *Not Quite an Angel* 1995 by Simon & Schuster

This revised and updated edition first published 2015 by Pan Books
an imprint of Pan Macmillan
The Smithson, 6 Briset Street, London, EC1M 5NR
Associated companies throughout the world
www.panmacmillan.com

ISBN 978-1-4472-8844-2



15

A CIP catalogue record for this book is available from the British Library.

Typeset by Ellipsis Digital Limited, Glasgow
Printed and bound by CPI Group (UK) Ltd, Croydon, CR0 4YY

*For my sister, Georgia*

*Christmas Eve, 1985*

*Marchmont Hall,*
*Monmouthshire, Wales*

# 1

David Marchmont glanced towards his passenger as he steered the car along the narrow lane. The snow was falling in earnest now, making the already dangerously icy road even more precarious.

'Not far now Greta, and it looks as if we've made it just in time. I reckon this lane will be impassable by morning. Does anything seem familiar?' he asked tentatively.

Greta turned towards him. Her ivory skin was still unlined, even though she was fifty-eight years old, and her huge blue eyes dominated what David had always thought of as her doll-like face. Age hadn't dimmed the vividness of their colour, but they no longer shone with excitement or anger. The light behind them had disappeared long ago, and they remained as blank and innocent as the inanimate china facsimile she reminded him of.

'I know I once lived here. But I can't remember it, David. I'm sorry.'

'Not to worry,' he comforted her, knowing how much it distressed her. And also thinking that if he could edit out of *his* memory that first grisly, devastating sight of his childhood home after the fire – the pungent smell of charred wood and smoke remained with him to this day – he almost certainly would. 'Of course, Marchmont is well on its way to being restored now.'

'Yes, David, I know. You told me that last week when you came over to me for supper. I cooked lamb cutlets and we had a bottle of Sancerre,' she said defensively. 'You said we were staying in the house itself.'

'Exactly right,' David agreed equably, understanding that Greta always felt the need to give him exact details of recent events, even if the past before her accident was inaccessible to her. As he navigated the ice-rutted lane, the tyres struggling to maintain a grip on the slight incline, he now wondered if bringing Greta back here for Christmas was a good idea. Frankly, he'd been amazed when she'd finally accepted his invitation, after years of trying to persuade her to leave her Mayfair apartment and receiving a firm 'no'.

At last, after three years of painstaking renovation to restore the house to some semblance of its former glory, he'd felt it was the right moment. And for some reason, out of the blue, so had she. At least he knew the house would be physically warm and comfortable. Although emotionally – for either of them, given the circumstances – he didn't know . . .

'It's getting dark already,' Greta commented blandly. 'And it's only just past three o'clock.'

'Yes, but I hope the light will hold long enough so we can at least see Marchmont.'

'Where I used to live.'

'Yes.'

'With Owen. My husband. Who was your uncle.'

'Yes.'

David knew that Greta had simply memorised the details of the past she'd forgotten. As if she were taking an exam. And it was he who had been Greta's teacher, told by the doctors who cared for her to steer clear of any traumatic events but to mention names, dates and places that might stir something in her subconscious and provide the key to recovering her lost memory. Occasionally, when he went to visit her and they chatted, he thought he saw a flicker of recognition at something he mentioned, but he couldn't be sure whether that was through what he had told her since or what she actually remembered. And after all these years, the doctors – who'd once been certain that Greta's memory would slowly return, as there was nothing to indicate it wouldn't on the numerous brain scans she'd had since the accident – now talked of 'selective amnesia' brought on by trauma. In their opinion, Greta did not *want* to remember.

David steered the car slowly around the treacherous bend in the lane, knowing that within a few seconds the gates that led to Marchmont would come into view. Even though he was the legal owner and had spent a fortune on the renovation of the house, he was only the caretaker. Now the restoration was almost complete, Ava, Greta's granddaughter, and her husband, Simon, had moved from the Gate Lodge to take up residence at Marchmont Hall. And when David died, it would legally pass to Ava. The timing couldn't be better, given the couple were expecting their first baby in a few weeks' time. And just maybe, David thought, the past few years of a family history which had gone so badly wrong could be finally laid to rest with the breath of new, innocent life.

What complicated the situation further were the events that had happened *since* Greta's memory loss . . . events he'd protected her from, concerned about the effect they might have on her. After all, if she couldn't remember the start of it all, how could she possibly deal with the end?

All in all, the situation meant that he, Ava and Simon walked a tightrope during conversations with Greta, wanting to prompt her memory but constantly wary of what was discussed in front of her.

'Can you see it, Greta?' David asked as he drove the car between the gates and Marchmont came into view.

Of Elizabethan origin, the house sat low and gracefully against the skyline of undulating foothills that graduated into the majestic peaks of the Black Mountains beyond. Below it, the River Usk meandered through the wide valley, the fields on either side sparkling with the recent snowfall. The mellow red brick of the ancient walls rose into triple gables along its frontage, while the intricate panes of glass in the mullioned windows reflected the winter sun's last, rosy rays.

Even though the old timbers – bone dry as they were – had given the hungry flames of the fire a healthy supper that had resulted in the roof being destroyed, the outer shell had survived. As the fire services had told him, it was partly due to the luck of a huge downpour an hour or so after the first small ember had caught light. Only nature had saved Marchmont Hall from total destruction and there had at least been something left for him to restore.

'Oh, David, it's far more beautiful than it looked in the

photographs you showed me,' Greta breathed. 'What with all the snow, it looks like a Christmas card.'

And indeed, as he parked the car as close to the front door as he could, David saw the warm glow of lamps already lit and the twinkling lights of a Christmas tree through a window. The picture painted was so at odds with the dark, austere atmosphere of his childhood home – indelibly imprinted on his memory – that he felt a sudden sense of euphoria at its apparent transformation. Perhaps the fire *had* burnt away the past, metaphorically as well as physically. He only wished his mother were still here to see its remarkable rehabilitation.

'It does look rather lovely, doesn't it? Right,' he said, opening the car door and causing a shower of snow to slide off the roof, 'let's make a run for it. I'll come back for the cases and presents later.'

David walked around the car to open the passenger door and Greta climbed out cautiously, her slip-on town shoes disappearing, along with her ankles, into the deep snow. As she looked up at the house and then down at her snow-submerged feet, a sudden memory stirred.

*I've been here before . . .*

Standing stock-still, in shock that this moment had finally come, she desperately tried to grasp the fragment of remembrance. But it was already gone.

'Come on, Greta, you'll catch your death standing out here,' said David, offering her his arm. And together they walked the few yards to the front door of Marchmont Hall.

After they'd been greeted by Mary, the housekeeper who had worked at Marchmont for over forty years, David showed Greta to her bedroom and left her to take a nap. He imagined that the stress of deciding to actually leave her home for the first time in years, coupled with the long journey from London, must have worn her out.

Then he wandered into the kitchen in search of Mary. She was rolling out pastry for mince pies at the newly fitted central island. David cast his eyes around the room, admiring the gleaming granite worktops and the sleek, integrated units that lined the walls. The kitchen and bathrooms had been David's only concession to modern design when he'd planned Marchmont's restoration. All the other rooms had been modelled on the original interior, a daunting task that had involved weeks of research and days spent poring over archive photographs in libraries, as well as dredging his own childhood memories. Armies of local craftsmen had been employed to ensure that everything from the flagstone floors to the furniture was as close as possible to the old Marchmont.

'Hello, Master David.' Mary's face broke into a smile as she looked up. 'Jack telephoned ten minutes ago to say your Tor's train was delayed because of the snow. They should be here in about an hour or so. He took the Land Rover, so they'll be fine getting back.'

'It was good of him to offer to pick her up. I know how hard it is for him to spare time away from his duties on the estate. So, how do you like the new facilities, Mary?'

'It's wonderful, *bach*. Everything is so fresh and new,' she replied in her soft Welsh accent. 'I can't believe it's the same house. It's so warm in here these days, I hardly need to light the fires.'

'And your flat is comfortable?' Mary's husband, Huw,

had died a few years ago and she had found it isolated in the estate cottage all alone. So, whilst he was working with the architect on the new plans for the house, he had incorporated a suite of rooms in the spacious attic for Mary. After what had happened before, he felt happier having someone permanently on site if Ava and Simon had to go away.

'Oh yes, thank you. And it has a wonderful view over the valley, too. How's Greta? To be honest with you, I was amazed when you told me she was coming here for Christmas. Indeed to goodness, I never thought I'd see the day. What does she think?'

'She didn't say much,' said David, not sure whether Mary was referring to Greta's reaction to the renovations or her return to the house after all these years. 'She's resting at the moment.'

'You saw that I put her in her old bedroom, to see if it would jog her memory. Although it looks so different now even I don't recognise it. Do you really think she doesn't know who I am? We went through a lot together when she lived at Marchmont.'

'Please try not to let it upset you, Mary. I'm afraid it's the same for all of us.'

'Well, maybe it's best if she *doesn't* remember some of what happened,' she replied grimly.

'Yes,' David agreed with a sigh. 'It's going to be a very odd Christmas, one way and another.'

'You can say that again, *bach*. I keep looking for your mother in the house, then realise she's no longer here.' Mary bit back her tears. 'It's worse for you, of course, Master David.'

'Well, it's going to take some getting used to for all of us. But at least we have Ava and Simon, with their baby on the way, to help us get through it.' David put a comforting arm around Mary's shoulder. 'Now, can I try one of your delicious mince pies?'

Ava and Simon arrived back at the house twenty minutes later and joined David in the drawing room, which smelt of fresh paint, and woodsmoke from the vast stone fireplace.

'Ava, you look wonderful. Positively burgeoning with good health.' David smiled as he embraced her and shook hands with Simon.

'I seem to have suddenly ballooned in the past month. I'm obviously having a rugby player, be it a boy or girl,' Ava answered, looking up fondly at Simon.

'Shall I ask Mary to make us a pot of tea?' enquired David.

'I'll go,' said Simon. 'Ava, darling, you sit down with your uncle and put your feet up. She was called out in the middle of the night to a distressed cow in labour,' he added to David with a despairing shrug as he left the room.

'And I hope someone will be there for *me* when I'm in labour and distressed,' Ava retorted with a chuckle, sinking into one of the newly upholstered chairs. 'Simon's always nagging at me to slow down, but I'm a vet. I can hardly leave my patients to die, can I? I mean, the midwife wouldn't leave me, would she?'

'No, Ava, but you're due to give birth in six weeks' time, and Simon is concerned that you're doing too much, that's all.'

'When the locum arrives at the practice after Christmas

it'll make things a lot easier. But in this weather I can't promise I'm not going to get called out to warm up sheep suffering from hypothermia. The farmers have done a good job of bringing them down from the hills before the bad weather set in, but there's always the odd one that gets left behind. Anyway, Uncle David, how are you?' Ava had always called him 'Uncle', even though they were, technically, first cousins once removed.

'I'm very well, thank you. I recorded my Christmas show in October and since then, well . . . as a matter of fact' – David reddened with sudden embarrassment – 'I've been writing my autobiography.'

'Have you now? That must make interesting reading.'

'My life does certainly, and that's the problem. There are parts of it I can't talk about, obviously.'

'No—' Ava's expression became serious. 'Speaking honestly, as you know I always do, I'm surprised you agreed to write it. I mean, you've always kept your private life scrupulously private.'

'Yes, but sadly some gutter journalist has decided he's going to pen the unauthorised version, so I decided I'd better put the record straight first. As far as I can under the circumstances, that is.'

'Right. Then I can see why you'd want to do it. Goodness,' Ava breathed, 'having had a movie star for a mother and a famous comedian as a cousin has made me loathe the thought of celebrity. You won't mention anything about . . . what happened to me, will you, Uncle David? I'd die if you did. Especially after last time, when I was splashed all over the front page of the *Daily Mail* with Cheska.'

'Of course not, Ava. I'm doing my utmost to keep the

family out of it. The problem is, that doesn't leave much to tell. There've been no drugs, nervous breakdowns, drink problems or womanising in my life, so it makes for a very boring read.' David sighed and gave an ironic smile. 'Talking of women, Tor should be here soon.'

'I'm glad she's coming, Uncle David. I'm very fond of her. And the more of us here this Christmas, the better.'

'Well, at least we've finally managed to get your grandmother to join us.'

'Where is she?'

'Upstairs, resting.'

'And how is she?'

'The same, really. But I'm so proud of her for finding the courage to come here.' Car lights flashed beyond the window. 'That must be Tor. I'll go and help her in with her luggage.'

When David had left the drawing room Ava mused on his enduring and loyal relationship with Greta. She knew the two of them had known each other forever, but she wondered just what it was about her that appealed to him so much. Ava's great-aunt, David's mother LJ, who had died only a few months ago, had said that her son had always loved Greta. And certainly, Greta still looked very youthful, almost as if her memory loss had erased the physical signs of fifty-eight years of living, which normally manifested themselves on a face like an outer emotional map.

Ava hated to admit it, but she found her grandmother rather vacuous and childlike. On the few occasions she'd seen Greta over the years she'd felt it was like talking to a perfectly formed but hollow Fabergé egg. But then again, perhaps any depth and personality she'd once had had been wiped away by the accident. Greta lived like a recluse, rarely venturing out of the front door of her apartment. This was the first time Ava had ever known her to leave it for longer than a few hours.

She knew she shouldn't judge her grandmother, having never known her before the accident, but at the same time she acknowledged that she had always compared Greta to LJ, whose indomitable spirit and zest for life made Greta – even after everything that had happened to her – seem weak and colourless. *And now*, Ava thought, biting her lip, *Greta is here for Christmas, and LJ isn't.*

A lump came to Ava's throat, but she swallowed it down, knowing her great-aunt wouldn't want her to grieve.

'Best foot forward,' she'd always said when tragedy had struck.

Ava couldn't help but wish with all her heart that LJ had been here for a little longer so she could have witnessed the birth of her baby. At least she'd lived to see her marry Simon, and had known when she died that Marchmont – and Ava – were safe.

David came back into the drawing room with Tor.

'Hello, Ava. Merry Christmas, and all that. Goodness, I'm cold. What a journey!' Tor said, walking to the roaring fire and warming her hands by it.

'Well, you made it, and just in time, apparently. Jack told me they've cancelled any further trains to Abergavenny tonight,' said David.

'Yes, I must admit I didn't fancy spending Christmas in a bed and breakfast in Newport,' Tor said drily. 'And the house looks wonderful, Ava. You and Simon must be thrilled.'

'We are,' said Ava. 'It's so beautiful, and we're so grateful to you, Uncle David. Simon and I would never have had the resources to renovate it ourselves.'

'Well, as you know, one day it will pass to you, anyway. Ah, Simon.' David looked up as he entered the room. 'A nice fresh pot of tea. Just what we all need.'

Greta awoke from her nap feeling disoriented and unable to remember where she was. Panicking, she fumbled for a light in the pitch blackness and switched it on. The strong smell of fresh paint jogged her memory as she sat up in the comfortable bed and admired the newly decorated room.

Marchmont Hall . . . the house she'd heard so much about from David over the years. Mary, the housekeeper, had told her earlier this had once been her bedroom, and it had been in here that she'd given birth to Cheska.

Greta got out of bed and walked to the window. The snow was still falling. She tried to access the fleeting memory that had been kindled when she'd stood outside the house, and sighed in despair when her mind stubbornly refused to give up its secrets.

After freshening up in the smart en-suite bathroom, she dressed in a new cream silk blouse she'd bought a few days ago. Adding a dab of lipstick to her mouth, she stared at her reflection in the mirror, feeling anxious about leaving the sanctuary of her bedroom.

It had taken everything that was left of her to make the decision to join her family here at Marchmont for Christmas. So much so that after she'd said yes, and watched

David's astonished expression as she did so, Greta had experienced severe panic attacks which had rendered her sleepless, sweating and shaking into the small hours. She'd visited her doctor, who had prescribed beta blockers and sedatives. With his encouragement, plus the thought of spending yet another miserable Christmas alone, she had managed to pack, climb into David's car and get here.

Perhaps the doctors would disagree with her motivation; they would argue in their usual psychobabble that maybe at last she was ready, that her subconscious finally deemed her strong enough to cope with returning. And certainly, since she'd taken the decision, she'd been dreaming vividly for the first time since the accident. None of her dreams made sense, of course, but the shock of having what the doctors would term a 'flashback' when she'd stepped out of the car and looked at Marchmont Hall a couple of hours ago gave some credence to their analysis.

She knew there was a lot still to face. 'Company', for a start, and for an extended period of time. And among those gathering here for the festive season there was one person she was particularly dreading spending time with: Tor, David's lady-friend.

Even though she had met Tor occasionally when David had brought her round for tea at Greta's Mayfair apartment, she had never spent longer than a few hours with the woman. Even though, on the surface, Tor had been sweet and polite and seemed to be interested in what she had to say – which wasn't a lot – Greta had felt patronised, as if Tor were treating her as some kind of mentally deficient, senile old lady.

Greta looked at her reflection in the mirror. She may be many things, but she wasn't *that*.

Tor was an Oxford don. Intellectual, independent, attractive – in a practical sort of way, Greta had always thought, and then reprimanded herself for her instinctive female derision of a rival.

Put simply, Tor was everything Greta wasn't, but she made David happy and Greta knew she must be happy for that.

At least David had said that Ava would be here with her husband, Simon. Ava, her granddaughter . . .

If anything about her memory loss particularly upset her, it was Ava. Her own flesh and blood, her daughter's daughter . . . Yet though she'd seen Ava periodically over the past two decades and liked her very much indeed, Greta felt guilty that she was unable to connect with her granddaughter like a close relative should. Surely, even though she had no recollection of Ava's birth, she should instinctively feel some deeper emotional bond?

Greta thought Ava suspected – just as LJ had – that she remembered more than she did and was somehow shamming. But despite years of sessions with psychologists, hypnotists and practitioners of any other form of treatment for memory loss she'd read about, nothing stirred. Greta felt she lived in a void, as if she were merely an onlooker to the rest of humanity, all of whom found it easy to *remember*.

The closest she felt to another human being was her darling David, who'd been there when she'd finally opened her eyes after nine months in a coma and had spent the past twenty-four years caring for her in any way he could. If it hadn't been for him, given the emptiness of her existence, she was sure she would have lost all hope many years ago.

David had told her that they met forty years ago, when she was eighteen and working in London at a theatre called the Windmill just after the war. Apparently, she'd once explained to him that her parents had died in the Blitz, but had never mentioned any other relatives. David had told her that they had been very good friends, and Greta had surmised that their relationship had been nothing more than that. David had also said that, soon after they'd met, she had married a man called Owen, his uncle, once the squire of Marchmont.

Over the years Greta had wished endlessly that the friendship David had described to her had been something more. She loved him deeply; not for what he had been to her before the accident but for all he meant to her now. Of course, she knew her feelings were not reciprocated and she had no reason to believe they ever had been. David was a very famous and successful comedian and still extremely attractive. Besides, for the past six years he'd been with Tor, who was always on his arm at charity events and awards ceremonies.

In her darkest moments Greta felt she was little more than a liability; that David was merely doing his duty, out of the kindness of his heart and because they were related by marriage. When she'd finally come out of hospital, after eighteen months, and moved back into her apartment in Mayfair, David had been her only regular visitor. Her guilt at being dependent on him had grown over the years and, although he told her that popping in to see her was no hardship, she'd always tried not to be a burden, so she often pretended she was busy when she wasn't.

Greta moved away from the window, knowing she must pluck up the courage to go downstairs and join her family. She opened the bedroom door, walked along the corridor and stood at the top of the magnificent dark oak staircase, its carved balustrades and elaborate acorn-shaped finials gleaming softly in the light of the chandelier overhead. Gazing down upon the large Christmas tree which stood in the hall beneath her, she smelt the fresh, delicate scent of the fir and, again, something stirred. She closed her eyes and breathed deeply, as the doctors had told her to, trying to encourage the faint memory to grow.

The residents of Marchmont Hall woke up on Christmas morning to an idyllic, snowy scene outside. At lunchtime, they tucked into a goose, and vegetables grown on the estate. Afterwards, they gathered in the drawing room by the fire to open their gifts.

'Oh Granny,' said Ava as she unwrapped a soft white baby blanket, 'that will be so useful. Thank you.'

'Also, Tor and I would very much like to buy you a pram but, given that neither of us has a clue about all those new-fangled contraptions parents use these days, we've written you a cheque,' David said, handing it to Ava.

'That's more than generous, David,' Simon said, topping up his glass.

Greta was touched by Ava's gift of a framed photograph of the two of them, taken when Ava was a tiny baby and while Greta was still hospitalised.

'That's just to remind you of what's to come,' Ava said

with a smile. 'My goodness, you'll be a great-grandmother!'

'I will, won't I?' Greta chuckled at the thought.

'And you look barely a day older than the first time I met you,' David commented gallantly.

Greta sat on the sofa, watching her family with pleasure. Perhaps it was the effect of far more wine over lunch than she was used to but, for once, she didn't feel unwanted.

After the presents had been unwrapped, Simon insisted he take Ava upstairs for a rest, and David and Tor left for a walk. David asked Greta to accompany them, but she tactfully declined. They needed time together, and three was always a crowd. Greta sat by the fire for a while, dozing contentedly. Coming to, she glanced out of the window and saw that the sun was now low but still shining, the snow glittering beneath it.

On impulse, deciding she could do with a breath of fresh air, too, she sought out Mary and asked if there were any boots and a thick coat she could borrow.

Five minutes later, dressed in a pair of wellingtons that were far too big for her and an old Barbour, Greta strode out across the virgin snow, breathing in the wonderful, clean, crisp air. She paused, wondering which way to go, hoping some inner instinct would guide her, and decided to take a stroll through the woods. As she walked, she looked upwards at the deep blue sky above and a sudden joy filled her veins at the sheer beauty of the scene. It was such an unusual and rare feeling that she almost skipped as she zigzagged her way through the trees.

Arriving in a clearing, she saw a majestic fir tree standing in the centre of it, the rich green of its bushy, snow-laden branches a contrast to the tall, bare beech trees that made up the rest of the wood. Walking towards it, she noticed there was a gravestone beneath it, the inscription covered by snow. Surmising that it was almost certainly the grave of a family pet – perhaps one she had known – Greta reached down and scraped away the hard, icy flakes with her gloved hand.

Slowly, the inscription began to appear.

JONATHAN (JONNY) MARCHMONT

Beloved son of Owen and Greta
Brother of Francesca

BORN 2ND JUNE 1946
DIED 6TH JUNE 1949

May God guide his little angel up to Heaven

Greta read and reread the inscription, then fell to her knees in the snow, her heart pounding.

Jonny . . . The words on the gravestone said that this dead child was *her* son . . .

She knew Francesca – Cheska – was her daughter, but there'd never been any mention of a boy. The inscription said he'd died at just three years of age . . .

Weeping now with frustration and shock, Greta looked up again and saw that the sky was beginning to darken. She gazed around the clearing helplessly, as if the trees might speak to her and give her answers. As she knelt there, in the distance she heard the sound of a dog barking. An echo of another moment created a picture in her mind; she'd been here in this place once before and had heard a dog . . . Yes, *yes* . . .

She turned and focused on the grave. 'Jonny . . . my son . . . please let me remember. For God's sake, let me remember what happened!' she cried, half-choking on her tears.

The sound of the dog's bark faded away and as it did so she closed her eyes and immediately saw a vivid image of a tiny baby wrapped in her arms, nestling against her chest.

'Jonny, my darling Jonny . . . my baby . . .'

As the sun dipped below the trees and into the valley below, heralding the arrival of night, Greta's arms reached wide to clasp the gravestone as, finally, she began to remember . . .

# Greta

## London, October 1945

# 2

The cramped dressing room in the Windmill Theatre smelt of Leichner No. 5 panstick perfume and sweat. There weren't enough mirrors, so the girls jostled for space as they painted on lipstick and teased their hair into curls on top of their heads, fixing the elaborate styles with spritzes of sugar water.

'I suppose there's something to be said for appearing half naked; at least you don't have to worry about laddering your nylons,' laughed an attractive brunette as she checked her reflection and deftly arranged her breasts to better advantage in her low-cut, sequinned costume.

'Yes, but carbolic soap doesn't exactly leave your skin looking as fresh as a daisy after you've scrubbed the make-up off, does it, Doris?' replied another girl.

There was a sharp knock at the door and a young man peered into the dressing room, seemingly oblivious to the scantily-clad bodies that met his eyes. 'Five minutes, ladies!' he shouted before retreating.

'Oh well,' sighed Doris. 'Another shimmy, another shilling.' She stood up. 'I'm just thankful there's no more air raids. It was bloomin' freezing a couple of years ago, sitting in that bloody basement in not much more than your undies. My backside turned positively blue. Come on, girls, let's go and give our audience something to dream about.'

Doris left the dressing room and the others drifted out behind her, chattering amiably, until there was only one girl left, hurriedly applying red lipstick with a small brush.

Greta Simpson was never late. But today she'd overslept until after ten, even though she was due at the theatre at eleven o'clock. Mind you, it had been worth having to run the half-mile to the bus stop, she thought dreamily as she stared into the mirror. Last night with Max, when they'd danced until the small hours then wandered hand in hand along the Embankment as the sun came up over London, made it all worthwhile. She hugged herself tightly at the memory of his arms around her and his passionate kisses.

It was four weeks since she'd met Max in Feldman's nightclub. Usually, Greta was too exhausted after five shows at the Windmill to do anything other than go home to bed, but Doris had begged her to come and help celebrate her twenty-first birthday, and in the end she'd agreed. The two girls were chalk and cheese; Greta quiet and reserved, Doris brash and blowsy with a loud cockney twang. Yet they'd become friends of sorts and Greta hadn't wanted to let her down.

The pair had treated themselves to a taxi for the short journey to Oxford Street. Feldman's was packed with demobbed British and American servicemen, as well as the cream of London society who frequented the most popular swing club in town.

Doris had bagged a table in the corner and ordered a gin and It for each of them. Greta glanced around and thought how the atmosphere in London had changed since VE Day, just five short months ago. A sense of euphoria pervaded the air. A new Labour government had been elected in July, with Clement Attlee at the helm, and their slogan 'Let us face the future' summed up the fresh hopes of the British people.

Greta had felt suddenly light-headed as she'd taken a sip of her cocktail and soaked in the club's atmosphere. The war was over after six long years. She'd smiled to herself. She was young, she was pretty and it was a time of excitement and new beginnings. And God knew, she could do with one of those . . .

It was as she was looking around that she'd noticed a particularly handsome young man standing with a group of GIs at the bar. Greta had remarked on him to Doris.

'Yeah, and he'll be randy as they come, I'll bet. All them Yanks are,' Doris had said, catching the eye of one of the group and smiling boldly at him.

It was no secret at the Windmill that Doris was free with her affections. And five minutes later a waiter arrived at their table with a bottle of champagne, 'With the compliments of the gents by the bar.'

'Easy when you know how, dear,' Doris had whispered to Greta as the waiter poured the champagne. 'This evening won't cost either of us a penny.' She'd winked conspiratorially and instructed the waiter to tell the 'gents' to come over so she could thank them in person.

Two hours later, high on champagne, Greta had found herself dancing in Max's arms. She had discovered that he was an American staff officer working at Whitehall.

'Most of the guys are on their way home, which is

where I'll be headed in a few weeks,' Max had explained. 'We just got a few things to tidy up first. Boy, I'm gonna miss London. It's a swell city.'

He'd looked surprised when Greta told him she was in 'show business'.

'You mean you're on the stage? As an actress?' he'd said, his brow creasing into a frown.

Greta had sensed immediately this wasn't something that was going to impress him and she'd quickly changed her story. 'I work as a receptionist to a theatrical agent,' she'd added hurriedly.

'Oh, I see.' Max's features immediately relaxed. 'Show business sure doesn't fit with you, Greta. You're what my mother would call a real lady.'

Half an hour later Greta had extricated herself from Max's arms and told him she must go home. He'd nodded politely and walked her outside to find a taxi.

'It's been a wonderful evening,' he'd said as he helped her inside. 'Can I see you again?'

'Yes,' she'd replied, before she could stop herself.

'Great. I could meet you here tomorrow night?'

'Yes, but I'm working until half past ten. I have to see a show one of our clients is in,' she'd lied.

'Okay, I'll be waiting for you here at eleven. Night, Greta, don't be late tomorrow.'

'I won't.'

As the taxi had driven her home, Greta found that her mind was a mixture of conflicting emotions. Her head told her it would be futile to begin a relationship with a man who had only a few weeks left in London, but Max seemed like a gentleman, and that made such a pleasant change from the often rowdy male audience that frequented the Windmill.

As she'd sat there, she'd thought sombrely of the circumstances that had landed her at the stage door of the Windmill barely four months ago. In all the magazines and newspapers she'd read as a teenager 'The Windmill Girls' had always seemed so glamorous, dressed in their beautiful costumes with an array of British celebrities pictured smiling between them. Having had to make a hasty exit from the all-too-different world she'd previously occupied, the Windmill had been her first port of call when she'd arrived in London.

The reality, as she now knew, was very different . . .

After she'd arrived back at her boarding house and climbed into the narrow bed, with a cardigan over her pyjamas to keep out the autumnal chill of the unheated room, Greta had realised that Max was her passport to freedom. And whatever it took to convince him that she was the girl of his dreams, she'd decided she'd do it.

As planned, Max and Greta had met at Feldman's the following night, and from then on they'd seen each other almost every evening. And despite all Doris's warnings about overpaid and oversexed Yanks, Max had always behaved like a perfect gentleman. A few days ago he had taken Greta to a dinner dance at the Savoy. As she'd sat at the table in the grand ballroom and listened to Roberto Inglez and his Orchestra, she'd decided she loved being wined and dined by her rich, handsome American officer. And, more and more, she was learning to love him as well.

Through their conversations, Greta had begun to realise

that Max had lived a very privileged but somewhat sheltered life before arriving in London a few months ago. He told her he'd been born in South Carolina, the only son of wealthy parents, and lived just outside the city of Charleston. Greta had gasped when he'd shown her a photograph of the elegant, colonnaded white house where they lived. Max had told her his father owned several lucrative businesses in the Deep South, including a large automotive factory which had apparently fared well during the war. When Max left England and arrived back home he would be joining the family business.

Greta knew from the flowers, nylons and expensive meals he paid for that Max had money to burn, so when he started talking about 'our' future, a glimmer of hope that they just might have one had begun to ignite in her heart.

Tonight, Max was taking her out for dinner at the Dorchester and had told her to wear something special. He was due to ship out to America in a couple of days and had said time and time again how much he'd miss her. Perhaps he'd be able to come back to London to visit, or maybe, just maybe, she thought, she could save up enough money to make a trip across to the States to see him . . .

Her romantic reverie was interrupted by a light tap on the door. She looked up as a familiar, friendly face appeared around it.

'Ready yet, Greta?' asked David Marchmont. As always, Greta was taken by surprise at the clipped, upper-class English accent that was so at odds with his stage persona. As well as working as assistant stage manager, David doubled up as a comedian at the Windmill, going by the name of Taffy – a sly reference to his Welsh roots, and how he was commonly addressed by everyone at the theatre – and delivering his amusing spiel in a broad Welsh brogue.

'Give me two minutes?' she requested, remembering abruptly what she had to do tonight.

'No longer than that, I'm afraid. I'll walk you up to the wings and sort your props out.' He frowned slightly as he looked at her. 'Are you sure you're okay about this? You look awfully pale.'

'I'm fine, really, Taffy,' she lied, feeling her heart rate increase. 'I'll be out in a jiffy.'

As he closed the door, Greta sighed deeply as she applied the finishing touches to her make-up.

The work at the Windmill was far harder than she'd ever imagined. *Revudeville* played five times a day and, when the girls weren't performing, they were rehearsing. Everyone knew that most of the men in the audience didn't come to see the comedians or the other acts in the variety show but rather to gape at the gorgeous girls as they paraded around the stage in revealing costumes.

Greta grimaced and glanced guiltily at her beautifully tailored cherry-red coat, hanging on the peg by the door. She'd been unable to resist it during a particularly expensive shopping spree at Selfridges, wanting to look her best for Max. The red coat was an all-too-vivid symbol of the money problems that had brought her to where she was now – Greta swallowed hard – about to stand virtually naked in front of hundreds of leering men.

A few days ago, when Mr Van Damm had asked her to perform in the Windmill's daring *tableaux vivants* – which meant standing stock-still in an elegant pose as the other Windmill Girls walked around her – Greta had baulked at the thought of stripping off almost completely. A few sequins to cover each nipple and a tiny G-string were all she would have to protect her modesty. But, egged on by Doris, who had been appearing in the *tableaux* for over a year, and the thought of her unpaid rent, she had reluctantly agreed.

She shuddered at the thought of what Max – whom she had discovered was a Baptist from a devout family – would think of her career progression. But she desperately needed the extra cash that appearing in the *tableaux* would bring.

Glancing at the clock on the wall, Greta realised she'd better step on it. The show had already started and she was due to make her grand entrance in less than ten minutes. She opened the drawer of the dressing table and took a hasty sip from the hip flask Doris kept secreted there, hoping that Dutch courage might help to see her through. There was another knock on the door.

'I hate to rush you, but we'd better get going,' Taffy called from behind it.

Taking a last glance at her reflection in the mirror, Greta stepped out into the dim corridor, clutching her robe protectively around her.

Seeing her apprehensive expression, Taffy walked forward and gently took her hands in his. 'I know you must be nervous, Greta, but once you get out there you'll be fine.'

'Really? Do you promise?'

'Yes, I promise. Just imagine that you're an artist's model in a studio in Paris, posing for a beautiful painting. I've heard they strip off at the drop of a hat over there,' he joked, trying to lift Greta's spirits.

'Thank you, Taffy. I don't know what I'd do without

you.' She smiled gratefully and allowed him to lead her down the corridor towards the wings.

Seven hours and three nerve-wracking performances later, Greta was back in the dressing room. Her *tableau vivant* had gone down a storm and, thanks to Taffy's advice, she'd managed to conquer her fears and stand under the bright lights with her head held high.

'Well, that's thc worst over with – the first time's always the hardest,' said Doris with a wink as they sat next to each other, Greta removing her heavy stage make-up whilst Doris retouched hers in readiness for the evening show. 'Now, you just concentrate on looking gorgeous for tonight. What time are you meeting your American bloke?'

'Eight o'clock, at the Dorchester.'

'Ooo, get you, eh? Living the high life and no mistake.' Doris grinned at Greta in the mirror, before standing up and reaching for her feathered headdress. 'Well, I'm off to tread the boards yet again, while you gallivant around the West End like Cinderella with your handsome prince.' She gave Greta's shoulder a squeeze. 'Enjoy yourself, dear.'

'Thanks,' Greta called as Doris made her way out of the dressing room.

Greta knew she'd been lucky to get the evening off. She'd had to promise Mr Van Damm that she'd work extra hours next week. In a state of heightened excitement, she slipped into the new cocktail dress she'd bought with the extra shillings she knew her new-found promotion would earn her and carefully repainted her face before donning her beloved red coat and dashing out of the theatre.

*

Max was waiting for her in the lobby of the Dorchester. He took her hands and gazed at her. 'You look so darned beautiful tonight, Greta. I must be the luckiest guy in all of London. Shall we?' He proffered his arm and the two of them walked slowly towards the restaurant.

It wasn't until they'd finished their desserts that he asked her the question she'd been longing to hear drop from his lips.

'You want to marry me?! I . . . oh Max, we've known each other for such a short time! Are you sure this is what you want?'

'*Certain* sure. I know love when I feel it. It'll be a different kind of life for you in Charleston, but it'll be a good one. You'll never want for anything, I promise. Please, Greta, say yes, and I'll spend the rest of my life doing my best to make you happy.'

Greta looked at Max's handsome, sincere face and gave him the answer they both wanted to hear.

'I'm sorry I don't have a ring to give you yet,' he added, tenderly taking her left hand in his and smiling into her eyes, 'but I want you to have my grandmother's engagement ring when we get to the States.'

Greta smiled ecstatically back at him. 'The only thing that matters is that we're going to be together.'

Over coffee, they discussed their plans: Max would sail home in two days' time and Greta would follow him as soon as she'd worked out her notice and packed up her few possessions.

On the dance floor later that night, dizzy with romance and euphoria, Max pulled her closer to him.

'Greta, I understand if this is inappropriate, but as we

just got engaged and we've got so little time left before I sail, would you come back to my hotel? I swear I won't compromise you, but at least we can talk in private . . .'

Greta could see that he was blushing. From what he'd said to her, she'd guessed that he was probably still a virgin. And, if he was going to be her husband, surely a kiss and a cuddle wouldn't hurt?

Later, at his hotel in St James's, Max took her in his arms and began to embrace her. Greta could feel his growing excitement, and hers, too.

'Can I?' he ventured, his fingers resting tentatively on the three buttons at the nape of her neck.

Greta reasoned with herself that a few hours earlier she'd appeared almost naked in front of men she didn't even know, so what was there to be ashamed about in giving the gift of her innocence and making love to the man she was going to marry?

The following day, as Greta sat in the Windmill's dressing room securing her hair with a couple of kirby grips, she couldn't help feeling anxious. Was she making the right decision in marrying Max?

Appearing on the big screen had been her ambition for as long as Greta could remember, and her mother had done nothing to discourage it. She'd been so obsessed with the cinema herself she'd even named her only daughter after the legendary Garbo. As well as taking Greta to endless matinees at the Odeon in Manchester, her mother had also paid for elocution and acting classes.

But surely, Greta mused, if a career in the movies was her destiny, wouldn't someone have spotted her by now?

Directors were always popping in to cast their eye over the famous Windmill Girls. During her four months at the theatre, two of her friends had been whisked off to become Rank starlets. It was the reason a lot of the girls, herself included, were here. They all lived in hope that one day there would be a knock on the dressing-room door and a message would be passed to the girl in question that a gentleman from a film studio would 'like a word'.

She shook her head as she stood up and prepared to leave the dressing room. How could she even think about not marrying Max? If she stayed in London, she might still be at the Windmill in two, or three, or four years' time, enduring the degradation and up to her ears in debt. With so many young men killed in the war, she knew she was lucky to have found a man who seemed to love her and, from what he'd said, could also give her a life of security and comfort.

Today was Max's last in London. He was due to sail back to America the following morning. Tonight they were meeting at the Mayfair Hotel for dinner and to finalise plans for Greta's passage. Then they would spend a last night together before he left at dawn to join his ship. Although she would miss him, it would be a relief to end the deceit about what she really did for a living. She hated lying to him constantly, having to make up stories about working late at the office for her demanding boss.

'Greta, darling! The curtain's about to go up!' Taffy broke into her daydream.

'Keep your hair on, I'm coming!' She smiled at him, and followed him along the dimly lit corridor towards the stage.

'I was wondering, Greta, if you fancied a drink after the performance?' he whispered as he stood behind her in the wings. 'I've just spoken with Mr Van Damm, and he's giving me a regular slot. I feel like celebrating!'

'Oh, Taffy, that's wonderful news!' Greta was genuinely thrilled for him. 'You deserve it. You really are talented,' she said, reaching up to give him a hug. At over six feet tall, with unkempt sandy hair and merry green eyes, she'd always thought him attractive and she had an inkling he had a soft spot for her. They'd sometimes go out for a bite to eat together and he would practise new jokes on her for his 'Taffy' routine. She felt guilty that she hadn't yet told him about her engagement.

'Thank you. So how about that drink?'

'Sorry, Taffy. I can't tonight.'

'Perhaps next week, then?'

'Yes, next week.'

'Greta! We're on!' called Doris.

'Sorry, got to go.'

David watched Greta disappear onto the stage and sighed. The two of them had shared some lovely evenings together but just as he'd started to think she might reciprocate his feelings, she'd begun to cancel their meetings. He knew why, as did the whole theatre. She had a rich American officer in tow. And how could a poorly-paid comedian, set on bringing his brand of laughter into a world that had seen so little of it in the past few years, possibly compete with a handsome American in uniform? David shrugged to himself. Once this Yank had gone home . . . well, he would bide his time.

*

Max Landers sat down and glanced round uncomfortably at the noisy, all-male audience. He hadn't been keen on coming here, but the guys from his Whitehall office, out to celebrate their last night in London and already half-cut, had insisted the show at the Windmill was something they shouldn't miss before they left town.

Max didn't listen to the comedians or the singers but instead sat counting the minutes until he could slip away and meet his darling girl, his Greta, later tonight. It was going to be tough for her when he sailed tomorrow, and of course he'd have to pave the way with his parents, who wanted him to marry Anna-Mae, his high-school sweetheart back home. They'd have to understand that he had changed. He'd been a boy when he'd left, but now he was a man, and a man in love. Besides, Greta was a real English lady and he was sure her charm would win them over.

Max hardly glanced up as applause rang around the theatre and the curtain fell on the opening act.

'Hey!' His friend Bart thumped him on the arm and he jumped. 'You gotta check the next act out. This is what we came to see.' Bart made the shape of a woman's body with his hands. 'Apparently, it's really hot, man,' he said, grinning.

Max nodded. 'Yeah, Bart. Sure thing.'

The curtain rose once more, to thunderous applause and the sound of shrill wolf whistles. Max looked up at the virtually naked girls on the stage in front of him. *What kind of woman could do that?* he found himself asking. In his opinion, they were little better than whores.

'Hey, aren't they great?' said Bart, his eyes shining with

lust. 'Look at that broad in the centre. Wow! Hardly a stitch on her, but what a cute smile.'

Max gazed at the girl, who was standing so still she could almost be a statue. She looked a little like . . . He leant forward and did a double take.

'Jesus H. Christ!' He swore under his breath, his heart pounding in his chest as he studied the big blue eyes that gazed out above her audience, the sweet lips and the thick blonde hair piled on top of her head. He could hardly bear to look at the familiar full breasts with their pert nipples barely concealed by a few sequins, or the seductively curved belly that led down to her most intimate part . . .

Without a shadow of a doubt, it was his Greta. He turned and saw Bart gazing hungrily at his fiancée's body.

Max knew he was going to throw up. He stood and hurriedly left the auditorium.

Greta took her third cigarette from the silver case Max had given her and lit it, checking her watch for the umpteenth time. He was over an hour late now. Where on earth was he? The waiter kept giving her suspicious glances as she sat alone at a table in the cocktail bar. She knew exactly what he was thinking.

She finished the cigarette and stubbed it out, glancing at her watch once more. If Max hadn't turned up by midnight, she would go home and wait for him there. He knew where she lived – he'd collected her from her lodging house on a couple of occasions – and she was sure he'd have a good reason for not showing up.

Midnight came and went, and the cocktail bar emptied. She stood up slowly and left, too. When she got home, she was disappointed not to see Max waiting for her outside. She let herself in and put the kettle on the small stove.

'Don't panic,' she told herself as she spooned a tiny amount of the precious coffee powder Max had given her into a cup. 'He's bound to be here soon.'

Greta sat stiffly on the edge of the bed, jumping at every tap-tap of footsteps that passed the house and willing them to stop in front of it and mount the steps. She didn't want to change or to take off her make-up in case the bell rang. Finally, at three o'clock, shivering with cold and fear, she lay down on the bed, tears coming to her eyes as she gazed at the damp, peeling wallpaper.

Panic rose inside her: she had no idea how to contact Max. His ship was sailing from Southampton and she knew he had to report to it by ten o'clock this morning. What if he didn't get in touch with her before then? She didn't even have his address in America. He'd promised to give her all the details of her passage and onward journey over dinner.

As the stars disappeared with the dawn, so did Greta's dreams of her new life. She knew now for certain that Max wouldn't be coming; by now he was surely on his way to Southampton, ready to sail out of her life forever.

Greta arrived at the Windmill the following morning, feeling numb and exhausted.

'What's the matter, love? GI sailed off into the sunset and left poor little you behind?' cooed Doris.

'Leave me alone!' cried Greta sharply. 'Anyway, you know he's not a GI, he's an officer.'

'No need to get nasty, I was only asking.' Doris stared

at her, clearly offended. 'Did Max enjoy the show yesterday?' she enquired.

'I . . . What do you mean?'

'Your boyfriend was in the audience last night.' Doris turned away from Greta and concentrated on applying her eyeliner. 'I presumed you'd invited him,' she added pointedly.

Greta swallowed, torn between wanting to conceal the fact that she hadn't known Max was there and making sure that what Doris had said was true.

'Yes, I . . . of course I did. But I never look into the audience. Where was he sitting?'

'Oh, on the left-hand side. I noticed him because just after the curtain went up on us *jolies mesdames* he got up and left.' Doris shrugged. 'There's none so strange as folk, 'specially menfolk.'

Later that night Greta let herself into her room, knowing with absolute certainty she would never hear from Max Landers again.

# 3

Eight weeks later Greta realised that Max had left her a legacy which would mean she was unlikely ever to forget their brief but passionate affair. She was absolutely sure she was pregnant.

Miserably, she entered the stage door of the Windmill. She felt dreadful, having spent the early morning fighting sickness and, in between running to the lavatory, trying to work out what on earth she was going to do. Apart from anything else, a burgeoning stomach would cut short her employment at the Windmill in a matter of weeks.

She hadn't slept at all last night, the fear in the pit of her stomach making it impossible. As she'd tossed and turned, Greta had even considered going back home. But she knew in her heart that could never be an option.

Shuddering at the unbidden memory, she forced herself to concentrate on her current predicament. As she sat in front of the mirror in the dressing room, despair overwhelmed her. It was all very well to leave the Windmill to go into the arms of a wealthy American husband, but what she faced now was, at best, a place in one of the homes that dealt with women in her position. Although the management were kind, the moral rules laid down for the girls at the Windmill were unbreakable. And being unmarried and pregnant was the biggest sin a girl could commit.

Greta knew her life was in ruins. All her plans for a future marriage or a film career were over if she had this baby. Unless . . . she stared at her terrified reflection in the mirror but realised there was nothing else for it. She would have to ask Doris for the address of a 'Mr Fix-it'. Surely it would be fairer on her unborn baby? She had nothing to give it: no home, no money and no father.

The curtain came down at ten forty-five and the girls made their way back wearily to the dressing room.

'Doris,' Greta whispered, 'can I have a quick word?'

'Of course, love.'

Greta waited until the other girls had gone into the dressing room before she spoke. As calmly as she could, she asked for the address she needed.

Doris's beady eyes scrutinised her closely. 'Oh, dearie me. That GI gave you a goodbye present, didn't he?'

Greta hung her head and nodded. Doris sighed and laid a sympathetic hand on Greta's arm. She could be as hard as nails on occasion, but underneath the brashness there beat a heart of gold.

'Of course I'll give you the address, dear. But it'll cost you, you know.'

'How much?'

'Depends. Tell him you're a friend of mine and he might do it cheaper.'

Greta shuddered again. Doris made it sound as if she were going for a perm. 'Is it safe?' she ventured.

'Well, I've had two and I'm still here to tell the tale, but

I have heard some horror stories,' Doris remarked. 'When he's done it, go home and lie down until the bleeding stops. If it doesn't, get yourself to a hospital sharpish. Come on, I'll write down the address. Pop along and see him tomorrow and he'll fix you up with an appointment. Do you want me come with you?'

'No, I'll be fine. But thanks, Doris,' Greta said gratefully.

'No problem. Us girls have got to look after each other, haven't we? And remember, dear, you're not the first and you won't be the last.'

Early the following morning Greta took a bus up the Edgware Road to Cricklewood. She found the street where Mr Fix-it lived and walked slowly along it. Stopping in front of a gate, she glanced up at a small red-brick house. Taking a deep breath, she opened the gate, walked up the path and knocked on the front door. After a moment, she saw a net curtain twitch, then heard the sound of a bolt being drawn back.

'Yes?'

A diminutive man, who bore an unsettling resemblance to the pictures of Rumpelstiltskin from Greta's childhood storybooks, answered the door.

'Hello. I . . . er . . . Doris sent me.'

'You'd better come in, then.' The man opened the door wider to let Greta through and she entered a small, dingy hall.

'Please wait in there. I'm just finishing with a patient,' he said, indicating a sparsely furnished front room. Greta sat down in a stained armchair and, wrinkling her nose at the smell of cat and old carpet, picked up a tatty copy of *Woman* and flicked through the pages. She found herself looking at a knitting pattern for a baby's matinée jacket and abruptly closed the magazine. She sank back into the armchair and stared at the ceiling, her heart pounding against her chest.

A few minutes later, she heard someone moaning softly from a room nearby. She swallowed hard as the man came back into the front room and shut the door.

'Now, miss, what can I do for you?'

It was a silly question, and they both knew it. The moaning was still audible, despite the closed door. Greta's nerves were in shreds.

'Doris says you maybe could sort out my . . . er, problem.'

'Perhaps.' The man stared at her intently, his fingers moving to his head and smoothing the few greasy brown strands that covered his bald patch. 'How far gone are you?'

'About eight weeks, I think.'

'That's good, good.' The man nodded.

'How much will it cost, please?'

'Well, I normally charge three guineas but, seeing as you're a friend of Doris, I'll do it for two.'

Greta dug her nails into the armchair and nodded her acceptance.

'Good. Well, if you care to hang on for half an hour or so, I could fit you in immediately. No time like the present, is there?' he said with a shrug.

'Will I be able to go to work tomorrow?'

'That depends on how things go. Some girls bleed a lot, others hardly at all.'

There was a knock at the door and a dour-looking woman poked her head around it. Ignoring Greta, she beckoned the man with her finger.

'Excuse me, I have to go and check on my patient.' He stood up and abruptly left the room.

Greta put her head in her hands. *Some girls bleed a lot, others hardly at all . . .*

She stood up, stumbled out of the grim front room and ran along the hall to open the front door. She slid back the rusty bolt, turned the latch and opened it.

'Miss, miss! Where are you goi—'

Greta slammed the door behind her and fled away up the street, tears blurring her vision.

That night, after the show, Doris sidled up to her.

'Did you see him?'

Greta nodded.

'When are you . . . you know?'

'I . . . some time next week.'

Doris patted her on the shoulder. 'You'll be fine, dear, honest you will.'

Greta sat without moving until the other girls had left the dressing room. Once the room was empty, she laid her head on the table and wept. The sound of the unseen woman she'd heard moaning had haunted her since she'd left the miserable house. And even though she knew she was sentencing herself to dreadful uncertainty, she knew she couldn't go through with an abortion.

Greta didn't hear the soft tap-tap on the dressing-room

door and jumped violently when a hand was laid on her shoulder.

'Hey! Steady on, it's only me, Taffy. I didn't mean to startle you. I was just checking to see that you'd all left. What's wrong, Greta?'

She looked up at Taffy's kind face watching her sympathetically in the mirror and searched for something to wipe her running nose. She was touched by his concern, especially since she knew she'd hardly given him a backward glance since she'd met Max. A spotlessly clean checked handkerchief was passed to her.

'There you go. Would you like me to leave?' He hovered behind her.

'Yes, er, no . . . oh, Taffy . . .' she sobbed miserably. 'I'm in such trouble!'

'Then why don't you tell me about it? It'll make you feel better, whatever it is.'

Greta turned to face him, shaking her head. 'I don't deserve sympathy,' she whimpered.

'Now you're being silly. Come here and let me give you a hug.' His strong arms closed around Greta's shoulders, and he held her until her sobs were little more than hiccups. Then he began to wipe away her tear-streaked make-up. 'We are in a state, aren't we? Well, as my old nanny used to say, nothing's ever as bad as it seems.'

Greta pulled away from him, suddenly uncomfortable. 'I'm sorry about this, Taffy. I'll be fine now, really.'

He looked at her, unconvinced. 'Have you eaten? You could pour out your sorrows over a nice plate of pie and mash. I find it always helps with affairs of the heart. Which I presume is where your problem lies.'

'Try a little further down,' mumbled Greta, then regretted it immediately.

He did his best not to let his true emotions register on his face. 'I see. And that Yank's upped and left you, has he?'

'Yes, but—' She looked at him in astonishment. 'How did you know about him?'

'Greta, you work in a theatre. Everyone from the doorkeeper to the manager knows everyone else's business. A nun on a vow of silence couldn't keep a secret in this place.'

'I'm sorry I didn't tell you about him. I should have, but—'

'What's past is past. Now, I'm going to wait outside while you change and then I'm going to take you for some supper.'

'But, Taffy, I—'

'Yes?'

Greta offered him a weak smile. 'Thank you for being so kind.'

'That's what friends are for, isn't it?'

He took her to their usual café across the road from the theatre. Greta found she was starving and devoured her pie and mash as she recounted her plight to him.

'So, I got the address from Doris and I went to see him this morning. But, Taffy, you have no idea what it was like there. This Mr Fix-it . . . he had dirty fingernails. I can't . . . I can't—'

'I understand,' he soothed. 'And your American doesn't know you're pregnant?'

'No. He shipped out the morning after he went to the Windmill and saw me starkers. I don't have an address for him in America and, even if I did, after seeing me on stage he's hardly likely to take me back, is he? He comes from a very traditional family.'

'Do you know whereabouts he lives in the States?'

'Yes, in a town called Charleston. It's somewhere in the South, apparently. Oh, Taffy, I was so excited about seeing the bright lights of New York.'

'Greta, if Max lived where you say, I doubt you'd ever have seen New York. It's hundreds of miles away from Charleston, nearly as far as London is from Italy. America's a vast country.'

'I know, but all the Americans I've met seem to be so forward-thinking and not at all stuffy like us Brits. I think it would have suited me.'

He gazed at her, his emotions a conflicting mixture of irritation and sympathy at her naivety. 'Well, if it makes you feel better, dear girl, the town you were about to move to is slap bang in the centre of what is known as the Bible Belt. Its inhabitants adhere so rigidly to the Scriptures that they make the morals of even our most devout English souls seem relaxed.'

'Max did say he was a Baptist,' Greta mused.

'There you are, then. I know it's no consolation, but honestly Greta, Charleston is about as far from the atmosphere of New York as my family home in the wilds of the Welsh mountains is from London. You'd have been a fish out of water there, especially after the life you've lived here. Personally, I think you've had a lucky escape.'

'Perhaps.' Greta understood that he was trying to comfort her, but everyone knew America was the New World, the land of opportunity, whichever part of it you lived in.

'But if you say they have such strict morals, then why did Max . . . well, you know . . .' Greta blushed.

'Maybe he thought he could bend the rules if you were engaged to be married,' he suggested lamely.

'I thought Max loved me, really. If he hadn't proposed, then I'd never, ever have—'

Greta's voice dried up in shame and embarrassment. He reached for her hand and squeezed it. 'I know you wouldn't,' he said gently.

'I'm not like Doris, really. Max . . . he was the first.' Tears appeared again in Greta's eyes. 'Why does my life always seem to go wrong?'

'Does it, Greta? Do you want to talk about it?'

'No,' she answered quickly. 'I'm just being self-indulgent, feeling sorry for myself because I've made such an awful mistake.'

As he watched Greta force her features into a smile, Taffy wondered what had led her – a girl who was obviously educated and whose accent told him she was well bred – to the Windmill. Greta was a cut above the rest of the girls, which, if he was frank, was the reason he'd been drawn to her. However, now was obviously not the moment to ask, so he changed the subject.

'Do you want the baby, Greta?'

'To be honest, I don't know, Taffy. I'm confused and frightened. And ashamed. I really believed Max loved me. Why did I ever . . . ?' Her voice trailed off miserably. 'When I was in that dreadful house waiting to see Doris's Mr Fix-it I didn't run away just because I was frightened of the procedure. I kept thinking of this little thing inside me. Then, on my way home, I passed two or three mothers wheeling their babies in prams. And it made me realise that, however tiny, it's alive, isn't it?'

'Yes, Greta, it is.'

'Then can I really commit murder for a mistake I've made? Deny the baby its right to life? I'm not a religious person, but I don't think I'd ever forgive myself for killing it. On the other hand, what future can there be for either of us if I bring it into the world? No man will ever look at me again. A Windmill Girl in the club at the age of eighteen? Hardly a good track record, is it?'

'Well, what I suggest you do is sleep on it. The most important thing is that you're not alone. And . . .' He voiced the thought that had been slowly brewing as he listened to her story of woe. 'I may well be in a position to sort something out, put a roof over your head if you do decide to go ahead with the pregnancy. This Mr Fix-it really doesn't sound too good, does he? You might end up killing both of you, and we wouldn't want that, would we?'

'No, but I'm still not convinced I have any choice.'

'Believe me, Greta, there is always a choice. What about going to see Mr Van Damm? I'm sure he's had to deal with this kind of thing before.'

'Oh, no! I couldn't do that! I know he's kind, but Mr Van Damm expects his girls to be whiter than white. He's terribly protective of the Windmill's image. I'd be out on my ear tomorrow.'

'Steady on, it was only a thought,' he replied, getting up to pay the bill. 'Now, I'm going to put you in a taxi. Go home and get some rest. You look exhausted, Greta.'

'No, really Taffy, I can take the bus.'

'I insist.'

Hailing a taxi outside the café, he pressed some coins into her small hand and put a finger to her lips as she began to protest again. 'Please, I'll worry if you don't. Pleasant dreams, Greta, and don't worry, I'm here now.'

'Thank you again for being so kind, Taffy.'

As David waved after the taxi, he asked himself why he was trying to help Greta, but the answer was simple. No matter what she'd done, he'd known from the moment he'd set eyes on her that he loved her.

# 4

The next morning the two of them were once again sitting in the café across the road from the Windmill. Greta had slipped out of the morning's rehearsal to meet David, claiming she was feeling faint and needed some fresh air, which wasn't far from the truth.

'You look awfully pale,' he said. 'Are you all right?'

Greta took a big gulp of her watery tea and added another lump of sugar. 'I'm tired, that's all.'

'I'm not surprised. Here, have half of my sandwich.'

'No, thanks.' Just the smell of it made her feel nauseous. 'I'll eat something later.'

'Mind you do. Well then?' He looked at her expectantly.

'I've decided I can't go through with the . . . procedure, so that leaves me no choice. I'm going to have the baby and suffer the consequences.'

'Right.' David nodded slowly. 'Well, now your mind's made up, I'm going to tell you how I may be able to help. What you need is a roof over your head and a bit of peace and privacy until the baby arrives. Yes?'

'Yes, but . . .'

'Hush, and listen to what I have to say. I have the use of

a cottage in Monmouthshire, on the Welsh borders. I was thinking you could go and stay there for a while. Have you ever been to the area before?'

'No, I haven't.'

'Well, then you won't know what a special place it is.' He smiled. 'The cottage is on a big estate called Marchmont. It's near the Black Mountains, in a beautiful valley not too far from the town of Abergavenny.'

'What a funny name.' Greta managed a half-hearted smile.

'I suppose you get used to the language when you're brought up there. Anyway, with me working in London, I don't need the cottage at the moment. My mother lives on the estate, too. I telephoned her last night and she's prepared to keep an eye on you. A lot of the land is farmed, so there's enough fresh produce to feed you during the coming winter. The cottage is small, but clean and cosy. It would mean you could leave the Windmill, have the baby and if you wanted to, come back to London without anyone even knowing. Well, there it is. What do you think?'

'It sounds lovely, but—'

'Greta, all I can do is offer you an alternative,' he said, seeing the doubt and fear in her eyes. 'And yes, it's very different from London. There are no bright lights, there's nothing to do in the evenings and you may be lonely. But at least you'll be safe and warm.'

'This – er – estate is where you were brought up, is it?'

'Yes, although I was at boarding school from the age of eleven and, after that, university. Then the war came and I was away with my regiment, so I haven't been back as often as I'd have liked. But Greta, you've never seen anything more lovely than a sunset over Marchmont. We have over five hundred acres, the house is surrounded by woodland that's home to endless plant and bird life, and a salmon river runs right through it. It really is a very beautiful place.'

A glimmer of hope for her hitherto devastated future began to glow in Greta's mind.

'You say your mother has said she won't mind if I stay? Does she . . . does she know about the baby?'

'Yes, she does, but don't worry, Greta. My mother is unshockable and very broad-minded. And, to be honest, I think she'd enjoy the company. The main house on the estate was used as a convalescent home in the war and, since all the staff and patients left, she misses the activity.'

'It really is very kind of you, Taffy, but I wouldn't want to impose. I have very little money to pay rent. In fact, none at all.'

'You don't have to pay anything. You'd be there as my guest,' he confirmed. 'As I said, the cottage is empty and it's yours if you want it.'

'You really are very generous. If I did take you up on your offer,' she said slowly, knowing that whatever this cottage was like, it had to be preferable to an unmarried mothers' home, 'how soon could I go?'

'As soon as you would like to.'

Two days later Greta went to tell Mr Van Damm that she was leaving the Windmill. When he asked her why, despite strongly suspecting that he already knew the reason, Greta merely said that her mother was unwell and she had to return home to care for her. She came out of the office apprehensive, but feeling better that she'd made a decision. Later that day she informed her landlady that she'd be vacating her room at the end of the week, and spent her last few days at the theatre trying not to worry about the future. All the girls signed a card for her and Doris hugged her goodbye, at the same time discreetly handing her an envelope containing a tiny pair of bootees.

It took Greta no time at all to pack her few belongings into two small suitcases. She paid her landlady and said goodbye to the room that had been her home for the past six months.

David accompanied her to Paddington Station on a foggy December morning to see her off on the long journey to Abergavenny.

'Oh, Taffy, I do wish you were coming with me,' she said, leaning out of the window as he stood on the platform.

'You'll be as safe as houses, Greta. Trust me. I wouldn't do wrong by you, now would I?'

'Your mother will be there to pick me up from the station?' Greta asked anxiously for the third time.

'Yes, she'll be there. And one word of warning – try and remember to refer to me as David. She won't be very impressed with my Windmill nickname, I can assure you,' he said with a chuckle. 'And I'll come and visit as soon as I can, promise. Now, here's a little something for you.' He pressed an envelope into her hand as the guard blew his whistle. 'Goodbye, sweetheart. Safe journey and take care of the both of you.'

Kissing her on both cheeks, David thought Greta resembled a ten-year-old evacuee being billeted out to an unknown location.

Greta waved until he was a tiny speck on the platform, then made her way to her carriage and sat down amongst a group of demobbed soldiers. They were smoking and talking excitedly about friends and relatives they hadn't seen for months. The contrast between them and her was almost unbearably poignant – they were returning to their loved ones and she was on a journey into the unknown. She opened the envelope David had put into her hand. It contained some money and a note telling her it was for emergencies.

As she watched London's familiar buildings give way to undulating fields, Greta's fear began to grow. She comforted herself with the thought that if David's mother turned out to be a madwoman and the cottage no more than a chicken shed, she now had enough money to return to London and rethink her plans. As the train travelled west, stopping at numerous stations, the soldiers gradually disembarked to be greeted on the platforms by joyful parents, wives and girlfriends. There were only a handful of passengers left by the time she'd changed trains at Newport, then, eventually, Greta was alone in the carriage. She began to relax slightly as she stared out of the window at the unfamiliar Welsh landscape. As the sun began to set, she became aware of a subtle change in the scenery; it was wilder and more dramatic than anything she'd seen before in England. Snow-capped mountains appeared on the darkening horizon as the train chugged nearer to Abergavenny.

It was past five o'clock and already pitch black when the train finally drew in to her destination. Greta pulled her suitcases from the rack above her head, straightened her hat and stepped out onto the platform. A chill wind was blowing and she pulled her coat closer to shield her body. She walked uncertainly towards the exit, glancing around for anyone who might be expecting her. She sat on a bench outside the tiny station as her fellow passengers greeted those there to meet them and subsequently departed into the night.

Ten minutes later, the narrow forecourt was almost deserted. After shivering on the bench for a few more minutes, Greta stood up and walked back into the relative warmth of the station itself. The clerk was still working behind the window, and she tapped on it.

'Excuse me, sir.'

'Yes, *fach*?'

'Can you tell me what time the next connecting train to London leaves?'

The clerk shook his head. 'No more trains tonight. The next one's tomorrow morning.'

'Oh.' Greta bit her lip, feeling tears pricking the back of her eyes.

'I'm sorry, miss. Have you anywhere to stay tonight?'

'Well, someone's meant to be meeting me to take me to a place called Marchmont.'

The clerk rubbed his brow. 'Look you, that's a good few miles from here. Not walking distance. And Tom the Taxi is over in Monmouth tonight with his missus.'

'Oh dear.'

'Don't panic yet, see. I'll be here for another half-hour or so,' the clerk said kindly.

Greta nodded and retraced her steps to the bench. 'Oh

goodness,' she sighed and breathed on her hands, trying to stop them going numb. Then she heard the sound of a car approaching. A loud horn assaulted her ears and bright lights dazzled her eyes. Once the noisy engine of the vehicle in front of her had died into silence, a female voice called out, 'Damn! Damn! Hello there! Are you Greta Simpson?'

Greta tried to make out the figure sitting in the driving seat of the open-topped car. The driver's eyes were shielded behind huge leather goggles.

'Yes. Are you Taff— David Marchmont's mother?'

'I am. Jump in then, quick smart. Sorry I'm late. The blasted car got a puncture and I had to change the tyre in the dark.'

'Er, right.' Greta stood, picked up her suitcases and hauled them across to the car.

'Throw those in the back, dear, put these on and grab that travel rug. It can be a bit breezy if the old girl gets above twenty miles per hour.'

Greta took the proffered goggles and blanket. After a few false starts the engine burst into life and the driver reversed rapidly out of the station forecourt, narrowly missing a lamp post.

'I thought you weren't coming,' Greta ventured as the car hit the open road and sped down it at frightening speed.

'Don't talk, dear girl. Can't hear a word above this racket!' shouted the driver.

Greta spent the following half-hour with her eyes tightly shut and her hands balled into fists, the knuckles white with tension. At last the car slowed, then it stopped abruptly, almost throwing Greta over the small windscreen and onto the bonnet.

'Do be a darling and open those gates, will you?'

Greta stepped shakily out of the car. She walked in front of the headlights and pushed open two enormous wrought-iron gates. On the wall to one side of them there was an ornate bronze plaque with the word 'MARCHMONT' engraved upon it. The car drove through and Greta shut the gates behind them.

'Buck up, dear. Nearly there now,' the driver shouted over the roar of the engine.

Greta scurried back into the car and they set off along the rutted drive.

'Here we go. This is Lark Cottage.' The car shuddered to a halt and the driver leapt out, grabbing Greta's cases from the back seat. 'Home sweet home.'

As Greta stepped down, she watched the woman making her way through a glade of moonlit trees. Following nervously behind her, she sighed in relief as a small cottage came into view. Oil lamps illuminated the interior, giving out a soft yellow glow. The woman opened the front door and they went in.

'So.' The woman peeled off her goggles and turned to face Greta. 'This is it. Will it suffice, do you think?'

It was the first opportunity Greta had had to study her companion, and she was immediately struck by the woman's resemblance to her son. She was very tall and long-limbed, with piercing green eyes and a shock of windswept greying hair cut in a short, sensible style. Her outfit of corduroy breeches, knee-length leather boots and a tailored tweed jacket was both mannish and strangely elegant.

Greta glanced around the cosy interior of the cottage, looking gratefully at the fire, with its burning embers.

'Yes. It's lovely.'

'Good. Bit basic, I'm afraid. No electricity in here yet. We were just about to install it when war broke out. The privy's outside and there's a tin bath in the kitchen for high days and holidays, but it takes so damn long to fill it's easier to use the sink.'

The woman strode towards the fire, picked up a poker, stirred the embers and threw on three logs from the basket beside the fireplace. 'There. I lit it before I came to fetch you. The oil for the lamps is in a canister in the privy, the logs are in the shed out back, and I've put some milk, fresh bread and cheese in the pantry for your supper. I'm sure you're parched. Put the kettle on the range and it'll boil in no time. And don't forget to stoke it with wood every morning. It's a hungry beast, if I remember rightly. Now, got to be off, I'm afraid. We've lost a ewe, you see. Gone over a gulley, we suspect. David said you're a pretty self-sufficient kind of gel, but I'll drop in on you tomorrow when you've got your bearings. I'm Laura-Jane Marchmont, by the way' – she thrust out her hand to Greta – 'but everyone calls me LJ. You should too. Goodnight.'

The door slammed and she was gone.

Greta shook her head in confusion, sighed and then sank into the threadbare but comfortable armchair in front of the fire. She was hungry and desperate for a cup of tea, but first she needed to sit down for a few minutes and recover from the ordeal of her day.

She stared into the fire, pondering on the woman who had just left. Whatever she had expected Taffy's mother to be, it was not Laura-Jane Marchmont. In truth, she'd imagined an unsophisticated country widow with plump, ruddy cheeks and child-bearing hips. She glanced round her new home and began to take full note of her surroundings. The sitting room was snug, with a charming beamed ceiling and a large inglenook fireplace taking up an entire wall. The furnishings were minimal: just the armchair, an occasional table and a crooked shelf stacked untidily with books. She pushed open a latched door and walked down two stone steps into the small kitchen. There was a sink, a Welsh dresser filled with mismatched crockery, a scrubbed pine table with two chairs and a pantry, in which she discovered a loaf of fresh bread, a slab of cheese, butter, some tins of soup and half a dozen apples. She opened the back door and found the icebox masquerading as a lavatory to her left.

A creaking staircase led off from the kitchen to a door at the top, beyond which was the bedroom. The low-ceilinged room was almost entirely taken up by a sturdy wrought-iron bed covered in a cheerful patchwork quilt. An oil lamp cast a warming, shadowy glow. Greta looked longingly at the bed but knew that, for the baby's sake as much as her own, she needed to eat before she slept.

After a supper of bread, soup and cheese in front of the fire, she yawned. She washed as best she could in the kitchen sink, realising she'd have to boil the kettle in future if she wanted warm water. Then, shivering, she picked up her suitcases and finally made her way up the staircase.

Pulling her nightdress over her head, and adding a jumper on top of that, she pulled back the quilt and sank gratefully into the comfortable bed. She closed her eyes and waited for sleep to wash over her. The silence, after her noisy London room, was deafening. Eventually, exhaustion overtook her and she fell into a dreamless slumber.

# 5

Greta woke the following morning to the sound of two pigeons cooing outside her bedroom window. Feeling disoriented, she reached for her watch and saw that it was past ten o'clock. She rose from the bed, drew the curtains back and peered out of the window.

The sky was a soft blue and the frost of the night before had been melted away by the weak winter sun, leaving a heavy dew. Below her, there was a gently sloping valley, its sides planted with a dense wood, the huge trees now bare of leaves. The sound of rushing water told her a stream must be close by. Across from the river that bisected the floor of the valley she could see undulating fields sloping upwards, populated with small white dots which must be sheep. And away to her left, presiding over the valley, stood a low red-brick house surrounded by sweeping lawns and tiers of stone terraces. Its many mullioned windows glinted in the sun and she could see smoke coming from two of the four majestic chimneys. She assumed this must be Marchmont Hall. To the right of the house there were barns and other outbuildings.

The sight of the peaceful, natural landscape surrounding Greta filled her with unexpected pleasure. She dressed quickly, eager to go outside and explore. As she was walking down the narrow staircase, there was a knock on the front door and she hurried to open it.

'Morning. Just came to check that you're settling in all right.'

'Hello, LJ,' said Greta self-consciously. 'I'm fine, thank you. I've only just woken up.'

'Good grief! I've been up since five nursing that blessed ewe. She *had* fallen over the gulley, and it took the men hours to coax her up. Looks as if she'll make it, though. Now, we need to have a chinwag about logistics whilst you're staying here, so why don't you come over to me tonight for a spot of supper?' suggested LJ.

'That would be lovely, but I don't want to put you to any bother.'

'No bother at all. To be honest, it'll be nice to have a bit of female company.'

'Do you live in that big house over there?' enquired Greta.

'Used to, dear girl, used to. But nowadays I live in the Gate Lodge by the main gate. Does me fine. Just turn right out of here and follow the path. A brisk walk of five minutes should do it. There's a hurricane lamp in the pantry. You'll need it. Pitch bloody black around here, as you saw last night. Now, I must be off. See you at seven.'

'Yes, I'll look forward to it. Thank you.'

LJ smiled at Greta, then turned round and waved as she marched briskly down the path.

*

Greta spent the day settling into her new home. She unpacked her cases then went for a walk, following the sound of running water. After a while she found the stream and knelt to take a drink of the clear, sparkling water. The air was bracing and bitterly cold, but the sun was shining and the leaves that had fallen from the many trees formed a natural carpet for her to walk on. She arrived home weary, but with a hint of pink in each of her normally pale cheeks. She changed into her best skirt and jacket, looking forward to supper with LJ.

At five to seven Greta knocked on the door of the Gate Lodge. By the dim light of the moon, she could see it was a modest but handsome red-brick building whose gable-fronted architecture echoed that of Marchmont Hall itself. The small front garden looked immaculate.

LJ opened the door a few seconds later. 'Bang on time, I see. I like that. I'm a stickler for punctuality. Come in, my dear.' She took the hurricane lamp Greta was carrying and extinguished it before helping her off with her coat.

Greta then followed LJ through the hall and into a formal but reassuringly cluttered sitting room.

'Sit down, dear girl. Drink?'

'Yes, please. Anything soft, thank you.'

'I'll mix you a small gin. Do you and the baby no harm at all. Drank like a fish myself when I was carrying David, and look at the size of him! Won't be a second.'

LJ left the room and Greta sat down on a chair by the fire. She glanced around the room and took in the mahogany dresser filled with expensive-looking china and the framed pictures depicting lurid hunting scenes. It was obvious that the furniture in the room was valuable, but had seen better days.

'There we go.' LJ handed a large glass to Greta and sat down in the armchair opposite her. 'Welcome to Marchmont, my dear. I hope that for the time you're with us, you'll be very happy.' LJ took a large gulp of her gin as Greta tentatively sipped her own.

'Thank you. It's so kind of you to have me here. I don't know what I'd have done if it hadn't been for your son,' she murmured shyly.

'He always was a soft touch for a damsel in distress.'

'Taffy's doing awfully well at the Windmill, too,' Greta said. 'Mr Van Damm has just given him a regular slot. His routine is very funny. All us girls fall about when we listen to it.'

'Yes, well, could I ask one favour? While you're here, please could you try to remember to call my son by his proper Christian name? I'm afraid it offends my sensibilities to hear his extremely unimaginative nickname. Especially as he's only half Welsh in the first place.'

'Of course, I apologise, LJ. So his father is Welsh, I suppose?'

'Yes, as you might have guessed, I'm as English as you. Such a shame that David barely knew his father. Robin, my husband, died in a riding accident when David was twelve, you see.'

'Oh, I'm sorry,' murmured Greta.

'So was I, my dear, but the one thing you learn, living on an estate such as this is that death is as much a part of life as life itself.'

Greta took another small sip of her gin. 'You said this morning you used to live in the big house?'

'We did. David was born there. When the house was taken over as a nursing home during the war I moved out to the Gate Lodge. I decided it suited me much better and never moved back, especially since—' LJ stopped suddenly. 'My husband's elder brother lives there now.'

'I see. It looks like a beautiful place,' ventured Greta, sensing LJ's tension.

'I suppose so. Huge though, and the maintenance bills are a nightmare. Cost a fortune to have electricity put in. Mind you, with ten large bedrooms, it served well as a nursing home. It held twenty officers and a team of eight nurses at one time. Rather came into its own, I think.'

'So, do you help run the Marchmont estate?' asked Greta.

'No, not any more. After my husband died, yes, I did. I looked after the upkeep of the place, which I can tell you is a full-time job. Owen, Robin's brother, was in Kenya but returned home when war broke out and naturally he took over the running of things. The farm produced milk and meat for the Ministry of Agriculture and it meant that we here were self-sufficient. Rationing hardly touched us. It was all hands to the pump then, I can tell you. I worked on the farm from dawn until dusk. Then, when the house was requisitioned as a nursing home, I worked alongside the medical staff. I know I should be relieved the war is over, but I rather enjoyed all the activity. Feels a bit like I've been put out to pasture now,' she said with a sigh.

'But you still help on the farm?'

'For the present, yes. Some of the young men from

around here are yet to return, so the farm manager's always short-handed. I'm roped in to help milk the cows or hunt for lost sheep when necessary. It's quite a big operation, you know. Nowadays, one has to make one's land pay its way. The milk and meat we produce earn sufficient income to keep the estate going. Now, that's enough about me. Tell me about you.'

'There's nothing much to tell, really. I used to work with Taff— David, at the theatre and we became friends.'

'You were one of the Windmill Girls, then?'

Greta blushed and nodded. 'Yes, but only for a few months.'

'No need to be embarrassed, dear girl. Women have to earn their living somehow and, until the world wakes up and sees the inner steel of us females, one has to get by any way one can. Take me, for example. The very model of an upper-class Englishwoman. Even had an "honourable" before my name. Being a girl, I had to stay at home and learn cross-stitch while my brothers – who in my opinion did not have a decent brain between them – were educated at Eton and Oxford. One's a drunk and managed to squander the family pile in a matter of years, and the other got himself shot whilst hunting in Africa.'

'Oh dear, I'm sorry to hear that.'

'Don't be. He deserved it,' LJ said brusquely. 'I've spent the past thirty years at Marchmont working in some capacity or another and it's been the happiest time of my life. Anyway, we seem to have got back to me again. My fault. I digress all the time. One of my bad habits, I'm afraid. We were talking about you. I don't wish to seem rude, but just what is your relationship with David?' LJ's aquiline nose almost quivered with inquisitiveness.

'We're good friends. That's all, really.'

'Would it be impertinent to suggest that I have the feeling that David is more than a little keen on you? After all, it's not as if he lends the cottage to every stray girl he meets.'

'As I said, we're just good friends.' Greta felt herself blushing. 'David helped me because I had no one else.'

'What about your family?'

'I . . . they died in the Blitz.' It was a lie, but LJ wasn't to know.

'I see. Poor you. And the baby?'

'The father was an American officer. I thought he loved me and—'

LJ nodded. 'Well, it's happened through the centuries and will continue for time eternal, I'm sure. And there are lots less lucky than you, my dear. At least you have a roof over your head, thanks to my son.'

'And I'll always be grateful,' said Greta, feeling suddenly tearful and overwhelmed.

'Now, you don't mind if we eat off trays in here, do you?' LJ said, changing the subject. 'The dining room's so damned cold and gloomy. Only to be used for funeral wakes, in my book.'

'Not at all.'

'Good. I'll go and fetch our supper, then.'

LJ was back shortly, carrying two plates piled high with a hearty beef stew and buttery mashed potatoes.

'This tastes wonderful,' Greta said, tucking in hungrily. 'What we ate at home during the war was pretty awful.'

'I heard those powdered eggs were something of an acquired taste.' LJ raised her eyebrows. 'Well, you won't want for fresh produce around here. We have sheep galore, poultry, game birds and home-grown vegetables to boot. Plus the dairy, of course.'

'Goodness me! I was starving,' Greta said a few minutes later as she put her knife and fork together on the empty plate.

'A combination of fresh air and pregnancy. Now, come and help me wash up. I do so hate coming down to dirty dishes in the morning.'

Greta picked up her tray and followed LJ into the kitchen.

'Talking of food, I'll bring eggs, milk, vegetables and meat for you weekly. If you want anything else, you can catch the bus into Crickhowell, the nearest village. Not that they stock hampers from Fortnum's, but there's a nice wool shop. Maybe you could knit some things for the baby – and for yourself, for that matter. You'll need some warmer clothing, winter can be bitter here.' LJ glanced at Greta's thin jacket and skirt.

'I don't know how to knit, LJ.'

'Well, then, we'll have to teach you, won't we? During the war I must have knitted about a hundred jumpers for our boys. It's amazing the things you learn when you have to. And David has a stack of books that should keep you occupied. I've just finished *Animal Farm* by that chap George Orwell. Wonderful book. I'll lend it to you if you like.'

Greta nodded eagerly. She'd always been an avid reader.

They went back into the sitting room, drank cocoa and listened to the nine o'clock news on the wireless.

'Lifeline for us here, that ugly box of wire mesh,' said LJ. 'I've become quite addicted to Tommy Handley in *ITMA*, and David idolises him.'

'May I ask why David left Marchmont to work in London?' asked Greta. 'If I'd been born here, I certainly wouldn't have left.'

LJ sighed. 'Well, for starters, David really left Marchmont a long time ago. He boarded at Winchester and was in his final year at Oxford when the war broke out. Although he didn't need to, he enlisted straight away and was injured a few months later at Dunkirk. Once he recovered, he was sent to Bletchley Park and, from all accounts, was working on some pretty top-secret stuff down there. Clever boy, David. Has an excellent academic record. Seems such a shame he didn't have a chance to finish his degree, or decide to pursue a career in which he can use his brains.'

'Well, I've seen David perform. The way he reels off his patter is wonderful. I think you have to be very clever to be a good comedian,' said Greta defensively.

'Yes, well, not quite what one would have chosen for one's only son, but he's dreamt about the bright lights since he was a small boy. Lord knows where he gets it from. There aren't many performers in his father's family or mine,' sniffed LJ. 'I did wonder whether his stint in the army might change his mind, but no. Eight months ago he was relieved of his duties. He came home and told me he was off to London to try his luck on the stage.'

'Well, if it's any comfort, he's doing extremely well. Everyone at the Windmill thinks he'll go far.'

'It is indeed a comfort. When you have your little one in

a few months' time you'll understand the agony of being a parent. Even if I had other plans for David when he was younger, I'm just grateful he lived through the war to pursue his dreams. My main concern now is that he's happy.' LJ yawned suddenly. 'Excuse me. After last night's debacle with the ewe, I'm exhausted. I'm sorry to throw you out, but I have to be up early to milk the cows. Will you be all right to make your own way home?'

'I'll be fine,' promised Greta.

'Good. I'll pop in to see you whenever I can and, if you need anything, I'm always around somewhere.'

LJ walked into the hall and retrieved Greta's coat from the banister. She stooped down and picked up a pair of wellington boots.

'Here, take these. They'll probably be far too big for you, but those town shoes you're wearing won't last you more than a few days here.'

Greta put on her coat and took the wellingtons. 'Thank you so much for supper. It really is good of you to look after me like this.'

'I've always been a sucker for my darling David.' LJ's face softened as she relit Greta's hurricane lamp and handed it to her. 'You'll understand what I mean soon enough.' She indicated Greta's stomach. 'Goodnight, Greta.'

'Goodnight.'

LJ stood at the door and watched the girl make her way carefully down the path. She shut the door, deep in thought, and went to sit in her favourite armchair by the fire, trying to work out why she was filled with unease.

When David had telephoned her and told her he wanted

Greta to come and stay in his cottage, LJ had heard the warmth in his voice when he spoke about her. Maybe he was hoping that Greta's gratitude would spill over into something more, that she would one day reciprocate his feelings. Greta seemed a nice enough sort of girl, but LJ could see that she wasn't in love with her son.

As she climbed the stairs to bed LJ prayed that her precious David wouldn't regret his kind-hearted action.

She had a strong feeling that the arrival of Greta at Marchmont was going to have an effect on David's destiny. And, for some reason she could not fathom, on her own, too.

# 6

After a week of living at Marchmont and with Christmas approaching, Greta knew that in the months to come, bore dom would be her greatest enemy. Introspection had never been something that appealed to her; in truth, it frightened her. The thought of having hour after hour to contemplate her life and the mess she had made of it was not one she relished. But here, with nothing to do but read books – several of which were classics by Charles Dickens and Thomas Hardy, whose tales of tragedy only served to mirror her own misery – Greta found herself watching the clock and willing the time to pass.

She spent hours thinking about Max, where he was, what he was doing. She even contemplated getting in touch with Whitehall and trying to trace him, but there seemed little point. Max wouldn't want her now.

She missed him. Not the presents, nor the life she could have had, but the man himself. His soft Southern drawl, his laughter, the gentleness of his touch as he'd made love to her . . .

In the afternoons she'd taken to going for a long walk, just to get out of the cottage. She would walk past the Gate

Lodge, praying that its occupant might see her from the window and come out to have a chat. LJ had popped in a few days ago with food supplies, a pair of knitting needles and some wool. She had sat patiently with Greta for an hour, teaching her the basics, but Greta hadn't seen her since and would set off alone into the woods.

Then, yesterday, LJ had arrived with a hamper filled with Christmas treats.

'I'm off to my sister's house in Gloucestershire in an hour or so. I'll be back bright and early on Boxing Day,' she'd imparted in her usual brusque manner. 'This lot should keep you going, and I've asked Mervyn, the farm-hand, to drop off some fresh bread and milk whilst I'm away. Merry Christmas, dear girl. Snow is forecast for tomorrow, so make sure you keep your fire stoked.'

As Greta watched LJ leave, her sense of isolation had deepened. And as the snow LJ had predicted began to tumble from the sky on Christmas Eve, even the pleasure of a home-made mince pie and a small glass of sweet sherry from the hamper hadn't cheered her spirits.

'We're completely alone, little one,' she'd whispered to her stomach as the nearby chapel bells chimed midnight. 'Merry Christmas.'

On Christmas Day Greta drew back the curtains to see a fairy-tale picture in front of her.

The snowfall overnight had transformed the landscape. Every branch of every tree was covered with the pure white powder, as though someone had sprinkled them with icing sugar. The floor of the woods, with the occasional dark twig piercing the snow's perfect surface, resembled a carpet of ermine. A thick frost added twinkling highlights to the idyllic scene as the morning sun rose higher over the frozen valley.

Walking downstairs, Greta pondered that on any other Christmas Day, she'd have been delighted that snow had fallen, but as she relit the fire and put the kettle on the range to boil, she thought she'd never felt so miserable.

Later, as she cooked and ate the chicken LJ had left her, then demolished the rest of the mince pies – her appetite seemed to be insatiable these days – she reflected on past Christmases and how very different they had been.

Not wishing to look back, but with nothing to distract her and unable to prevent the memories flooding in, she put on her coat, hat and wellington boots and set off for her afternoon walk.

Opening the back door, Greta stepped out, the snow crunching underfoot as she did so, her breath crystallising into thin wisps of white in the freezing air. Roaming through the woods, her mood lifted briefly as she drank in the magical surroundings, stopping here and there to examine the glistening, frosty patterns that had formed on tree trunks and fallen branches. Yet it wasn't long before her mind began to wander once again.

Perhaps, she thought, the reason she felt so low was that it had been a year ago today when the problem that had precipitated her abrupt move to London had first arisen.

She'd had a happy childhood, living in a respectable suburb of Manchester, the only child of adoring parents. Then, one dreadful day when she was thirteen and the German air raids had begun in earnest, her father had gone out in his black Ford car and never returned. Her sobbing, hysterical mother told her the following day that he had died in a bombing raid at the Manchester Royal Exchange. A week later Greta had watched what was left of her beloved father being lowered into the ground.

In the two years that followed, in an atmosphere of tension as the war raged on, her mother went into a deep depression – sometimes taking to her bed for weeks on end – while Greta concentrated grimly on her schoolwork and buried her nose in books. The one other thing she derived comfort from was the cinema, which her mother had taken her to regularly. The world of fantasy, in which everyone was beautiful and almost all the stories had happy endings, had provided a blessed relief from reality. Greta had decided that when she was grown up she was going to be an actress.

When she was fifteen, her situation changed. Her mother arrived home one night in a big car with an overweight, grey-haired man and told Greta that he was to be her new father. Three months later they had moved to her stepfather's enormous house in Altrincham, one of the most desirable towns in Cheshire. Her mother, relieved to have found another man to take care of her, became her old self and their home was once again filled with guests and the sound of laughter. And, for a while, Greta was happy.

Her new stepfather, a brusque but wealthy Mancunian industrialist, was a distant figure whom initially Greta rarely saw. But as she matured into a young woman, his attention had begun to wander from his wife to her young, and prettier, daughter. It became a habit of his that, every time they were alone together in the house, he would seek her out. Things had come to a head on Christmas Day last year, when, during a party at the house, while her mother was downstairs entertaining guests, he had followed her upstairs . . .

Greta shuddered at the memory of his stinking breath, the heavy weight of his bulk pinning her against a wall as his hands had groped for her breasts and his wet lips had sought hers.

Luckily, on that occasion, the sound of footsteps climbing the stairs had prevented him going any further, and Greta had run to her room in a state of terrified shock, praying the incident had merely been a drink-fuelled one-off.

Sadly, this hadn't been the case, and Greta spent the following few months doing all she could to avoid her stepfather's advances. One hot June night he had burst into her bedroom as she was removing her stockings ready for bed. Grabbing her from behind, he'd thrown her onto the mattress with a hand over her mouth to prevent her screams. Somehow she'd been able to manoeuvre her knee upwards and, as he shifted his weight off her to open his trouser buttons, she'd managed to butt her knee hard into his groin.

With a howl, he'd rolled off the bed, then staggered to the door, screaming obscenities at her.

Knowing she now had no alternative, Greta had packed her suitcase, then, when the house was silent, stolen downstairs after midnight. She remembered that once, her stepfather had invited her into his study and insisted she sat on his knee. Revolted, but not wanting to incur his anger, she'd done so. He'd opened a drawer, taken out a key, unlocked his safe and shown her a diamond necklace he said would be hers if she was a good girl. Greta had noticed that the safe was stacked with cash. So that fateful night, walking swiftly to the drawer and taking the key from its hiding place, she'd unlocked the safe and grabbed a large wad of notes.

Then she had left the house, walked to Altrincham train station and sat on the platform until the five o'clock milk train arrived to take her to Manchester. From there she'd caught the train to London and gone straight to the Windmill to enquire about a job.

Greta looked up at the fast-darkening sky, wondering whether her mother had ever tried to find her after she'd left. She'd sometimes thought about writing to her, but how could she explain her sudden departure? Even if her mother believed her, which was doubtful, Greta knew the truth would break her heart.

Sadness overwhelmed her as she came to a halt in a clearing, suddenly realising she'd been so deep in thought she hadn't been concentrating on where she was going. Standing amongst the tall trees that glistened in the fading light, Greta searched for a landmark, something to guide her home. But everything familiar was masked by the white covering of snow.

'Oh God,' she muttered, turning in a fruitless circle, desperate to find her bearings.

Pulling up her collar against the cold, trying frantically to decide which direction to head in, she heard a dog bark close by. She stopped, glanced back and saw an enormous black hound charging towards her. Rooted to the spot with fear, she watched as it pounded closer, its pace not letting up. With a great effort, Greta managed to galvanise her body into action and turned and ran as fast as she could.

'Oh God! Oh God!' she cried, hearing the dog panting only a few yards behind her. The light had almost gone now, and she couldn't see clearly where she was going. As her too-big wellingtons struggled to maintain a grip on the icy snow, she stumbled and fell, hitting her head against the base of a tree. Everything went black.

Greta awoke to the sensation of hot breath on her face and a rough tongue licking her cheek. She opened her eyes, stared into the big red eyes of the dog and let out a high-pitched scream.

'Morgan! Morgan! Heel!'

The dog immediately left Greta and ran obediently to the side of a tall figure walking swiftly towards her. Greta tried to sit up, but dizziness overcame her. She closed her eyes and slumped back down with a groan.

'Are you all right?'

The voice was male and deep.

'I—' Greta opened her eyes once more and saw a man standing over her. 'I don't know,' she whispered, and started shivering uncontrollably.

The man bent down. 'Did you fall? You have a nasty gash on your forehead.' He reached out a hand and pushed away her hair. He studied the cut, then fumbled for a handkerchief and used it to clear the blood.

'Yes. That dog was chasing me. I thought it was going to kill me!'

'Morgan? Kill you? I rather doubt it. Coming to bid you welcome in a rather boisterous manner, maybe,' the man said gruffly. 'Can you walk? We need to get you up to the house so we can dry you off and look at that wound properly. It's too dark out here to see what we're dealing with.'

Greta made a valiant effort to stand, but when she put pressure onto her right ankle the pain made her yelp. She sank back again, shaking her head pathetically.

'Righto. Only one thing for it, then. I'll have to carry you. Put your arms round my neck.' The man knelt next to her, and Greta did as he'd asked. He lifted her from the ground without difficulty.

'Hold on tight. Soon have you in the warm.'

Greta hid her face in the waxed-cloth shoulder of her saviour. She felt so dizzy it was all she could do to will herself not to faint again. Ten minutes later she looked up and saw that they were out of the woods and heading towards the glowing lights of the big house. They reached the porticoed entrance and the man pushed the large oak door open with his shoulder.

'Mary! Mary! Where are you, woman?' he shouted as he crossed the cavernous entrance hall. Through a haze of pain, Greta took in the enormous Christmas tree positioned in the well of the heavy Elizabethan staircase. The candlelight reflecting off the delicate glass baubles danced hypnotically in front of her eyes and a wonderful smell of pine scented the air. The man carried her into a spacious drawing room, where a fire blazed in the grate of a huge stone fireplace. He laid Greta gently down on one of the two large velvet sofas arranged around the hearth.

'Sorry, Master Owen. Did you call?' A rotund young woman in an apron appeared at the drawing-room door.

'Yes! Get some warm water, a towel, a blanket and a large glass of brandy.'

'Yes, sir. Of course, sir,' Mary said, and left the room.

The man shrugged off his coat and threw it over a chair, then started to bank up the fire. Soon the heat began to travel towards Greta. She watched him silently as she tried to control her shivering. He was not as tall as she'd first thought from her prone position on the ground in the woods. His weathered yet handsome face was deeply tanned and framed by thick, grey, curly hair. He was dressed practically for the outdoors, in moleskin trousers and a tweed jacket with a high-necked woollen jumper beneath it, and Greta deduced he was probably in his mid-fifties.

'Here we go, sir.' Mary, the maid, hurried back into the room with the things he had requested. She set them down on the floor by the sofa. 'I'll just pop and get the brandy from the library, sir.'

'Thank you, Mary. Now' – the man knelt by Greta and dipped a corner of the towel into the water – 'let's get this wound clean, then Mary can find you something dry to put on.' He dabbed at the cut on her forehead and Greta winced. 'Not a poacher, are you? You don't look like you are, but one can never tell these days.'

'No.'

'Well, that's as maybe, but you were still trespassing. You were on private land.' He rinsed the blood-stained towel in the water and pressed it once more against her temple.

'I wasn't trespassing,' Greta managed. 'I live here on the estate.'

One of the man's thick brown eyebrows rose in surprise. 'Do you, indeed?'

'Yes, in Lark Cottage. It's David Marchmont's, and he's letting me borrow it for a while.'

The man's brow furrowed. 'I see. Girlfriend of his, are you?'

'Oh no, nothing like that,' Greta clarified hurriedly.

'Well, I do wish Laura-Jane would tell me when her son offers one of Marchmont's cottages to a stray young lady. I'm Owen Marchmont, David's uncle, by the way. I own this estate.'

'Then I'm sorry you didn't know I was here.'

'Not your fault, but typical, typical,' Owen grumbled. 'Ah, here comes the brandy. Thank you, Mary. Find this young lady something dry to wear then help her out of those wet clothes. I'll return shortly and have a look at that ankle,' he added to Greta, then nodded briefly at her and left the room, with Mary following close behind.

Greta lay back against the arm of the sofa, her head throbbing, but at least she no longer felt faint. She looked around the gracious, comfortable room and saw that it was filled with an eclectic mix of tasteful antique furniture. The ancient stone floor was softened by several faded Aubusson rugs, and plum-coloured silk curtains framed the large windows. The ceiling was supported by one huge beam and the oak-panelled walls were hung with oil paintings.

Mary was soon back, and she helped Greta undress then wrapped her up in a thick woollen robe.

'Thank you,' Greta said as the girl handed her the glass of brandy. 'I'm sorry to be a nuisance.'

'Now, you rest, *fach*. You've had a nasty fall, see. Master Owen will be along soon to look at your ankle,' Mary said kindly, as she retreated once more.

A few minutes later Owen entered the room and walked towards Greta. 'Feeling better?' he asked.

'I think so,' she said uncertainly, taking a cautious sip of brandy.

'Let's have a look.' He sat down on the sofa and examined Greta's ankle. 'It's badly swollen, but as you can move it I doubt you've broken it. My guess is it's a bad sprain. The only thing for that is rest. Given the snow, I'm afraid you'll have to stay here for the night. You've had a nasty shock and it wouldn't do to put any weight on that ankle at present.'

'Oh no, sir, I . . . I wouldn't like to impose. I—'

'Nonsense! We have nine empty bedrooms and Mary has only me to worry about. I'll have her light a fire in one of the spare rooms. Are you hungry?'

Greta shook her head. She still felt sick.

Owen rang for Mary and when she reappeared, he issued further instructions then sat down in an armchair opposite Greta.

'Well, this is an interesting turn of events on Christmas Day. My guests left a couple of hours ago, after lunch, and it seems I now have another. What were you doing in the woods when darkness was falling anyway, my dear? You were a long way from Lark Cottage when Morgan found you. I doubt you could have found your way home. You might have frozen to death out there.'

'I . . . got lost,' Greta admitted.

'Well, all in all, despite a sprained ankle, I think you've had a lucky escape.'

'Yes. Thank you so much for rescuing me,' she said, stifling a yawn.

'Right, by the looks of you, it's time to put you to bed. Let's carry you up the stairs, shall we?'

Fifteen minutes later Greta was wearing a clean pair of Owen's pyjamas and installed in a large, comfortable, canopied bed. It and the room itself, with its heavy damask drapes, oriental rugs and exquisite walnut furniture, reminded her of something a queen might sleep in.

'Any problems, ring the bell and Mary will attend to you. Goodnight, Miss—?'

'Simpson, Greta Simpson. And I'm truly sorry for putting you to all this trouble. I'm sure I'll be fine tomorrow.'

'Of course. And please call me Owen.' He gave her an almost embarrassed half-smile and left the room.

After Mary had delivered a mug of cocoa, of which Greta could manage only a few sips, a wave of exhaustion overcame her. She closed her eyes and slept.

Mary knocked on the door the following morning and quietly entered the room. She set down a breakfast tray and drew back the curtains.

'Morning, miss. How are you feeling today?' she asked as Greta stirred in the big bed and stretched luxuriously.

'As a matter of fact, I slept better than I have in a long time.' She smiled weakly as she watched Mary bend down to light the fire. 'I need to use the lavatory,' she said, pulling back the bedcovers and climbing out. 'Ouch!' Greta grabbed onto the mattress as a searing bolt of pain shot through her ankle.

'Oh dear, miss.' Mary was by her side in an instant, and helped her back onto the bed. She studied the ankle, which had turned a lurid dark purple during the night. 'I'll help you to the lavatory, but I think I'd better ask the master to call Dr Evans.'

A short while later, Owen stood up from his desk, reached for the doctor's hand and shook it. 'Thank you for coming at short notice, Dr Evans. What's the verdict on our guest, then?'

'I gave her a thorough examination and the head wound isn't as bad as it looks, but the young lady's ankle is very badly sprained. I'd suggest complete rest for the next few days at least. Especially under the circumstances,' added Dr Evans.

'And what might those be?'

'By my reckoning, the young lady in question is just under three months pregnant. I wouldn't want to risk her taking another tumble and harming her unborn child, especially with this lethal weather. I suggest she stays in bed. I'll come by in couple of days' time and check on her progress.'

Owen's face was expressionless. 'Thank you, doctor. And I hope I can rely on your discretion in this matter.'

'Of course.'

When Dr Evans had left, Owen climbed the stairs and walked down the corridor to Greta's bedroom. He knocked softly and opened the door. He saw she was dozing and stood watching her from the end of the bed. She looked vulnerable and tiny lying there, and he realised she was little more than a child herself.

Owen moved over to a chair by the window and sat down, contemplating the circumstances that had brought Greta to the estate. He stared out over Marchmont, which would, as things stood, pass into his nephew's hands when he died.

Ten minutes later he left the bedroom, then made his way downstairs and out of the front door.

LJ was in the shed, milking the last of the cows. She heard footsteps and looked up. A frown crossed her forehead when she saw who it was.

'Hello, Owen. The Marchmont rumour mill tells me you're housing an unexpected guest. How's the patient?'

'Her ankle's not too good, I'm afraid. The doctor has prescribed complete rest, so it seems she'll be staying at the Hall for a few days. She can hardly return to the cottage alone at present. The poor thing can hardly stand.'

'Oh dear,' sighed LJ. 'I am sorry about this.'

'I presume you know of her . . . condition?'

'Yes, of course I do.'

'David's child, is it?'

'Good grief, no! Some GI left her in the lurch and David stood in to help. She had nowhere else to go.'

'I see. Very generous of him, under the circumstances.'

'Yes. David is a generous boy.'

'She has no other family, then?'

'It seems not,' LJ said curtly, standing up. 'Now, if you'll excuse me—'

'Of course. I'll let you know how she progresses. Pretty little thing, isn't she?'

'Yes, I suppose she is.'

'Goodbye, Laura-Jane.' Owen turned and walked outside into the yard.

LJ watched him, confused by his questions. She picked

up the pail, now brimming with fresh milk, and dismissed the conversation as just another example of Owen Marchmont's complex personality.

It was only later that night when, unusually, she was still awake in the early hours, that she realised the significance of what he had said about Greta.

'No . . . surely not?' she groaned, horrified at the thought that had entered her head.

# 7

It was four days before Greta was able to hobble across the room unaided. Propped up comfortably in the large bed with its lovely view over the valley, and with Mary attending to her every need, she began to enjoy herself. Owen popped in to see how she was every afternoon and, having discovered her love of books, would sit reading to her. Greta found his presence oddly comforting and loved the sound of his deep voice.

As Owen finished *Wuthering Heights* and closed the book, he saw there were tears in her eyes.

'My dear Greta, what's the matter?'

'I'm sorry. It's such a beautiful story. I mean, to love someone like that and yet never to be able to . . .' her voice trailed off.

Owen stood up and patted her hand gently. 'Yes' – he nodded, touched by the way the book had moved her – 'but it's only a story. Tomorrow, we'll start *David Copperfield*. It's one of my favourites.' He smiled at her and left the room.

Greta lay back on her pillows and thought how lovely it would be if she didn't ever have to return to the loneliness of the small, cold cottage. Here, she felt cocooned. She wondered why Owen wasn't married. He was educated, intelligent and, even if the years were passing, he was still an attractive man. She found herself imagining what it would be like to be his wife; the mistress of this house and the Marchmont estate, safe and secure for the rest of her life. But of course it was a dream. She was a penniless woman bearing an illegitimate child and soon she'd have to face reality again.

The following afternoon, after Owen had read some *David Copperfield* to her, Greta stretched and sighed heavily.

'What is it?' he asked.

'It's just – well, you've been so kind, but I really can't impose upon you much longer. The snow is thawing, my ankle's feeling better and I ought to go back to Lark Cottage.'

'Nonsense! I'm enjoying your company. The house has been more or less deserted since our last officer left a few months back. And that cottage of my nephew's is damp, cold and in my view, completely unsuitable until you've fully recovered. How on earth will you get up the stairs to bed at night?'

'I'm sure I can manage.'

'I insist you stay at least another week until you're back on your feet, so to speak. After all, it was my fault this happened in the first place. The least I can do is extend my hospitality until you're properly better.'

'If you're sure, Owen,' Greta replied, trying to hide her euphoria that her stay had been prolonged.

'Absolutely. It's a delight having you here.' Owen gave her a warm smile and stood up. 'Well, I'll leave you to rest.'

He walked towards the door, then stopped and turned back. 'And, if you're feeling strong enough, perhaps you would afford me the pleasure of joining me downstairs for dinner tonight?'

'I . . . yes, I'd love to. Thank you, Owen.'

'Until eight, then.'

Later that afternoon, Greta enjoyed the luxury of a deep, hot bath. Then she sat at the dressing table in the bedroom and did what she could to style her hair. Devoid of make-up, and with her cheeks flushed from her bath, she looked particularly young.

She arrived in the drawing room twenty minutes later, wearing a freshly laundered blouse and bouclé wool skirt and leaning on a crutch that Owen had found for her.

'Good evening, Greta.' He stood up to take her arm and helped her to an armchair. 'May I say how well you're looking tonight.'

'Thank you. I told you I was getting better. I feel a bit of a fraud staying in bed all day.'

'May I get you a drink?'

'No, thank you. I think alcohol would go straight to my head at present.'

'Maybe a little wine with dinner, then.'

'Yes.' The room felt chilly and Greta held out her hands towards the fire.

'Are you cold, my dear? I had Mary light the fire earlier, but I don't often use this room. I find the library much more practical when I'm alone.'

'No, I'm fine, really.'

'Cigarette?' Owen offered Greta a silver case.

'Thank you.' She took one and he lit it for her.

'So, tell me a little about yourself.'

'There isn't much to tell.' She took a nervous puff of her cigarette.

'Laura-Jane says you worked with David at a theatre in London. Are you an actress?'

'I . . . yes, I am.'

'Never had much time for the theatre myself. More of an outdoor sort of fellow, really. But tell me, what plays have you appeared in?'

'Well, I wasn't so much an actress. More a . . . dancer, really.'

'Musical comedy, eh? I do like that Noël Coward chap. Some of his songs are very jolly. So you were in London during the war?'

'Yes,' Greta lied.

'Must have been dreadful when the doodlebugs were landing.'

'Yes. But everyone pulled together. I suppose you have to when you're all shoved on the platform at Piccadilly Circus underground station for the night.' Greta smoothly repeated Doris's description of how it had been.

'The great British spirit. It's what got us through and won us the war, you know. Now, shall we go in to dinner?'

Owen helped Greta into the dining room, which – like the other rooms she'd encountered so far – was beautifully furnished, with flickering sconces adorning the walls and a long, highly polished table. There were two places set at one end. He pulled out a chair for her and she sat down.

'This house is so beautiful, but very big. Don't you find it lonely living here by yourself?' she asked him.

'Yes, especially since I'd got used to it being full of

patients and nurses. And in winter the place is damned draughty, too. Costs a fortune to heat but I'm not fond of the cold. I lived out in Kenya before the war. Climate there suited me a lot better, but not necessarily the lifestyle.'

'Will you go back?' ventured Greta.

'No, I decided to get shot of the farm when I left. And besides, I'd left Marchmont in Laura-Jane's hands for long enough and I felt I should do my duty.'

They both looked up as Mary entered the room. 'Ah, the soup. And Mary, would you pour the wine?'

'Certainly, sir.'

Owen waited until Mary had served them and left before saying, 'I don't wish to pry, but what exactly is a pretty young thing like you doing leaving London for the wilds of Monmouthshire?'

'Oh, it's a long story,' Greta replied evasively, reaching for her glass.

'No rush. We have all evening.'

'Well,' said Greta, realising she wasn't going to get away without an explanation. 'I'd had enough of London and needed a change. David offered me his cottage and I decided to take it to give me some time to think.'

'I see.' Owen watched Greta drink her soup, knowing full well she was lying. 'Tell me if I'm being indiscreet, but was there a young man involved?'

Greta put down her spoon with a clatter, deciding it was pointless to deny it. 'Yes.'

'Ah, well. His loss is my gain. Fellow must have been blind.'

Greta stared into her soup bowl, her eyes swimming with tears. She exhaled slowly. 'And there's another reason.'

Owen said nothing, just waited for her to speak.

'I'm pregnant.'

'I see.'

'I'll understand if you want me to leave.' Greta reached into her sleeve for her handkerchief and wiped her nose.

'There, there, my dear. Please don't upset yourself. I think what you've told me is all the more reason why you need to be taken care of at the moment.'

She stared at him in complete surprise. 'You're not shocked?'

'Greta, I may live in the middle of nowhere, but I have seen a little of life. It's very sad, but these things happen. Especially during wartime.'

'He was an American officer,' Greta whispered, as if that somehow made it better.

'He knows about the baby?'

'No. And he never will. He . . . he asked me to marry him. I agreed, but then, well, he went back to America without even saying goodbye.'

'I see.'

'I don't know what I'd have done if it hadn't been for David.'

'Are you two—?'

'Absolutely not,' Greta replied firmly. 'We're just good friends. David's been very kind.'

'So, what are your plans for the future?'

'I've absolutely no idea. To be honest, since I moved here, I've been trying not to think about it.'

'What about your family?' Owen asked, as Mary returned carrying a silver salver of roast beef, which she set on the sideboard before clearing away the soup bowls.

'I don't have one. My parents died in the Blitz.' Greta dipped her eyes in case he read the lie in them.

'I'm sorry to hear that. But you're obviously well educated. Your knowledge of literature, for example, is extensive.'

'Yes, I've always loved books. I was lucky. Before my parents died, I went to a private girls' school.' This, at least, was the truth.

'So now you really are alone in the world, aren't you, my dear?' Owen hesitantly reached out a hand and covered Greta's with it. 'Well, don't worry, I promise to do my best to look after you.'

As the evening progressed and the conversation moved away from the past Greta began to relax. After dinner, they went back into the drawing room and she sat by the fire stroking Morgan, the black Labrador, who lay stretched out beside the hearth. Owen drank a whisky and talked of his life out in the bush in Kenya. He told her he'd owned a large farm near Nyeri in the Central Highlands and had loved the wild landscape and the local people.

'But I rather tired of the high jinks of my ex-pat neighbours out there. Although "Happy Valley", as it was known, was in the middle of nowhere, they certainly found ways to entertain themselves, if you understand my meaning.' Owen raised an eyebrow. 'I was easy meat for certain female vultures, being a single man. I was glad to come back here to some sort of moral normality.'

'You've never married?'

'Well, there was someone, a long time ago. We were engaged, but—' Owen sighed. 'Anyway, it's true to say I've never felt the urge to ask anyone since. Besides, who'd want a grumpy old man like me?'

*I would*. The thought leapt into Greta's head but she squashed it down immediately. The wine and the heat from the fire were making her sleepy, and she yawned.

'Bed for you, young lady. You look exhausted. I'll call for Mary to help you up to your room,' he said, ringing the bell.

'I am, I'm sorry. It's been some time since I was up this late.'

'Don't apologise, and thank you for being such charming company. I do hope you haven't been bored.'

'No. Not at all.' Greta stood up as Mary came into the room.

'Then would you find it acceptable to dine with me again tomorrow?'

'Of course I would. Thank you, Owen. Goodnight.'

'Greta?'

'Yes?'

'Just remember that you're not alone any longer.'

'Thank you.'

Walking slowly up the stairs with Mary, and then, as the maid chattered away whilst helping her into bed, Greta tried to make sense of the evening. She had been convinced that the minute she told Owen she was expecting a baby he would change his attitude towards her. Yet as she settled down under the blankets and Mary left the room, she realised that in his own brusque way, he had been flirting with her. But surely he couldn't possibly be interested in her now he knew the truth?

Over the next week, as the New Year came and went, Greta dined with Owen every night. Now her ankle was better, instead of reading to her in the afternoons he took her for short walks across the land that formed the Marchmont estate. She began to see that, in his old-fashioned way, he was courting her. She couldn't understand it. After all, the squire of Marchmont could hardly marry a woman bearing another man's child. Could he . . . ?

Yet – despite her heartfelt protestations that she must return to Lark Cottage – when she had been living at the big house for almost a month, Greta knew for certain that Owen didn't want her to leave.

One evening after supper they were sitting in the drawing room together after dinner discussing *David Copperfield*. Owen closed the book and silence fell. His expression suddenly became serious.

'Greta. I have something I want to ask you.'

'I see. It's not something dreadful, is it?'

'No . . . at least, I hope not. Well' – he cleared his throat – 'the thing is, Greta my dear, I have become remarkably fond of you in the short time you've been here. You've brought an energy and a zest back to me I thought had long passed. In short, I dread you leaving. So . . . the question I have to ask is: would you do me the honour of marrying me?'

Greta stared at him, open-mouthed with shock.

'Of course I'll understand completely if you couldn't countenance being the wife of a man so much older than yourself. But it seems to me you need things that I can give you. A father for your child, and a safe, secure environment for both you and the baby to flourish in.'

She managed to find her voice. 'I . . . you mean you're

prepared to bring up the baby I'm going to have as your own?'

'Of course. There's no need for anyone to know it isn't mine, is there?'

'But what about LJ and David? They know the truth.'

'Don't worry about them.' Owen used his hand to metaphorically flick the problem away. 'So, what do you say, my dear Greta?'

She remained silent.

'You're asking yourself why I'd want to do this, aren't you?'

'Yes, I am, Owen.'

'Would it be too simplistic if I told you your presence here has made me realise how lonely I've been? That I feel an affection for you I hadn't previously thought possible? Marchmont needs youth . . . life, or it will wither away with me. I believe, in turn, we can give each other what we lack in our respective lives.'

'Yes, but—'

'I don't expect you to make up your mind now,' he said hastily. 'Take some time to think about it. Go back to Lark Cottage, if you wish.'

'Yes. No . . . I—' Greta rubbed her forehead. 'Would you excuse me, Owen? I'm feeling dreadfully tired.'

'Of course.'

They stood up. Owen reached for her hand and kissed it softly. 'Think long and hard, dear girl. Whatever your decision, it's been a pleasure having you here. Goodnight.'

Greta lay in bed, turning Owen's proposal over and over in her mind. If she accepted, her baby would have a father and both of them would escape the stigma that haunted illegitimate children and their mothers. She'd be the mistress of a beautiful house and never have to worry where the next meal was coming from ever again.

The one thing she wouldn't have was a man she loved. Although Owen was kind, thoughtful and attractive in his own way, if she were brutal about it, Greta didn't relish the thought of sharing a bed with him.

But if she said no, it was back to the cottage to face having her baby alone. And beyond that, who knew? What chance would there be of finding the real love she craved in the years ahead? Let alone providing for herself and the baby?

A picture of Max drifted into her mind. She shook her head quickly to clear it. He was never coming back and she had to forge a life for herself and her child.

Greta wondered what David and LJ would say. She hoped they would understand. Besides, she was currently in no position to take other people's finer feelings into consideration.

'There's no one else to look after us, is there?' she asked, patting her stomach.

The following evening Greta went down for dinner and told Owen that she would accept his offer of marriage.

Two days later Mary came bustling into the dining room while Owen was having his breakfast and reading *The Times*.

'Excuse me, sir, Mrs Marchmont is here to see you.'

'Tell her she'll have to wait until I've finished my breakf—'

'I don't think this can wait, Owen.' LJ appeared in the doorway behind Mary and pushed past her.

Owen grunted. 'Very well. Thank you, Mary. Close the door behind you, will you?'

'Yes, sir.'

Mary left, and LJ stood at the other end of the table glaring at him. Owen calmly wiped his mouth on a napkin and folded his newspaper neatly.

'Well, what is this thing that cannot wait?'

'You know very well what it is.' LJ's voice was barely more than a whisper.

'You're upset because I'm marrying Greta, is that it?'

LJ sank into a chair at the other end of the table and sighed heavily. 'Owen, I don't profess to be party to your private thoughts, nor am I your keeper, but for God's sake, you know nothing about the girl.'

Owen took a piece of toast from the rack and proceeded to butter it. 'I know all I need to.'

'Really? Then you're happy that the new mistress of Marchmont will be a woman who used to earn her living parading around a stage at the Windmill with hardly a stitch on?'

'I've done my research, and I'm aware of what she did before she came here. I'm simply grateful I've found someone who has given me the kind of happiness I didn't think I'd find again.'

'So you're saying you're in love with her? Or are you just blinded by her pretty face?'

'As you implied earlier, Laura-Jane, this really is none of your business.'

'Oh yes it is, if it means that Greta's illegitimate child will inherit Marchmont instead of my son!' LJ's voice was quavering with emotion. 'If this is about punishing me, then you've succeeded.'

'Well, *your* son has hardly shown a great passion for the place, has he?'

'It's his by rights, Owen, and you know it.'

'I'm afraid that isn't true, Laura-Jane. Marchmont will be left to any child that I may have. And no one other than yourself and David is aware that Greta's baby isn't mine. There might be speculation that the child was conceived out of wedlock and a marriage hastily arranged, but that's as far as it will go.'

'You think so, do you?' LJ's hands were shaking as she tried to keep her anger under control. 'So you expect me to stand by and watch while my son's inheritance is passed to some bastard child of a GI?!'

'It would be your word against ours but, if you wish to take the case to court, please do so,' Owen replied calmly. 'There's no way of proving it, so I suspect that people will just think it's sour grapes on your part. And it's the kind of scandal the papers love. Rest assured, our reputations would be dragged through the mud, but please do what you think you must.'

'I just don't know how you can do this to David, Owen. After all—'

'*You* don't know how *I* can do this?' He laughed scornfully. 'Just cast your mind back thirty years, my dear Laura-Jane, and remember what *you* did to *me*.'

LJ was silent as she stared at him. Eventually, she sighed. 'So is that what all this is about? Revenge?'

'No, although you must remember that you've brought this problem on yourself. If it hadn't been for you marrying my younger brother while I was away fighting for king and country, then *we* might have had a son and this situation would not have arisen.'

'Owen, you were away for almost five years, and for three of those we all believed you were dead!'

'Then shouldn't you have waited for me? After all, I had asked you to marry me before I left and you'd accepted my proposal. You even wore my engagement ring! Can you imagine how I felt arriving back in England from that ghastly POW camp in Ingolstadt to find that my fiancée was married to my brother and living in my family home? Not only that, but you were pregnant with his child. Good God, Laura-Jane! The war nearly destroyed me, but the one thing that kept me going was the thought of you waiting for me here.'

'Do you think that I haven't torn myself apart over and over for what I did?' LJ wrung her hands in despair. 'But it's me you should hate, not my son, not David. He doesn't deserve to be treated the way you've treated him. You've never been able to bear to look at him!'

'No, and I never shall.'

'Well, you may think I betrayed you, but don't you think I've been punished enough by living with the guilt and seeing how you felt about David? And now this!'

'Then why do you stay here?'

'Are you asking me to leave?'

Owen chuckled and shook his head. 'No, Laura-Jane. Don't cast me in the role of a complete villain. Marchmont is your home as much as it's mine. And remember, it was your decision to move out of the main house and into the Gate Lodge when I arrived home from Kenya.'

Laura-Jane put her head in her hands wearily. 'Please, Owen, I beseech you. Don't deny David his rightful inheritance because you want to punish me. You know I would never publicly fight you, so I leave it to your conscience. It's not only wrong to deny David, but to hand Marchmont over to a child without one ounce of Marchmont blood in its veins seems a very high price to pay for revenge.' LJ stood up slowly. 'I've nothing more to say, except that I've decided you're right. I should leave Marchmont. I shall be gone within the week. As you point out, there's nothing to keep me here, especially now.'

'As you wish.'

'And you didn't answer my question. Are you in love with Greta?'

Owen looked at LJ, and wavered only for an instant. 'Yes.'

'Goodbye, Owen.'

He watched her stalk from the room without a backward glance, the air of elegance that had so entranced him when she was a girl of sixteen still visible in her gait. She had been a fine-looking woman in those days, and he'd loved her very much.

Owen stood up, walked over to the window and watched Laura-Jane striding away from the house. Once more he experienced a pang of regret. He'd gone to Kenya to escape the pain of her betrayal, unable to watch his brother, Robin, and his ex-fiancée together. When he'd heard that Robin had died in a riding accident all those years ago, it would have been the easiest thing in the world to return to Marchmont and ask LJ to marry him. But his pride had not allowed him to do that. So he had stayed away until the war had forced him home.

Even so, the thought of her leaving Marchmont filled him with sadness. Should he run after her, confess that after all these years, he was still in love with her? That the reason he'd never married was because even after what she'd done to him, it was her, and only her, that he'd ever wanted?

*Go now, quickly! Tell her, before it's too late*, a voice inside him urged. *Forget about Greta and go to Laura-Jane. Make the most of the years you have left . . .*

Owen slumped into a chair by the window. He whimpered and shook his head, knowing that, whatever his heart told him he should do, the pride which had dominated and ruined his life thus far would once again deny him the freedom to go to the woman he loved.

# 8

David's career as a stand-up comic was beginning to take off. His contract at the Windmill had been extended and the warmth of the audience's response was growing in tandem with his confidence. He'd been taken on by a good agent who had seen his act one night and thought he was destined for bigger things. The regular income from the Windmill meant that he'd been able to move out of his room in Swiss Cottage and into a one-bedroom flat in Soho, nearer to the theatre. The move and the punishing schedule at work meant there had been no time to make his planned trip to visit his mother and Greta at Marchmont. But next weekend he was determined to go.

As he rose and dressed, neatly making the bed and tidying away a sock and a tie, he felt his heart skip a little faster than usual. This morning he was due at the BBC in Portland Place to record his first sketch for a comedy show which would air at seven o'clock on Friday nights – prime-time radio listening. The show introduced up-and-coming comic talent, and he knew that many a great comedian had used it as a stepping-stone to fame and fortune.

David went into his tiny kitchen and put the kettle on

the stove to boil. He heard the click of the letterbox and padded into the hallway to pick up his post. Going back into the kitchen, he studied the envelope in surprise. There was no mistaking his mother's individual script, but the postmark was Stroud, not Monmouth.

Making himself a pot of tea, he sat down at the small table and began to read.

*72 Lansdown Road*
*Stroud*
*Gloucestershire*

*7th February 1946*

*My dear David,*

*I know you will already have seen that I do not write to you from Marchmont but from my sister Dorothy's house. To come straight to the point, I have moved out of the Gate Lodge and am staying here until I have decided what I shall do. I won't bore you with the details, but suffice it to say that I have decided it is time to move on, start afresh, so to speak. Anyway, please don't worry about me. I'm fine, and Dorothy has made me both welcome and extremely comfortable. With William dying last year, she rattles around in this big house, and it seems we are company for each other. I may stay here, I may not. Time will tell, but I shall not be returning to Marchmont.*

*My darling boy, I have some news. Owen rather fell for your friend Greta; he subsequently proposed to her and she has accepted. I'm afraid we had a bit of a set-to over it. You know how stubborn your uncle can be on occasions. Anyway, I do hope that this news does not disturb you too deeply. I fear that your feelings for Greta are more than those of a friend. However, having studied her from a distance, my belief is that Greta has done what is best for both her and her baby. We have both been invited to the wedding and I enclose your invitation. I will not be attending.*

*I do hope that you will find the time to visit me, or perhaps I will take the train up and come and see you in London.*

*I hope all is well with you. Do write if you have a moment,*

*All my love to you, Ma x*

David reread the letter, shaking his head in disbelief.

Greta marrying Owen . . . He felt the unfamiliar sensation of tears pricking the backs of his eyes. He understood why, of course. Owen could give Greta everything she needed. She couldn't possibly have fallen in love with him, surely? He was old enough to be her father. He berated himself for not making his feelings clearer. If he had, it might have been he who would be walking down the aisle with her. Now, he'd probably lost her forever.

And as for his mother leaving Marchmont . . . David couldn't help wondering whether it was because of the marriage. He knew how much she loved her life there and what it would have taken for her to say goodbye to it. He was aware that she didn't see eye to eye with Owen, that their relationship was cool and distant, but he'd always put this down to a clash of personalities.

He checked his watch and poured himself another cup of tea. As he sipped it, a thought crossed his mind. If Greta was marrying Owen and he was taking on her baby, did this mean that her child would inherit Marchmont one day? He supposed it did. Surprisingly, this fact meant very little to him. Since he was young, he'd always known his future was not at his family home. And any material possessions he wanted, he aimed to earn through his own efforts and talent. Even so, he was fully aware of how much it meant to his mother for him to inherit it. The thought of a child with an unknown American as its true father standing to claim what she felt was rightfully his was one he knew LJ would find impossible to stomach.

David sighed heavily. There seemed little point in going to Marchmont under the circumstances so, instead, he decided he'd visit Gloucestershire this weekend, or perhaps meet with his mother in London, on more neutral territory.

'Damn!' he exclaimed, suddenly realising he had only fifteen minutes to get to Portland Place.

He hurriedly put on his overcoat, stuffed the letter in his pocket and ran out, slamming the door behind him.

Owen Jonathan Marchmont married Greta Harriet Simpson ten weeks after he'd first set eyes on her in the woods. On a grey March day they exchanged vows in the chapel on the estate in front of a small congregation.

Greta had invited no one to attend. She'd received a sweet letter from David, declining the wedding invitation from her husband-to-be but wishing her all the best for the future. LJ was also absent. She had moved out of the Gate Lodge a month ago without saying goodbye. Feeling somewhat guilty – knowing that it must have been the announcement of her engagement that had precipitated LJ's departure – Greta could not help also feeling relieved. LJ's presence and palpable disapproval would only have served to unsettle her.

With LJ gone, she was determined to forget about her past. The wedding signified a new start, a chance to look forward to the future. As she stood at the altar next to Owen, she prayed with all her heart that this would be possible. Her empire-line brocade wedding dress had been purposely tailored to be long and loose-fitting. It would have taken a very keen pair of eyes to spot the bulge in her stomach. And from now on, she thought, as Owen led her out of the church, the baby inside her belonged to him.

At the wedding breakfast, which was held at Marchmont Hall, Greta watched the guests drinking champagne and chatting to each other, feeling strangely removed from the proceedings. Owen had invited three officers from his old army regiment, Dr Evans, a couple of distant cousins and four local farm owners. Mr Glenwilliam, Owen's solicitor, had acted as his best man.

Although the guests spoke to her kindly enough, she could almost smell their surprise that Owen should have married after all this time. And, more to the point, taken such a young wife. She knew that when the baby was born considerably less than nine months after the wedding, they'd all nod their heads knowingly.

'All right, my dear?' asked Owen, handing her a glass of champagne.

'Yes, thank you.'

'Good. I'm just going to say a few words, thank people for coming, that sort of thing.'

'Of course.'

Her husband stood up. The guests stopped talking and turned towards him.

'Ladies and gentlemen, thank you very much for joining myself and my wife' – Owen looked down fondly at Greta – 'on this happy occasion. Some of you may have been surprised when you received your invitation, but now that you've met Greta you'll understand why I proposed. It's taken almost six decades to get me down the aisle and I'd just like to say how grateful I am to my new wife that she accepted my offer of marriage. I can't tell you the amount of courage I had to pluck up before I asked her!' he joked. 'And, before I close, I'd just like to thank Morgan, my Labrador, for introducing us in the first place. There's life in the old dog yet, you know!'

There was a round of applause as Mr Glenwilliam raised his glass for the toast.

'To the bride and groom!'

'The bride and groom!'

Greta took a sip of the champagne and smiled at Owen, her protector and saviour.

The guests left in the early evening and Greta and Owen sat drinking the remains of the champagne by the fire in the drawing room.

'Well, Mrs Marchmont, how does it feel to be a married woman?'

'Exhausting!'

'Of course, my dear. The day must have been draining for you. Why don't you pop on upstairs and I'll have Mary bring you some supper in bed?' Owen immediately saw the surprise on Greta's face. 'My dear, in your present condition, I don't think that it would be fair of me to expect you to . . . consummate our union. I suggest that we keep the sleeping arrangements just as they are for the present. Once you are . . . unencumbered, well, we'll think again.'

'If that's what you want, Owen,' she replied sedately.

'It is. Now, off you go.'

Greta stood up and walked over to him, bending down and kissing him on the cheek. 'Goodnight. And thank you for such a lovely wedding day.'

'I enjoyed it, too. Goodnight, Greta.'

When she'd left the room Owen poured himself a whisky and sat staring morosely into the fire. All he'd been able to think of earlier as he'd stood at the altar and slipped the ring onto Greta's finger was that it should have been Laura-Jane next to him, the two of them plighting their troths for eternity. Since she'd left Marchmont, he'd missed her dreadfully. Not for the first time, he wondered if marrying Greta had been the right decision.

But what was done was done, and Owen promised himself he would never reveal to Greta the truth of his feelings. She would have everything she needed.

Except his heart.

As the last of the snow melted away and the first fresh scent of spring arrived with April, Greta watched her previously neat bump enlarge and spread. She became very uncomfortable and found it difficult to sleep. She also noticed that her ankles were swelling and that she got out of breath very quickly. Seeing her discomfort, Owen insisted on calling Dr Evans.

The doctor examined her gently, pressing her stomach and listening to it through an instrument that resembled an ear trumpet.

'Is everything all right?' Greta asked anxiously as he packed up his medical bag.

'Oh yes, absolutely fine. But I hope you're prepared for double trouble in a couple of months' time. I believe you're expecting twins, Mrs Marchmont. That's why you've been so uncomfortable. I think it would be best if you took it very easy from now on. And, for the moment, I'd suggest complete bed rest until we get the swelling in your ankles under control. You are very slight, Mrs Marchmont, and two babies is a lot for your body to cope with. Stay in bed and rest. There's no reason to expect any problems, as both babies' heartbeats are strong and you're in good health yourself. We might transfer you to the cottage hospital for the last few weeks, but we'll see how you're doing closer to the time. I'll go downstairs and tell the father the good news.' Although he smiled at her kindly, she saw the hint of irony in his eyes. 'I'll pop in and see you again in the next few days.'

'Thank you, doctor.' Greta lay back and let out a sigh of relief. If there'd ever been any doubt in her mind as to the wisdom of marrying Owen, it had just been banished. Twins: two babies to feed, clothe and look after. God knows what would have become of the three of them if she'd been alone . . .

Ten minutes later there was a knock at the door. Owen walked across the room, sat on the bed and took her hands in his.

'The good doctor has told me the news, my dear. Now, you're to take care of yourself and rest. I'll tell Mary to bring all your meals to your room.'

'I'm sorry, Owen.' Greta looked away as tears came to her eyes.

'Why are you sorry?'

'It's just that you've been so kind. And I'm sure you didn't expect two young babies under your roof.'

'Come now. You did me the greatest kindness by marrying me. Twins, eh? They'll liven the old place up! And now we have double the chance of having a boy.' He kissed her on the cheek. 'I have to go out to Abergavenny, but would you like me to come and read to you later?'

'Yes, if you have time. And also, Owen, would it be possible to get me some knitting patterns and some wool on your way? I want to try and knit some clothes for the babies. Mary said she'd help me.'

'What a lovely idea. That will keep you occupied at least.'

When Owen had left Greta thought about what he had said. It wasn't the first time he'd hinted how happy he'd be if the child was a boy. She supposed it was what all men wanted.

'Please, God,' she whispered, 'let me have a son.'

Greta went into labour in the middle of the night a month before her due date. Dr Evans was called, and the local midwife, Megan. The doctor was eager to get her into hospital, but when he arrived he saw she was in no state to be moved.

Five hours later, Greta gave birth to a tiny girl weighing just over five pounds. Twenty minutes after that, a boy of four pounds and seven ounces arrived. An exhausted Greta cuddled her baby girl and watched as Dr Evans slapped her son's tiny bottom.

'Come on, come on,' he muttered, and eventually the little thing gave a cough and a squeal. Dr Evans cleaned up the baby, wrapped him tightly in a blanket and handed him to Greta.

'There you go, Mrs Marchmont. Two beautiful babies.'

Greta felt the tears running down her cheeks as she stared at the perfectly formed human beings she had brought into the world. She was overcome with a feeling of tenderness so powerful it took her breath away.

'Are they all right?' she asked anxiously.

'They're both fine, Mrs Marchmont, but after you've had a cuddle I'm going to take them both away and check them over. The boy is very small and will need extra care. I'm going to suggest to your husband that he employs a nursemaid for the next few weeks to help you. You must get some rest now. Megan will stay with you and tidy you up.'

Reluctantly, Greta handed first her boy and then her girl to Dr Evans. 'Don't keep them too long, will you?' she said, then lay back on the pillows and gritted her teeth as the midwife began to stitch her up.

Later, as she was drifting off to sleep, she felt a rough sensation against her cheek. She opened her eyes and saw Owen smiling down at her.

'Oh, my big, brave girl. How clever you are. We have a beautiful son.'

'And a daughter.'

'Of course.'

'Might we call the boy Jonathan – Jonny, for short – after me, and my father?' he asked.

'Yes, of course. And what about the girl?'

'I thought I'd leave you to choose.'

'Francesca Rose,' she said softly. 'Cheska, for short.'

'Whatever you like, my dear.'

'How are the babies?'

'Fine. They're both fast asleep in the nursery.'

'Can I see them?'

'Not now. You must get some rest. Doctor's orders.'

'All right, but soon, please.'

'Yes, of course.' Owen kissed her forehead and left the room.

Greta didn't see her son for the next forty-eight hours. Too weak to get out of bed, she begged the nursemaid Owen had employed to bring Jonny to her, but she refused, bringing only Cheska.

'He's sick, isn't he?' she asked fretfully.

'No. He just has a slight fever and the doctor doesn't want him moved.'

'But I'm his mother. I must see him! He needs me!' Greta fell back onto her pillows with a cry of frustration.

'All in good time, Mrs Marchmont,' said the nurse brusquely.

Later that evening Greta managed to sit upright and haul herself out of bed. She staggered along the corridor to the nursery, where she found Owen holding her whimpering son in his arms, cooing quietly to him. Cheska was sleeping peacefully in her crib.

'What are you doing out of bed?' A frown crossed Owen's brow.

'I wanted to see my son. Is he all right? The nurse wouldn't tell me anything. I'm not even allowed to give him his bottle.' Greta reached for the baby, but Owen cradled him protectively.

'No, Greta. You're too weak. You might drop him. He's had a slight temperature, but the doctor says that has passed. My dear, why don't you go back to bed? You need to rest.'

'No! I want to hold Jonny.' Greta reached towards her husband and almost wrenched the baby out of Owen's grip. She stared down at her child. She had forgotten just how small he was and noticed that his tiny cheeks were slightly flushed. 'I'm taking him back to bed with me,' she said firmly.

'Now, Mrs Marchmont, don't be silly. The baby is being well cared for and you must build up your strength.' The nurse bustled into the room behind her.

'But I—' Suddenly, all the fight went out of Greta. She let the nurse take Jonny from her and return him to his cot, while Owen led her back to her bedroom as though he were escorting a naughty child. Once in bed, Greta began sobbing uncontrollably.

'I'll get the nurse to come to you, my dear,' Owen said, obviously embarrassed by her emotional state, then abruptly left the bedroom.

'There, there, Mrs Marchmont. All new mothers feel

like this. Here.' The nurse handed Greta a pill and a cup of water. 'It'll calm you down and help you sleep.'

But sleep didn't come. Greta lay there, staring into the dark, remembering the fiercely protective look in Owen's eyes when she'd asked to hold her son.

Not for the first time, she wondered whether that was what he'd hoped for when he had married her. An heir to Marchmont.

And now she'd given him what he'd wanted.

Over the next few days Greta regained her strength and her equilibrium. She began to take an active part in the care of her babies – brooking no refusal from the nurse – and watched happily as they both grew stronger by the day. Her life became one long round of feeding, changing and grabbing sleep when she could. Mary and the nurse were there to help, but she wanted to do as much as possible herself.

No longer were her thoughts focused on her own needs. At every cry and whimper she was beside her babies, calming, nurturing and protecting them. Greta realised she had never been happier. Her life had taken on a wonderful new meaning simply because she was needed; she was an irreplaceable guardian for these two tiny humans. Rather than resenting the challenge, she revelled in it, and the twins blossomed under her tender care.

Owen appeared like clockwork in the nursery at two o'clock every afternoon. He'd barely glance at Cheska but would pick up Jonny and spirit him off for an hour or two. Greta would sometimes find the boy balanced on Owen's knee in the library or glance outside and see her husband pushing the big, heavy perambulator across the gravel, Morgan padding along at his master's side.

'He hardly notices you, does he, darling?' Greta kissed her daughter's downy blonde hair. 'Well, never mind. Mummy loves you. She loves you very much.'

As the months passed, Greta began to think more about the strange relationship she had with her husband. In the mornings, she was caught up with the twins, while Owen was either out on the estate or in town on business. He spent at least a couple of hours each afternoon with Jonny while she was with Cheska in the nursery, so, during the day, husband and wife saw each other very little. In the evenings they would still eat together at the long, polished table in the dining room, but Greta noticed that their conversation was becoming more stilted. The only subject they really had in common was their children. Owen's eyes would light up as he told an anecdote about Jonny pulling Morgan's tail or squealing in delight as he was tickled, but then there would be long silences. Greta usually retired to her room straight after supper, exhausted after her day and grateful for the fact that Owen had so far not suggested changing their sleeping arrangements.

Sometimes, in the small hours when she was in the nursery watching over Jonny, who seemed to regularly catch colds or have a mild fever, Greta would brood on the odd state of her marriage. She felt she knew Owen no better than the day they had first met. He was still kind and considerate, but she felt more like an indulged niece than a wife. She'd even begun to wonder whether she'd effectively married the father she'd lost and missed so terribly when she was younger.

Often, she'd dream of being in a pair of young, strong arms, but on waking she'd decide that the lack of them was a small sacrifice to make. Her babies had a father, they all had a roof over their heads and would never want for anything material for the rest of their lives. Her own private yearnings were not a priority.

A year passed, and then another. Greta delighted in watching Jonny and Cheska say their first words and take their first steps. The twins were very close, communicating in their own, often indecipherable, language and content to play together for hours. Their special game was Hansel and Gretel, in which they would pretend to be the brother and sister from their favourite fairy story and imagine that a clearing in Marchmont's woods held the witch's fabled gingerbread house. They would run back to Greta, screaming with a mixture of fear and excitement when they reached the end of the tale, Jonny holding Cheska's hand tightly in his own.

Greta thought her children's laughter was the most beautiful sound in the world. She loved watching the way Jonny was so protective of his sister, and how equally attentive Cheska was to her more delicate sibling when he caught one of his coughs or colds.

The relationship between Owen and Jonny also grew and flourished. Jonny would give 'Da', as he called him, a beaming smile when he entered the nursery and hold his arms up to be cuddled. Greta often watched from the window as her husband and son disappeared into the woods, the boy's little hand held fast in Owen's and his legs struggling to keep pace. If Greta resented the obvious favouritism, she didn't show it. Instead, she built a bond between herself and her angelic, golden-haired daughter.

Occasionally, there were visitors: Mr Glenwilliam would come for dinner with his wife, and sometimes Jack Wallace, the farm manager, would join them for Sunday lunch. A couple of Owen's army chums came once for the weekend, but Greta had always known that he was not a great socialiser.

Greta's friendship with Mary grew apace, even though she was the mistress and Mary the servant. Mary had confided in her that Huw Jones, a young farmhand on the estate, had been gently courting her for the past few months. She confessed that he'd kissed her the last time they had met and how nice it had been. Greta had felt a sudden pang of envy at the fact Mary had a young suitor, but lived vicariously through their romance. They often leafed through Greta's weekly copy of *Picturegoer* together or giggled over the twins' antics. Greta thanked God Mary was here. She was the only young, female company she had.

# 9

'Darling boy! How wonderful to see you! My, you look well!' LJ reached up and kissed her son on both cheeks.

'And it's good to see you, Ma. Shall we go through?'

'Yes. But are you sure you can afford this?' LJ looked around the Savoy Hotel reception as they made their way through to the Grill Room.

'Absolutely. Things are going rather well for me, Ma. I've waited a long time to be able to do this,' David replied with a grin.

LJ watched in surprise as the maître d' greeted her son warmly and escorted them to a secluded banquette in a corner of the room.

'Do you come here often, David?'

'Leon, my agent, always brings me here for lunch. Now, shall we have champagne, Ma?'

'Are you sure, David? It must be frightfully expensive,' said LJ, making herself comfortable.

David summoned a waiter. 'We'll have a bottle of Veuve Clicquot, please. Today is a celebration.'

'What of, darling?'

'The BBC, in their wisdom, have at last decided to give me my own radio show.'

'Oh, David!' LJ clapped her hands together in delight. 'How absolutely wonderful! I'm thrilled for you.'

'Thanks, Ma. My show will go out on Monday night between six and seven. I'll be compering, and we'll be having different guest comedians and crooners every week.'

'You *must* be doing rather well if you can afford to treat your mother to a champagne lunch at the Savoy Grill.'

'Not from the BBC, I might add, but then no one ever became rich working for them,' David replied, irony in his voice. 'It's all the other things I'm starting to do. They add up. Leon thinks I may have secured a small part in a film at Shepperton Studios, then there's the Windmill and—'

'Do you still have to work there, David, dear? It's just the thought of, well . . . you know I've never been terribly keen.'

'For the moment, yes. Remember, they gave me a job when no one else would, Ma. Anyway, I want to play it safe until I've got at least six months' definite work and the radio show proves it's going to be a runner. You won't like the name of the show, though.'

'Won't I? What is it?'

'*Taffy's Ticklers.*'

'Gracious! That confounded name has really stuck, hasn't it? Well, you'll always be David to me, dear boy.'

The champagne arrived and the waiter poured out two glasses. David raised his. 'To you, Ma. For all your support.'

'Silly boy! I've done nothing. You've done it all by yourself.'

'Ma, you've done so much. When I first told you I wanted to be a comedian you didn't pour scorn on me, however ridiculous it may have seemed at the time. And when I left for London after the war to try my luck, you didn't chastise me for being irresponsible.'

'Well, I'm thrilled things have turned out so well for you. Here's to you, darling. Down the hatch, as they say.' LJ took a sip of champagne, but then her face became serious. 'David, I must ask you, have you had any second thoughts on the Greta and Owen situation? You know as well as I do that their deception is little less than a crime. The two of them have cheated you out of your rightful inheritance. I'm sure that if you decided to take it to court, you'd have a very strong case. After all, those babies were born less than six months after Owen first laid eyes on Greta. And Dr Evans must know the truth. He delivered them, after all.'

'No, Ma,' David said firmly. 'We both know that Dr Evans would never speak out against Owen. They've known each other for years. And besides, with my career finally headed in the right direction, a scandal like that could destroy it before it really begins. Anyway, I'm very happy living my own life. The best thing I ever did was to leave Marchmont. I have everything I need right here, really. How are Owen and Greta?'

'I have absolutely no idea. I've had no contact with Owen since I left. Mary writes me the occasional letter, but I haven't heard from her for months either. Honestly, David, I don't understand how you can take all this so calmly. I know I can't,' she muttered, taking a large slug of champagne.

'Perhaps it's because I never expected to inherit Marchmont in the first place. When I was growing up, I realised Owen didn't like me. I never understood why, though.'

LJ gritted her teeth. She had never told her son about her relationship with Owen or explained his subsequent antipathy towards David. And she didn't intend to do so now. 'I really don't know, David. Suffice to say, the entire situation is quite ghastly. Now, shall we order? I'm famished.'

The two of them enjoyed a lunch of lobster soup, rack of lamb and fruit salad, over which they chatted about the format of David's radio show.

'And what about female company? Picked up any new waifs and strays recently?' asked LJ, raising an eyebrow.

'No, Ma, I'm far too busy with my career at the moment to even contemplate a relationship. So, tell me, how's life in Gloucestershire?'

'Well, I've never been a great one for bridge parties and the petty gossip of the suburbs, but I mustn't complain.'

'Admit it, Ma' – David eyed her – 'you miss Marchmont, don't you?'

'Perhaps. Mind you, not many women of my age would say they missed getting up at five to milk the blasted cows, but at least it gave me a purpose. I find all this spare time I have now makes the day drag. I may be getting on a little, but I'm not in my dotage yet. Mind you, Dorothy's a brick.' LJ paused, then sighed. 'Yes, dammit! I *do* miss the old place dreadfully. I miss waking up in the morning and looking out at the mist on the tops of the hills and hearing the sound of the stream beneath me. It's so very beautiful there and—' Her voice trailed off and David could see tears in her eyes.

'Ma, I'm so sorry.' He reached out a hand to cover hers.

'Listen, I could take steps to fight for Marchmont if it means that much to you. Forgive me for being selfish. It's been more your home than mine, and now you've lost it – all because I sent Greta to you.'

'Goodness, David, don't blame yourself for simply trying to help a damsel in distress. No one could have foreseen what would happen. Anyway' – LJ took a handkerchief from her handbag and surreptitiously wiped her eyes – 'don't listen to me, I've had far too much champagne and I'm just being a silly old woman, looking back to the past.'

'Are you sure you can't go back to Marchmont, Ma?'

'Never.' LJ stared at her son, her eyes suddenly hard. 'Now, I really must be heading for the train home. It's gone three o'clock and Dorothy gets in a fearful panic if I'm not back when I say I'll be.'

'Of course.' David signalled for the bill, hating to see his mother's distress. 'It's been wonderful to see you.'

Five minutes later he escorted his mother outside and into a taxi.

'Please take care of yourself, Ma,' he said, kissing her.

'Of course I will. Don't worry about me, darling. I'm as tough as old boots.'

David watched the taxi drive off, feeling vaguely depressed. Over the years he'd often had the feeling that there was more to the cool relationship his mother had with Owen than met the eye.

But he was damned if he knew what it was.

# 10

On the afternoon of the twins' third birthday Greta held a tea party on the terrace. Owen, herself, Mary, Jonny and Cheska spent two hours eating sandwiches and chocolate cake, then playing Blind Man's Buff and Hide and Seek in the woods.

At bedtime Greta felt Jonny's forehead, as his cheeks looked a little too rosy. She crushed half an aspirin into some juice and made him drink it. This usually did the trick to bring his fever down. Jonny had a nasty cough, the legacy of a bout of bronchitis a week ago, but had seemed bright enough this afternoon.

She mentioned her concern to Owen when Jonny had at last fallen asleep and she'd joined her husband for dinner.

'Overexcitement, I'll bet,' Owen had said with a fond smile. 'He'll soon perk up when I take him out on his new tricycle tomorrow. He's turning into a fine, sturdy young man. I'll have him up on a pony in the next few months.'

Despite his reassurances, Greta couldn't settle once she'd climbed into bed. Although she was used to dealing with Jonny's frequent illnesses, this time her maternal alarm bell was ringing loudly. She padded into the nursery and found Jonny tossing and turning in his cot. His coughing had developed a deep, rasping edge to it. Putting her hand on his forehead, she could feel immediately that he was burning up. She stripped him and wiped him down gently with a cool sponge, but still this didn't ease the fever. She sat watching him for a while, trying to suppress her panic. After all, Jonny had often run a temperature before and she didn't want to overreact. But an hour later, when Greta yet again leant over the cot to feel his forehead, he didn't open his eyes at her touch. Instead, he lay there, coughing and murmuring incoherently to himself.

'Jonny's really ill, I know he is!' she cried, as she flew into Owen's bedroom.

Her husband was awake immediately, his eyes full of fear. 'What's wrong with him?'

'I'm not sure,' said Greta, choking back a sob, 'but I've never seen him as bad as this. Please call Dr Evans. Now!'

Forty minutes later the doctor was bent over Jonny's cot. He took his temperature and listened to the toddler's shallow breathing through his stethoscope.

'What is it, doctor?' asked Greta.

'Jonny has a particularly nasty case of bronchitis, and it may well be turning into pneumonia.'

'He'll be all right, won't he?' asked Owen, his face grey with fear.

'I suggest we take him to the hospital in Abergavenny. I don't like the sound of those lungs. I suspect they're filling with fluid.'

'Oh God,' Owen moaned, wringing his hands in anguish.

'Let's try not to panic. I'm only taking precautions. Can

you take your car, Mr Marchmont? It'll be faster than calling the ambulance. I'll telephone the hospital and let them know you're coming in with Jonny, then I'll join you there.'

Owen nodded as Greta scooped up her son and the three of them made their way hastily down the stairs to the car. On the journey to the hospital, clutching her sick child in her arms, Greta watched her husband's hands shaking as he drove towards Abergavenny.

Jonny's condition deteriorated seriously over the next forty-eight hours. Despite the best efforts of the doctors and nurses, Greta listened helplessly to her son struggling for every breath as he grew weaker. She thought her heart might break in despair.

Owen sat silently on the other side of Jonny's bed, neither of them able to provide any comfort for the other.

Jonny died at four in the morning, three days after his third birthday.

Greta held him for the last time, studying every tiny detail of his beloved face: his perfect rosebud lips, and his high cheekbones, which were so like his father's.

The two of them drove home in silence, too devastated to speak. Greta went straight up to the nursery and held Cheska close to her, crying into her hair.

'Oh, my darling . . . my darling, why him? Why him?'

Later that day, she staggered downstairs to find Owen. He was in the library. A bottle of whisky was beside him and his head was in his hands. He was crying; dreadful deep, rasping sobs.

'Please, Owen, don't . . . don't.' Greta went to him and placed her arms around his shoulders.

'I . . . I loved him so much. I knew he wasn't mine, but from the first moment I held him in my arms I . . .' Owen shrugged miserably. 'He felt like my son.'

'And he *was* your son. He worshipped you, Owen. No father could have done more.'

'Having to watch him die so painfully . . .' Owen put his head into his hands once more. 'I can't believe he's gone. Why him? He hadn't had a life yet and here am I, fifty-nine years old. It should have been me, Greta!' He looked up at her. 'What have I got to live for now?'

Greta sighed deeply. 'You have Cheska.'

Greta hoped that the funeral might bring some form of closure for herself and her husband. Owen looked as though he had aged ten years in ten days and she'd had to physically support him at the graveside as they watched the tiny coffin being lowered into the ground.

She had suggested to Owen and the vicar that they lay Jonny to rest in the clearing in the woods where he had loved playing with his sister. 'And I'd prefer to think of him amongst the trees than surrounded by old bones in a cemetery,' she'd added.

'Whatever you want,' Owen had murmured. 'He's gone. Where he lies in death makes no difference to me.'

Greta had been undecided whether to take Cheska with them to the burial. She didn't understand where her brother had gone. 'Where's Jonny?' she would ask, her huge blue eyes filling with tears. 'Will he come back soon?'

Greta would shake her head for the hundredth time and explain that Jonny had gone to heaven and was now an angel, looking down at them from a big, puffy cloud.

Finally, having decided it was better that Cheska didn't see her beloved Jonny being put beneath the earth, a few days after the funeral Greta took her daughter into the woods and showed her the spot. She'd planted a small fir tree to mark Jonny's grave until the stone was erected.

'This is a special tree,' she explained to Cheska. 'Jonny loved the woods and this is where he comes with his angel friends to play.'

'Oh,' said Cheska, walking slowly towards it and touching one of its delicate branches. 'Jonny's here?'

'Yes, darling. People we love never leave us.'

'The Angel Tree,' Cheska murmured suddenly. 'He's here, Mummy, he's here. Can you see him in the branches?'

And, for the first time in two weeks, Greta saw Cheska smile.

Devastated as Greta was, she knew she had to maintain some semblance of normality for her daughter. But Owen had begun to drink regularly, and heavily. She could smell the alcohol on his breath at breakfast time and, by suppertime, he could hardly sit upright. After the initial devastation, he'd become morose and withdrawn and it was impossible to hold any sort of rational conversation with him. Greta began to take her evening meals up in her room, hoping that with time, as the sorrow lessened, he would pull himself together. But, as the months ground past and autumn arrived, it became clear to her that her husband's condition was deteriorating.

One morning she heard a shout from along the corridor and ran to find Mary outside Owen's bedroom nursing a swollen cheek.

'What happened?' she asked in alarm.

'The master threw a book at me. He complained his egg wasn't done to his satisfaction. It was, Greta. Indeed to goodness, it was.'

'Go and bathe that cheek, Mary. I'll see to my husband.' Greta knocked on the door, then entered Owen's room.

'What do you want?' he asked aggressively. He was sitting in a chair with Morgan at his feet. His breakfast tray was untouched and he was pouring himself a glass of whisky from an almost empty bottle.

'Don't you think it's a bit early for that?' Greta indicated the glass and noticed how thin he looked in his pyjamas.

'Just mind your own damned business, will you? Can't a man have a drink in his own house if he feels like it?'

'Mary's very upset. She's going to have a nasty bruise on her cheek where the book you threw hit her.'

Owen looked off into the distance, ignoring her.

'Don't you think we should talk, Owen? You're not well.'

'Of course I'm well!' he bellowed, draining his glass and reaching for the bottle.

'I think you've had enough for today, Owen,' she said quietly, walking towards him.

'Oh, do you indeed? And what gives you the right to pass judgement on my life?'

'Nothing, I . . . I just don't like to see you like this, that's all.'

'Well, it's your fault, anyway.' Owen sank back into his chair. 'If I hadn't married you and taken on your two bastards, then I wouldn't need to drink, would I?'

'Owen, please!' Greta was horrified. 'Don't call Jonny a bastard! You loved him.'

'Did I?' He leant forward and grabbed Greta's wrists. 'And why should I love some illegitimate Yankee brat, eh?' He began to shake Greta, slowly at first, then harder. Morgan started to growl.

'Stop it! You're hurting me. Stop it!'

'Why should I?' Owen roared. He let go of one of Greta's wrists and slapped her hard across the face. 'You're just a silly little whore, aren't you? *Aren't you?*'

'*Stop it!*' Greta managed to free herself and made for the safety of the door, tears of shock pouring down her face.

Owen looked across at her, his eyes dimmed by alcohol. Then he began to laugh. It was a harsh, cruel sound that sent her running from the room and into her own bedroom. She collapsed onto the bed and put her head in her hands in despair.

Owen's behaviour got steadily worse. His moments of lucidity became rare. Greta's presence seemed to ignite a flame of rage inside him, and the only person he would allow near him was Mary.

After several minor physical attacks, Greta called Dr Evans, fearing that the situation was getting out of control. Dr Evans was sent running out of Owen's bedroom by a hail of books, glasses and anything else her husband could lay his hands on.

'He needs help, Mrs Marchmont,' Dr Evans said as Greta offered him a cup of coffee. 'Jonny's death has sent him into a depression and he's trying to find solace in drink. He nearly died in the First World War, you know, had a bad case of shell shock when he returned to England, before he left for Kenya. I wonder whether his bereavement has touched on old wounds.'

'But what can I do?' Greta rubbed her forehead in agitation. 'He attacks me every time he sees me, and I'm starting to fear for Cheska's safety. He's not eating, just downing bottle after bottle of whisky.'

'Is there anywhere you could go and stay for a while? Any relatives? If you left, maybe it would shock him into pulling himself together.'

'No. I have nowhere to go. And anyway, I could hardly leave him like this, could I?'

'Mary seems to cope admirably. She appears to be the one person who can handle him. Of course, what we really need to do is to send him somewhere that could help him, but—'

'Not in a million years would he leave Marchmont.'

'Well then, the last resort would be to have him committed to an appropriate institution, but we'd have to go to court and have the judge agree. And in my opinion, he's not mad, just a depressed drunkard. I wish there were more I could do. I'm concerned for the safety of both you and your daughter. Do try and think if there's anywhere you could go, and don't hesitate to call me if you need help or advice.'

'I will, Dr Evans, thank you.'

Night after night, as Greta heard the sounds of loud snoring emanating from Owen's room, she'd swear to herself that, come the morning, she'd pack a suitcase and leave with Cheska. But when dawn broke reality would hit her. Where could she possibly go? She had nothing: no money or home of her own. All she had was here with Owen.

Eventually, it wasn't Owen's physical and mental abuse that made up Greta's mind for her.

One afternoon, when she put her head round the door of the nursery to check whether Cheska was still napping, she saw that her small bed was empty.

'Cheska! Cheska!' she called. There was no reply. She ran down the corridor and was about to knock on Owen's bedroom door when she heard chuckling from within. As silently as she could, Greta turned the door handle.

What she saw when she peered through the crack in the door made her shudder with horror. Owen was sitting in his chair, with Cheska perched happily on his knee as he read her a story.

It was a scene of perfect contentment.

Except for the fact that Cheska was dressed from head to toe in her dead brother's clothes.

# 11

Greta arrived back in London with Cheska on a cold, foggy October evening, realising it was almost four years since she had left. She had with her one suitcase, which contained some clothes for her and her daughter and fifty pounds in cash – the money David had given her when she'd left London, plus twenty pounds she'd taken from Owen's wallet.

After finding Cheska in Jonny's clothes, she'd finally known she had no choice but to leave. Days of agonising followed, and Greta had confided in Mary, feeling guilty for leaving her alone with Owen but knowing she had little choice.

'You must go, Miss Greta, for Cheska's sake, if not yours. I'll handle the master. If he throws things at me, I'll just duck!' Mary had smiled bravely. 'And Dr Evans is only a telephone call away, isn't he now?'

Owen had been in his bedroom, as usual, starting on his daily path towards drunken oblivion. Greta had knocked on his door and told him she was taking Cheska into Abergavenny to do some shopping and might be gone all day. He'd gazed at her out of bleary eyes; she doubted he'd even heard what she'd said. Huw, Mary's young man, had agreed to drive them to Abergavenny Station. Greta had thanked him profusely, purchased two rail tickets to London and boarded the waiting train.

As it sped away from Wales and her shambles of a marriage, Greta stared numbly out of the window. Although she had no idea where she and her daughter were going to sleep that night, anything seemed better than living in constant fear of her increasingly unstable husband. She couldn't allow herself to look back, despite her devastating loss. Cheska lolled against her, a rag doll clutched under one arm. Greta closed her arms protectively around her remaining child. And even though she knew she was returning to London with little more than she'd left with, Greta felt surprisingly strong and strangely unafraid.

When the train finally pulled into Paddington, she stepped onto the platform, struggling to carry a sleepy and confused Cheska and their suitcase. She walked to the taxi rank and asked the driver to take her to the Basil Street Hotel in Knightsbridge. She'd been there once with Max and knew it was respectable, if expensive.

Used to the silent tranquillity of Marchmont, the noise of the busy London streets thundered in Greta's ears as she paid the taxi driver and walked into the hotel lobby. But at least the quaint atmosphere of the hotel comforted her. They were shown up to their twin-bedded room, and she immediately ordered two rounds of sandwiches and a pot of tea from the porter.

'Here we are, darling.' Greta sat Cheska up at a small table. 'Cheese and tomato. Your favourite.'

'Don't want, don't want!' Cheska shook her head and started to cry.

Greta quickly gave up trying to persuade the little girl to eat. Instead, she unpacked the suitcase and put her into her nightgown.

'There you go, sweetheart. Isn't this a treat? Staying at a hotel in London and sharing a room with Mummy?'

She shook her head. 'Cheska wants to go home,' she whined.

'Well, why don't you pop into bed and Mummy will read to you?'

This seemed to cheer her up and Greta read a story from *Grimms' Fairy Tales*, her daughter's – and hitherto, she reflected miserably, her son's – favourite book, until Cheska's eyelids drooped, then finally closed. She sat on the bed studying her daughter for a long time. The high cheekbones, retroussé nose and rosebud lips were framed in a heart-shaped face. The natural curl in Cheska's soft golden hair made night-time rags unnecessary; it hung in perfect ringlets to her shoulders. Long, dark lashes rested against the perfect, unmarked skin under her eyes. Lying asleep, she looked like an angel.

A powerful wave of love washed over her. Cheska had always been undemanding, seeming to accept without question the way Owen had fussed over Jonny and ignored her. Although Greta still battled daily with her grief over Jonny's death, she hated the tiny part of her that felt almost grateful that it was he who'd been taken and not her beloved daughter.

Greta undressed, then leant over and kissed the little girl softly on the cheek. 'Goodnight, my darling. Sleep tight.' She climbed into her own bed and turned out the light.

Despite Greta's resolve, the first few days in London proved hard. Her first priority was to find a place for the two of them to live, but Cheska soon tired of being dragged round apartment after apartment and became irritable and tetchy. Greta didn't like the suspicious look in potential landladies' eyes when she explained she was a widow. The stigma of being a single mother was one she supposed she would have to get used to.

After three days of searching she found a clean, bright set of rooms on the top floor of a house very near to where she had lived before she'd fled to Wales. Kendal Street was just off the Edgware Road, and it gave Greta a feeling of security to move back to an area she already knew. The other advantage was the landlady, who had seemed very sympathetic when Greta told her that Cheska's father had died just after the war.

'I lost my husband and my son, Mrs Simpson. A terrible business.' She sighed. 'So many young 'uns growing up without their dads. Luckily, my husband left me this house, and it gives me a living. It's a quiet building, mind. I live in the basement and we have a couple of old ladies on the ground floor. Your little one's a good girl, is she?'

'Oh yes, very good. Aren't you, Cheska?'

Cheska had nodded and given the landlady a big smile.

'What a sweet little daughter you have, Mrs Simpson. When would you like to move in?' the landlady had asked, obviously charmed.

'As soon as possible.'

Greta handed over a deposit and a month's rent. She moved the two of them into the rooms two days later, pulling one of the twin beds into the sitting room so that Cheska could have her own bedroom and wouldn't be disturbed at night.

The first evening in the flat Greta put Cheska to bed, then went into her sitting room-cum-bedroom and sank into an armchair. After the spaciousness of the big house at Marchmont she felt horribly claustrophobic. But for the present, it was the best she could do. The money she had brought with her was dwindling already and she knew she had to find a job quickly.

She picked up the copy of the *Evening News* she had bought earlier and turned to the 'Situations Vacant' section. She skimmed through the advertisements, ringing possibilities with a pencil. Feeling depressed at the lack of suitable vacancies, and her lack of qualifications for any of them, Greta went into the kitchen, made herself a cup of tea and lit a cigarette. Her job at the Windmill was hardly the sort of thing one could tell a prospective employer about, and she really didn't want to go back there, as the punishing hours would mean leaving Cheska for long periods in the evenings. Ideally, she wanted some kind of respectable clerical position in an office in the City or the West End. Once she found a job, she'd have to advertise for a child-minder to look after Cheska while she was at work.

The next day Greta bought Cheska a chocolate bar then dragged her into a public phone box while she arranged interviews. She lied through her teeth, telling prospective employers that yes, she could type, and yes, she did have office experience. Having organised two appointments for the following morning, she now had the problem of what to do with Cheska while she attended them. Greta walked slowly back home, dragging her daughter behind her and feeling disheartened. In the hallway, an old lady was picking up the leaves that had made their way inside from the street.

'Hello, dearie. You new?'

'Yes. We've just moved into the top-floor flat. I'm Greta Simpson, and this is my daughter, Cheska.'

The old lady's eyes settled on the little girl. 'Have you been eating chocolate, dear?'

Cheska nodded shyly.

'Here.' The woman pulled a handkerchief from her sleeve and wiped Cheska's face. Surprisingly, the little girl didn't complain. 'There. That's better, isn't it? I'm Mabel Brierley, by the way. I live in number two. Husband at work, is he?'

'I'm a widow, actually.'

'So am I, dear. Died in the war, did he?'

'Yes, well, just afterwards. He was injured during the Normandy landings and never recovered. He passed away just after VE Day.'

'Oh, I am sorry. Lost mine in the First World War. Tragic times we live in, ain't they, dearie?'

'Yes,' agreed Greta sombrely.

'Any time you want a cup of tea and a bit of company, I'm always here. Nice to have a little one around the place. And such a pretty thing, aren't you?' She bent forward, smiling, and chucked Cheska under her chin.

Greta watched her daughter smile back at Mabel and decided to take the bull by the horns. 'I was wondering,

Mrs Brierley, do you know anyone who would be able to look after Cheska for a few hours tomorrow morning? I've got a job interview and I can't really take her with me.'

'Well, now let me think.' Mabel scratched her head. 'No, I can't say I do. Unless . . .' She looked down at the little girl. 'I suppose I could mind her, as long as it wouldn't be for too long.'

'Oh, would you? I'd be so grateful, and I'll be back by lunchtime. Of course, I'll pay you.'

'All right, then, dearie. We widows have to help each other out, don't we? What time?'

'Could I bring her down at nine?'

'Yes. See you then.'

Relieved, Greta carried Cheska up the stairs to their rooms.

Dressed in the one smart suit and hat she had brought with her, Greta took Cheska down to Mabel the following morning. The little girl whimpered when her mother explained that she had to go out for a while, but would be back by lunchtime.

'Don't you worry, Mrs Simpson. Cheska and me'll be fine,' Mabel reassured her.

Greta left before she could witness the tears that were bound to come and caught a bus to Old Street for her first interview.

The position was as a clerk in a bank, performing menial tasks such as filing, combined with a little bit of typing. Greta was nervous and her lies were unpractised. She came out of the interview with the office manager knowing she wouldn't be hearing from him.

The next interview was for the position of sales assistant on the perfume counter in the Swan & Edgar department store at Piccadilly. Her prospective boss was a woman in her mid-forties with sharp features, crisply dressed in a masculine suit. She asked Greta if she had any dependants and Greta lied more smoothly this time but still came out of the shop knowing it would be a miracle if she were offered the position. Feeling depressed, she walked along the road to a news stand to buy a paper.

Every day for a week Greta dropped Cheska off at Mabel's and spent the mornings going to interviews. She'd begun to realise that mass post-war unemployment, a problem that had seemed so distant and unrelated to her while she was at Marchmont, was having a marked effect on her prospects of finding a job. Greta soldiered on, though, the thought of returning to Wales and Owen making her all the more determined.

On Friday she deposited Cheska with Mabel as usual and set off on the bus for Mayfair. She wasn't optimistic about her interview, which was for the position of receptionist with a firm of solicitors. Yesterday a prospective employer had given her a typing test, which she'd failed miserably.

Taking a deep breath, Greta rang the bell on the side of the imposing black front door.

'Can I help you?' The woman who opened it was young, with a friendly smile.

'Yes. I have an appointment with Mr Pickering at half past eleven.'

'Right. Follow me.'

Greta walked behind the girl and was ushered into the

reception area. The room had oak-panelled walls, a thick carpet and leather armchairs.

The girl indicated one of the chairs. 'Do sit down. I'll go and tell Mr Pickering you're here.'

'Thank you.' Greta watched the girl open a door at the back of the room and disappear, closing it behind her. She wondered whether it was worth staying. In a smart practice like this, she was sure they'd want someone with years of experience.

She looked up as the door at the back of the room reopened.

'Greta Simpson, I presume?'

Greta stood up and held out her hand to a tall, very attractive man, whom she guessed was in his mid-thirties, dressed impeccably in a pinstripe suit. He had piercing blue eyes and thick black hair that was receding slightly at the temples. 'Yes. How do you do?'

Mr Pickering took her hand and gave it a firm shake. 'Very well, thank you. Would you like to follow me?'

'Certainly.' Greta accompanied him to the door at the back of the room, which he held open as she passed through.

'In here.' Mr Pickering guided Greta into a large, untidy office. The desk was laden with papers, and heavy legal books lined the shelves behind it. 'Do sit down, Mrs Simpson. I apologise for the mess, but I'm afraid it's the only environment in which I can work.' He smiled pleasantly as he sat down behind the desk and studied her, his fingers forming a steeple under his chin. 'So, tell me a little bit about yourself.'

Greta went through her story, but didn't mention Cheska.

'Right. Any experience working in an office?'

After a week of lying Greta decided to come clean.

'No, but I'm extremely eager and willing to learn.'

'Well –' Mr Pickering tapped a pencil on his desk – 'the position we're offering is not really a technical job. We deal with some very wealthy, important people and we like to make sure they're looked after from the minute they walk into the building. We'd expect you to greet our clients, offer them tea and, above all, to be discreet. Most of the clients are coming to visit us because they have a . . . personal problem of some sort. The telephone on the desk in reception would be your responsibility, as would the appointments diary for myself and my partner, Mr Sallis. We also have Moira, our secretary, who handles the typing and office administration very efficiently, but you'd be called upon to help her out on occasions. You'd be replacing Mrs Forbes, whom you met in reception. We're sorry to lose her, but she's having a baby in the New Year. You're – er – not thinking along those lines, are you, Mrs Simpson?'

Greta managed to look suitably shocked. 'In my present circumstances as a widow, I doubt that is an option open to me.'

'Good. Continuity, you see, is key. The clients like to establish a rapport. And I'm sure, with your pretty face, you'll be able to charm them. So, would you like to give it a try? Start on Monday?'

'I . . .' Greta was so surprised she couldn't think of what to say.

'Or would you prefer to go away and think about it?'

'No, no,' she said quickly. 'I'd love to take the job.'

'Excellent. I think you'll be perfect.' Mr Pickering stood up. 'I do apologise, but I have a lunch appointment. If you want to know any more, have a word with Sally . . . I mean, Mrs Forbes. She'll fill you in. The salary is two hundred and fifty pounds a year. Is that acceptable?'

'Oh yes, absolutely.' Greta stood and reached her hand across the desk. 'Thank you very much, Mr Pickering. I won't let you down, I promise.'

'I'm sure you won't. Good day, Mrs Simpson.'

As Greta left the office and walked into the reception area, a wave of euphoria overwhelmed her. Not even three weeks in London, and she'd managed to find herself somewhere to live and a means of supporting herself and her daughter.

'How did it go?' asked Sally.

'He offered me the position. I start on Monday.'

'Thank goodness for that! He's seen lots of girls, you know. I was beginning to think I'd be giving birth at my desk if he didn't find someone soon. No one seemed to be quite charming enough, if you know what I mean!'

'I think so. Have you been happy here?' asked Greta.

'Very. Mr Pickering is easy to work for, and the old man – sorry – Mr Sallis, the senior partner, is a sweetie. Mind you, just watch out for Veronica. That's Mr Sallis's daughter. She's married to Mr Pickering and an absolute harridan! She floats in here from time to time on her way to somewhere frightfully grand for lunch. She rules her husband with a rod of iron. She's the real power behind the throne. If she doesn't like you, you're out. My predecessor left because of her.'

'I see.'

'But don't worry. Her Majesty doesn't grace us with her presence too often, thank goodness. Anything else you'd like to know while you're here?'

Greta asked a few questions, which Sally answered in detail, then she looked at her watch. 'Oh dear. I didn't realise it was so late! I must be going.'

'Well, nice to meet you. I'll be here for a few days after you've started, to show you the ropes, but I'm sure you'll do fine.'

'Thank you. When is your baby due? I—' Greta only just managed to stop herself before she launched into sympathetic conversation about the last tiring months of pregnancy. 'See you on Monday. Goodbye.'

Greta hurried out into the street and treated herself to a taxi, anxious to get home as soon as possible. She decided she would ask Mabel if she was interested in minding Cheska on a permanent basis during the day. If she wasn't, she'd have to place an advertisement in the local newsagent's window.

When Greta arrived home, a smiling Cheska, her face smeared with chocolate, came running out of Mabel's flat to greet her.

'Hello, darling.' Greta swept her daughter up in her arms. 'Have you had a nice time?'

'We made fairy cakes, Mummy.' Cheska snuggled into her mother.

'Has she been good?' she asked Mabel, who'd appeared at the door.

'As gold. You have a lovely little girl there, Mrs Simpson.'

'Oh, please call me Greta. Do you have a spare five minutes, Mabel? There's something I'd like to ask you.'

'Yes. Come in, dear, do. I've just brewed up.'

Greta picked Cheska up and carried her into Mabel's flat, which was cluttered with heavy, old-fashioned furniture. It smelt faintly of violets and disinfectant.

Mabel sat them down in her sitting room, then brought through a tray on which was a teapot covered in a bright, knitted tea-cosy, cups and a plate of rather burnt fairy cakes.

'There you go.' Mabel passed Greta a cup of strong tea. 'Now, what was it you wanted to ask, dearie?'

'Well, this morning I managed to find myself a job working for a firm of solicitors in Mayfair.'

'Ooh, aren't you the clever one? Never learned to read and write meself. Women didn't in them days, see.'

'Well, the problem I've got is Cheska. I have to go out and earn a living but obviously I can't take her with me.'

'No. 'Course you can't.'

'So I was wondering whether you'd be interested in minding her on a regular basis? I'd pay you, naturally.'

'Well, let me see. What hours are we talking about?'

'I'd have to leave at eight-thirty and I wouldn't be back until six.'

'Five days a week?'

'Yes.'

'Well, we could give it a go, couldn't we?' Mabel smiled at Cheska, who was happily eating a cake on her mother's knee. 'She'd be company for me an' all.'

They then agreed a wage of fifteen shillings a week.

'That'll be fine,' said Mabel. 'Any extra pennies come in

handy these days. My husband's pension only just covers the rent and food.'

'Well, I really am very grateful. Anyway, we mustn't take up any more of your time today. Come on, Cheska, let's go and have some lunch.' Greta stood up.

'You know what you want to do, don't you, dear?' said Mabel as she led them to the front door.

'What's that?'

'Find a new husband. I'm sure a good-looking girl like you could find herself a nice wealthy gentleman to marry and take care of the two of you. It's not right for a mother to have to work.'

'That's kind of you, Mabel, but I don't think any man would be interested in a widow and her daughter,' Greta said with a rueful smile. 'See you on Monday.'

'Yes, dear. Mind how you go.'

As Greta carried Cheska upstairs to their flat, she thought about what Mabel had said. Even if she were free to do so, she doubted she'd ever marry again.

# 12

Greta and Cheska spent an enjoyable Saturday afternoon shopping in the West End. Fashionable boutiques had been few and far between in Wales. At Marchmont, all she'd needed were warm, practical garments.

Now the stores seemed to be overflowing with the kind of clothes Greta hadn't seen since before the war. Cheska was fascinated by the huge department stores, trotting after her mother with an expression of wonder on her face. Greta bought two inexpensive suits and three blouses for work and also a cream Aran sweater and a tartan kilt for Cheska.

On Sunday night Greta sat her daughter down and explained that Mummy had to go out to work so the two of them could have nice things to eat and pretty dresses to wear. She told her that Mabel would look after her during the day, but Mummy would be back home to put her to bed at night. Cheska seemed to accept this with little fuss. She announced that Mabel was nice and gave her chocolate.

The next morning Greta left Cheska at Mabel's flat. The little girl went to her without a whimper. Feeling relieved, Greta caught a bus to work.

By the end of her first week she had settled down and

was enjoying her job. The clients who came in were friendly and courteous. Moira, the middle-aged secretary, was very helpful and Terence, the office boy, was a cockney lad with a wisecrack for every occasion. She rarely saw old Mr Sallis, who only came in three days a week. Mr Pickering was either locked away with a client or rushing off for a lunch appointment. To her relief, the dreaded Veronica did not make an appearance.

Cheska seemed quite happy with her new routine and, although Greta arrived home tired from her day's work, she always found the energy to cook a nice supper, then read to her daughter for an hour before she went to bed.

At the weekends, even though money was very tight, Greta made a special effort to organise treats. Sometimes they visited Hamleys toy shop and went for tea afterwards at a Lyons Corner House. And once, she'd taken Cheska to London Zoo to see the lions and tigers.

Greta was surprised at how easily they had both adapted to their new life in London. Cheska rarely mentioned Marchmont, and as for Greta, her busy new schedule meant she had far less time to think about the loss of her precious son. She felt a pang of guilt each time she received a badly spelt letter from Mary telling her of Owen's continuing decline. He'd had a couple of nasty falls and Dr Evans had tried to admit him to a hospital, but he'd refused to go. Morgan, his beloved Labrador, had died recently, and this had apparently sent him into further sustained bouts of drinking. He was too sick to look after the estate and Mr Glenwilliam, his solicitor, had taken over the running of Marchmont.

Mary stoically told Greta not to worry, that she'd done

the right thing for Cheska by leaving. Greta wondered when Mary would write to say that she was resigning, especially as she'd mentioned that Huw, the young estate worker who'd been courting her, had asked her to marry him. They were engaged and saving up for the wedding, but for now, Mary still seemed to be taking her master's erratic behaviour in her stride.

It was a month after starting her job that Greta first met Mr Pickering's wife. She had just arrived back from her lunch break and sat down at her desk when an elegant woman dressed in a luxurious fur coat and matching hat walked through the front entrance and into reception without ringing the bell. Greta smiled up at her.

'Good afternoon, madam. May I help you?'

'And who might you be?' The women's gimlet eyes swept over Greta.

'I'm Mrs Simpson. I replaced Mrs Forbes a few weeks ago. Did you have an appointment?' asked Greta pleasantly.

'I hardly think I need to make an appointment to see either my husband or my father, do you?'

'No, of course not. I do apologise, Mrs Pickering. Which of them would you like to see?'

'Don't bother. I'll go through and find my husband myself.' Veronica Pickering peered down at Greta's hands. 'And I rather think you should find yourself an emery board. Those nails look dirty and unpolished. Can't have our clients thinking we employ riff-raff, now can we?' She gave Greta one last patronising glance, then turned and swept through the door leading to her husband's office.

Greta looked down at her perfectly clean, if unmanicured, fingernails and bit her lip. Then a client appeared in reception and she was kept busy making tea and chatting to him.

Ten minutes later Mrs Pickering emerged with her husband in tow.

'Take Mr Pickering's calls, Griselda. We're going out to buy me a Christmas present, aren't we, darling?'

'Yes, dear. I'll be back by four, Greta.'

'Very good, Mr Pickering.'

As they walked towards the front door Veronica Pickering turned to her husband. 'Not sure about that accent, James dear. Don't they teach standard English in schools these days?'

Greta gritted her teeth as the door shut behind them.

Meeting Veronica Pickering unsettled her for the rest of the day. Mr Pickering didn't return to the office, and the next time she saw him was the following morning. He stopped beside her desk as he walked through reception.

'Good morning, Greta.'

'Good morning, sir.'

'I just wanted to apologise for my wife. I'm afraid it's the way she is, and you mustn't take anything she says to heart. We – I mean, Mr Sallis and I – are very pleased with your work so far.'

'Thank you, sir.'

'Good. Carry on, then.' Mr Pickering smiled at her in that sweet way of his and Greta wondered why on earth he had married such a ghastly woman.

After that, Mr Pickering would often stop and have a chat with Greta when he passed her desk, as if to reassure her that he did not share his wife's opinion of her. During one such chat Greta asked if she could have a typewriter so she could help out with any extra letters. Mr Pickering agreed and, with Moira's patient assistance, she began to teach herself to type.

There were only a few days to go until Christmas and Greta was looking forward to the week she had off over the festive season. She had already spent far too much money on Cheska's presents, not wanting her little girl to think Father Christmas had forgotten her, and had booked two seats at the Scala Theatre to see Margaret Lockwood in *Peter Pan*. Greta was determined to make sure their first Christmas without Owen and Jonny was as happy as the circumstances permitted.

'Father Christmas will know where I am, Mummy, won't he?' asked Cheska anxiously as Greta tucked her up in bed for the night.

'Of course, darling. I wrote to the North Pole and told him we'd changed our address. Next week we'll go out and buy a tree and lots of nice decorations to hang on it. Would you like that?'

'Oh yes, Mummy.' Cheska smiled in pleasure and snuggled down under her covers.

Moira went down with influenza and was sent home the following afternoon, and Mr Pickering began to hand Greta piles of typing.

'I do apologise, Greta, but there are so many loose ends to tie up before the office closes for Christmas. Mr Sallis has already gone to the country, so I'm having to do everything. You couldn't by any chance stay late tomorrow night, could you? We'll pay you extra, of course.'

'Yes, I think that will be all right,' she replied.

That evening Greta asked Mabel if she'd give Cheska her tea tomorrow, then put her to bed and stay with her until she arrived home.

'I'd be so grateful, Mabel. I've seen a gorgeous doll in Hamleys that I'd love to buy her, and the extra money will pay for it. And you will be joining us for Christmas lunch, won't you? Cheska has asked if you could come. She adores you, you know.'

'Then I'm happy to help you out. As long as you don't make a habit of it, mind,' Mabel replied.

It was past seven the following evening before the last letter was neatly typed, ready for Mr Pickering to sign. Greta picked them up and knocked on his door.

'Come in!'

'Here you are, Mr Pickering. All done.' Greta put the letters on his desk.

'Thank you, Greta. You are a wonder, really. I don't know what I'd have done without you.' He scrawled his signature at the bottom of each letter and passed them back to her.

'Well, that's it for the day, I think. Now, how about I buy you a drink for all that hard work and to celebrate Christmas?'

'I'd love to, but—' Greta was just about to say that she ought to be getting home to Cheska, but managed to stop herself.

'We could hop to the Athenaeum.' Mr Pickering was

already reaching for his overcoat. 'I can't stay long, as I'm meeting Veronica in an hour to go to a party.'

Greta knew she ought to say no and go straight home, but it was a very long time since she'd been out anywhere in the evening. Besides, she liked Mr Pickering. 'All right then,' she agreed.

'Good. Grab your coat, and I'll meet you out front.'

'Fine, but I need to put these letters into their envelopes and stamp them.'

'Of course. We'll post them on the way.'

Ten minutes later the two of them were walking along Piccadilly to the Athenaeum. The cocktail bar was crowded, but they managed to find seats and Mr Pickering ordered them two pink gins.

'So, what are you doing for Christmas, Greta?' he asked as he lit a cigarette. 'Oh, and by the way, please call me James now we're out of office hours.'

'Oh, nothing much,' she answered.

'Going to your family, are you?'

'Er, yes.'

Their drinks arrived and Greta took a sip of hers.

'They live in London, do they?'

'Yes. And you?'

'Oh, the usual stuff. We've a party at our place in London tomorrow to celebrate Christmas Eve, then we go down to Mr and Mrs Sallis's house in Sussex until the New Year.'

'You don't sound terribly thrilled about going to your in-laws,' Greta ventured.

'Don't I? Oh dear. That's what Veronica keeps saying.'

'Don't you like Christmas?'

'I used to, when I was a boy, but these days it just seems to be one long round of socialising with people I rather dislike. I suppose it would be different if we had some little ones. I mean, that's who Christmas is really for, isn't it?'

'Yes,' agreed Greta. 'Have you . . . I mean, are you and Mrs Pickering planning to have children?'

'I'd like to think so, one day, but my wife is hardly the maternal type.' James sighed. 'Anyway, tell me more about you.'

'There's nothing much to tell.'

'Surely a lady as attractive and intelligent as yourself must have a man in tow?'

'No, I'm single at the moment.'

'I find that most difficult to believe. I mean, if I were a single man, I'd find you hard to resist.' He took a sip of his pink gin and eyed her over the rim of the glass.

Greta, lightheaded from the alcohol, blushed and realised she was enjoying the attention. 'What did you do during the war?' she asked him.

'I have asthma so the army refused me. Instead, I worked at the Ministry of Defence in Whitehall and studied for my law exams at night. Mr Sallis made me a junior partner on VE Day, just after I passed,' said James.

'Did it help that you were Mr Sallis's son-in-law?'

'Of course it did, but I'm actually quite a good solicitor too, you know.' He smiled, taking her pointed comment good-naturedly.

'Oh, I don't doubt that for a moment. So, how did you meet your wife?'

'At a party shortly before the war. I was just down from

Cambridge. Veronica set her sights on me and . . .' He laughed. 'To be honest, Greta, I didn't stand a chance.'

There was a short silence as Greta digested this information. 'I don't think she likes me very much. She accused me of being slovenly and having an accent.'

'That's only jealousy, Greta. Veronica's not so young any more and she resents anyone who is. Particularly someone as lovely as yourself. Now, I'm afraid I'm going to have to leave you. The drinks party starts in fifteen minutes and it's more than my life's worth to be late.' He paid the bill, then handed Greta some coins. 'Here, take a taxi home, will you?'

They stood up, walked through the lobby and out of the front entrance.

'I enjoyed that,' he said. 'Maybe you'd like to have dinner with me one evening?'

'Maybe.'

'Well, for now, Merry Christmas, Greta.'

'And to you, James.'

He waved back at her as he walked briskly along the pavement. The hotel doorman hailed a taxi for Greta and she stepped inside. As it drove off, she allowed herself to think back over the conversation. She found James attractive, and there was little doubt the feeling was reciprocated. It had been such a long time since she had been in the company of a man who had complimented her. For a few seconds Greta imagined James pulling her into his arms and kissing her . . . then stopped herself abruptly.

It was madness even to think about it. He was married. And not only that, he was her employer.

Even so, as she lay alone in bed that night, her body

tingling with desire for him, Greta knew it was doubtful she'd be able to resist the temptation if it was offered to her.

# 13

Over the Christmas holidays Greta struggled to put thoughts of James to the back of her mind and concentrated on giving her daughter the best Christmas she possibly could. Cheska's face on Christmas morning was a picture of wonder as she unwrapped her numerous presents, including the doll from Hamleys whose eyes opened and closed. Mabel came upstairs to share their small roast chicken and the day was very cheerful. But after Cheska had gone to bed and Mabel had left, Greta felt a wave of emptiness wash over her. She looked up at the stars and sent a whispered message to her lost son: 'Happy Christmas, Jonny, wherever you are.'

On Boxing Day she took Cheska to see *Peter Pan* at the Scala Theatre.

'Do you believe in fairies?' cried Peter Pan.

Cheska jumped out of her seat in her eagerness to save Tinkerbell. 'Yes! Yes!' she shrieked with every other child in the theatre.

Greta spent more time watching her daughter's face than she did the stage. The sight gladdened her heart and made all the sacrifices worthwhile.

When she returned to work after New Year James was not yet back from the country.

A week later, when he walked into reception, her heart almost missed a beat.

'Hello, Greta. Happy New Year to you,' he said, then strode through the door to his office and closed it behind him. A deflated Greta spent that evening wondering if she'd imagined the way he'd been at the Athenaeum.

Ten days later the telephone on her desk rang.

'Hello, Greta, it's James. Has Mr Jarvis arrived yet?'

'No, he just telephoned to say he'd be slightly late.'

'Fine. Oh, and by the way, are you doing anything tonight?'

'No.'

'Then let me take you out for that dinner I promised you.'

'That would be lovely.'

'Good. I have a meeting at six, so hang on for me here until it's finished.'

Heart beating with excitement, Greta made a quick phone call to Mabel, who said she was prepared to babysit, and that evening, when James's meeting was finished, she walked with him round the corner to Jermyn Street.

Once seated in the cosy, candlelit restaurant, they were handed large leather-bound menus.

'We'll have a bottle of Sancerre, thank you. And the special of the day. It's always the thing to go for here,' he said with a smile when the waiter had left. 'And I got something for you.' He fumbled in his jacket pocket and produced a beautifully gift-wrapped package which he handed to her. 'A small, belated Christmas present.'

'Goodness, James, you really shouldn't have.'

'Nonsense. I wanted to. Go on, open it.'

Greta did so. Inside the Harrods box was a brightly patterned silk scarf. 'It's beautiful, thank you.'

Over dinner, they chatted, with Greta doing most of the listening at first. But, as the lovely wine entered her system, she began to relax – although she knew she had to keep her wits about her, given the web of lies she'd told him to get the job in the first place.

'So your Christmas was pleasant?' she asked him.

'Yes, it was . . . fine. Although a little bit too formal for me.'

'And Veronica is well?'

'Yes, as far as I know. She's in Sussex still with her parents. Mrs Sallis isn't well at the moment. I have a feeling Mr Sallis may retire soon, and I'll be taking over the practice.'

'That must be good news for you.'

'Yes. In many ways, the firm is stuck in the Dark Ages. It needs modernising, but my hands are tied, for the present at least.'

Listening to him, Greta sensed that James was not particularly happy with his lot. There was something intrinsically sad about him, which rather appealed to her.

'Greta, if you've finished your coffee, would you like to come back to my house for a nightcap?'

Knowing she should refuse but desperate to say yes, Greta checked her watch. It was already ten o'clock and she'd sworn to Mabel she'd be home before eleven.

'Is it far?'

'No, five minutes from here, if that.'

When they arrived, James unlocked the front door and switched on the lights in the hall.

'Here, let me take your coat,' he offered.

He led Greta into an imposing drawing room. It was sparsely but stylishly furnished, with three cream leather sofas forming a U-shape around a large fireplace, above which hung a brightly coloured modern painting.

'Sit down and I'll get us both a brandy.'

'This is a lovely house, James,' she said as he took the decanter from a tray.

'Yes, Geoffrey . . . Mr Sallis, that is, gave it to us as a wedding present. Not my choice of decor. I'd prefer something a bit warmer, but Veronica likes it.' James sat down far closer to Greta than was necessary, given the vastness of the sofa.

After ten minutes of inconsequential chat, during which James's gaze never left her, Greta rose from the sofa. The inappropriateness of their situation, not to mention the undeniable sexual tension, was making her jittery and nervous. 'Thank you for dinner, but I really must be getting home now.'

'Of course. I enjoyed the evening immensely, and I'd like to do it again.' He got up too, and took her hands in his. 'Very much.' Then he reached forward and kissed her gently on the lips.

Greta felt his arms wind around her waist and pull her tightly against him. After a while she began to kiss him back, feeling a long-forgotten heat spread through her.

James began to undo the buttons on her jacket. His hand found its way under her blouse and he cupped his fingers around her breast.

'Oh God . . . I've dreamed of this since I first set eyes on you,' he murmured, and pulled her down on to the rug.

It was almost midnight when Greta left and hailed a taxi, bracing herself for the clucking annoyance of Mabel when she arrived home. Thankfully, Mabel had dozed off in a chair and was snoring loudly. Greta shook her awake gently and, still groggy from sleep, Mabel offered no complaint at the late hour as she left. Greta checked Cheska, who was sleeping peacefully, arms wrapped tightly around her new doll. Then she undressed for the second time that evening and climbed into bed.

The smell of him still lingered on her skin, and her body felt relaxed, sated.

As she lay there, sleepless, she decided she would handle this affair like the mature woman she was, taking what she needed and using James as he was using her. She would not come to depend on him or, even worse, fall in love with him.

As she finally drifted into unconsciousness, her lips turned up in a tiny smile of contentment.

One sunny June morning Greta realised that her affair with James had been going on for almost six months. She could no longer deny that he had become part of her life and that if he were no longer in it the void would be huge. They saw each other every time Veronica went away, which was often.

Recently, Greta had told him that she felt what they were doing was wrong and they ought to end it. At these moments James would once more confess his unhappiness with Veronica and start talking about a future together. He'd open a practice down in Wiltshire, he told her, where the two of them could make a fresh start. He just had to pick the right moment to tell Veronica. But he absolutely would, he said. And soon.

Despite her initial misgivings, Greta began to believe him. The thought of having a man to take care of her and Cheska – she was sure he wouldn't mind about her when she told him, he'd said he loved children – was so appealing.

And even though she'd sworn to herself to keep her heart locked away, slowly, her resolve had been worn down. Greta knew she had fallen in love with him.

Veronica was in the drawing room on her hands and knees, searching for an expensive earring she'd just dropped onto the floor. She and James were due to go out to dinner soon, and she couldn't find it. She put her hand underneath the sofa and groped around. Her fingers touched something soft and she pulled the object out. It was the silk scarf James had given her for Christmas. How odd, she thought to herself, she was sure she'd folded it away in her drawer earlier that day. She picked it up and put it on the sofa, then continued to search for her missing earring.

The following morning Veronica opened a drawer and saw her silk scarf lying exactly where she thought she'd put it the day before. She took it out and went downstairs to the drawing room, picked up the one she had found underneath the sofa and smelt it. Cheap perfume.

Veronica knew exactly who the scarf belonged to.

*

Greta looked up when Veronica came through the door.

'Good morning, Mrs Pickering. How are you today?' she asked, as pleasantly as she could.

'Actually, I just popped in to return something of yours.' Veronica took the silk scarf out of her coat pocket and dropped it on Greta's desk. 'It does belong to you, doesn't it?'

Greta felt herself blushing.

'Do you want to know where I found it? I'll tell you. Under the sofa in my drawing room.' Veronica spoke in a low, cold voice. 'How long has it been going on? You do realise you're not the first, don't you? Just one in a long line of common little tarts who flatter my husband's ego.'

'You're wrong! It's not like that. Anyway, it doesn't matter that you know. He was going to tell you tonight in any case.'

'Really? Tell me what, exactly?' Veronica sneered. 'That he's going to leave me for you?'

'Yes.'

'He told you that, did he? Yes, he usually does. Well, let me tell *you* something, my dear. He'll never leave me. He needs what I give him too much. He doesn't have a penny of his own, you know. He came into the marriage with nothing. Now, I suggest you pack your things and leave this office immediately. There's no reason why we can't handle this in a civilised way, is there?'

'You can't take that decision! I work for James.' Greta rallied, anger getting the better of her.

'Yes, my dear, but when my father retires he's passing over his practice to James and me. We'll own it jointly, and

I'm sure I'll have his full backing when I say I want you out now.'

'We're both leaving anyway. He loves me. We have plans!'

'Is that so?' Veronica raised a perfectly groomed eyebrow. 'Well then, why don't we go into his office and hear about them?'

Greta followed Veronica into James's office. He looked startled as they both marched in.

'Hello, darling. And Greta. What can I do for you?'

'Well, the problem is that I've found out that the two of you have been having a grubby little affair behind my back. I put it to Greta that the best thing she could do was to leave quickly and quietly, but she insisted she hear it from you.' Veronica seemed perfectly calm, almost bored. 'Tell her, darling, and we can go out for lunch.'

Greta studied James's expression, wondering why he wasn't speaking. Their eyes met, and she saw the sorrow in his. Then he looked away and she knew she'd lost.

Eventually, James cleared his throat. 'Yes, I . . . I think it would be best if you left, Greta. We'll pay you until the end of the week, of course.'

'You'll do no such thing!' said Veronica sharply. 'Greta has made her own bed, so to speak, and she must lie in it. I hardly think we are under obligation to pay her anything, do you?'

James looked at his wife and, for a second, Greta saw the uncertainty in his eyes. Then it faded and his whole body seemed to droop. He shook his head sadly.

Greta fled out of his office, grabbed her coat and handbag and left the building.

# 14

Greta spent the afternoon wandering around Green Park, unable to go home and face Cheska, or Mabel's questions as to why she was home early. She sat on a bench in the June sunshine and watched people go by: nannies chatting as they pushed perambulators, businessmen carrying briefcases, young couples strolling hand in hand.

'Oh dear Lord,' she moaned, as she put her head in her hands. Not since Max had deserted her had she felt so alone. And she knew she only had herself to blame. She should have known from the start that her affair with James could never have a happy ending.

Greta pondered on why she seemed destined to choose the wrong kind of man. Other women managed to find lifetime partners, so why couldn't she? Surely she'd done nothing bad enough to deserve the kind of luck she'd had? And yet, she asked herself brutally, wasn't it her own weakness that kept putting her in this position? She was like a moth, helplessly drawn to the flame of a candle that would inevitably destroy her.

She sat staring into the distance. The thought of having to find another job, with no real hope of ever getting the love and security she craved, seemed too much to contemplate.

But she had to pull herself together. She knew she had to fight on, if not for her own sake, then for her daughter's.

One thing was for certain: she was finished with men for good. Never again would she allow another man close enough to wreak havoc in her life. From now on, any love she had to give was for Cheska alone.

Greta stood and wandered up towards Piccadilly. She crossed the road and headed for the Windmill, wondering whether she should walk inside and beg for a job rather than embarking on another round of fruitless interviews. If she wasn't going to receive any pay for her last week's work, she had to earn some money straight away. Yes, she decided, it was the best solution. No references required, no questions asked. Greta pushed open the stage door and asked the doorman if she could see Mr Van Damm.

Fifteen minutes later she was outside once more, feeling even more depressed. Mr Van Damm was sorry, but he had no vacancies. He'd taken Greta's new address and promised to write to her as soon as something came up, but she knew he wouldn't. She was five years older than she'd been when she'd first arrived, and he was aware that she had a child, thanks to the theatre rumour mill.

Disconsolately, Greta stood outside the stage door and looked at the group of prostitutes chatting in the doorway on the other side of Archer Street. She recognised some of the faces that had been there when she'd worked at the Windmill. Greta had always looked down her nose at them, but had she really been any better than they were? After all, she had given herself to James for free but had performed the same function: she had satisfied a need his wife didn't fulfil.

'Greta! Greta, it is you, isn't it?'

A hand was placed on her shoulder from behind. She heard the familiar voice and turned around.

'Taffy!' Her face lit up. 'I mean . . . David.' She chuckled despite herself.

'I thought I saw you coming out of Mr Van Damm's office so I dashed after you. What on earth are you doing here?'

'I . . . well, actually, I was asking for my old job back.'

'I see. Ma told me you'd left Owen a few months back, but we'd no idea where you'd gone. We've both been desperately worried about you and your little one. Look, have you got time for a cup of tea? We've got a lot to catch up on.'

Greta looked at her watch. It was ten to four. She still had a couple of hours before she needed to be home.

'On one condition.'

'Anything you say,' he said with a smile.

'That you won't tell your mother, or *anyone*,' she emphasised, 'that you've seen me.'

'It's a deal.' David offered Greta his elbow. She slipped her arm through his and they walked companionably down the road to a nearby café.

While he was busy ordering a pot of tea for two, Greta lit a cigarette and wondered how much David knew about her departure from Marchmont.

'So, where have you been hiding since you arrived in London?' he asked her.

'Near where I used to live, actually. Cheska and I share a small flat.'

'I see. I understand you left Owen because of his . . . problem.'

'Yes. When Jonny died, he fell apart completely.'

'I was so very sorry to hear about the little chap's death. It must have been heartbreaking for you.'

'It was . . . terrible.' Greta felt a lump rise in her throat. 'And when Owen became violent I didn't really have any alternative. I feel very guilty about leaving him in his condition, but what else could I do?'

'Well, for a start, you could have come to me when you arrived in London,' he admonished her.

'Oh, David, after all you'd done to help me, I couldn't ask you again.'

'You should have. From the sound of things, my uncle doesn't know what day it is. Glenwilliam, the solicitor, telephoned me to say he's had a fall after a particularly heavy drinking binge and is now confined to a wheelchair with a fractured pelvis.'

'Oh God, how awful.' Greta stared guiltily into her teacup. 'I should have stayed, shouldn't I?'

'No, Greta. You did the right thing. From what Glenwilliam has said, you and Cheska had no choice but to leave. How have you survived money-wise?'

'I have . . . *had* a job, until this morning, but there was a disagreement with my employer and I left. That's why I was at the Windmill, to see if they could offer me anything.'

David studied Greta across the table. Although she was still as beautiful as he remembered, he saw that her eyes were red from crying and she looked exhausted. 'Poor you.

You really should have come and found me here. You know I would have helped.'

'It's awfully sweet of you to say that, but—'

'You thought I'd be angry because you married my uncle,' he finished for her.

'Yes.'

'Well, before we go any further, I want to say that I don't hold what you did against you in the slightest. Although I wouldn't presume to know what your feelings for Uncle Owen were.'

'I didn't love him, David, if that's what you mean. I was desperate, and he was very kind to me in the beginning,' she replied with brutal honesty. 'Having said that, I think he was using me, too. I've realised since that Owen only married me because he wanted an heir for Marchmont.'

'Sadly, I believe there's some truth in what you say. The thought of passing Marchmont on to me when he died was never something he was keen on,' said David with a wry laugh.

'You must believe that I didn't know anything about all this when he started courting me. I'm quite sure your mother left Marchmont because I was marrying him. I feel very bad about that, too.'

'Well, I've always thought there was something Ma hasn't told me about her relationship with my uncle. But if it makes you feel any better, she's perfectly happy living with her sister in Gloucestershire.'

'David, I'm so sorry for all the trouble I've caused you and your family. You were so kind to help me and I just seem to have brought disaster on you all. Oh dear, why do I always cry when I'm with you?'

'I don't know whether I should take it as a compliment or an insult. Here.' He handed her his handkerchief. 'Now, on to happier matters, when do I get to see this . . . now what would she be? Er—' He scratched his head. 'Cousin, I suppose. Do you think Cheska is "once removed"? I've always wanted to have a "removed" relative!'

Greta giggled and blew her nose. 'David, you don't know how good it is to see you.'

'And you, Greta. So, what are you going to do for money now you've lost your job?'

'Try and get another one, I suppose. Anyway, tell me, how are things for you?'

'Very good, as a matter of fact. Next week is my last at the Windmill. I have my own radio show on the BBC, and next month I begin shooting my first major film, at Shepperton Studios. I have a very nice cameo role playing a hapless card sharp. Always was rubbish at Snap,' he said with a grin.

'My goodness, that's wonderful.'

'I can't complain, certainly. Look, why don't you bring Cheska to Sunday lunch at my apartment? I'd love to meet her. My agent's coming, too. We're celebrating my leaving the Windmill and starting the film.'

'We'd love to come, if it isn't too much trouble.'

'No trouble at all.' He scribbled his address down on a piece of paper. 'It's just round the corner from here. I've written my telephone number down, too. If you need anything, Greta, please call me. After all, we are family, in an odd sort of way.'

'Thank you. I'll see you on Sunday, then.' Greta stood

up. 'I have to go now. Cheska's childminder gets worried if I'm late.'

'Of course. Goodbye.'

After paying the bill, David made his way across the road to the stage door. As he entered his dressing room, he realised he was whistling. He stared at his reflection in the mirror and saw a brightness in his eyes that had nothing to do with his blossoming career.

It was because of Greta.

Fate had sent her back to him when he'd thought she was lost to him forever.

And this time, he wouldn't let her go.

On Sunday Greta dressed Cheska in her best blue dress and tied a matching ribbon into her blonde curls.

'Who are we going to see, Mummy?' her daughter asked as they left the flat.

'Your Uncle David. He's a famous comedian, which means he's very funny. He's about to be in a film.'

Cheska's huge china-blue eyes were round with expectation as they climbed aboard the bus, eventually alighting at Seven Dials. They then walked along Floral Street to the address David had given Greta.

'Come in, come in!' David greeted them warmly at the door. He bent down and looked into Cheska's eyes. 'Hello. I'm your cousin, David, possibly once removed . . .' He winked at Greta. 'But why don't you call me Uncle? That's a beautiful dolly. What's her name?'

'Polly,' said Cheska shyly.

'Polly the Dolly. It suits her very well. Do you know, you're beautiful, just like your mummy.' He stretched out his arms to Cheska and lifted her up into them. 'Follow me,' he said, and the three of them went into the bright, airy sitting room, where a middle-aged man sat, drinking a whisky.

'This is my cousin, Cheska, and her mother, Greta. Greta, this is Leon Bronowski, my agent.'

The man stood up and held out his hand to Greta. 'My pleasure,' he said, in a faintly foreign accent.

David settled Cheska on the sofa and took Greta's coat. 'What can I get you both to drink?'

'A gin would be lovely, and some squash, if you have it, for Cheska.'

He went into the kitchen to organise the drinks.

'Did you first spot David at the Windmill, Mr Bronowski?' Greta asked as she sat down.

'Please, call me Leon. And the answer is yes. He's a very talented young man and will go far, I think. He tells me you used to work there with him?'

'Yes, although it feels like a lifetime ago now.'

'It's a rare breeding ground for new talent. There are many ladies in the chorus who have gone on to become successful film actresses. That was your intention too, I presume?'

'The arrival of Cheska rather stopped me in my tracks, but of course I had dreamed of it. Doesn't every girl?'

Leon nodded thoughtfully as he studied Cheska. 'Of course.'

Their host came back with two glasses.

'Thank you. Here's to you, David. Well done. You must be very excited about the film.' Greta raised her glass.

'I am. But it's all down to Leon. If it weren't for him, I'd probably still be slaving away at the Windmill, looking for my first big break. Now, excuse me whilst I see to the lamb.'

Shortly afterwards, David served up a very palatable roast, which the four of them ate at the table in a corner of the sitting room. Greta felt a glow of pride as she watched Cheska sit quietly as David and Leon discussed the latest showbusiness gossip.

As they drank their coffee after the meal, Leon's glance fell once more on the child, who had left the table and was sitting cross-legged by the fire, looking through her favourite picture book, *Grimms' Fairy Tales*, which Greta had brought with her.

'Is she always this good?' he asked.

'Most of the time. She has her moments, as all children do.'

'She's very beautiful. She reminds me of a cherub with that golden cloud of curls and those wonderful eyes,' mused Leon. 'Have you ever thought of putting her into films?'

'No. Surely she's too young?'

'How old is she?'

'Just four.'

'Well, Greta, the reason I ask is that the director of the film David is making at Shepperton is searching for a child to play the part of the heroine's daughter. It isn't a big role, just two or three scenes. Cheska looks like Jane Fuller, who is playing the part of the mother.'

'Jane Fuller's very beautiful,' said Greta.

'You know, Leon, you're right,' agreed David.

All three of them gazed down at Cheska, who looked up and gave them a sweet smile.

'How would you feel, Greta, if I mentioned to the director that I knew a little girl who might be right for the part?'

'I really don't know.' Greta looked at David. 'What do you think?'

'Well, if Cheska did get the part, her Uncle David would be there on set to keep an eye on her, wouldn't he, sweetheart?' he winked at the little girl.

'Think about it, Greta. I'm sure I'd be able to secure you a position as her chaperone. The pay is good, and you'd be able to make sure she was well cared for. Of course, all this really depends on whether Charles Day, the director, thinks she's suitable. And in any case, he may already have chosen a child. Time is running short.'

'Well, I suppose it won't do any harm for this man to see Cheska. I presume she'd be paid, too? Not that it's that important, of course,' Greta added quickly.

'Absolutely. Why don't I give Charles a call in the morning? See if he's cast the part yet? If he hasn't, I'll fix up an appointment for the two of you to go and meet him.'

'Yes, why not?' agreed Greta.

'Here's my card. Give me a call around noon tomorrow and I should have some news. Now, I'm sorry to leave such delightful company so soon but, unfortunately, I have to go to the Dorchester to meet another of my clients.' Leon rose from the table. 'The luncheon was excellent, as always, David.' He went across to Cheska and knelt down next to her. He held out his hand and she took it solemnly. 'Goodbye,' he said.

'Goodbye, sir,' she replied.

Leon stood up and chuckled. 'She could melt the hardest

heart. I think you just might have a little star on your hands, Greta. Goodbye, all.'

Greta and David took the dirty dishes into the small kitchen. David washed, while Greta and Cheska dried. They went back into the sitting room and Cheska climbed onto David's knee at his beckoning, stuck her thumb in her mouth and promptly fell asleep.

Greta sat on the rug and watched him looking down fondly at her daughter. The wine she'd had with lunch, combined with the humidity of the day, had made her feel sleepy and relaxed. She yawned and stretched like a cat, feeling unusually peaceful. 'It's a lovely place you have here, David. No one would think it was right in the centre of London.' She looked at him askance when he didn't reply.

'Sorry, Greta, I was in another world. What did you say?'

'Nothing important. Just how peaceful it is here.'

'Yes it is, isn't it, although I'm thinking of moving. I've got some money in my bank account and my accountant has advised me to invest it in property. This place is only rented. I might look for somewhere on the outskirts of London. Growing up at Marchmont has given me a yearning for more space outside my front door.'

'If I had any money I'd buy a big apartment in Mayfair with two pillars outside and a flight of steps leading up to the front door,' said Greta dreamily, thinking of James's house. 'Now, I'm afraid I should be getting Cheska home and into the bath.'

'Let me drive you, Greta. Cheska's tired,' David suggested as the child opened her eyes sleepily.

'If you're sure, that would be lovely.'

*

'Do you want to come in for coffee?' asked Greta when they pulled up outside her lodgings fifteen minutes later. 'I'm afraid it's not very luxurious.'

'No, thanks. I have to go through the script for tomorrow night's show. Do listen, if you can.'

'Of course I will,' she said, too ashamed to admit that she couldn't afford a radio set. 'Come on, darling,' she added to Cheska.

'Goodnight, Cheska.' David bent down and planted a kiss on her cheek.

'Goodnight, Uncle David. Thank you for the nice food.'

'Any time, sweetheart. You were a pleasure to have as a guest. Call me when you know whether she and I will be working together,' he added to Greta.

'I will, and thank you, David. I haven't enjoyed myself so much for ages.'

'Remember: any problems, you know where I am.'

She nodded gratefully and disappeared inside.

# 15

The following day at noon Greta telephoned Leon's office from a phone box. She had spent much of the previous night wondering whether it was right to allow Cheska to appear in a film at such a young age. However, if Cheska did get the job, she'd be able to spend much more time with her daughter than if she were out at work. And she knew how well films could pay.

'Greta, thank you for calling,' said Leon. 'I've fixed up for you and Cheska to meet Charles Day, the director, at ten o'clock tomorrow morning. If you give me your address, I'll send my driver round at nine to take you to Shepperton Studios. It's quite a trek by public transport.'

'That's awfully kind of you, Leon.'

'Think nothing of it, my dear. And can I contact you at home when I've heard? They'll make a quick decision because filming starts so soon.'

'You'll have to take my neighbour's number. I don't have a telephone at the moment.'

'Right.' Leon jotted down Mabel's number and the address of the house. 'If all goes well, I think you can allow yourself the luxury of having a telephone installed. You'll need it. Put Cheska in the dress she wore on Sunday and tell her to break a leg.'

Greta hung up with a shiver of excitement. Cheska was standing patiently, waiting for her mother to finish the conversation. She swung her daughter up into her arms and hugged her.

'How would you like to go and have our tea at Lyons Corner House?'

'Yes please, Mummy!' said Cheska, her eyes lighting up.

Greta was up bright and early in the morning. While Cheska slept, she washed and styled her own hair, then dressed in her best work suit. She went to wake Cheska, then made her breakfast and put her in the blue dress.

'Where are we going, Mummy?' Cheska had picked up on her mother's excitement and the fact she was in her best frock once again.

The doorbell rang.

'We're going in a car to see a nice man. He might want to put you in a film, darling.'

'Like Shirley Temple?'

'Yes, darling.'

They climbed into the back of a big black car, Cheska's eyes widening at the sight of its soft leather interior. As it drove through the streets of London and out into the leafy Surrey suburbs, the little girl listened as Greta told her she had to be on her very best behaviour.

Greta felt like a star herself as the car stopped at the gates of Rainbow Pictures and the driver gave their names to the security guard. They were waved through and Greta looked in fascination as they drove past a number of what resembled large aircraft hangars. She thought of how she'd once dreamed of getting the call to come here to audition herself, and a tingle ran through her.

The driver pulled up in front of the main reception. 'I'll wait out here until you've finished. Good luck, miss.' He tipped his hat and smiled at Cheska as they climbed out.

Greta took Cheska's hand and walked through the entrance doors, explaining to the receptionist who they were.

'Please do sit down over there, Mrs Simpson. Mr Day's secretary will be down to collect you shortly,' the receptionist said, pointing to a sofa.

'Thank you.' Greta led Cheska over to the small waiting area and gazed at the stills from various famous films that decorated the walls. I mustn't build my hopes up, or Cheska's, she told herself firmly. After a while a smart young woman holding a clipboard appeared from a lift and walked towards them.

'Mrs Simpson and Cheska?'

'Yes.'

'Would you like to follow me?'

Greta hastily smoothed her daughter's curls and squeezed her hand before they were shown into a big office dominated by a large desk behind which a man of about thirty-five was sitting.

'Mrs Simpson and Cheska, sir,' announced the secretary.

'Thank you, Janet.' The man stood up. 'Mrs Simpson, a pleasure to meet you. I'm Charles Day, the director of *Dark Horse*. Please do come and sit down.' He gestured to two chairs in front of his desk. Greta sat Cheska in one and took the other herself.

'And this, I presume, is Cheska?'

'How do you do, sir?' said Cheska in a small voice.

His eyes twinkled in amusement. 'Very well indeed, thank you. Well, young lady, do you know why you're here?'

'Oh yes. So I can be in a film and wear pretty dresses like Shirley Temple.'

'That's right. And would this be something you'd like to do?'

'Oh yes, sir,' repeated Cheska.

Charles turned his attention to Greta. 'Leon Bronowski is absolutely right. Your daughter does resemble Jane Fuller. Could you turn to look at Mummy, Cheska?' he asked.

She did as she was told, and Charles studied her.

'A likeness in profile as well. Good, good. Now, Mrs Simpson, Mr Bronowski says you'd be prepared to chaperone your daughter?'

'I would, yes.'

'Although we start shooting on Monday week, Cheska's scenes won't be filmed until a couple of weeks after that. We'd contract her for a month, but we obviously wouldn't have her working more than a few hours a day. Would that fit into your plans comfortably?'

Greta nodded. 'Yes, that sounds fine.'

'Excellent. Mr Bronowski tells me Cheska behaves like an angel.'

'She's a good little girl, yes.'

'Well, that stands very much in her favour. There's nothing worse than a spoilt brat having a temper tantrum when one has the cameras rolling. Time is money. Are you a good girl, Cheska?'

'I think so, sir.'

'And I think so, too. If we put you in this big picture, you'd have to promise to be on your best behaviour.'

'I promise, sir.'

'Right. I think I've seen all I need to, Mrs Simpson. We're interviewing two more little girls this morning and I'll be in touch with Leon when I've made my decision. Thank you very much for coming all this way to see me. It's been a pleasure to meet the two of you. Goodbye.'

'Thank you, Mr Day.' Greta stood up. 'Come on, darling.'

Cheska wriggled out of her chair and, of her own volition, stood on tiptoe to reach over the big desk. She put out her hand and Charles took it, smiling.

'Goodbye, sir,' she said, then turned and trotted out of the room after her mother.

'Charles Day on the telephone for you, Leon.'

'Thank you, Barbara. Hello?'

'Leon, it's Charles. That kid you sent to me today is everything you said she was. If she can act as well, we've got an English Shirley Temple on our hands.'

'Cute, isn't she?'

'Adorable. Apart from looking like an angel, she has that wonderful vulnerability of a young Margaret O'Brien or Elizabeth Taylor. Needless to say, we want her for the part. Even though it's a small one, it'll give the studio a chance to take a look at how she comes across on camera without there being any pressure on her. Have you signed her up yet?'

'No. I was waiting to hear from you.'

'Then wait no longer. I could be wrong, but Cheska has star quality, and you know what a rare commodity that is. I see big things ahead for her.'

'Indeed.'

'We'll need to change her surname. Simpson is far too dull.'

'Right. I'll put my thinking cap on.'

Having heard the excitement in Charles Day's voice, Leon discussed terms and was able to extract a generous fee for Cheska, and for Greta as her chaperone. He put the telephone down feeling the kind of buzz he only experienced when his nose for talent was proved right.

Mabel knocked on Greta's front door at half past four that afternoon, out of breath from hurrying up the stairs.

'There's a Mr Leon Bronosk— somebody on the telephone for you, Greta.'

'Thank you, Mabel. Could you watch Cheska for a few minutes while I go and talk to him?'

She hurried down to Mabel's flat and picked up the receiver.

'Hello?'

'Greta. It's Leon. Charles Day just called and he wants Cheska for the part.'

'Oh, that's wonderful!'

'I'm glad you're pleased. Charles was very impressed with her. He thinks Cheska might be a real find.'

'You are sure this won't do Cheska any harm, Leon? I mean, she's so young.'

'Well, Shirley Temple was even younger when she appeared in her first film. And besides, even though Charles liked her, it's wrong to get carried away until we've seen what she looks like on the big screen. The camera either loves you or it doesn't. We'll have to wait and see whether it'll be her friend or her enemy.'

'Of course.'

'Now, I think you'll be pleased with the fee I've extracted for Cheska. If she does well, Rainbow Pictures may want to sign her up long term. Then we'll really be talking. But for now, how does five hundred pounds sound?'

Like two years of hard work at my old job, thought Greta. 'Fine,' she squeaked. 'Thank you.'

'Good. And you'll also be paid ten pounds a day for chaperoning Cheska. Can you come to my office on Friday morning? I'll need you to sign the contract on her behalf. Oh, and Greta, Charles Day wants to change her surname to something a bit more glamorous. You wouldn't object to that, would you?'

'No, not at all.' Simpson wasn't Cheska's real surname anyway, she thought.

'Right, see you on Friday, then. Goodbye.'

Greta put down the receiver, did a little jig of excitement in Mabel's hall, then dashed upstairs to tell her daughter.

'Starring in a film, are we? Cor, you'll soon be too posh to speak to the likes of me.' Mabel smiled at Cheska and chucked her cheek affectionately.

David arrived a little later with a big bar of Nestlé chocolate for Cheska and a bottle of champagne for Greta.

'Who's a clever girl, then?' He picked Cheska up and hugged her. 'I knew she'd get it, Greta. She's such a little angel, aren't you, sweetheart?'

'Yes, Uncle David.' Cheska nodded seriously and the adults laughed.

'To bed with you, young lady. You're not Elizabeth Taylor yet, you know.' Greta winked at David.

When Greta had tucked her in, and David had told her a story, acting out all the characters, which brought gales of giggles from the bedroom, Greta and David sat down in the cramped sitting room and drank the champagne.

'You do think I'm doing the right thing, don't you?' Greta asked.

'It is only a few days' filming, Greta. If Cheska hates it, she never has to do it again. My guess is she'll be spoilt rotten by the rest of the cast and have a wonderful time. And, let's be honest, the money will come in handy for both of you, won't it?' David hadn't failed to notice the shabbiness of the flat, nor the fact that Greta's skirt and blouse looked distinctly threadbare.

'Yes, it will, although I feel awfully guilty that Cheska has to earn it for us.'

'Well, at least you'll see more of her, instead of leaving her with your neighbour all day.'

'Yes, I suppose so.'

'Good. Now, stop worrying, and have another glass of champagne.'

Greta arrived with Cheska at Leon's office in Golden Square in Soho at eleven thirty on Friday morning. She looked at the photographs on the wall of his large office as the two of them were ushered in to sit down.

'That's you with Jane Fuller, isn't it?'

'Yes, on the set of her first picture, ten years ago now,' Leon replied. 'Now, let's get down to business.'

Greta listened as Leon explained that he would handle Cheska's career and take ten per cent of her earnings. She signed where he indicated and he smiled.

'Right, now it only leaves us to think of a new surname for Cheska. If we don't come up with one, the studio will pick it for her, and I think it's your right to choose. What about family names? What was your mother's maiden name?'

'Hammond.'

'Cheska Hammond. I like that. We'll put it to the studio and see what they think. Well, I believe that's everything.' He rose to his feet to signal that the meeting was over. 'I'll be in touch as soon as I know her official call date and I'll send you a script. Thank you for coming, Greta. I'm sure Cheska will do us both proud, won't you?'

'Yes, Mr Leon,' Cheska replied. 'Goodbye.'

Three weeks later Cheska went in front of the camera for the first time. Greta hovered off set and watched her daughter sitting on Jane Fuller's knee.

'Right, quiet studio!' called out Charles. 'Okay, we're going to try Cheska with a line. Cheska, when I say "Go!", can you put your arms around Jane's neck and say, "I love you, Mummy"?'

'Yes, Mr Day.'

'Good girl. All right. Let's go for a take.'

A hush fell over the studio.

'Scene ten. Take one.' The clapperboard snapped shut and Charles smiled encouragingly at Cheska. 'Go!'

Cheska put her arms round Jane Fuller's elegant neck and hugged her.

'I love you, Mummy,' she said, gazing up at the actress as the camera zoomed in for a close-up of her face.

Greta watched with tears in her eyes. 'And I love you, Cheska,' she whispered.

Charles Day watched the rushes with one of Rainbow Picture's top executives. Cheska Hammond was the most natural, beguiling child actress either of them had ever seen.

'You said she'll remember lines if you tell her what to say?' asked the executive.

'She did today, anyway,' answered Charles.

'Right, get as many one-liners in as you can, without offending Jane, of course. We don't want her to know she's being upstaged by a four-year-old,' he said with a chuckle.

**Excerpt from *Picturegoer Monthly***
**March 1951**

> *Dark Horse* is the new release from Rainbow Pictures. Its director, Charles Day, is being hailed as the new English Selznick, and it is acclaim that is justified by what can only be described as a moving and powerful film.
>
> Jane Fuller and Roger Curtis star, both giving excellent performances as estranged husband and wife, with the comedian David (Taffy) Marchmont making his film debut and adding a touch of sensitive humour to his role as a failed card sharp. But what they say about never acting with children and animals

comes home to roost in this film. Four-year-old Cheska Hammond's cameo as the couple's daughter is a scene-stealer. Word is that her part was enlarged as soon as Charles Day saw her potential. Rainbow Pictures have placed her under a three-picture contract and her next film is already in production.

Go and see *Dark Horse*; I guarantee there won't be a dry eye in the house when Miss Hammond's final, poignant scene hits the screen. I predict a glittering future for her.

*Christmas Day, 1985*

*Marchmont Hall,*
*Monmouthshire, Wales*

# 16

'Mary, have you seen Greta recently?' David asked as he walked into the kitchen to find her setting out cold turkey and ham with pickles and salad.

'Last time I saw her was a few hours ago, when she asked me for some boots and a coat so she could go for a walk. Look you, maybe she's back and up in her room taking a nap.'

'Yes, probably.'

'Shall I bring up this supper now or later?' Mary asked him.

David looked at his watch and saw it was almost half past seven. 'Why don't you leave it in here instead of carting it all into the dining room, and we can come in and pick at what we want? You've had a long day, Mary, and it's about time you put your feet up.'

'Are you sure?'

'Completely.'

'All right then, Master David, I will,' she said gratefully. 'And thank you for my cashmere cardigan. I've never owned anything so luxurious.'

'You deserve it, Mary. I don't know what this family

would do without you,' David smiled at her before leaving the kitchen to go upstairs and check on Greta. He knocked on the door of her bedroom and, receiving no response, after a second try he opened it quietly.

'Greta? Greta?' The room was in darkness and David fumbled on the wall to find the light switch. There was no one there and, judging by the neatly made bed, Greta hadn't been up to take a nap. David's heart somersaulted. He searched all the upstairs rooms, and asked Ava if she'd seen her grandmother. She hadn't, so David conducted a search downstairs as well.

'Have you lost something, David?' Tor looked up from the biography of Mao Zedong he had bought her for Christmas.

'Greta, actually. She went out for a walk earlier and she hasn't reappeared yet.'

'Do you want me to come and help look for her?'

'No, it's absolutely freezing out there. I'm sure she won't have gone far. Back in a bit.' David opened the front door, his conversation with Tor not betraying the fear he felt. If Greta had been out there since mid-afternoon, and perhaps got lost, she could be freezing to death by now.

He switched on the powerful torch he'd brought with him and trudged off through the snow. As he walked, it crunched and crackled under the weight of his boots.

'Think, David, think . . . Where could she have gone?' he muttered to himself.

The truth was, the answer was anywhere, for if Greta couldn't remember Marchmont, then it was highly unlikely there was any specific place she'd want to head for. After checking both the front and back gardens, he decided to walk into the woods. It was as good a place as any to look.

He remembered then how Greta had originally arrived at Marchmont Hall on a Christmas Day long ago, having sprained her ankle in the woods, and felt a sense of déjà vu as he walked through the trees, the light of his torch illuminating the glittering fairyland surrounding him, which belied the danger Greta might be in if she was still somewhere out here.

Arriving at the clearing which contained Jonny's grave, he called out to Greta and, to his relief, heard a faint cry of response.

'Greta, are you all right? Keep talking to me, and I'll head in the direction of your voice!'

After a few moments the beam of his torch picked her up; she was stumbling through the snow towards him. He ran to her and saw that she was shivering uncontrollably, her cheeks streaked with ribbons of mascara.

'What on earth are you doing out here, darling?' David said, taking off his thick ski jacket, putting it round her shoulders and closing his arms about her to try to warm her up.

'David! I've remembered! I've remembered all about my parents, and Jonny, and the reason I came to Marchmont, and . . .' With that, she crumpled into his arms, sobbing.

Sweeping her up, David carried Greta back through the woods towards the house. On the way back she continued to tell him what she now knew, the words tumbling out in a disjointed torrent.

'I've remembered all about the GI, and being at the

Windmill and why I ended up there and . . . everything! Oh God, David, I can remember it all. Up to Marchmont, that is, and Jonny's death, but after that it's all still a bit unclear.'

'Right,' David said, as he carried her into the kitchen where Tor, Ava and Simon were helping themselves to supper. 'Greta got lost in the woods and I'm taking her upstairs for a hot bath. Tor, could you make a hot-water bottle, please, and a cup of strong, sweet tea and bring them upstairs?'

'Of course. Anything else?'

'Not for now. Let's get her warm, and then she might have some wonderful news for us all.'

Upstairs, David helped Greta off with her outer clothes, as she was still shivering violently, then closed the bathroom door behind him. He turned and found Tor standing in the bedroom with the tea.

'What's happened, David? You looked almost euphoric when you arrived back with Greta. Not exactly the reaction I'd expect after rescuing someone who might have died from hypothermia.'

'Tor,' he said, keeping his voice to a whisper so Greta couldn't hear, 'I don't know the details yet, but Greta told me she's remembered. Some things, anyway. Isn't that wonderful? After all these years.'

Tor could see David had tears of joy in his eyes. 'Yes, it is. A real Christmas miracle.'

'It must be coming back here to Marchmont that's done it. Goodness, if only I'd been able to persuade her to come years ago . . .'

'Well, perhaps she wasn't ready. Anyway, I can't wait to

hear all about it. I'm amazed she didn't freeze to death out there; you must have found her in the nick of time.'

'I think she was so full of adrenalin that she kept on the move, which probably saved her. Anyway, you go downstairs and have your supper. I'd better wait for her here.'

Tor nodded and left the room. David sat down heavily on the bed and ten minutes later, Greta emerged from the bathroom in her robe.

'Have you stopped shivering yet?' he asked, studying her expression to try and gauge how she was feeling.

'Oh yes. I don't feel cold at all.'

'How *do* you feel?'

'I don't know . . . I'm not sure. I . . . remembered some more things in the bath, and what I need to do is try and put them in some kind of order. Maybe you can help me with that, David?'

'Of course I can.'

'But not tonight. I'm going to stay up here and try to put the pieces together a little bit more. You go downstairs with the family. The last thing I want to do is ruin everyone's Christmas Day or be a bother, which, unfortunately, I have been already.'

'Greta, don't be silly! This is a huge moment for you. Surely I should stay?'

'No, David. I need to be by myself.' As she said the words, they glanced at each other, both understanding their significance.

'Okay then. There's some tea by your bed and a hot-water bottle in it. Shall I bring up a tray? You should eat something.'

'Nothing for now, thank you. Oh David, even though I'm shocked and confused at the moment, isn't it amazing?'

David looked at her lovely blue eyes, and saw them – for the first time in twenty-four years – shining with life.

'It is, Greta, it is.'

The following morning Greta came down for breakfast and was hugged and congratulated by her family.

'I do apologise for it all happening in such a dramatic fashion,' she said guiltily, looking at Tor.

'Do you know what triggered it?' asked Ava, fascinated not only by what had happened but also the visible physical change in her grandmother. It was as if she really had been frozen inside for years and now the thaw had begun, her eyes sparkled and her cheeks were tinged with pink.

'I had the tiniest flashback when I first stepped out of the car on Christmas Eve, and another when I looked down from the upstairs landing and saw the Christmas tree in the hall. And then of course, I went for a walk in the woods, randomly, because I couldn't remember where to go, and found myself by Jonny's grave. Maybe something was leading me there, but that was the beginning of it. Please don't ask me just now what I remember and what I don't, because it's all a bit of a mix-up in my head. But at least this morning when I saw Mary I knew exactly who she was. And also how kind she'd been to me when I first arrived at Marchmont. And you, David, of course.'

'Have you got to me yet, Granny?'

'Give her time, Ava,' David admonished her gently, seeing a momentary flicker of fear cross Greta's face. 'I'm sure that now it's begun, Greta, and the metaphorical door has been unlocked, the memories will continue to come back.'

'Perhaps you should go and see a psychotherapist, Greta,' Tor commented. 'I don't know much about this sort of thing, but it might be a bit overwhelming for you.'

'Thank you, but for the moment I'm coping well. Now, I'm going to take a short walk whilst the sun is still shining. I promise I won't get lost this time,' she added with an ironic smile.

David was about to offer to go with her, then thought better of it.

'I said I'd go and help Mary prepare lunch. She looks exhausted,' said Tor, also rising. 'I vote we give her the rest of the day off. I'm sure we can cope without her.'

'And, if no one minds,' said Simon, 'I'm going to head off to my music studio. I've still got two songs to write for Roger's new album.'

'Of course not, darling,' said Ava. 'Stay there as long as you want.'

'You make sure you rest.' Simon kissed his wife and left the room.

'So the studio's working out, is it?' asked David.

'God yes, so much so I think Simon would like to sleep in it as well.' Ava chuckled. 'I know I always seem to be saying thank you to you, Uncle David, but it really was a brainwave to convert one of the barns for him. All the recording artists love coming here because it's so peaceful and beautiful. And the Gate Lodge is going to work brilliantly for accommodation, now Simon and I have moved out. He'll pay you back, you know, and probably sooner than you think. The studio's fully booked for the next six months.'

'Which must be a blessing and a curse for *you*.'

'Yes,' Ava agreed, comforted by her uncle's intuitiveness. 'I could have done with Simon on hand for the next few months, but there we are. The good news is that he's happy. And you must be, too, given Granny's Christmas-night revelation.'

'To be honest, I'm still struggling to take it in. After all these years, it's quite a shock.'

'It is, but for the first time just now I got a glimpse of how she must have been before the accident. And I think that Tor is probably right about her seeing someone. I know Granny's on a high at the moment, but if her memories are starting to return, as she says, it's going to be a difficult time for her. Especially with what she still has to remember,' Ava said quietly.

'I know, but at least she's here with us and we can all support her.'

'She said she'd remembered up to her life at Marchmont this morning. And there were some difficult times back then. To suddenly know that you had a three-year-old son who died is dreadful enough.' Ava shuddered and put a protective hand to her bump. 'But the rest . . . well, I only hope she can cope with it.'

'Yes, but after the half life she's been living, surely it's better this way?'

'Well, the thing is, Uncle David, even if she does remember the night of the accident, perhaps she needn't ever know the whole truth about it?'

'I understand what you're saying, Ava,' David agreed,

'and I think the answer is that we'll all have to suck it and see, as they say. The one thing I do know about Greta is that she's a survivor. And, if anyone can deal with this, she can. Anyway, you're not to worry about your granny. I'll look after her. You concentrate on taking care of yourself. Right, I'm going to brave it in the Land Rover and see if I can get into the village and buy a *Telegraph*.'

Ava watched David leave the room and wondered if she was the only one of the gathering who could see how he felt about Greta. For Tor's sake, she hoped she was.

Later that day David walked into the drawing room, and found Greta alone, staring into the dying embers in the grate. 'Can I join you? Everyone else is either out or has gone for a nap.'

'You could certainly perk this fire up for me.' Greta smiled at him.

'Of course. How are you feeling?' he asked her, as he busied himself with logs and kindling.

'Would it be all right if I said I really don't know just now?'

'I think it would be fine. I doubt there are any rules for what you're going through. And if there are, I'm sure it's okay to break them.' David sat down opposite her and watched the fire reignite merrily in the grate. 'I'm here to listen, not judge, and to help you in any way I can.'

'I know, David,' Greta said gratefully. 'I have just one question for you, actually: why didn't you tell me about Jonny, and that he'd died when he was so young?'

'The doctors told me not to say anything that might

traumatise you. Forgive me, perhaps I should have done, but . . .'

'Please don't apologise. I know you were trying to protect me,' Greta said hastily. 'As you can imagine, it makes me a little scared to think about what *else* I have to remember beyond all this. But really, David, you've been wonderful to me. I've remembered what you did for me when I was pregnant and desperate and . . . thank you. The truth is, apart from the fact that I'm feeling I have to grieve all over again for the son I lost, when I went back to Jonny's grave today, more memories started to flood in. About' – Greta gulped – 'afterwards.'

'Such as what?'

'Cheska. David, can you help me remember, even if it's painful for me to hear? I need to piece everything together. Because so far, nothing makes sense. Do you see?'

'I think so,' he replied cautiously, 'but don't you think you should let it all happen naturally? I mean, maybe we should take advice from a professional on what's best for you?'

'I've dealt with shrinks and all manner of trick-cyclists for years, so please believe me when I say that I know my own psyche far better than anyone else,' Greta replied firmly. 'And, if I didn't feel I could cope, I wouldn't be asking you to fill in the missing links. Believe me, I can already tell you a lot of it. For example, I know, or believe I know, that Owen was a drunk and I had to leave Marchmont with Cheska. I went to London, and I remember quite a bit about what happened there; things I did that I can't say I'm proud of. But if you could tell me – and I mean the absolute truth – it really would help me. Please, David, I need to know.'

'If you really feel you're up to it, then I will, yes.'

'As long as you swear to me that it will be everything. No holds barred. Only then will I be able to believe it *is* real, and not my imagination playing tricks on me. The whole truth, please,' Greta entreated. 'It's the only way.'

David wished he could have a whisky, but as it was only three o'clock in the afternoon he resisted. Greta must have sensed his reluctance, because she said, 'And I know already that some of it's dreadful, so there's no need for you to worry about shocking me.'

'Okay, then.' David capitulated with a sigh. 'So you've said you remember coming to London. Do you also recall me getting Cheska an audition for her first film?'

'I do, yes. Go from there, David, because that's where it all begins to get hazy . . .'

# Cheska

## London, June 1956

# 17

Sometimes Cheska would have a dream. It was always the same dream, and she would wake shaking with fear. The dream always took place in a big, dark wood with lots and lots of tall trees. There was a little boy in the dream who looked just like her, and she played Hide and Seek with him through the trees. There was sometimes an older man there too, who always wanted to hug the little boy but never her.

Then the dream would change and it would become night. The older man, whose breath smelt horrid, would force her to look inside a coffin at the little boy. The little boy's face was white and his lips were grey and she knew he was dead. The man would remove the boy's clothes then turn to her, and the next thing she knew *she* was wearing the clothes. They smelt fusty and a big spider would climb up the front of the jacket towards her face. Then there was a tap on her shoulder and she'd turn round and stare into the frozen eyes of the small boy, who seemed to appear from the shadows of a small fir tree, his body shivering with cold as he reached out to her . . .

Cheska would wake up with a cry and reach out for the lamp that sat on her bedside cabinet. Switching it on, she'd sit upright, staring around at the familiar, cosy room, reassuring herself that everything was exactly the same as when she had gone to sleep. She'd find Polly, who'd usually be on the floor by her bed, and hug her, her thumb going guiltily into her mouth. Mummy kept telling her that if she continued with such a babyish habit her teeth would stick out and her career as a famous film star would be over.

The dream would eventually fade, and she would lie back on her pillows and stare at the pretty white lace canopy that hung above her. Her eyes would close and she'd drift back to sleep.

She didn't tell Mummy about the dream. She was sure Mummy would say she was being silly, that dead people couldn't come back to life. But Cheska knew they could.

At the tender age of ten Cheska Hammond was one of the best-known faces in Britain. She had just completed her seventh film, and in the past three her name had been above the title. Film reviewers had nicknamed her 'The Angel' early on in her career, and it had stuck. Her new picture was due to be released in four weeks' time and Mummy had promised she would buy her a white fur coat to wear to the premiere at the Odeon in Leicester Square.

Cheska knew she should enjoy the premieres of her films, but they scared her. There were always so many people outside the cinema when her car drew up and big men had to escort her inside very quickly through the surging crowd. Once, a lady had grabbed her arm and tried to pull her away from her mother. She had been told later the lady had been taken away by the police.

Mummy was always telling her what a lucky girl she

was: she had as much money as she'd ever need, a beautiful apartment in Mayfair and a mass of adoring, devoted fans. Cheska supposed she was, but then she didn't really know any different.

During the making of her last film, *Little Girl Lost*, which was set in an orphanage, Cheska had made friends with one of the children who played a minor role. The girl, Melody, spoke in a funny accent and Cheska had listened in fascination as she told her about her brothers and sisters. She said she slept with her sister in the same bed because there wasn't enough room for separate ones in their small flat in East London. Melody told her of the naughty pranks her four brothers got up to and of the big family Christmases they had. Cheska listened, enthralled, thinking of the elegant – but rather dull – festive lunches she and Mummy usually spent with Leon and Uncle David.

Melody introduced her to some of the other little girls and she discovered that they all went to stage school and had lessons together. It sounded like fun. Cheska herself had one crusty old tutor called Mr Benny, who taught her as often as her filming commitments allowed. She'd sit with him in her dressing room at the studio or in the sitting room at home, writing out reams of sums and learning dreary poems off by heart.

Melody gave her bubblegum, and they'd had a competition behind one of the scenery flats to see who could blow the biggest bubble. Cheska thought Melody was the nicest person she'd ever met. She'd asked Mummy whether she too could go to stage school with the other children, but Mummy had said that she didn't need to. Stage school taught you how to be a star and she – Cheska – was one already.

Melody had asked her once if she'd like to come back for tea at her house. Cheska had been so excited, but Mummy had told her she couldn't go. When she had asked why not her mother had set her mouth in a hard line, the way she did when Cheska knew her mind was made up. She'd told her that film stars such as Cheska couldn't make friends with common little extras like Melody.

Cheska wasn't sure what 'common' was, but she knew it was what she wanted to be when she grew up.

Melody's time on the film set had ended and she had gone back to school. The pair had swapped addresses and promised to write to each other. Cheska had written numerous letters and given them to Mummy to post but had never received a reply. She missed Melody. She was the first friend she'd ever had.

'Come on, darling, time to wake up.'

Mummy's voice broke into her dreams.

'We've got a busy day today. Lunch with Leon at twelve, and then to Harrods to pick up your new coat. That'll be fun, won't it?'

'Yes, Mummy.' Cheska nodded half-heartedly.

'Now.' Her mother walked towards the large fitted wardrobe that took up an entire wall of her large bedroom. 'Which dress would you like to wear to lunch?'

Cheska sighed. Lunches with Leon were long and boring. They always went to the Savoy and she had to sit quietly while Mummy and Leon discussed important business matters. She watched as her mother opened her wardrobe door to reveal a selection of thirty party dresses, all handmade for her from the finest silk, organdie and taffeta and wrapped carefully in polythene. Her mother pulled one out. 'What about this? You haven't worn it yet, and it's so pretty.'

Cheska stared at the pink dress with its layers of net petticoat peeping out from underneath the skirt. She hated wearing these dresses. The net made her legs itch and left red marks round her waist.

'You've got a pair of pink satin slippers somewhere that will match beautifully.' Greta laid the dress on Cheska's bed and went back to the wardrobe to hunt for them.

Cheska closed her eyes and wondered what it would be like to have the whole day to herself to play. The exquisite doll's house with its beautifully carved wooden family sat on the floor of her room, but she never seemed to have a moment to enjoy it. When she was making a film she was driven to the studio at six o'clock in the morning and they would rarely arrive home before half past six at night, when it was time for tea and a bath. After that, Cheska had to finish her homework, then practise her lines with Mummy so she was word perfect the next day. Mummy had said it was the gravest sin to forget a line on a take and, so far, Cheska had never 'dried', as so many of the adult actors did.

'Chop, chop, young lady! Your porridge will get cold.'

Greta pulled back Cheska's bedcovers, and the girl swung her legs over the side of the mattress. She put her arms inside the dressing gown her mother was holding out for her and followed her from the room.

Cheska sat at her usual place at the large, polished table

in a corner of the sitting room and surveyed the bowl of porridge in front of her.

'Do I have to eat this, Mummy? You know I hate it. Melody says her mother never makes her have breakfast and . . .'

'Honestly,' said Greta, sitting down opposite her daughter. 'All I ever hear is "Melody this" and "Melody that". And yes, you do have to eat your porridge. With your busy life, it's important you start off the day on a full stomach.'

'But it's yucky!' Cheska stirred her spoon in the thick mixture, picked up a dollop and let it drop back into the bowl. It splashed onto the table.

'Stop that, young lady! You're behaving like a little madam. You're not such a star that I can't put you over my knee and give you a good hiding. Now eat!'

Cheska sullenly spooned the porridge into her mouth.

'I've finished,' she said after a while. 'May I please get down now?'

'Go and get dressed and I'll be along shortly to brush your hair.'

'Yes, Mummy.'

Greta watched as her daughter stood up and walked out of the room. She smiled benevolently at the receding figure. Apart from the odd small tantrum, which was only to be expected from a growing girl, Cheska really did behave like an angel. Greta was sure her impeccable manners and politeness had helped in her climb to the fame she now had.

Cheska was a star because she had a beautiful, photogenic face and talent as an actress but also because Greta had instilled in her that she must be one hundred per cent disciplined and professional when she worked. It might have been Cheska's money that had bought their large, beautifully furnished Mayfair apartment and wardrobes full of clothes, but it was Greta who had guided and shaped her daughter's career. At first she'd had to steel herself to be more assertive when she met with studio executives or directors but, driven on by fear of going back to the life they'd led before, she'd learnt quickly. On the whole she'd surprised herself at how well she'd adapted to her role as Cheska's manager.

It was Greta who had taken the decisions on which scripts she should accept, knowing the kind of film that would show her daughter to the best advantage, and her instincts had always been proved right. She'd also become adept at getting the best financial deal. She'd ask Leon to go back for more money, saying she wasn't prepared to sign the contract on Cheska's behalf unless the studio offered what she wanted. A tense few days would follow, but the studio would eventually agree. Cheska was an asset they wanted to keep at any cost, and Greta knew it.

Her hard bargaining had made her daughter extremely wealthy. They lived very well and were able to buy whatever took their fancy, although they didn't spend anywhere near as much as Cheska earned. Greta had carefully invested the rest of Cheska's money for her daughter's future.

Greta's difficult past was now a distant memory. She had dedicated her life to Cheska's career, and if she'd toughened up in the process, was that such a bad thing? At least people no longer ignored her, or walked all over her, as they used to. She still experienced private moments of doubt and regret about the lonely path her personal life had taken, but to the outside world she was now a force to be reckoned with. She controlled one of the hottest properties on the British movie scene. She was the mother of 'The Angel'.

Occasionally, Greta would wrestle with a stab of guilt when David asked her if she thought Cheska was happy. She would become defensive and tell him that of course she was. What little girl wouldn't be, with the amount of attention and adulation she received? After all, wasn't David a big star, too, and hadn't he enjoyed achieving his goal? David would nod his head slowly and apologise for questioning her judgement.

Greta picked up a movie magazine from the table and flicked through the pages until she reached the large advertisement for *Little Girl Lost*. She smiled as she looked at her daughter's vulnerable face. In the picture she was clutching a threadbare teddy and dressed in rags. Yes, this would bring them in by the droves. Which reminded her: she had a meeting later on with Mrs Stevens, who ran Cheska's fan club. They had to decide which still they would use from the new film to send out to her army of fans.

Greta shut the magazine with a sigh. No wonder there had been no men in her life for such a long time. Even if she'd wanted it to be different, organising the schedule of a famous movie star was a full-time job and then some.

Cheska was her life, and there was no going back now.

# 18

David was up at the crack of dawn. No matter when he went to bed, which, once he'd wound down after a perfor mance, could be extremely late, he always woke up on the dot of six thirty.

Today, he was as free as a bird. His run at the Palladium had finished a week ago, his radio show was on its summer break, and he didn't need to write any new material for a couple of months.

He looked out of the window at the bright sunshine and felt a sudden pang of longing for the countryside. Although the Hampstead garden of his pretty cottage was large for the area, he still felt it had a synthetic feel. There was nothing rugged or dangerous about either the landscape or the climate. A man living in London was effectively sanitised, in danger of losing his basic instincts, he thought.

Maybe he would take a long holiday this summer. He'd been invited to a friend's villa in the South of France, but the thought of being away from Greta was not one that appealed.

He opened the French windows and stepped out into the garden. Hands in his pockets, he strolled around admiring the well-tended flower beds, with abundant roses and cascades of lobelia providing a wealth of colour in contrast to the smooth emerald-green lawn.

He was an intelligent, rational man, but he knew his logic went out of the window when it came to Greta. In the past six years they had seen each other regularly. He would often go round to their apartment for Sunday lunch with both Greta and his darling Cheska. Occasionally, he took Greta out to the theatre and to dinner afterwards.

Time had gone on, and he knew they had slipped into a comfortable intimacy, one that was almost akin, he thought morosely, to that of brother and sister. He was there as a sounding board on Cheska's career and he knew that Greta regarded him as a very dear friend. The right moment to change the basis of their relationship had never seemed to arrive. In all the years since Greta had reappeared in his life, he still hadn't plucked up the courage to tell her he loved her with all his heart.

David sighed as he deadheaded a wilting bloom on one of the rose bushes. At least he could take comfort from the fact that, as far as he knew, she'd had no other men. Of course, technically, she was still married to Owen, even though they'd had no contact with each other for the past seven years. Besides, he knew that all Greta's energy and love went into Cheska. There was simply no room for anyone else.

Her obsession with her daughter worried David. Greta was living through her, which was not only unhealthy for herself, but for Cheska, too. Often, when he looked at the little girl's slight body and pale face, he feared for her future. The strange, pressurised life she led in her bubble of fame was surely not right for a child. He felt guilty for having encouraged Greta to let Cheska undertake her first film, but how could he have known she would become such a huge star? He'd thought at the time it would just be a bit of fun that would earn them a few extra pennies.

When he visited them at home for Sunday lunch, even when it was just the three of them, Cheska would always be in one of the formal party frocks Greta insisted she wore. She would sit at the table looking so uncomfortable that David longed to pick her up and carry her off to the nearest park or playground. He wanted to see the little girl let her immaculate hair down, get her pretty dress dirty and, most of all, to scream in the excited way children were meant to.

He sometimes asked Greta gently if she thought Cheska should play with other children, as she spent so much time in the company of adults. Greta would shake her head firmly and say that Cheska's commitments didn't allow time for such activities.

David would say no more. He understood that despite the trappings of wealth Cheska's success had brought, Greta's life had not been easy, and that she was simply attempting to do the best for her daughter. There was no doubt that Cheska was loved and looked after. Besides, he hated the look on Greta's face when he questioned her.

He walked back towards the house, thinking that maybe he would go to the South of France after all. He did need a holiday and until he could pluck up the courage to tell Greta how he felt it was ridiculous to run his life around her.

He heard the telephone ringing in his study and hurried inside.

'Hello?'

'David, it's Ma.'

'Hello, Ma. How nice to hear from you.'

'Yes, well, I always say this thing is only used to bring bad news,' LJ said grimly.

'What is it, Ma?'

'It's your Uncle Owen. Dr Evans called me a little while ago. He's been ill for some time, as you know, but there's been a sharp deterioration in the past month. Apparently, Owen wants to see me. He insisted Dr Evans ask me to travel to Marchmont as soon as possible.'

'And are you going?'

'Well, I rather feel I have to. I was wondering, if you're not too busy, whether you'd come with me for moral support. Could you pick me up from Paddington in your car and drive me there? I do apologise, David, but I just don't think I could face returning to Marchmont alone.'

'Of course, Ma. I've nothing on for the next few weeks, anyway.'

'Thank you, David. I'm most awfully grateful. Can you possibly make tomorrow? From what the doctor says, Owen doesn't have much time left.'

'I see. Should I tell Greta?'

'No.' LJ's voice was sharp. 'Owen hasn't asked to see her. Best let sleeping dogs lie.'

The two of them discussed train times and David arranged to meet his mother at half past ten and drive on to Wales from there. He replaced the receiver and sat down at his desk, deep in thought.

He felt that Greta should be told about Owen's illness. After all, she was still legally married to him. However, he didn't want to upset any apple carts, when his mother was obviously distressed at the thought of returning to Marchmont and seeing Owen. And as he rose from the desk, he wondered just what Cheska had been told about her father.

The long drive to Wales was made easier by good weather and negligible traffic. David and LJ chatted comfortably together on the way.

'It feels awfully odd going back, doesn't it, David?' she said, as they navigated the winding valley road flanked by lush sloping fields on the last leg of their journey to Marchmont.

'Yes. It's been over ten years for you, hasn't it?'

'Amazing how one adapts, though. I've become quite a pillar of the Stroud community, and an adept bridge player to boot. If you can't beat 'em, join them, that's my motto,' she added drily.

'Well, it certainly seems to suit you. You do look well.'

'When one has time on one's hands, it seems to do the complexion good, if not the psyche.'

A silence fell between them as they turned off the valley road and began to climb the narrow lane towards Marchmont. As they passed through the gates and the house came into view, LJ sighed in sudden remembrance of its beauty. On this warm June afternoon the windows glinted in the strong sunlight, seeming to welcome her home.

David pulled up in front of the house and turned off the

engine. Immediately, the front door was opened and Mary came running out.

'Master David! Lovely it is to see you after all these years! I never miss your radio show! And not a day older do you look, *bach*.'

'Hello, Mary.' David gave her a warm hug. 'It's kind of you to say so, but I think I've put on a few pounds since those days. You know I was never one to refuse a biscuit or a piece of cake.'

'And look you, it suits you, with your height,' Mary replied.

LJ stepped out of the car and walked round to greet her. 'How are you, my dear?'

'Very well, thank you, Mrs Marchmont. All the better for seeing you back where you belong.'

The three of them walked towards the front door. Stepping into the hall, David could feel his mother's tension.

'It's been a long drive, Mary. Could you organise some tea before my mother sees Mr Marchmont?'

'Of course, Master David. Dr Evans is with him at the moment. He had a bad night. If you'd like to step into the drawing room, I'll tell the doctor you're here and bring you that tea.'

As Mary disappeared upstairs, David and LJ walked across the hall and into the drawing room.

'Good God, it's musty in here. Does Mary never air these rooms? And the furnishings look like they haven't been cleaned for months.'

'I wouldn't have thought she'd have much time for housework, what with caring for Owen, Ma.' But she was right: the graceful room, which he always remembered as immaculate, its furniture beautifully polished, now looked tatty and neglected.

'Of course not. She's been a brick to stay with him at all.' LJ went to one of the French windows, unlocked the latch and opened it wide. They both stepped outside onto the terrace and breathed in the fresh air.

'Give me a hand, will you, dear boy? If we dust these chairs down, we can drink our tea out here. It feels so terribly gloomy inside.'

LJ was heaving a rusty wrought-iron chair into position when Mary brought out the tea a few minutes later.

'Just put it down and we'll help ourselves, Mary dear,' directed LJ.

'Very good, Mrs Marchmont. I've told Dr Evans you've arrived.'

'Thank you. Will you suggest he joins us for a cup of tea?'

'I will, ma'am,' Mary said and went inside.

The two of them sipped their tea in silence.

'How could I ever have left this?' LJ murmured, gazing at the idyllic view. Below the woods that covered the gently sloping hillside the sunlight glittered on the glassy surface of the river as it meandered lazily down the summer-green valley.

'I know what you mean.' David sighed and patted his mother's hand. 'The sound of running water always reminds me of my childhood.'

They both turned as they heard footsteps behind them. 'Please, don't get up. Laura-Jane, David. Thank you for coming so quickly.' Dr Evans, his hair now streaked with grey, smiled at them.

LJ poured him a cup of tea as he sat down. 'So, how is Owen, doctor?'

'Not very well at all, I'm afraid. I know you're both aware that for some years Mr Marchmont has had a serious drink problem. I've told him time and again he ought to stop but, unfortunately, he's ignored my advice. He's had countless falls over the years and now his liver is letting him down, too.'

'How long has he got?'

David watched his mother closely. Her face betrayed no hint of emotion; as always, she was being practical. But he noticed her hands twisting round and round on her lap.

'To be honest, Mrs Marchmont, I'm amazed he's lasted this long. A week, perhaps two . . . I'm sorry, but there it is. I could move him to a hospital, but there's little they could do. And besides, he refuses point-blank to leave Marchmont.'

'Yes. Well, thank you for being so honest with us. You know I prefer it that way.'

'He knows you're here, Laura-Jane, and would like to see you as soon as possible. He's lucid at present, so I suggest you go in sooner rather than later.'

'Right you are, then.' LJ stood up and David watched her take a deep breath. 'Lead the way.'

Minutes later she stepped into Owen's bedroom, which was in shadow, the thick curtains half drawn. Owen was lying in his large bed, a frail, shrunken old man. His eyes were closed, his breathing shallow. She stood by the bed staring down at the face of the man she had once loved. She thought how, in the past, she'd always imagined a time in the future when they'd have a chance to put things right between them; apologies would be made, feelings of hurt exorcised. Now the finality of the situation horrified her. For Owen, and for the two of them, there was no future left.

LJ's hand went to her mouth as she choked back tears. Owen's eyes flickered open and she watched as he tried to focus. She sat down on the edge of the bed and bent her head forward so he could see her.

He lifted one of his hands shakily and touched her arm. 'For— Forgive me . . .'

LJ grasped the hand, put it to her mouth and kissed it gently but didn't reply.

'I . . . must explain.' He seemed to be struggling not only physically but mentally to voice the words. 'I . . . love you . . . always have . . . loved no other.' A tear trickled from his eye. 'Jealousy . . . a terrible thing . . . wanted to hurt you . . . forgive me.'

'Owen, you silly old fool, I thought you detested the very sight of me! That's why I left Marchmont,' she replied, stunned by what he'd just said.

'Wanted to punish you for marrying my brother. Wanted to ask you to marry me when he died . . . but pride . . . couldn't, you see.'

LJ's throat constricted with emotion. 'Oh God, Owen, why didn't you tell me? All those wasted years, years that could have been so happy. Was I the reason you went away to Kenya?'

'Couldn't bear to see you with my brother's child. Must apologise to David. Wasn't his fault.'

'Don't you know I went through hell when the letter

arrived from the War Office telling me you were missing in action? I waited three long years, praying you were alive. But everyone told me I must get on with my life. Your family wanted me to marry Robin. What else could I do?' said LJ despairingly. 'You know I never loved him the way I loved you. You must believe me, Owen. Good God, if only you had come home and asked me to marry you when Robin died, I would have agreed immediately.'

'I wanted to but—' Owen's face contorted in pain. 'I faced death many times in the war, and yet now I'm scared, so scared.' He gripped her hand. 'Stay with me until the end, please? I need you, Laura-Jane.'

*Were these last days enough to make up for the lifetime they had missed?* Never, but this was all they had.

'Yes, my darling,' she said quietly. 'I'll stay with you until the end.'

# 19

Greta was in the bath when the telephone rang.

'Drat!' She reached for a towel, hurried out of the bathroom and into the sitting room to pick up the receiver. 'Hello,' she said.

'It's me, David. Did I disturb you?'

'No, I was in the bath, that's all.'

'Well, I'm afraid I've got some bad news. I'm calling from Marchmont. Owen died an hour ago.'

'I'm sorry, David.' Greta bit her lip, not knowing what else to say.

'The funeral's here at Marchmont on Thursday afternoon. I'm letting you know because I thought you might want to come.'

'Er, well, thanks, David, but I'm afraid I won't be able to. Cheska has a photographic shoot all day.'

'I see. Well, even if you don't come to the funeral, you're going to have to come for the reading of the will. Owen insisted you attend just before he died. From what he said to my mother, I think it might be to your advantage.'

'Do I have to come? I mean, we don't need any more

money and, to be honest, as you can imagine, I'm not keen on going back to Marchmont.'

'That's exactly how Ma and I felt when we came here a couple of weeks ago. It holds some unpleasant memories for all of us. But now I've spent some time here, even under these circumstances, I'll be sad to return to London. One forgets how beautiful it is.'

'To be blunt, David, I'm nervous. And what about Cheska? She's never asked, so I've told her nothing about Owen. I never knew what to say.'

'Then maybe it's time you did enlighten her, Greta. After all, one day, she'll ask, so now's as good a time as any. Anyway, it would do Cheska good to get out of London.'

'I suppose so,' she said, but she sounded unconvinced.

'Look, Greta. I know how you feel but, legally, you are still Owen's wife and, to all intents and purposes, Cheska is his child. The solicitor won't read the will without you, which means if you won't come here, myself and Ma will have to travel to London. My mother has been nursing Owen almost non-stop for the past couple of weeks and she's exhausted. I'd prefer it if it could all be over quickly so she can start to recover.'

'Does she want me there?'

'She feels you should come, yes.'

Greta sighed. 'All right, then. I suppose we could cancel Cheska's shoot. The funeral will be family only, won't it?'

'Yes.'

'What time will it start?'

'Half past three.'

'I'll ask the studio to provide a car to drive us up. We'll leave early on Thursday morning.'

'As you wish. And Greta?'

'Yes?'

'Don't worry. I'll be there.'

'Thank you, David.' Greta put the telephone down, wandered over to the drinks cabinet and poured herself a small whisky from the bottle she kept for David when he visited. Still wrapped in a towel, she slumped onto the sofa and wondered what on earth she should tell Cheska about Owen. And about Marchmont.

'Darling, I . . . I had a telephone call last night.' Greta watched her daughter eating her porridge. 'It was bad news, I'm afraid.'

'Oh dear, Mummy. What about?'

'Well, we have to go away tomorrow for a few days. You see, darling, your daddy is dead.'

Cheska looked surprised. 'I didn't know I had a daddy. What was his name?'

'Owen Marchmont.'

'Oh. And why has he died?'

'Because he was a lot older than me to begin with and he got sick. And you know everyone dies when they get old. Is there anything else you want to ask me about him?'

'Where does . . . I mean, where did my daddy live?'

'Wales, where Uncle David comes from. It's a very lovely place. He lived in a beautiful house, and we'll be staying there.'

Cheska's face brightened. 'Will Uncle David be there, too?'

'Yes. And we'd better go and buy you some play-clothes. Marchmont isn't the place for party frocks.'

'Could I have some dungarees like Melody used to wear?'

'We'll see what we can find.'

'Thank you, Mummy.' Cheska slid from her place at the table and wrapped her arms round her mother in an unsolicited show of affection. 'Are you sad that my daddy died?'

'Of course. People are always sad when other people die.'

'Yes. They always are in my films. I'll go and wait in my room for you to brush my hair.'

'Good girl.'

Greta watched her walk out of the sitting room, realising she would need all her courage to face the past, for both their sakes.

The night before the funeral, David was inspecting some of the old books in the library when his mother appeared at the door.

'I've almost finished helping Mary with the food for tomorrow. Could we have a drink together in twenty minutes or so? I . . . need to talk to you, David.'

'Of course.'

LJ gave him a wan smile and left the room. He wandered over to inspect the contents of the drinks cabinet. There were many bottles, but they were all empty. Right at the back of the cupboard he found and retrieved the dregs of a whisky bottle. He took out two glasses and poured out what was left equally between them.

He and his mother had found empty whisky bottles all over the house, stashed behind sofas, in cupboards and under Owen's bed, to the extent that David was surprised his uncle had lasted as long as he had. He settled himself in an armchair with his glass and waited for his mother to join him.

'So, there it is, David.' LJ sighed deeply. She had talked for the past fifteen minutes, explaining to her son for the first time why Owen had always resented him so strongly. 'You mustn't think that I didn't love your father, because I did. I was devastated when Robin died. But Owen and I . . . well . . .' LJ paused. 'He was my first love and I believe that kind of love never really dies.'

David was surprised to discover that he wasn't shocked by what his mother had told him, just saddened. 'Why didn't Owen offer to marry you when Pa died?'

'Pride, mostly. I suppose it all comes down to lack of communication.' LJ stared into the distance. 'Owen took forty years to tell me he still loved me. A whole lifetime wasted.' She shook her head sadly. 'At least we had two precious weeks together at the end, which is some comfort.'

'So one of the reasons Owen asked Greta to marry him was to hurt you?'

'Undoubtedly, yes. And the thought of you inheriting Marchmont was just too much for him.'

'And what about Marchmont now? Will it go to Greta? After all, legally, she is his wife.'

'Owen wouldn't discuss it, so we'll have to wait until the reading of the will. I have no idea what he'll have decided.'

'Why is life so complicated?'

'Oh my dear boy, I have asked myself that time and time again during the past forty years. But if life has taught me anything, it's that you mustn't waste a day of it. And, more importantly, if you love someone, for goodness' sake, tell them how you feel.' She stared hard at her son. 'I wouldn't like to see you suffer the way I have.'

David had the grace to blush. 'No, of course not.'

'Do excuse me, but I'm going to retire. It'll be a long day tomorrow and the past couple of weeks have taken their toll.' LJ stood up and kissed David on the forehead. 'Goodnight, dear boy. Sleep well.'

David watched his mother leave the room, then sat pondering over what she had just told him.

Love could alter destiny and control lives. As it controlled his own.

Ma was right: life was too short.

And she could only say no.

# 20

Cheska watched from the back of the studio limousine as the London skyline disappeared and was replaced by green fields. She sat quietly, staring out of the window until, finally, the steady drone of the car's engine made her doze.

'Darling, we're almost there.'

Cheska felt her mother shaking her gently and opened her eyes.

'This is Marchmont, Cheska,' Greta said as the car approached the house.

The front door opened and David appeared, walking briskly towards the car.

'Hello, sweetheart,' he said, lifting Cheska out and into his arms.

'Did my daddy really live here?' she whispered to him, looking up in awe at the huge house.

'Yes, he really did. Hello, Greta.' He kissed her on both cheeks, then looked at her in admiration. The short black A-line dress she was wearing accentuated her slim figure, and her new 'Hepburn' haircut suited her delicate features. 'You look wonderful.'

'Thank you. You look very smart, too.'

'I rather like this suit but, unfortunately, I only get to wear it on sombre occasions such as this.'

The chauffeur had taken Greta's suitcase out of the boot and was standing waiting for further instructions.

'Thank you for such a pleasant journey,' Greta said, turning to him. 'Would you like some tea before you leave?'

'No, thanks. I'm off to see my cousin in Penarth. Have an enjoyable stay, both of you.'

David noticed how used to handling staff Greta had become. A far cry from the nervous, insecure young woman whom he'd packed off to Marchmont all those years ago. 'Come on, let's go inside,' he said. 'Ma is waiting to see you.'

Greta took Cheska's hand and followed David towards the front door. 'This is where you were born, darling,' she explained.

'Goodness!' said Cheska. 'It's as big as Buckingham Palace!'

'Almost.' David winked at Greta over Cheska's head.

'Are those real sheep?' Cheska pointed to the white dots on the misty hillside some distance away.

'They are.'

'Gosh! Could I possibly go and see one close up?'

'I'm sure we can arrange that.' David smiled.

Nervously, Greta followed David and Cheska into the house. The same smell of dogs and woodsmoke that she had noticed when she was first carried inside it assailed her nostrils. As they walked into the drawing room LJ stood up. Her hair had turned snow-white in the intervening years, but her posture was still ramrod-straight and she showed no other sign of her advancing years.

'Greta! How lovely to see you.' LJ walked towards her and kissed her on both cheeks. 'Was the journey horrendous?'

'No, it was fine, thank you,' Greta replied, grateful for LJ's generous welcome.

'And this must be Cheska.' LJ held out her hand to the girl, who put her small fingers into LJ's palm.

'I'm very pleased to meet you,' Cheska replied solemnly, as they shook hands.

'What beautiful manners,' LJ said approvingly. 'Now, the cars are arriving at three, which gives us half an hour or so. I'm sure you'd like to freshen up after your journey, Greta dear. I've put you in your old room and I thought Cheska could sleep in her old nursery.' LJ turned her attention back to the child. 'Are you hungry, Cheska?'

'Yes, I am. We didn't have any lunch.'

'Well, why don't you come down to the kitchen and meet Mary, who can't wait to see how you've grown up.'

'Yes, please.'

'Right then.' LJ offered her hand to Cheska, who took it happily.

The two of them disappeared from the room and Greta heard her daughter chattering to LJ as she led her down the corridor. She climbed the stairs to the bedroom in which her two babies had been born.

As memories of Jonny began to trickle back into her consciousness, Greta shuddered. Coming back here to Marchmont was extremely unsettling. The sooner it was over and they were back to their usual life, the better.

*

Cheska watched the coffin being lowered into the ground. She supposed she should be sad. When she'd stood by the grave of her father in the last film, the director had asked her to cry.

She didn't really understand about dying. Only that you never saw the person again and they went to a place called Heaven and lived on a fluffy cloud with God. She looked up at her mother and noticed that she wasn't crying. She was looking off into the distance, not down into the big, dark hole.

The sight of the coffin reminded Cheska of the nightmare she had all the time. She turned away and rested her head against her mother's arm, hoping it would all be over soon and they could go home.

'I think it's time to go to bed, young lady.'

Cheska was sitting contentedly on David's knee in the library.

'All right, Mummy.'

'How about I come up when Mummy has got you ready for bed and tell you one of my special stories?'

'Oh, yes please, Uncle David.'

'Right you are, then. See you in a minute.'

'Goodnight, Aunt LJ.' Cheska climbed down from David's knee and kissed her aunt on the cheek.

'Goodnight, my dear. Don't let the bedbugs bite.'

'I won't.' Cheska giggled and followed Greta out of the room. 'I like it here, Mummy, and Aunt LJ is so nice. I'm glad I've got another relation. Do you think she's very old?' she asked as they mounted the stairs.

'No, not very.'

'Older than Daddy?'

'Probably a bit younger.' Greta led Cheska along the corridor to the nursery, hoping the child couldn't sense her own apprehension at the thought of entering the room where she'd once spent so many hours with the twins. 'Here we are, sweetheart,' she said brightly, forcing a smile. 'See, this is where you slept when you were a baby. Cheska, what on earth's the matter?' Greta looked at her daughter, who had stopped at the entrance to the room. The colour had drained from her face.

'I . . . Oh, Mummy, could I sleep with you tonight instead?'

'You're a big girl now, and anyway, this is such a cosy room. See, this is one of your old dolls.'

Cheska remained rigid in the doorway.

'Don't be difficult, Cheska. Mummy's had a very long day. Come and put your nightie on for me.'

'Mummy, let me sleep with you, *please*. I don't like it in here,' she pleaded.

'Well, why don't you get changed like a good girl, then climb into bed and let Uncle David come and tell you a story? And afterwards, if you still don't want to sleep in here, you can come into my bed. How's that?'

Cheska nodded and took a tentative step into the room.

Sighing with relief, Greta helped her undress. That done, she tucked her into the narrow bed and sat down beside her. 'There, you see. This really is a nice, friendly sort of room.'

But Cheska was staring at something behind Greta. 'Mummy, why are there two cots over there? Was one of them my brother Jonny's?'

Greta turned and saw them. Not wanting to distress her daughter, she fought back her emotions. 'Yes, that's right.'

'So why are they still here?'

'Oh, I should think Mary forgot to move them after we left.'

'Why did we leave?'

Greta sighed, bent over and kissed Cheska on the forehead. 'I'll tell you tomorrow, darling.'

'Don't go until Uncle David gets here, *please*, Mummy.'

'All right, darling. I won't.'

'Is that my favourite girl all tucked up in bed?' David appeared at the door.

Cheska managed a smile as Greta rose to her feet. 'Goodnight, darling. Don't go telling her frightening stories, David. She's a little unsettled,' Greta murmured, as she passed him on her way out of the room.

'Of course I won't. I'm going to tell Cheska all about the famous Welsh gnome called Shuni, who lives in his cave on a hillside not so many miles from this house.'

Greta watched as David perched on the edge of the bed. She stood for a few moments at the doorway listening to him begin his story, before making her way quietly downstairs.

As David continued with the story, Cheska's face began to relax and she giggled at the funny voice David was using for the gnome.

'And everyone lived . . .'

'Happily ever after!'

'There now. I think it's time you got some sleep.'

'Uncle David?'

'Yes, my darling.'

'Why does no one ever die in fairy stories and films except the wicked people?'

'Because that's the way it is in those kinds of stories. Good lives on and evil dies.'

'Was my daddy evil?'

'No, sweetheart.'

'Why did he die, then?'

'Because he was a real person, not pretend.'

'Oh. Uncle David?'

'Yes.'

'Are there such things as ghosts?'

'No, they're only in fairy stories, too. Sleep tight, Cheska.' David kissed her lightly on the cheek and walked towards the door.

'Don't shut the door, please!'

'I won't. Mummy will be up to check on you later.'

David went downstairs and joined LJ and Greta in the library.

'I don't know whether it was such a good idea to allow Cheska to come to the funeral,' he sighed. 'She's just asked me the strangest questions.'

'She made a terrible fuss about going to bed in the nursery, which is most unlike her,' replied Greta. 'When we've been on location, she's stayed in hotels and gone to sleep in strange beds without a murmur. Still, she's only a little girl. I don't think she really understood what was happening today.'

'She's not that little any more. She'll be in her teens in three years' time,' LJ commented.

'I suppose I think of her as younger than she is,' agreed Greta. 'She usually plays seven or eight-year-olds on screen.'

'Greta, do you think that Cheska understands the difference between the fantasy of her films and reality?' asked David gently.

'Of course she does! Why do you ask?'

'Oh, just something she said upstairs, that's all.'

'Whatever it was, I wouldn't read too much into it. What with the journey and the funeral, we're both exhausted.' Greta stood up. 'I think I'll head upstairs for a bath.'

'Do you not want any supper, my dear?' asked LJ.

'No, thank you. I'm still full from the sandwiches this afternoon. Goodnight.'

Greta walked quickly from the room and David sighed as he turned to his mother. 'I've upset her. She hates anyone criticising Cheska.'

'Odd child though, isn't she?'

'Sorry, Ma?' David pulled himself from his thoughts and sat down in a leather armchair opposite his mother.

'I said that Cheska is an odd child. But then I suppose she's had an odd life.'

'Yes, she has.'

'Personally, I think all this film nonsense is no way for a young one to be brought up. She needs to run about in the fresh air, put some colour in her cheeks and some meat on that thin little body of hers.'

'Greta says she enjoys making the films.'

'Well, it rather seems to me that Cheska has little choice in the matter or, in fact, knows no different.'

'I'm sure Greta wouldn't have her do anything that made her unhappy, Ma.'

'Maybe not,' sniffed LJ. 'Poor little thing. Up until these

past few days, it seems she didn't even know she had a father, let alone the fact that he isn't her natural flesh and blood.'

'Come on now, Ma, this is hardly the moment.'

'Greta seems to have told the child almost nothing about her past,' LJ continued, ignoring her son's plea. 'For instance, what does she know about her twin brother, if anything?'

'I'm not really sure. Look, Ma, try to understand that Greta has said little to Cheska about her past because she felt it was for the best. When she and Cheska moved to London, it was under extremely difficult circumstances and she obviously wanted to make a fresh start. There was no point telling Cheska what had happened until she was old enough to understand.'

'You do know that you're always defending Greta, dear?' LJ said quietly. 'You don't seem to see how brittle she's become since leaving Marchmont. She used to be such a soft, gentle soul.'

'Well, if she's become brittle, it's because she's had a lot to cope with. It's hardly her fault.'

'See, David? You're doing it again. I know from personal experience that keeping your heart locked away, just because it's been bruised in the past, is not the answer. More to the point, neither is pouring all the pent-up love stored in it into one child. Anyway,' she said, briskly changing the subject, 'I have a suggestion for you: why don't you ask the two of them to stay on for a while here? If, as we presume, Owen has left the estate to Greta, she'll need time to sort a few things out. It would also give Cheska a chance to live like a normal little girl for a few days.'

'I doubt Greta will stay here any longer than she has to,' David said. 'Let's wait and see what happens tomorrow.'

'Well, if she does inherit, given your obvious feelings for her, marrying her would be the perfect solution to the entire jigsaw. Greta needs a husband, you need a wife, and little Cheska needs a father and a more stable existence. And Marchmont needs a man to run it, preferably a man with a blood tie to the place.'

'You're scheming, Ma! Stop it,' David warned her. 'Apart from anything else, I have no wish to run Marchmont, not even to please you.'

LJ saw the anger in her son's eyes and knew that she'd gone too far. 'My apologies, David. I just want to see you happy.'

'And I you. Now, no more talk of this,' he said firmly. 'Let's go and have supper.'

Cheska was having the dream again. *He* was here again, next to her . . . the boy who looked like her. His face was so pale, and he whispered things to her that she couldn't understand. She knew all she had to do was wake up and switch on her light to see her own cosy bedroom and the nightmare would disappear. She fumbled for the lamp on the table by her bed, but her hand reached into nothingness. Desperately, she searched around, groping the air, her heart slamming against her chest.

'Please, please,' she moaned, but as her eyes became accustomed to the dull greyness of early morning it was not the comforting shapes of her bedroom she could see. It was the room in her dream.

Cheska began to scream, '*Mummy! Mummy! Mummy!*'

She knew she should get out of the bed and leave the room and then the nightmares would stop. But she was too terrified to move and the ghostly outlines would reach out their clammy, dead hands and . . .

A light was switched on and her mother appeared at the door. Cheska leapt out of bed, ran across the room and threw herself into Greta's arms.

'Mummy, Mummy! Take me away from here! Take me away!' she sobbed.

'Come now, darling, whatever is the matter?'

Cheska pushed Greta out of the room, into the corridor and slammed the nursery door behind her. 'Don't make me go back in there, *please*, Mummy!' she begged.

'All right, all right, darling. Calm down. You come along into Mummy's bed and tell me what frightened you.' She steered Cheska along the corridor and into her bedroom. Greta sat her on the bed and the child buried her face in her nightgown. 'Did you have a bad dream, darling? Is that what's wrong?'

'Yes.' She looked up at her mother with genuine fear in her eyes. 'But it wasn't a dream. It was real. He lives' – Cheska shuddered – 'in that room.'

'In the nursery? Who lives there?'

Cheska shook her head and buried her face in Greta's chest.

'Come on, darling.' Greta stroked Cheska's hair gently. 'Everyone has nightmares. They're not real. It's simply your imagination playing silly games while you're asleep, that's all.'

'No, no. It was real.' Cheska's voice was muffled. 'I want to go home.'

'We'll be going home tomorrow, I promise. Now, why don't we climb into my bed and snuggle up? It's nippy now and you'll catch cold.'

Greta pulled Cheska under the covers with her and held her tightly. 'There. Feeling better?'

'A little bit.'

'No one can hurt my baby while Mummy's here,' crooned Greta, as her daughter's arms gradually slipped from around her neck. Greta lay back too, fretting over Cheska's reaction in the nursery and wondering how much she actually remembered about Jonny. *No matter*, she told herself firmly, by this time tomorrow they would both be safely in London and she could pull the protective curtain back around their past.

# 21

'Are you sure you don't mind looking after Cheska?' Greta asked Mary the following day. She studied her daughter, looking for further signs of anxiety.

'Of course not. Look you, we'll have a fine time, won't we, *fach*?'

Cheska, sitting on a stool at the big kitchen table, up to her elbows in flour from the pastry she was helping Mary to make, nodded in agreement.

'I won't be gone long. Are you sure you'll be all right?'

'Yes, Mummy,' Cheska said, a hint of exasperation in her voice.

'I'll see you later then.' Greta left the kitchen, relieved that Cheska didn't even look up as she went.

David and LJ were waiting for her in the car.

'How is she?' LJ had heard the child's screams last night.

'Absolutely fine,' replied Greta tersely. 'I think it was just a very bad nightmare. She seems to have forgotten all about it this morning.'

'Well, I'm sure she'll have a marvellous time with Mary. Right, let's be off.'

David drove the few miles to Monmouth, then the three of them walked along the picturesque main street to Mr Glenwilliam's office in tense silence.

'Hello, Greta, David, Mrs Marchmont.' Mr Glenwilliam shook them all by the hand. 'Thank you for that wonderful spread yesterday after the funeral. I think you did Owen proud. Now, if you would all like to come through to my office, we can get down to business.'

They followed him and settled themselves into seats in front of Mr Glenwilliam's desk. He opened a large safe and drew out a thick roll of documents secured with a red ribbon, then sat down behind his desk and untied the bundle.

'I should tell you that, at Owen's insistence, I went to visit him approximately six weeks ago to make a fresh will, and this negates any will he may have had before. Even though he was extremely poorly, I can confirm that he was neither drunk nor deranged at the time and therefore of sound mind and body. Owen was very definite about the contents of this will. He gave an indication of the delicacy of the situation.' Mr Glenwilliam coughed nervously. 'I think the best thing is to read it, and then we can discuss any points that arise.'

'Let's get on with it, then,' said LJ, speaking for all of them.

Mr Glenwilliam cleared his throat and began to read:

> I, Owen Marchmont, being of sound mind and body, declare that this is my final will and testament. I bequeath the Marchmont estate in its entirety to Laura-Jane Marchmont. This is on the sole condition that she

lives at Marchmont for the rest of her life. When she dies, the estate is hers to dispose of as she wishes, although it would please me if she left it to David Robin Marchmont, my nephew.

The monies held in the Marchmont bank account also pass to Laura-Jane Marchmont, for the upkeep and management of the estate. From my own, personal bank account, I bequeath the following sums:

To my daughter, Francesca Rose Marchmont, on the condition that she visits Marchmont at least once a year until she is twenty-one years of age, the sum of fifty thousand pounds, to be held in trust for her until she is of age. This trust is to be administered by Laura-Jane Marchmont.

To David Robin Marchmont, the sum of ten thousand pounds.

To my wife, Greta, the sum of ten thousand pounds.

To Mary-Jane Goughy, in recognition of the way she has cared for me during my final years, I leave the sum of five thousand pounds, plus the tenancy in perpetuity of River Cottage on the Marchmont estate.

Mr Glenwilliam continued, naming a few additional small bursaries, but the three people in the room were no longer listening, each lost in their own thoughts.

LJ was fighting the lump in her throat. She never cried in public.

David was watching his mother, thinking that at last justice had been done.

Greta was relieved it was over and that she and Cheska could return to London sixty thousand pounds richer, and only have to endure a short visit to Marchmont once a year.

Mr Glenwilliam finished reading and removed his glasses. 'One last thing. Owen left a personal letter for you, Greta. Here.' He passed the envelope across the desk to her. 'Any questions?'

Greta knew he was waiting for her to protest that, by rights, Marchmont should have gone to her. She remained silent.

'Mr Glenwilliam, could you possibly give us a few minutes alone?' LJ asked quietly.

'Of course.'

The solicitor left the room and LJ turned to Greta. 'My dear, there's every chance you could prove that Owen was not of sound mind when he had this will drawn up. After all, you are Owen's widow. If you wish to contest it, neither David nor I would stand in your way, would we, David?'

'Of course not.'

'No, LJ. Owen has done what is right and best for everyone. As a matter of fact, I'm relieved. Cheska and I have a new life in London. You know as well as I do that she isn't Owen's child by blood and that the marriage was a failure. I think Owen has been extremely generous to us both under the circumstances. And, to be honest, I'm just glad it's all over.'

LJ looked at her with renewed respect. 'Greta, let us be frank with each other. We all know why you married Owen. Apart from being fond of him,' she added hastily. 'And perhaps you feel some guilt for that.'

'Yes, I do,' Greta agreed.

'Equally, you're a bright woman, and I'm sure you have

realised since that it suited Owen, too. Your marriage gave him a new lease of life and, most importantly for him, an heir to Marchmont, if Jonny had lived. So you see, you really mustn't feel guilty any more, or think there is any ill-feeling on my part. You were – to some extent – an innocent pawn in a game that you knew nothing about.'

'Really, LJ, you don't need to say anything else. I'm happy for you to have the estate. I wouldn't know where to begin when it came to looking after it.'

'You're absolutely sure, Greta? You must know that I will leave Marchmont to David in my will? It's his by rights.'

'Absolutely.'

'All right then. But remember: both Marchmont and I will welcome you any time you would like to visit. Owen was obviously anxious that you and Cheska don't lose touch with us.'

'Thank you, LJ. I'll remember that.'

David called Mr Glenwilliam back into the room. 'Does everything seem to be in order?' he asked.

'Yes. Greta has decided she will not be contesting,' David replied.

Mr Glenwilliam looked relieved. 'Now, obviously there are some legal things I have to tie up, and there will be taxes to pay on the amount Owen has bequeathed. Mrs Marchmont, you'll need to come back and sign some documents once they've been through probate. And I'll be here to offer any assistance you may need as regards the future handling of the estate. As you're aware, I've been looking after the business side of things for quite some time.'

'Thank you. I appreciate all your help, both past and present.'

'It's my pleasure,' nodded Mr Glenwilliam, as the three of them stood up and filed out of his office.

'Mummy, Mummy! Guess what? Mary took me across to the field and I patted a sheep!' Cheska was ecstatic as Mary brought her into the drawing room after the others had returned from Monmouth.

'How lovely.'

'And the farmer says I can help him milk the cows tomorrow morning. But I shall have to be up at five o'clock.'

'But, darling, we're going back to London this afternoon.'

'Oh.' Cheska's face fell in disappointment.

'I thought you wanted to go home?'

'I do—' Cheska bit her lip. 'But couldn't we stay just one more day?'

'We really should be getting back, Cheska. We have that photo shoot on Monday and we can't have you looking tired.'

'Just one more day. *Please*, Mummy.'

'Why not stay on for a while, dear girl? I think it would do both of you the world of good. Look at the colour in Cheska's cheeks. And David and I would appreciate it,' LJ coaxed.

Greta was startled by the abrupt change in her daughter's mood. 'As long as there are no silly antics about going to bed tonight, young lady.'

'I promise, Mummy. Thank you!' Cheska ran to her

mother, threw her arms around her and kissed her on the cheek.

'Right, that's settled then,' said LJ. 'Now, I must go and find Mary and break the good news to her about River Cottage and her legacy. I'm sure it will make her and her fiancé very happy. He's hung on for years waiting for her. I hope she'll finally make an honest man of him. David, sort out some drinks will you, dear boy. I'm parched!'

That night, Greta climbed into bed, having checked Cheska was fast asleep in the bedroom next to her own. She'd decided it was unwise to put her back in the nursery after the previous disturbance.

Then she opened the letter from Owen.

*Marchmont*
*Monmouthshire*

*2nd May 1956*

*My dear Greta,*

*I write this letter knowing that you will only read it once I am dead, which is rather a strange thought. However, you now know the contents of my will and I thought I owed you an explanation.*

*I have left Marchmont to Laura-Jane not least because she truly loves the estate but also because I owed it to her and David. After much thought, I decided that even if I had left it to you, it would have been a burden rather than a pleasure and you would almost certainly sell it, which would break my heart. And Laura-Jane's.*

*I understand that you didn't have an easy time whilst you were living here and that is in part due to my latterly unpardonable behaviour, for which I am truly sorry. I was a weak man and you were caught up in something that happened many years ago. I hope that you can find it in your heart to forgive me and, through that forgiveness, come to look on Marchmont as a place of sanctuary, a retreat for both you and Cheska, away from your busy lives in London.*

*You must believe I cared very much for you and the children, even though they were not my own. You, Jonny and Cheska gave me a new lease of life, for which I am most grateful. I apologise that my grief over Jonny's death brought that time to an end. I was not there to support you and I recognise that I behaved selfishly.*

*Please tell Cheska that I loved her as my own child. Mary tells me she saw her in a film at the cinema and that she has become something of a star. I am proud I was her de-facto father, if only for a short time. The only thing that comforts me as I lie here approaching death is that soon I will see my beloved Jonny.*

*I wish you both a long and happy life,*

*Owen*

Greta folded the letter back into its envelope and placed it in her handbag. She felt a wave of emotion building, but she pushed it firmly away. Max, Owen, James . . . they were all part of her past. She couldn't allow them to touch her now.

# 22

Cheska lay on her back and stared up at the big branches of the oak tree hanging above her, outlined by a perfect, cornflower-blue sky. She sighed contentedly. The film studios seemed far away, there was no one here to recognise her and, for what seemed like the first time in her short life, she was able to be completely alone and free. She felt safe here. The dream hadn't returned since she had left the nursery after the first night.

She sat up and looked into the distance. On the terrace, she could see Mummy and Uncle David having lunch. They'd been at Marchmont for a week now, the result of her begging and begging Mummy for them to stay longer. She lay back down again and thought how wonderful it would be if Mummy and Uncle David were to fall in love, get married and live here for ever and ever. Then she could help milk the cows every morning, have breakfast in the kitchen with Mary and go to the local school with other boys and girls.

But it was a dream. Cheska knew that tomorrow she and Mummy would have to go back to London.

She stood up, checked once more that Mummy wasn't

looking for her and wandered off towards the woods, stuffing her hands into the pockets of her new dungarees. She listened to the birds singing and wondered why their song sounded so much sweeter than the birds in London.

Walking through the tall trees reminded Cheska of the set for *Hansel and Gretel*, a film she had made last year which Mummy had said had been a big Christmas hit. As she walked deeper into the woods, she wondered if there was a wicked witch in a house of sugar-icing waiting to eat her, but as a leafy glade appeared, all she saw was a dear little fir tree, with a piece of stone underneath it.

Moving towards it, Cheska realised it was a gravestone and shuddered at the thought of the person lying under the earth. She knelt down in front of it. The inscription was embossed in gold and very clear.

JONATHAN (JONNY) MARCHMONT

Beloved son of Owen and Greta
Brother of Francesca

BORN 2ND JUNE 1946
DIED 6TH JUNE 1949

May God guide his little angel up to Heaven

Cheska gasped.

Jonny . . .

Fleeting memories she could not quite hold on to came into her head.

Jonny . . . Jonny . . .

Then she heard someone whispering.

'*Cheska, Cheska . . .*'

It was the voice of the boy in her dream. The dead boy, lying in the coffin. The one who had come to her in the nursery that night.

'*Cheska, Cheska . . . come and play with me.*'

'*No!*'

Cheska stood up and covered her ears with her hands, then ran from the woods as fast as her legs would carry her.

'Greta, as it's your last night tonight, I thought I might take you out to dinner in Monmouth,' David suggested as they sat on the terrace drinking coffee.

'I . . . Goodness me, Cheska looks as though she's being chased by a hungry lion!' Greta's attention was diverted as she watched her daughter racing towards them. She arrived, panting hard, and threw herself into Greta's arms.

'What is it, darling?'

Cheska looked up at Greta. Then she shook her head firmly. 'Nothing. I'm fine. Sorry, Mummy. Can I go and see Mary in the kitchen? She said I could help her make a cake to take home to London with us.'

'Yes, of course you can. Cheska?'

'Yes, Mummy?'

'Are you sure you're all right?'

'Yes, Mummy.' She nodded and disappeared into the house.

The interior of the Griffin Arms was bathed in soft candle-light as David and Greta entered the restaurant. They were shown to an intimate corner table beneath the ancient rafters, set with gleaming silver cutlery and delicate crystal wine glasses.

'Sir, madam, may I get you something to drink?' asked the head waiter.

'Yes, a bottle of your best champagne, please,' said David.

'Very good, sir,' he said, handing them both menus. 'I would recommend the prawns, which were freshly caught today, and also the Welsh lamb. And may I also say, sir, how much I enjoyed your last film.'

'Thank you. You're most kind,' said David, embarrassed, as always, to be recognised.

After ordering what the head waiter had recommended, they sat drinking champagne and chatting about LJ and Marchmont.

'It's such a shame that Cheska has to go back to London tomorrow. She seems to have blossomed in the past few days,' David commented.

'Yes, I'm sure it's done her good, but we can't have her public disappointed, can we?'

'I suppose not,' murmured David, hoping Greta was being ironic but realising she probably wasn't. 'Oh, by the way, I read in the *Telegraph* this morning that Marilyn Monroe and Arthur Miller have married. They're flying over to London, as she's making a film with Larry Olivier.'

'Really? They seem an unlikely couple,' said Greta, as the waiter arrived with their prawns. 'It seems everyone's getting married at the moment. Did you watch Grace Kelly marry Prince Rainier on the television earlier this year? Cheska was transfixed.'

During dinner David was so nervous that his normally healthy appetite deserted him and he hardly touched his food, even refusing dessert. Greta ate fresh strawberries as

David sipped the remains of the champagne. Ordering coffee and two brandies, he realised that time was running out. It was now or never.

'Greta, I . . . well, I want to ask you something.'

'All right. What is it?' She smiled at him quizzically.

'The thing is . . .' Time and again David had rehearsed the next few sentences in his mind, but now he actually needed to say them out loud, he couldn't remember a single word.

'Well, the . . . er . . . thing is, that I . . . I love you, Greta. I always have and I always will. There'll never be anyone else for me. Would you . . . I mean, might you . . . consider marrying me?'

A stunned Greta stared at David, taking in his earnest expression and flushed cheeks. She saw his kind eyes were filled with hope. She swallowed hard and reached for a cigarette. David was her best friend. Yes, she loved him dearly, but not in the way he wanted her to. She'd sworn to herself that she'd never love like that again.

'The point is, Greta,' he fumbled on, 'I think you need someone to take care of you. And Cheska needs a father. Your rightful home is Marchmont and don't you see that if we married, Marchmont would be ours one day, which would sort of put things right? Of course, we wouldn't have to live there now. You could move into my house in Hampstead, and . . .'

He paused mid-flow as Greta raised her palm towards him.

'Stop, David, please stop. Oh, I can hardly bear this!' She put her head in her hands and began to weep.

'Greta, please don't cry. The last thing I want to do is upset you.'

'David, darling David.' Greta eventually looked up at him, then used his proffered hanky to dry her eyes. She knew that whatever she said next would hurt him terribly. 'Let me try and explain. When I met Max all those years ago and he left me pregnant, I was young enough to pick up the pieces – with your help – and start again. Then I came to Marchmont and married Owen, simply because I was alone, frightened and about to become a mother. I needed security and, for a while, Owen gave me that. But it was short-lived and relying on Owen nearly destroyed both Cheska and me. Then we left and returned to London and I fell in love with my employer, who was a married man. Maybe it was the years with Owen that had made me crave a little romance, a little physical satisfaction.' Greta blushed at her own words. 'Owen and I never consummated our marriage, you know. Besides, James – that was his name – was talking of leaving his wife for me and, stupidly, I began to believe him. Then his wife found out about the affair and I discovered that he was a weak, selfish man who had never been worth my love in the first place. I lost my job into the bargain. In fact, it was on the very day I met you outside the Windmill again.'

'I see,' he said, struggling to digest all that Greta had just imparted.

'Anyway' – Greta paused, her brow furrowed in concentration – 'it was after that awful James business that I made a vow to myself: that I would never allow myself to become close to a man, in the romantic sense at least, again. All they've ever done is bring me pain and heartache. I relied on them to give me what I thought I needed. And in the past six years I've been happier in some ways than I've ever been. My life is Cheska, and there's no room in my heart for a husband.'

'I see.'

'You must know I care for you deeply, David, more than any other person in the world apart from Cheska, but I could never marry you. I'd worry it would all go wrong and besides' – Greta shook her head – 'I don't think I know how to love like that any more. Do you understand?'

'I understand that you've been badly hurt, but *I've* never hurt you. I love you, Greta. You must believe that.'

'I do, David, really I do. You've been wonderful to me. But it would be wrong of me to accept your proposal, because my heart is closed off – numb, I suppose. And I don't think that will ever change.'

'You say your life is Cheska. One day, she'll have her own life, too. What will you do then?' he asked quietly.

'Cheska will always need me,' Greta said firmly. 'David,' – her voice softened – 'I am overwhelmed by your offer. I had no idea you felt like this. And if I *were* thinking about marriage, you'd be the only man under consideration. But I'm not. And sadly, I never will be.'

David was silent and devastated. There seemed little point in pursuing the subject further. His dreams were shattered and there would be no second chances.

'I should have married you all those years ago when you were pregnant.'

'No, you shouldn't have. Don't you see, David? We have something far better than marriage. We have friendship. I just hope it won't disappear after tonight. It won't, will it?'

He reached for her hand across the table, wishing he were about to place the ring in his pocket on her finger, and smiled a small, sad smile. 'Of course it won't, Greta.'

A little later the two of them left the restaurant and walked back to the car in silence.

LJ thought she could hear voices upstairs. She left the library and the Marchmont estate account ledgers and tiptoed upstairs to check Cheska's room. The bed was empty. She knocked on the bathroom door, pushed it open and saw it was in darkness. Quickening her pace, LJ looked in Greta's room and the other bedrooms along the corridor until she came to the nursery. The door was closed, but she could hear high-pitched laughter inside. She opened the door slowly.

LJ caught her breath and her hand flew to her mouth.

Cheska was sitting on the floor, her back to the door. She seemed to be talking to someone as she tore the head off an old teddy bear and began to remove the stuffing. She twisted the bear's arm until it ripped off completely. Then she reached for the head of the bear and began to pull at the two button eyes. One came away in her hand and she poked her finger through the hole the missing button had left and laughed. It was a chilling sound.

LJ stood there watching, horrified by the sight of such violence from a child. Eventually, she stepped into the room and walked quietly across it to stand in front of her. Cheska didn't seem to notice. Still trying to pull the remaining eye off the teddy's face, she was now muttering to herself.

LJ saw the child's glassy eyes. She looked as though

she was in some kind of trance. She bent down. 'Cheska,' she whispered. 'Cheska!'

The child jumped then looked up at her, and her eyes cleared. 'Is it time for bed, Mummy?' she asked.

'It's not Mummy, it's Aunt LJ. What have you done to that poor teddy bear?'

'I think I should like to go to bed now. I'm tired, and so is my friend. He's going to bed, too.' She dropped what remained of the teddy bear and reached out her arms to LJ, who, with an effort, picked her up. Cheska's head rested on her shoulder and her eyes closed immediately. LJ carried her along the corridor and put her into bed. The child didn't stir as she closed the door behind her.

LJ went back to the nursery and, with distaste, gathered up the bits of stuffing and material that had once been a well-loved children's toy. She carried the remains down to the kitchen and placed them in the bin.

She went to sit in the library, praying that Greta would say yes to her son's proposal. When David had told her he was finally going to pluck up the courage to ask her, LJ had presented him with the engagement ring Robin had given to her. It was a family heirloom and only right that the next generation of Marchmont men should give it to his intended.

Even if Greta would never be her first choice for David, there was no doubt he loved her and needed a wife. And Cheska needed not only a father, but some kind of normality brought back into her strange, artificial world. And, after what LJ had just witnessed, perhaps some form of psychological help, too.

Later, LJ heard the front door open. David came into

the library and she stood up, searching his face anxiously. He smiled at her sadly and gave a slight shrug. She went to her son and put her arms round him.

'I'm so sorry, dear boy.'

'Well, at least I asked. It was all I could do.'

'Where's Greta?'

'Gone to bed. She and Cheska are leaving first thing tomorrow.'

'I wanted to have a word with Greta about something I saw Cheska do while you were out.'

'If that child did something naughty, then good for her. It's time she started having a will of her own,' David countered. 'Don't tell Greta, Ma. She won't believe you anyway, and it'll only cause tension.'

'It wasn't so much naughty as strange. To be honest, I think the child might be a little disturbed.'

'As you said, Cheska just needs to be allowed to act like a normal little girl sometimes. Most children do odd things occasionally. For my sake, leave it, will you? I want Greta to come back to Marchmont, and criticising her precious daughter will not help that happen.'

'If you insist,' sighed LJ.

'Thank you, Ma.'

'There are other women in the world, you know.'

'Maybe. But none like Greta.' David kissed her gently on her forehead. 'Goodnight, Ma.'

# 23

The change in Cheska was so slow and subtle that, as she approached thirteen, Greta was unable to identify exactly when it had begun. Over the two and a half years since Owen's death, Greta watched her daughter gradually turn from a sunny little girl into a morose, introverted child whose smile was saved only for the camera.

Cheska distanced herself from Greta, no longer responding to cuddles and displaying little affection towards her. Sometimes, in the middle of the night, Greta would hear her talking to herself and moaning. She would creep along the corridor and open her door. Cheska would stir slightly, turn over and become silent. On numerous occasions, Greta would ask her if everything was all right, if there was anything she wanted to talk to Mummy about but Cheska would shake her head and say no, she was fine, it was a friend who was unhappy. Greta would ask who this friend was, and Cheska would shrug and say nothing.

Greta remembered that she, too, had had an imaginary friend when she was younger, to help while away the lonely hours of being an only child. She decided she would just have to wait until Cheska grew out of it. The child was healthy enough: she ate, she slept – but the sparkle had disappeared from her eyes.

No one else seemed to have noticed the change and she was only glad that Cheska's continual frown and monosyllabic speech disappeared when she arrived on set.

Physically, Cheska was changing, too, and the sight of her burgeoning maturity had set alarm bells ringing in Greta's head. She began to insist that Cheska wore tight, thick vests that flattened her chest. The odd spot that appeared on her nose or chin was doused in antiseptic and covered with concealer. Chocolate and fatty foods were removed from her diet.

Although Leon had assured Greta that there was no reason why Cheska shouldn't make the transition from child to adult star, Greta knew the longer Cheska remained capable of playing innocent little girls, the better the public would like it.

To celebrate her daughter's thirteenth birthday, Greta had decided to hold a party at their house. She invited the cast of Cheska's latest film, as well as David, Leon and Charles Day, Cheska's principal director. She hired caterers and the party was to be photographed for *Movie Week*. A few days before, she had taken Cheska to Harrods to buy a new satin party dress, which Greta had hung in the wardrobe alongside her extensive collection.

On the morning of her birthday, Greta roused Cheska with breakfast in bed.

'Happy birthday, darling. Here, I've brought you orange juice and one of those pastries you like so much – just this once!'

'Thank you, Mummy,' said Cheska, sitting up.

'Are you feeling all right, darling? You look very pale.'

'I didn't sleep very well last night, that's all.'

'Never mind, this will cheer you up.' Greta went to the door and reached into the corridor. She returned to the bedside, brandishing a large box covered in wrapping paper, and placed it in front of her daughter. 'Go on, open it.'

Cheska tore at the paper and opened the box. Inside was a large doll.

'Isn't she beautiful? Do you recognise the face? And the clothes? I had her made especially.'

Cheska nodded without enthusiasm.

'It's you, as Melissa in your last film! I gave the artist a photograph of you so he could copy your features onto her face. I think he's done a wonderful job, don't you?'

Cheska remained silent as she stared at the doll.

'You do like it, don't you?'

'Yes, Mummy. Thank you very much,' she replied mechanically.

'Now, eat your breakfast. I've got to pop out to collect a little something special for the party this afternoon. I won't be long. Why don't you have a bath when you've finished breakfast?'

Cheska nodded. When she heard the front door close, she threw the doll to the floor, buried her face in her pillow and wept.

She'd wanted a radio so much and, despite weeks of hinting, her mother had given her a stupid doll instead, a present for a baby. And she *wasn't* a baby any longer, but her mother just didn't seem to understand.

Cheska sat up and eyed the satin dress hanging on her wardrobe door.

It was a beautiful dress – for a baby.

The voice she'd first heard at Marchmont began to whisper in her head again.

Greta collected the birthday cake from Fortnum & Mason and carried it carefully to the waiting taxi. On the short drive home she went through a mental list of everything she had to do before the guests began arriving at four o'clock.

She unlocked the front door to the apartment, went hurriedly into the kitchen and slid the birthday cake inside a cupboard, out of sight.

'Darling! I'm home!'

There was no reply. Greta knocked on the bathroom door. It was something Cheska had started to insist on. There was nothing she hated more than Greta barging in on her naked.

'Can I come in?' Receiving no reply, Greta turned the handle of the door. It opened and she saw the room was empty. 'I thought you were going to have a bath!' she called, walking back down the corridor and opening Cheska's bedroom door. 'We've got lots to do before the—'

She stopped in mid-sentence at the sight that met her eyes.

Her daughter was sitting on the floor, holding a pair of scissors, amidst a crumpled cascade of satin, silk and net. As Greta watched, Cheska held up the remnants of her beautiful new party dress and carried on cutting the fine material to shreds, giggling as she did so.

'What on earth do you think you're doing?' Greta

marched forward to confront her daughter. 'Give me those scissors! *Now!*'

Cheska looked up, her eyes blank.

'Give me those scissors!' Greta repeated, grabbing them from Cheska, who continued to stare up at her, her face expressionless.

Greta sank to the floor, her eyes full of tears. She looked towards the open door of the wardrobe and saw it was empty. Casting her eyes around the room, she took in the slashed remnants of what had been a wonderful collection of dresses lying in a heap beside the bed.

'Why, Cheska? Why?' she asked, but the girl did nothing but stare back at her with the same blank look. Greta reached for her shoulders and shook her hard. 'Answer me, damn you!'

The physical action seemed to break Cheska out of her trance. She stared into her mother's eyes, fear entering her own. Then she glanced around her at the ruined dresses, seeming to take in what she had done for the first time.

'Why? *Why!*' Greta continued to shake her.

Cheska began to cry; terrible, choking sobs. She sank into her mother's arms, but Greta didn't close them around her as her daughter sobbed on her breast.

'It was him, my friend. He told me to do it. I'm sorry. I'm sorry, I'm sorry.' Cheska repeated the words over and over.

'Who is *he*?' Greta asked.

'I can't tell you. I promised him I wouldn't!'

'But Cheska, how can he be a friend if he makes you do things like this?'

But she only shook her head and moaned into Greta's shoulder. 'My head hurts so badly,' she whimpered.

'It's all right, it's all right. Mummy's not cross any more. Come on now, let's calm down and clear up this mess. We have to get you ready for your party.' Greta rushed to the kitchen and returned with an armful of black bin-bags into which she began stuffing the pathetic remains of her daughter's wardrobe. She'd have to ring the dry-cleaning service to see if they could deliver one of Cheska's other dresses for her to wear to the party.

As Greta reached for the last shredded dress and picked it up off the floor, she gasped as the head of the doll she had given Cheska for her birthday stared up at her. It had been torn from the neck-socket and the hair had been brutally hacked away.

Greta saw an arm peeping out from under the bed. Slowly, she crawled around the floor, tears rolling down her cheeks, collecting the limbs of the dismembered doll. She packed them on top of the ripped dresses in the bin-bags, then sank back to her knees, head in her hands.

She now knew she could ignore it no longer.

Cheska needed help badly.

'So, what's the verdict, doctor?' Greta shifted nervously in her seat in the plush Harley Street surgery.

'Well, the good news is that Cheska is in perfect health physically.'

'Thank God,' she murmured. She had imagined all sorts of terrible things whilst waiting for the doctor to finish his examination.

'However, I would say that her . . . psychological condition is currently not as good.'

'What do you mean?'

'Well, Mrs Simpson, I asked her about this imaginary friend of hers. She tells me he talks to her all the time, especially at night. Apparently, it's he who asks her to do these . . . unpleasant things. She also told me that she has recurring nightmares and suffers from bad headaches.'

'Yes,' said Greta impatiently, 'but what is it that's causing these problems?'

'It might be, Mrs Simpson, that her imagination is playing tricks on her because she's continually under such a high level of stress. After all, she has been in the limelight since she was four. But, from talking to Cheska and hearing what you have told me, there's also evidence that your daughter could be suffering from a condition called schizophrenia. So I'm going to refer her to a psychiatrist who can assess her properly.'

'Oh my God!' Greta had heard the term before and knew exactly what it meant. 'Are you telling me she might be mad?'

'Schizophrenia is an illness, Mrs Simpson. We don't refer to it as madness in this day and age,' cautioned the doctor. 'Besides, she must be professionally assessed before any potential diagnoses can be confirmed. Do remember that Cheska is also trying to deal with the onset of puberty, a disturbing time for any young girl. However, the one thing I would recommend without hesitation is that she be allowed immediate time off. Take her somewhere quiet for a few months. Give her time to relax and grow up out of the public eye.'

'But, doctor, Cheska has just signed a new contract for two pictures. She's due to start shooting the first one in a couple of weeks. She simply can't take a few months off. Besides, she loves it. It's our . . . *her* life.'

'Mrs Simpson, you pay me to recommend suitable treatment and this is what I'm suggesting. Now, I'm going to contact my colleague and make an immediate appointment for you and Cheska to see him. In the meantime, I'll give you a prescription for some mild tranquillisers. They're only to be used if Cheska seems particularly distressed. They'll calm her down but shouldn't affect her ability to function normally.'

'Do you really think she should see a psychiatrist?' Greta asked. 'As you say, it may just be growing up and working too hard that has brought this behaviour on.'

'Yes, I do. Cheska may need additional medication, such as chlorpromazine, and it's better to be safe than sorry. Here's the prescription for the tranquillisers.' The doctor handed it to her. 'Do you want me to tell Cheska what I've told you?'

'No, thank you, doctor. I'll explain it to her,' said Greta hurriedly.

'All right. And remember, Mrs Simpson, until she sees the psychiatrist, complete rest is the order of the day. I'll telephone you when I've confirmed the appointment.'

'Yes. Thank you, doctor. Goodbye.'

Greta left the room and collected a pale Cheska. They walked out into Harley Street and Greta hailed a taxi.

'What did the doctor say was wrong with me, Mummy?' asked Cheska quietly as they were driven home.

Greta squeezed her hand. 'Absolutely nothing, darling. He says you're in perfect health.'

'But what about my headaches? And the . . . funny dreams?'

'The doctor says you've been working too hard, that's all. Nothing to worry about. He's given me a prescription for some pills to help relax you. He also said you could do with a holiday. So I was thinking we might go to Marchmont for a couple of weeks.'

Cheska's face brightened. 'Oh, that would be lovely! Will Uncle David be there?'

'I doubt it, but we can stay with Aunt LJ and Mary and you can rest and get ready for the start of your new film.'

'Yes, Mummy.'

Greta stole a glance at Cheska and was relieved to see that her daughter's eyes looked brighter than they had done for days.

That night, after giving Cheska one of the pills and putting her to bed, Greta sat in the sitting room nursing a small whisky. The doctor had called earlier, confirming Cheska's appointment with the psychiatrist in two days' time. Greta had thanked him and assured him she'd keep the appointment. However, she'd already decided she'd take Cheska to Marchmont the following day and see how she was after the break. Postponing the next film was not an option, even if the contract allowed it. Out of sight was out of mind when it came to the film-going public, especially at this point in Cheska's career, as she made the transition through adolescence. Any prolonged absence from the screen would kill it stone dead.

As for Cheska being schizophrenic – which was still tantamount to madness in Greta's eyes, no matter what the doctor said – well, the very thought was ridiculous. Her perfect daughter: talented, beautiful, a huge star . . .

The poor thing needed some rest, that was all. And Greta would make sure she got it.

Cheska returned from her two-week break at Marchmont calmer, refreshed and on two tranquillisers a day. Although she seemed a little quieter than normal, the headaches and nightmares had stopped. Greta called the Harley Street doctor to ask for a repeat prescription for the tranquillisers. He refused to write it until Cheska had seen the psychiatrist. Greta explained that after a two-week holiday her daughter seemed much improved and she really didn't want to unsettle her with further examinations. The doctor stood firm, telling Greta that tranquillisers, however mild, were a temporary measure only and not to be taken long term. Irritated, Greta then called her own local doctor and made an appointment to see him. Later that week she went to the surgery and told him that she herself was suffering from tension and anxiety. She asked for a prescription for the same tranquillisers Cheska had been given, explaining that a friend had recommended them. The doctor wrote it out for her immediately, without any further questions.

A week later Cheska was on the set of her new film. Greta increased her daughter's medication to three tablets a day.

Cheska was sitting in her dressing room reading a magazine article about Bobby Cross, the latest British pop sensation. She preferred him to Cliff Richard, although, since she'd bought her gramophone, 'Living Doll' had hardly been off the turntable. She touched the photograph of Bobby's face dreamily and wondered whether she'd ever manage to convince her mother to let her go to one of his concerts.

She put down the magazine with a sigh and reached for the large pile of fan mail Greta had left for her to look through. She pulled out a letter at random and read it.

*5 St Benet's Road*
*Longmeadow*
*Cheshire*

*Dear Miss Hammond,*

*I am writing to tell you how much I enjoyed your film* Little Girl Lost. *It made me laugh and cry, and I think you are the most talented and beautiful film star on the screen. Best of all, I liked it that the film had a happy ending and that you found your long-lost father.*

*Please send me a signed photograph.*

*Yours,*

*Miriam Maverly (aged 53)*

Cheska put down the letter and stared at her reflection in the mirror. Things had been better since she'd started taking the tablets. The headaches and the voice that had haunted her dreams and made her do the bad things had stopped.

Yet now she felt nothing. It was almost as if she weren't real, only masquerading as a living, breathing person. There was a numbness inside her that made her feel she was looking at herself and others from a distance.

Touching her cheek, she felt its warmth and it comforted her somehow.

She sighed heavily. She had thousands of adoring fans and a successful career that gave her privileges others only dreamt of. Most people spent their lives trying to attain what she'd had from the age of four. Yet, at thirteen years of age, she felt as old as the hills. Everything seemed pointless.

There was a knock on the door.

'They're ready for you now, Miss Hammond.'

'Just coming.'

She stood up, ready to face an hour of illusion that seemed so much more real than her own existence. As she left the dressing room, Cheska wondered whether her own life would have a happy ending.

# 24

Leon ushered Greta and Cheska into his office and kissed them both warmly.

'You both look well. Sit down and make yourselves comfortable. Now, Cheska, you know your mother and I have been talking a lot over the past couple of months about where we take your career from here. And we have both agreed that as you have now reached the grand old age of fifteen we have to change the public's perception of you.'

'Yes, Leon,' answered Cheska, sounding bored.

'As you know, making the transition from child actress to adult star can be fraught with difficulties, but I think Rainbow Pictures has found just the vehicle to help you on your way.' Leon smiled again and pushed a script across his desk.

Cheska took it and looked at the title. *Please, Sir, I Love You*. The script was snatched out of her hands by her mother before she had time to turn the first page.

Greta glared at Leon. 'I thought we'd agreed that you clear scripts with me first?'

'I do apologise, Greta, but this only arrived at the office last night.'

'Who's it by?' she snapped.

'Peter Booth. A new screenwriter for whom Rainbow Pictures has high hopes.'

'Cheska would be playing the lead?'

'Of course,' Leon assured her. 'And the good news is that Charles thinks he's signed Bobby Cross, the pop singer, to play opposite her. It would be his first movie.'

'But Cheska would still have top billing?'

'At the very least, I'm sure we could swing it so that she shares it with Bobby,' Leon said tactfully. 'The point is, Greta, this picture will win her an army of new fans. All the teenage girls will go to see Bobby Cross, and their boyfriends will fall in love with Cheska. It's a wonderful script, totally different from anything she's done before. And you'll get your first screen kiss, to boot,' said Leon, winking at Cheska.

'You mean I'd have to kiss Bobby Cross?' Cheska blushed, her eyes lighting up.

'Yes, more than once, I believe.'

'Leon, there's a swear word here. That'll have to go,' Greta said, leafing through the script.

'Greta, it's 1961. You have to understand that the world is changing, and we in the movie business have to mirror that change. *A Taste of Honey* – Rita Tushingham pregnant without a ring on a her finger – is out in just a few weeks, and—'

'Really, Leon! Not in front of Cheska.'

'Okay, okay. I'm sorry, but what I'm trying to say is that teenage girls are no longer tied to their mother's apron strings, sitting at home learning to cook until the right husband comes along. Next year, MGM is releasing the screen version of *Lolita*, and Alan Bates is starring in *A Kind of*

*Loving*. Rainbow Pictures wants to keep up with the times. The youngsters are the people filling the movie theatres now. Weepies, war films and costume dramas are passé. The kids want to identify with what they're seeing on the screen.'

'Thank you for the sermon, Leon,' said Greta. 'I am perfectly well aware of the way things are changing. I'm not quite in my dotage yet. Now, what exactly is this film about?'

'It's about a teenage schoolgirl who falls in love with her young, handsome music teacher. They run away together and the teacher forms a band. Meanwhile, they're pursued around the country by the authorities—'

'That's ridiculous, Cheska's only fifteen!' Greta interjected furiously.

'Calm down, Greta. The character in the movie is sixteen and by the time it premieres next summer, Cheska will be too. Besides, the subject matter may sound a little risqué, but apart from the odd kiss, there's no other, er, physical stuff – it's essentially a fun film, light-hearted, with all the music written by Bobby Cross. It would be filmed on location – to give it that touch of reality which is so popular at the moment.'

'It sounds great, doesn't it, Mummy?' said Cheska eagerly, and rather desperately.

'I'll take the script home and read it, Cheska, then we'll decide,' Greta replied firmly.

'Well, don't take too long. As we both know, Cheska's career is at a critical point. There are lots of other pretty young girls around who the studio has signed.'

'But none with the army of fans that Cheska has. That's what gets bottoms on seats in the cinemas,' Greta reminded him. 'Come along, Cheska, we must get home.' She stood up and signalled to her daughter to do the same.

'Goodbye, sweetheart.'

'Goodbye, Leon.' Cheska replied sadly as she followed her mother out of the room.

When they'd left Leon sat back in his chair and thought about how the meeting had gone. He'd always admired Greta for the way she had doggedly steered Cheska to such success. But just lately she had become more and more domineering. Granted, Cheska was hugely famous, but her admirers came mainly from the older generation. She wasn't a little girl any longer, so had lost the innate innocent qualities that had made her such a big child star. Box-office receipts for her last film had been down on the previous one, and she hadn't been offered a script for nine months. Cheska now had to convince Rainbow Pictures and a whole new public that she was still worth paying to see as an adult actress. Greta simply had to realise that the balance of power had shifted and she could no longer call the shots.

Leon was at least relieved that Cheska was turning from a lovely-looking child into a beautiful young woman. Her waif-like slimness combined with her flowing blonde hair and exquisite features would make any pimply youth drool over her for weeks. Cheska's future lay in her ability to grow up and turn the male population on.

Leon wondered whether her mother would allow that to happen.

'*Please*, Mummy. I love the script! I think it's groovy!'

'Don't use such a silly word, Cheska.'

They were sitting at the table eating breakfast. Cheska

had read the script in bed last night. The few hours of sleep she did get had been filled with dreams of kissing Bobby Cross. For the first time in years she felt excitement.

'I don't know, Cheska. I've read the script too, and I just don't think your fans would like to see you in short skirts and false eyelashes.'

'But, Mother, I can't play little girls any more. I'm too old – even the reviewers have started to say that.'

'Yes, but maybe we ought to have a look at other scripts before we decide. For goodness' sake, there's one scene when your character comes out of her bedroom in her underwear!'

'So what? I'm not ashamed of my body. It's more natural to be naked than it is to wear clothes, you know,' Cheska added, quoting directly from an article she had read recently in a magazine.

'Cheska, please! You may think you're grown up, but you're not sixteen yet and my opinion still counts for something!'

'Mother, there are girls not much older than me living in flats by themselves, having boyfriends and . . . and . . . other things!'

'And what do you know about boyfriends, young lady?'

'All I know is that other girls have them and that I want to do this film!' Cheska got up from the table, went to her bedroom and slammed the door behind her.

Greta made a mental note that she needed to call the doctor for another prescription of tranquillisers. Then she went to the telephone and dialled Leon's number.

'Hello, Leon, it's Greta here. I've read the script and I'm worried about it. I want the semi-nude scenes removed and the slang taken out. Then we'll consider it.'

'No can do, Greta. Cheska either takes the part as it is, or she doesn't.'

'Well then, it's a no from this end, too. Can't you look for other scripts for her?'

'Greta, I need to make it clear to you: as far as the studio is concerned, it's this or nothing. Should I tell them they should start screen-testing other girls for the part?'

Greta was silent. She had been backed into a corner and she knew it.

'What about Cheska?' Leon asked her. 'Does she want to do it?'

'Yes, but with strong reservations.'

Reservations my backside, thought Leon. He'd seen the excitement in Cheska's eyes when he'd mentioned Bobby Cross.

'Well, let me call Charles and tell him Cheska will take it before he runs out of patience and casts somebody else. We can sort out the details later. Come on, Greta,' he pleaded. 'We've worked together for a long time, and you must see that it's a golden opportunity for her.'

There was a long pause at the other end of the line. 'All right.'

'Wonderful! You won't regret this, I promise you.'

'I hope you're right,' Greta murmured to herself as she put down the telephone, then went to tell Cheska the news.

The expression of happiness on her daughter's face was one Greta hadn't seen for a very long time. 'Thank you, Mummy. I know this is the right thing to do. I'm so happy!'

And that, at least, made Greta glad.

*

'Okay, all done.' The make-up lady whipped the tissue from around Cheska's neck. 'They'll be ready for you in about fifteen minutes. Want some coffee?'

'No, thanks.' Cheska shook her head and stared at her reflection in the mirror, which was propped up against a wall on a school desk. Her face had been covered in foundation, then her eyelids lined with liquid black. False eyelashes had been added and blue shadow highlighted her big eyes. Her lips had been painted with pink lipstick, accentuating her pearly white teeth. Her head felt strangely light, used as she was to her long hair which had been cut into a pageboy and now hung just above her shoulders in a golden halo.

She was wearing a traditional school blazer, shirt and tie, but the pleated hemline of the skirt finished four inches above her knees, leaving her long legs to taper down to her ankle socks and shoes.

Cheska giggled. Mummy would have a fit when she saw her. But she didn't care. She felt wonderful.

The floor manager came into the room to take her on set.

'You look great, Cheska.' The girl smiled. 'I can hardly believe it's you.'

Cheska followed her out of the room, down the draughty corridor and into the large school hall.

'You know which scene we're shooting first?'

'Yes.' Cheska's eyes darted around the hall, searching for a glimpse of Bobby Cross. 'It's the assembly scene, when the new music teacher is introduced to the pupils for the first time.'

'That's right. Sit here, Cheska, and we'll call you when we're ready.'

The room was filled with chattering girls, all dressed in the same uniform as Cheska. There was a sudden hush as the hall doors opened and Bobby Cross entered with Charles Day. Cheska turned with the rest and drew in her breath as she saw him in the flesh for the first time. He was more handsome in real life than he was in any of his photos. His dirty-blond hair was swept up into a quiff and his chestnut eyes were framed by long, curly lashes. His lean body, with those infamous gyrating hips, was covered by a sober, grey suit.

'Hi, girls, how you doin'?' Bobby called out in his cheeky cockney accent, flashing his famous smile at the same time.

A collective sigh echoed around the hall.

'Come and meet Cheska Hammond, your co-star,' said Charles Day.

Cheska stood transfixed as Bobby walked towards her. 'Hello, darlin'. We're gonna have fun making this movie, aren't we?'

She managed to nod and mutter a yes.

Cheska felt a blush rise to her cheeks as Bobby's eyes travelled up from her ankle socks and came to rest pointedly on the swell of her breasts. He turned to Charles Day. 'I think all my dreams have come true!'

'Hello. I'm Cheska's mother, Greta Simpson. Pleased to make your acquaintance.' Greta pushed past Cheska and held out her hand graciously to Bobby.

'Hi there,' Bobby replied, ignoring it. 'See you on set.' He winked at Cheska and turned to walk away with Charles. 'Is that dragon gonna be chaperoning the best piece of crumpet I've seen in months? It'll ruin all my fun,' he said to Charles Day, in a voice loud enough for them both to hear. Greta's face was expressionless. Cheska could have fallen through the floor, but there was pleasure mixed in with the embarrassment.

'All right, everyone.' Charles Day clapped his hands together. 'Let's get to work.'

'Mummy, I want to go to the studio by myself from now on.' Cheska, fresh from a bath and ready for bed, had joined Greta in the sitting room.

Greta looked up from the magazine she was reading, a frozen expression on her face.

'Why on earth do you want to do that?'

'Because I'm nearly sixteen years old now and I don't need a chaperone any more.'

'But Cheska, I've always come with you! You need someone with you to sort out any problems that might crop up, you know that.'

Cheska sat down on the sofa next to her mother and took her hand. 'Mummy, please don't think I don't want you there, but none of the other girls in the film bring their mothers . . . I feel like such a baby, and people laugh at me.'

'I don't think that's true at all.'

'But you've spent all these years looking after me.' Cheska tried another tack. 'You're only thirty-four yourself. Surely, you want some time for yourself now? Besides,' she sighed, 'I have to learn to stand on my own two feet.'

'It's very kind of you to think of me, but I love coming to the studios. It's my life as much as yours.'

'Well, would you mind awfully if I tried it by myself for a few days to see how I got on?'

'But what about when you go away on location? You'll need someone there to look after you then.'

'Perhaps. Oh, please let me try, Mummy. It's very important to me.'

Greta hesitated, looking into her daughter's pleading eyes. 'All right. If it's what you want. Just for a couple of days, though.'

'Thank you, Mummy.' Cheska gave her mother a rare hug. 'I'm going to bed now. Tomorrow will be a long day. Goodnight.' She gave Greta a peck on the cheek and left the sitting room.

At eight the following morning Greta watched Cheska leave in the studio car. She took a long, leisurely bath, then pottered around making the beds and tidying the kitchen, even though they had a cleaner who came in three days a week. She brewed herself a coffee and saw that it was only just past ten o'clock. She sipped it and wondered what she could do to fill the hours until Cheska came home. She could go shopping, but without her daughter to try on clothes with, it didn't seem like an attractive option. She decided she'd ring David and see if he was free for lunch.

Although she'd prayed that their relationship wouldn't change after David's proposal, inevitably, it had. Over the intervening years, they had kept in touch but they hadn't seen as much of each other as they had before. David was always incredibly busy and in demand; he now had his own evening television show on ITV, the new commercial television network, and had become a huge household name. Although she missed him, Greta understood. He had to find his own future, meet other women.

But today, she needed him. She picked up the receiver and dialled his number.

David answered straight away. 'Hello.'

'David, it's Greta.'

'Greta!' His voice was warm. 'How are you?'

'Very well, thank you.'

'And Cheska?'

'She's fine. She started her new film a few days ago.'

'Really? Aren't you with her?'

'Er, no, not today. I had a few things to do so Cheska gave me the day off. I was wondering, do you fancy meeting for lunch? I have to go in to town to do a little shopping. We could go to the Savoy. My treat.'

'Oh Greta, I'd love to, but I'm afraid I've got a prior engagement.'

'Not to worry. Next week, maybe?'

'Oh dear, I can't, I'm afraid. I'm very tied up with the television show at the moment, but I'd love to meet up when things calm down a little. Can I ring you later in the week and we'll make a plan?'

'Okay.'

'Good. Sorry to rush off, but the studio car's just arrived. Goodbye, Greta.'

'Yes, goodbye, David.'

Greta put the telephone down, walked slowly to the window and stared down onto the street below. She checked her watch again and saw it was only five to eleven. Without Cheska, she had nothing.

And Greta knew she was losing her.

# 25

Cheska spent the next two weeks in a haze of love and confusion.

Most of her scenes were with Bobby Cross. He was chatty, very flirtatious and treated her like a grown-up. She longed to fire back some witty retorts, but she found herself totally tongue-tied when they were standing together waiting for a take. Unlike the other girls, who fluttered their eyelashes and flirted back, Cheska had no idea what to say or how to act.

And now she had her freedom during the day, the evenings at home with her mother felt uncomfortable. When she arrived back at the apartment after the day's filming, Greta would be eagerly waiting for her and Cheska would have to spend the evening going over every detail of the day's events. A delicious supper would be placed in front of her and she would do her best to eat it, even though she'd had a large lunch on set. The atmosphere was claustrophobic and she was always grateful when it was time for her to go to bed and she could shut her door and fall asleep, dreaming of Bobby.

*

'Okay, folks. That's a wrap. We meet bright and early in the foyer of the Grand Hotel in Brighton on Monday morning. If you haven't finalised your travel arrangements, speak to Zoe. She has all the details.'

'It'll be fun, won't it?'

'Sorry?' said Cheska, turning to Bobby.

'I said, Brighton will be fun. We're staying in the same hotel, you know.' Bobby winked.

'Yes,' she replied, blushing furiously.

At that moment, Zoe came up to them. 'Now, Cheska, I've booked a twin room for you and your mother. The car will pick you both up on Sunday afternoon at four.'

Cheska turned and saw Bobby frowning.

'Er, no, Zoe, I won't be needing a twin room. My mother isn't coming with me.'

She looked at Bobby, who smiled in approval. 'See you Sunday night, darlin'.'

'Okay, then,' said Zoe. 'Any problems, you have my home number.'

Later that night she and Greta had their first major argument. Cheska was adamant that she was going to Brighton alone; her mother just as vehement that she was going with her.

'You're too young to be by yourself in a strange town, Cheska! I'm sorry, but you're not going alone, and that's final.'

'Mother, don't you understand that I'm not a baby any more? Why won't you let me grow up? If I can't go by myself, then I'm not going at all!' She burst into tears, ran from the sitting room and slammed her bedroom door behind her.

In despair, Greta picked up the receiver and dialled Leon's home number. He listened sympathetically as she explained the problem.

'The point is, Leon, that Cheska is too young to be staying by herself. She thinks she's so grown-up, but she's not. She says she refuses to go if I insist on accompanying her.'

'Greta, I understand your concern, but Brighton is hardly the end of the universe, is it? It's only an hour or so from London, and Cheska will be staying in a hotel full of cast and crew. As a matter of fact, I'm going to be down there next week, anyway, so I can keep an eye on her. This is probably just an adolescent tantrum. If I were you, I'd let her go by herself and find out how much she misses you. And, to be frank, for the sake of the film, we want Cheska as happy and relaxed as possible. Charles says she's turning in a great performance so far.'

'All right,' said Greta eventually. 'I'll tell her she can go alone. But I want you to promise me you'll make sure that she's in bed by ten every night. No going out in the evenings. I know what location parties can be like.'

'I promise, and really, try not to worry. Cheska will be absolutely fine. Oh, and by the way, could you fit in a lunch at some point in the next couple of weeks? I've had a very interesting call from an American producer. He operates from LA, but he's a friend of Charles's and has been over here for the past few days. He's seen some of the rushes and thinks Cheska might be able to make it really big in Hollywood.'

'Well, I have a few things on next week,' Greta lied, wanting to keep up appearances, 'but I could make it the following Monday.'

'Good, good,' replied Leon. 'Let's meet at the Ivy at one. And don't worry, I'll look after Cheska for you.'

She put down the receiver and wondered what on earth she was going to do by herself whilst Cheska was away.

Cheska sat in the bath in her suite at the Grand Hotel in Brighton, soaping her legs, and feeling miserable and depressed. The day's filming had been a nightmare. They had been trying to shoot the scene on Brighton beach where she and Bobby had their first kiss. The weather had been dreadful – a gale howling around their ears – and she had been so nervous about The Kiss she'd kept fluffing her lines.

In the end, with the weather worsening and tempers fraying, Charles Day had called an early wrap.

'Don't worry,' Charles had said earlier as they had walked along the promenade back to the hotel. 'We'll go again tomorrow after a good night's sleep, okay?'

Cheska had nodded, run upstairs to her suite and flung herself onto her bed in tears.

'Oh, Jimmy, isn't this wonderful? I've never felt so happy!' Cheska repeated the simple line that led into The Kiss as she stepped out of the bath and dried herself. The rest of the cast and crew were having dinner downstairs, but she didn't feel like joining them. She was too embarrassed. She decided to order some sandwiches from room service and have an early night.

The telephone in her bedroom rang and she walked from the bathroom to answer it. 'Hello?'

'Darling, it's Mummy. How are you?'

'Fine.'

'How did filming go today?'

'Very well.'

'Good. Are you eating?'

'Of course I am!'

'No need to shout, Cheska. I'm just concerned about you.'

'Mummy, I've only been away a day.'

'You're not too lonely by yourself, are you?'

'No. I've got to go now and learn my lines for tomorrow.'

'Yes, of course. As long as you're all right.'

'I am.'

'Oh, and Cheska, don't forget to take your pills, will you?'

'No, Mummy. Goodnight.'

Cheska put down the receiver and fell back onto the bed in irritation.

Charles Day was having a drink with Bobby in the hotel bar. As they talked, they were constantly interrupted by blushing teenagers holding out scraps of paper for Bobby to sign.

'The problem is there's no chemistry between you and Cheska Hammond at the moment. This is her first adult role and she's having problems. Every time you tried to kiss her on camera today she looked scared out of her wits.'

'Yeah, she definitely needs to loosen up,' agreed Bobby.

'The whole point of the film is the sexual buzz between the two of you. If that doesn't jump out at the audience, then the film goes up in smoke. Maybe she'll have calmed down by tomorrow. Cheska's a great actress, but she's used to playing Little Girl Lost, not Sex Kitten.'

'I'll bet she's a right little goer under all that uptightness,' muttered Bobby. 'Listen, do we need to shoot that beach scene tomorrow?'

Charles shrugged. 'I suppose we could reschedule it to later in the week. Why?'

'Give me a few days, and I'll have your little problem sorted for you, okay?'

'All right, but tread carefully. Cheska may look like a blonde bombshell but she's a complete innocent. Her mother has kept her under lock and key up until now.'

'Kid gloves, mate, kid gloves,' murmured Bobby, grinning.

The telephone rang again in Cheska's room at half past nine, just as she had switched off the light.

'Hello?'

'Cheska, Bobby here. Where've you been hiding yourself all night?'

'Oh—' She gulped in shock at the sound of his voice. 'I was tired, that's all.'

'Well, now you've had a little rest get your backside down here. I'm taking you partying.'

'Well, I . . . I'm in my nightie, I—'

'Sounds good to me. Wear that. See you in the bar in ten minutes. Goodbye.'

The line went dead in Cheska's hand.

'Hey, baby doll! Love the outfit!'

Bobby was standing by the bar with some of the crew when Cheska came downstairs. She blushed at his comment on her corduroy pinafore dress and woollen tights.

'I was cold,' she said quietly.

'Come here.' Bobby opened his arms to her. 'I'll soon warm you up. I won't eat you, promise.'

Reluctantly, Cheska stepped closer, and he pulled her towards him.

'You shouldn't be hiding that great body, that's all,' he whispered, nuzzling her ear. 'Now, you already know Ben, the electrician, commonly known as Sparks, and Jimmy, or Boom, who picks up our dulcet tones on his mikes.'

''Ow do,' nodded Sparks, lighting a cigarette.

'Drink?' asked Bobby.

'Er, Coke, please.'

'One Coke, please, with a dash of rum to warm her up,' Bobby said to the barman.

'Oh, I don't think—'

'Come on, Cheska, try it. You're a big girl now.' Bobby handed her the glass. He pulled up a stool and she perched on it uncomfortably as he chatted to Sparks and Boom.

'All right, baby?' Bobby smiled at her.

'Yes, fine.'

'Okay, drink up and let's shift. Got a coat?'

'It's in my room.'

'You'll just have to cuddle up to me, then, won't you?' Bobby helped her down from the stool and they followed Sparks and Boom through the hotel lobby and out into the cold night. Bobby put his arm around her and they set off along the seafront.

'Where are we going?' she asked.

'To a club I know. You'll enjoy it. When I was an unknown singer, the owner gave me a spot. It's a great place.'

A few hundred yards along the street, Cheska followed

Bobby down a flight of steps. The room was packed with young people jiving to an Elvis Presley number played by a band on a small stage.

'Sit there and I'll get you a drink.' Bobby indicated a table in a corner and ambled off with Boom to the bar.

Cheska sat down and Sparks sat next to her. He opened a tin and began rubbing something brown between his fingers and letting it drop into a cigarette paper. He added tobacco, rolled up the cigarette and lit it.

'Smoke?' he offered Cheska.

'I don't, thanks.'

Sparks shrugged. He dragged hard on the reefer, letting the smoke stream slowly out of his nostrils. He nodded contentedly. 'Good stuff, good stuff.'

Bobby arrived back with the drinks and sat down next to her. 'All right, darlin'?'

She nodded, wide-eyed, and reached for her drink.

Bobby placed a proprietorial arm around her shoulder. 'You know, I've been waiting for a chance for you and me to get together.'

'Have you?' Cheska said in surprise.

'Yeah. You're one of the cutest chicks I've seen in years. C'mon.' Bobby pulled her to her feet. 'Let's go and dance.'

As they stepped onto the crowded floor, the band began to play a haunting melody.

'This song's called "Moon River" and it's the theme tune from that new film *Breakfast at Tiffany's*. I've heard the version they're releasing over here next month and it's gonna be a monster hit.' Bobby held Cheska close and crooned the words into her ear. 'Maybe I'll take you to see the film. That Audrey Hepburn's a bit of all right.'

When the song finished, they separated and clapped. 'Having a good time?' he asked her.

'Yes, thank you.'

'Ladies and gentlemen,' came a sudden voice from the microphone. 'I'm sure you've all noticed we have a star in our midst. I'm proud to say that it was this very club that gave Bobby Cross his first break. Bobby, please would you return the favour now and come up here and sing for us?'

A rousing cheer went up as Bobby waved modestly and made his way up onto the stage. He took the microphone and Cheska made her way back to the table.

'Thanks, ladies and gents. I'd like to perform my new song "The Madness of Love", which I dedicate to a friend of mine, the lovely Miss Cheska Hammond.' Slinging a borrowed guitar over his shoulder, Bobby began to sing the slow ballad. 'Yes, that's the madness of love . . .' he crooned, staring right at her, and Cheska watched transfixed, unable to break eye contact. When the song finished there was loud applause and calls for more. Bobby went into another of his hits, an up-tempo song that soon filled the dance floor.

Cheska reached for her drink and Bobby winked at her. Could he be interested in her? He was certainly acting as if he was. She giggled, as a sudden delicious feeling of happiness rose up inside her.

Bobby came over to her and pulled her up for a dance.

'Having fun, sweetheart?'

'Oh yes, Bobby. This place is great.'

'Yeah, it is.' His hands gently caressed her waist. 'And you're beautiful, do you know that?'

After a heavenly couple of dances, Bobby introduced Cheska to Bill, the club's owner.

'I remember coming to see you in *Little Girl Lost*. Grown up a bit since then, haven't you?' he said approvingly.

'She sure has,' nodded Bobby, as he ran a hand down her back.

The club had begun to empty and when Cheska and Bobby got back to their table Boom and Sparks had vanished.

'Probably pulled a couple of chicks and slunk away,' Bobby remarked as he led Cheska by the hand up the stairs and outside.

The wind had picked up since earlier, whipping Cheska's hair into a wild mane around her face.

'C'mon, let's brave the walk back to the hotel. I love the weather when it's stormy like this.' Bobby pulled her across the road and leant on the railing that overlooked the beach. 'Those waves are so powerful. We may think we're in control, but no one can stop that.' He pointed at the dark mass of crashing sea.

Cheska shivered involuntarily, from the freezing wind but also from excitement.

'Sorry, baby. Take this.' He took off his jacket and wrapped it around her shoulders. He tipped her chin up towards him. 'You know, you really are gorgeous. I understand why, in the film, Jimmy's prepared to throw up everything for you. So, have you ever been kissed?'

'No.'

'Well, give me the honour of being the first.' Bobby put his lips to hers and touched them gently.

Cheska felt the tension in her body ease away as he teased her mouth open. Tentatively, she allowed her own tongue to touch his and, realising there was nothing much more to it than that, she relaxed and began to enjoy it.

Eventually, Bobby broke away. 'Boy, you're a fast learner,' he quipped as he wrapped his arms around her. 'Romantic this, isn't it? Alone on a deserted seafront in the middle of the night, the wind howling, the sea crashing. You never forget your first kiss, Cheska.'

'Where was yours?'

'I can't remember!' He laughed. 'Come on. We'll both be in bed with double pneumonia by tomorrow if we don't get our backsides inside soon! Mind you, if I was snuggled up next to you, I wouldn't half mind.'

They ran back to the warmth of the hotel and Bobby escorted Cheska up to her suite.

'You know I'd like to come inside with you, baby, but I won't rush you. Dinner tomorrow night?' he asked her, kissing her gently on the forehead.

Cheska could only nod silently in agreement.

'Night. Sleep tight.' With a wave, he disappeared along the corridor.

Back in her room, she changed back into her nightdress. Sitting down to brush her hair, she looked at the tranquilliser and the glass of water sitting on the bedside table.

She wouldn't take it. Tonight she felt fabulous and she didn't want anything to dull the feeling. She lay down in the cold bed and put her head under the sheets to try to warm up, reliving every second of the wonderful evening she'd just had.

# 26

'All right, Bobby, I want you to swing Cheska round in your arms. Cheska, you throw your head back and laugh, then look into Bobby's eyes. Bobby, lean forward and kiss her.'

Standing on the windswept, freezing beach, Bobby winked at Cheska. 'Right, let's go for a take before it pisses down,' said Charles, looking up at the sky.

'You all right, sweetheart? You look half frozen. Come here,' said Bobby, cuddling her against him.

Cheska relaxed into his arms. Her feet were numb, the wind was making her eyes water, but she had never felt happier.

'Scene five. Take one.' The clapperboard snapped in front of their faces.

'Action!' shouted Charles. Bobby lifted Cheska off her feet and swung her round in his arms. She threw back her head, laughing, then looked into his eyes. He smiled at her and moved his lips towards her. Cheska shuddered involuntarily as he kissed her. She put her arms round his neck and closed her eyes.

'Cut! . . . I said "Cut!", you two,' laughed Charles, and

eventually Bobby and Cheska pulled apart. Cheska blushed. Most of the crew were grinning at her. She glanced at Leon, who was standing behind the camera. He winked and gave her a thumbs-up sign.

'I'll just check the gate, but if that's okay, then the scene's in the can. Great stuff, you two,' said Charles, walking over to congratulate them. 'Cheska, you've finished for the day. Get back to the hotel and straight into a hot bath. I don't want that agent of yours suing me for negligence.'

'I'll walk her back to the hotel and make sure she does just that,' said Leon. Putting an arm round Cheska's shoulder, he led her away. She turned and gave Bobby a small wave goodbye.

'See you later, sweetheart,' shouted Bobby, before turning to Charles with a grin. 'Told you I'd sort it, didn't I? Not that it hasn't been an enjoyable process.'

'Thanks, but just watch your step. With your – er – situation, we don't want anyone upset.'

'Discretion is my middle name, Charles, you know that.'

'I'm just pointing out that it's obvious to everyone that Cheska's got a huge crush on you, and we don't want any tantrums holding up production.'

'I'll treat her like a piece of Dresden china for the next few weeks, promise.' Bobby nodded at Charles, then set off up the beach towards the billowing make-up tent.

'Charles is thrilled with you,' said Leon as he and Cheska were propelled by the wind along the seafront towards the hotel. 'He says it's the best performance you've ever given. I was telling your mother that I've had a call from an

American producer. If this film is the hit everyone expects it to be, I think Hollywood will be beckoning.'

'But I didn't think Hollywood was interested in me.'

'They weren't when you were younger. They had their own crop of child stars. But now you've matured things are different. Look at what a big star Liz Taylor has become over there. Your mother is arranging passports for you both and I'm helping to sort out the visas. When this film is in the can, we'll fly you out.'

'Leon' – Cheska pulled her hair away from her face – 'I'm not going home this weekend.'

'Right. Have you told your mother?'

'No. I wondered, well . . . would you tell her? Say we're running over schedule or something and we have to do some extra filming on Saturday and Sunday?'

'You want me to lie for you, Cheska?'

She stopped walking and faced him. 'Oh Leon, please! You know what my mother's like! She's so overprotective I can hardly breathe.'

'I presume the real reason you want to stay in Brighton is to do with your co-star?'

'Sort of, but mainly I just thought it would be really nice to have a whole weekend to myself for the first time in my whole life.'

Leon regarded his client thoughtfully. Now that Greta wasn't there to speak for and organise her, Cheska's personality was slowly beginning to assert itself. The chemistry between her and Bobby was obvious. Morally, he knew he should tell her, warn her what she was getting into and try to steer her away. Yet, he equivocated with himself, surely the worst that could happen was that she would nurse a broken heart for a while? Everyone had to fall in love for the first time and it would do her no harm whilst she did so to convey that emotion on film. And, after all, her private life was really none of his business.

'Okay, Cheska,' he said finally. 'I'll tell your mother for you.'

'Anyway, Cheska asked me to send her love and apologies. She says she'll see you next week.'

'Didn't she ask if I would come down to Brighton?' Greta asked, nervously lighting a cigarette. It was a habit she'd taken up again recently, out of sheer boredom.

'To be honest, the weather is dreadful down here and it's played havoc with the film schedule. For the next few days they're out on location most of the time and doing some night shoots, too.' The lies fell smoothly from Leon's lips. 'If I were you, I'd stay indoors in London.'

'I suppose you're right. Just promise me that my little girl's all right and that you're keeping an eye on her.'

'She's just fine, Greta, believe me. And turning in a great performance. So, see you at the Ivy on Monday?'

'Yes, thank you, Leon. Goodbye.'

Greta put down the telephone and listened to the silence in the apartment. It was broken only by the clock on the mantelpiece slowly ticking away the seconds. The past few days had seemed endless. Only the thought of Cheska arriving home tonight had been keeping up her spirits. She had cooked shepherd's pie, Cheska's favourite, and could smell its enticing aroma emanating from the kitchen. She glanced at the table, already set for two.

She had no girlfriends to call, nothing to do and

nowhere to go. Her mind flickered for a moment towards David. Perhaps she had been mad to refuse his marriage proposal, to devote her life to Cheska's career, when she might – just might – have found happiness for herself. *No*, she told herself firmly; she'd chosen to close that door and it would never be opened to her again.

All that was left was to face the harsh reality that Cheska was making her redundant after nearly sixteen years of devoted service.

Greta had believed it could never happen to her again. But it seemed that, once more, she was entirely alone.

'Oh darlin', if you only knew how much I've wanted to do this,' Bobby whispered into Cheska's ear as he removed the last piece of clothing from her slim young body. 'Let me look at you.'

Bobby knelt above her on his hotel bed, taking in the newly developed contours of her hips, waist and breasts, the soft light casting dancing shadows over her creamy skin. He normally preferred a little more flesh on his women, but still, Cheska's adolescent body made for an enticing sight.

She smiled shyly up at him as he stripped off his shirt, trousers and then his underwear. Bobby leant forward and licked her ear with his tongue. 'Let's take it slowly. I want to enjoy all of you.'

Cheska closed her eyes as Bobby's tongue moved from her ear and down to her neck. She felt his teeth give her skin gentle nips as his mouth moved down to caress each of her breasts in turn. She lay wondering if what she was allowing Bobby to do was terribly wrong, but her body was telling her it was the most natural thing in the world.

Bobby rose above her again, his hands reaching for something on the bedside table. 'Gotta keep you safe, darlin',' he said. 'Right, ready?'

As he positioned his body over hers, Cheska raised her head. 'Bobby?'

'Yes?'

'Do you . . . do you love me?'

''Course I do, baby. You're so gorgeous.' He kissed her then, hard on the mouth, and as she responded she felt him enter her.

Cheska gasped loudly as a sharp pain ripped through her.

'It'll get better from here on, you'll see,' he soothed. 'Oh baby, you feel so great.'

Cheska watched Bobby's face just inches above hers as he began to move faster, his muscular arms either side of her body. Then, with a sudden moan he rolled away and fell onto the pillows beside her.

Cheska lay watching the flickering flames in the fireplace, wondering if what she'd just experienced was how it was meant to be. A hand trailed across her breast.

'You okay? You're very quiet.'

'I think so.'

'Don't worry. The first time is always the worst, but the night is young and I'm gonna show you what lovemaking can really be like.'

Cheska arrived on set on Monday morning feeling as though she'd been caught in a tornado and set down in the land of Oz. Her body was covered in small bruises, the result of elbows and knees jamming together in moments of passion. After forty-eight hours spent in bed with Bobby, the centre of her was sore and tender, her legs wobbly, like jelly.

'Hi, Cheska. Have a good weekend?' Charles took in her dancing eyes and high colour.

'Oh yes, thank you,' she assured him. 'The best weekend of my life.'

# 27

'I won't be in until late, Mummy. We're shooting some night scenes. Bye,' Cheska called, opening the front door to leave the apartment and slamming it behind her before Greta had a chance to reply.

She breathed a sigh of relief as she slid onto the soft, butter-coloured leather seat of the waiting studio car. After the freedom she'd experienced in Brighton, coming back to London and her mother had felt more claustrophobic than ever. She couldn't wait to leave in the mornings. Bobby had found them a small bed and breakfast in Bethnal Green, close to the school being used as the location for the film. The two of them would disappear off at the end of the day's shoot to make love. Cheska usually just told her mother filming had run over. Lying to her had become second nature.

Half an hour later the car pulled up at the school gates. Cheska checked her reflection in the rear-view mirror and got out, her heart beating in anticipation of seeing Bobby.

'Wouldn't it be wonderful if we could stay together for the whole night like we did in Brighton?' murmured Cheska.

'Yeah,' Bobby replied, throwing her underwear to her as she lay on the bed. 'Shake a leg, baby. I gotta go.'

'Where to?'

'Oh, just meeting some people.'

'Can I come with you?'

'Not tonight. Anyway, that mother of yours will have you for breakfast if you're not home by ten.'

'Could we go out together some other night? You know, to a club?' Cheska climbed reluctantly out of the rumpled sheets and began to dress.

'Maybe.'

'When?'

'Soon.' Bobby sounded irritated.

'Filming's nearly over. Only a week left. Then what will we do?'

'We'll work something out. C'mon, Cheska. It's gone half past nine.'

'Sorry, Bobby.' She followed him obediently out of the room and they walked down the stairs.

'See you tomorrow.' Bobby kissed her on the cheek as he hailed her a taxi outside.

'I love you,' she whispered before stepping inside.

'Me too. Bye, baby.'

Cheska waved at him through the back window of the taxi and wondered where he was going. She knew so little about him, she realised, not even where he lived. But soon she would know everything about him, share his life completely, not just be a small part of it.

She was sure Bobby would ask her to marry him. After all, in her films, when two people fell in love, marriage was always the next step.

When she arrived back at the apartment she turned the key in the lock, hoping her mother would have gone to bed. With a sigh, she saw that the lights were still on in the sitting room. Greta was on the sofa in her dressing gown, watching television.

'Hello, Mummy.'

Greta smiled tightly. 'Hard night, was it?'

'Yes.' Cheska yawned. 'Would you mind if I went straight to bed? I'm exhausted.'

'Come and sit down while I make you a cup of tea. I want to talk to you about something.'

Cheska sighed as Greta went into the kitchen and filled the kettle. She sat down on the sofa and wished it wasn't the weekend tomorrow. It meant there were two whole days until she saw Bobby again.

Greta came back into the sitting room carrying a tray with a teapot, milk jug and two cups. She set it down and poured the milk and tea very slowly and deliberately. 'There you are. It should warm you up after a long night out in the cold. That is where you've been, isn't it?'

'Yes. It was freezing.' Cheska gave a shiver and sipped the tea.

'It's odd, because I had a telephone call from Charles Day tonight. At about seven o'clock.'

'Oh? What about?'

'A change of schedule next week. It seems the actress playing your mother has gone down with a nasty stomach bug and they want to leave her scenes until the end of the week to give her time to recover.'

'Oh.'

'It's peculiar, isn't it?' Greta sipped her tea.

'What is?'

'That Charles Day would have to call to tell you something when he was meant to be directing you in a scene at the very same time.'

'Oh, well, the thing was that Charles wasn't feeling too well either tonight, so the assistant took over,' lied Cheska frantically.

'Really? And what about the past two weeks? I asked Charles if you'd been filming in the evenings, and he said no. So the question is, Cheska, if you haven't been on set, where on earth *have* you been?'

'Just out,' Cheska replied quietly.

'"Just out". May I ask with whom?'

'People from the film. Friends, you know, Mummy.'

'And would "people" by any chance include Bobby Cross?'

'Sometimes.'

'Don't you *dare* lie to me, Cheska! You're insulting my intelligence!'

'I'm not lying, Mummy.'

'Cheska, please. It's bad enough that, because of you, I made a fool of myself on the phone to Charles Day, but to continue to lie so blatantly to my face, well—'

'All right, Mummy!' Cheska stood up. 'Yes! I have been with Bobby! I love him and he loves me, and we're going to be married one day! I didn't tell you because I knew that, not in a million years, would you allow me to have an ordinary thing like a boyfriend!'

'Boyfriend? I hardly think Mr Cross fits into that category, do you? He must be at least ten years older than you, Cheska!'

'What does age matter? What about my father? You told me he was much older than you. If you love someone, it makes no difference, does it?' Cheska spat out the words venomously.

'Let's both calm down, shall we?' Greta wiped her hand across her forehead, trying to control her anger. 'Look, darling, please understand that I'm hurt because you didn't tell me what you were doing. I thought we always told each other the truth?'

'But can't you see I'm growing up? I have to be allowed to have some secrets.'

'I know that. I do appreciate that you have your own life to lead, and that I can only play a small part in it from now on.'

'Oh, please! Don't try and make me feel guilty. I'm going to bed.' Cheska began walking towards the door.

'I'm sorry. I didn't mean that to sound the way it did,' Greta said quickly, knowing that, whatever she felt, she was in danger of losing Cheska completely if she didn't change tack. She forced a smile. 'Why don't you tell me about Bobby?'

Cheska stopped in her tracks and turned back, her eyes filling with warmth at the sound of his name. 'What do you want to know about him?'

'Oh, what's he like, the things you do together. I understand you're growing up and I want to be your friend as well as your mother.'

'Well,' she began tentatively, then, as her mother smiled at her encouragingly, she opened up and talked about Bobby, pouring out the way she felt.

'So, Bobby was the reason you stayed down in Brighton for the weekend?'

'Yes. I'm really sorry, Mummy. We just wanted to spend some time together, that's all.'

'Did Leon know the truth?'

'Er, no, not really,' Cheska replied shiftily. 'Don't blame him. I asked him to ring you.'

'So you think you're in love with Bobby?'

'Oh yes, definitely.'

'And you think he's in love with you?'

'I'm sure of it.'

'Cheska, you're not . . . you're not sleeping with him, are you?'

'Of course not!' Cheska's years of experience in front of the camera came into play and she managed to look suitably horrified.

'Well, that's something. Men are strange creatures, you know. I'm sure Bobby isn't like that, of course, but you need to be aware that some of them are only after one thing. I know the world has changed, but it's still best to wait a while, until you're absolutely sure.'

'Of course, Mummy.'

'You will tell me, won't you, if Bobby asks you to sleep with him?'

Cheska blushed and lowered her eyes. 'Yes.'

'We've never really discussed the facts of life, but I suppose you know by now how everything . . . works. And what can happen if you're not careful. If anything . . . happened to you, it could destroy your future. Come and sit next to me, darling.' She patted the sofa next to her and folded her arms around her daughter as she stroked her hair. 'I remember my first love well. I don't think you ever forget.'

'Bobby said something like that. Who was yours?'

'He was an American officer, over here in London during the war. I was devastated when he left, thought I'd never get over it. Of course, I did, in time. Uncle David helped me a lot.'

'Do you love David? You used to see him all the time and now you don't.'

'Yes, I do, Cheska, we've known each other a very long time. But we're also great friends, which is very important too.'

'Like a brother, you mean?'

'I suppose so, yes. To be honest, men and I have never seemed to be a good combination. They've caused me more problems than they've given me happiness. Love is a very strange thing, Cheska. It can change your life, make you do things that, in the cold light of day, you'd know were wrong.'

'The madness of love,' murmured Cheska. 'That's Bobby's new song.'

'And I hope you can understand that I don't want to see you tread the same path as I did. Fall in love by all means, but always keep something for yourself. Forge your own future, without depending on a man. Now, I think it's time you went to bed.'

Cheska sat up. 'Thank you, Mummy, for being so . . . understanding. I'm sorry I lied to you.'

'I know, darling. I just want you to remember that I'm your friend, not your enemy. And I'm always here if there's something you want to talk about.'

Cheska hugged Greta impulsively. 'I love you, Mummy.'

'And I love you, too. Now, off to bed with you.'

'Goodnight, then.' She rose from the sofa.

'Oh, by the way, our passports arrived this morning, and Leon is organising the visas for America. It'll be exciting to visit Hollywood, won't it?'

'Yes,' Cheska answered half-heartedly.

'Goodnight, darling, and don't forget to take your tablet.'

'I won't.'

Greta watched her daughter walk slowly out of the room. She closed her eyes, in relief, feeling calmer than she had for weeks. It was imperative that Cheska trusted her. When the relationship with Bobby Cross ended, as Greta knew it would, she'd be there to pick up the pieces. It would be she to whom Cheska would turn for comfort. And her daughter would come back to her, where she belonged.

After Cheska had flushed the tablet down the lavatory, she lay in bed thinking about what her mother had said. It was the most grown-up conversation she'd ever had with her. She smiled. Rather than tearing them further apart, Bobby had brought them closer together. She liked the thought of that. And she was sure that when they married, even though she would have to live with Bobby, there was no reason why her mother couldn't be a big part of their future.

One part of the conversation disturbed her, though.

'Always keep something for yourself . . .'

She sighed and turned over. That was something she couldn't do. Bobby had all of her. If he asked her tomorrow to give up her career and move with him to the other side of the world, she'd go willingly.

Bobby Cross was her destiny. He owned her, body and soul.

# 28

On Sunday evening Cheska went down with the same stomach bug that had affected the actress playing her mother in the film. She spent most of the night in the bathroom being violently ill.

At seven o'clock on Monday morning, as she lay in bed feeling weak and wretched, Greta came into her bedroom.

'I've called Charles and told him you're far too poorly to work today. He sends his love and told me to tell you not to worry. They can shoot around you for the next couple of days.'

'Oh, but—' Cheska's eyes filled with tears at the thought of not seeing Bobby for another forty-eight hours.

'There, there, darling. Could you manage to take your tablet?' Greta offered it to her daughter with a glass of water.

Cheska shook her head and turned away miserably.

Greta arranged her covers and swept her matted hair back from her forehead. 'Try to get some sleep now, darling. I'm sure this'll pass as quickly as it came.'

*

The following day Cheska was feeling better and on Wednesday she told her mother she was well enough to go back to work.

'But you haven't eaten anything for the past two days. I think you should stay in bed another day at least.'

'No, Mummy, I'm going. The shoot's due to wrap on Friday and they've already had to change the schedule because of me. I'm a pro, remember? That's what you've taught me.'

Greta couldn't disagree, so Cheska got out of bed and dressed. However ghastly she felt physically, the strain of going another day without seeing Bobby was far worse. She wondered how she would possibly cope when filming finished and she no longer saw him every day.

She staggered through the day's shoot, feeling dizzy and faint, until Charles came up to her, put an arm round her shoulders and told her he was sending her home. 'Go and have an early night, sweetheart. We can do some exterior stuff with Bobby.'

Cheska looked over at Bobby, who was laughing with one of the make-up girls. She'd hoped he might suggest they slip away together, but he'd hardly spoken to her all day. She watched as he put an arm round the girl, hugged her, then walked off. She ran to catch up with him. 'Bobby, Bobby!'

He stopped and turned to her. 'Hello, baby. Boy, you look dreadful.'

'I'm okay. Shall we go to the bed and breakfast tonight?'

'I thought Charles was sending you home?'

'He is, but I could meet you later.'

'And give me your bug? I don't think so.' He chuckled.

'Sorry, baby, I didn't mean that the way it sounded. Look, you go home and tuck yourself up in bed.'

'What about tomorrow night, then?'

'Well, it sounds as if we're gonna be shooting for most of tomorrow evening to make up for lost time. But there's the end-of-shoot party on Friday. We'll see each other then, okay?'

'Okay.' Cheska felt crushed. At the party, they'd be surrounded by the rest of the cast and crew, which wasn't exactly what she'd had in mind.

'Bye, darlin'.' Bobby waved casually as he walked away.

All Cheska's scenes were finished by midday on Friday. Charles gave her a hug and told her she'd been wonderful. She hung around for lunch, just in case Bobby was there, but he'd disappeared. With a sigh, Cheska left the school and got into the car that was waiting for her.

'Home, miss?' asked the driver.

'Yes . . . er . . . no. Could you take me into the West End, please?'

'Sure.' He started the engine and they set off. Cheska stared out of the window as they drove down Regent Street. Shoppers were wrapped up warmly against the chilly October afternoon.

'Here we go, love. You take care now.'

'Thanks,' Cheska said, stepping out of the car. 'Now where should I start?' she murmured to herself. She looked in the window of Marshall & Snelgrove and decided it was as good a place as anywhere.

An hour and a half later she was staggering under the weight of the bags she was carrying. She'd had a wonderful time, buying her first denim jeans, a pair of brightly coloured checked ski-pants that hugged her slim hips and two turtleneck sweaters. At Mary Quant, she'd bought the most wonderful dress to wear to the party tonight – a little black number, similar to the one she'd seen Audrey Hepburn wearing in the publicity material for *Breakfast at Tiffany's*.

Cheska hailed a taxi, wondering what her mother would have to say about her purchases, and headed for home.

'Well, what do you think?' Cheska came into the sitting room and did a twirl for Greta.

Greta swallowed hard. Her daughter looked stunning. The skimpy black dress showed off her lovely figure and the way she had styled her hair on top of her head gave her an added air of elegance.

'You look absolutely beautiful, darling, but you need some jewellery. Wait here.' Greta stood up and disappeared into her bedroom, coming back with a string of pearls. 'There.' She fastened them around Cheska's neck. 'Have you got a coat? You'll catch your death in that dress.'

'Yes, Mummy.'

'Where's the party?'

'At The Village in Lower Sloane Street.'

'That's a very fashionable spot, isn't it? Well, have a wonderful time. What time will you be back?'

'I don't know. But late. Don't wait up. Goodbye, Mummy.'

'Goodbye, darling.' Greta gritted her teeth as she heard the front door shut. She faced another evening alone and thought yet again how hard it was to watch her daughter turning into an adult.

During the long, lonely days while Cheska was working, Greta had found plenty of time to think. And much of it had been spent analysing her true feelings for David.

It had begun on the night Cheska had confided in her about Bobby and asked her if she loved David. Ever since then, Greta had looked back on the once close relationship they'd shared. He'd been such a big part of her life before his proposal. And Greta had to admit she'd missed him terribly over the past five years. He'd always been there for her, undemanding and supportive, and she realised now that she had almost certainly taken him and his kindness for granted.

When he'd asked her to marry him, she'd been riding high, Cheska had filled her life, and this, added to her resolution not to allow any man near her heart, had elicited her firm refusal.

The thing she'd pondered on most was whether she missed him simply because Cheska had gone and there was now a void in her life that David was the obvious candidate to fill. Or whether it was *him* she missed.

Greta thought of the times they had spent together over the years. Not only had David provided a listening ear and sound advice, but he'd always had the ability to cheer her up when she'd been at her lowest ebb. She felt better when she was with him, and she longed now for the lightness he'd brought to her life.

She'd also begun to see a clearer picture of herself as she'd been over the past few years: her grim determination to make Cheska a star, to control her and her career to the detriment of everything else. With her heart firmly locked away, Greta knew she had become hard; all the softness that had once led her time and again into trouble had gone. Even though this meant she was safe from any further hurt, it meant there were rarely times of joy. She tried to recall the last time she'd actually laughed, and couldn't.

David made her laugh. His belief that any situation, however dire, had some humour in it somewhere provided the perfect antidote to her own tendency towards seriousness.

As Greta began to wake up from her emotional torpor, she contemplated how she had always considered love as a passionate madness that was all-consuming. Just as Cheska was feeling now with Bobby Cross. But she could see quite clearly that what her daughter was experiencing was infatuation, which was simply about physical chemistry.

And she realised that in the past, that had been her, too.

When she thought about David, it brought forth a completely different set of feelings: it was a wonderful, warm sensation that filled her and made her feel content, secure and loved. There was no play-acting like there'd been with other men; with David, she was completely herself. He knew her inside out, faults and all, yet he still loved her.

But . . . Greta closed her eyes. Was there that all-important stirring in her stomach when she thought about him? The two of them had never even kissed. She considered how she felt when she saw him on television; recently, she'd noticed how handsome he seemed to have become, but maybe he always had been and she simply hadn't noticed, caught up as she had been in the fulcrum of her own dramas.

Certainly, she felt proprietorial about him. She remembered the pang of jealousy she'd suddenly experienced a few weeks ago when she saw him in the newspaper, pictured at a premiere with a beautiful actress on his arm.

Her life had been hollow . . . empty, since she'd refused him. Greta admitted to herself that she'd been unhappy for years. Being busy with Cheska's career had papered over the cracks, but now . . .

She sighed, stood up and walked into the kitchen to make herself her nightly Horlicks. She imagined David being here with her, how he'd find a joke about something, then maybe take her in his arms and give her one of his huge cuddles, then kiss her . . .

Greta's stomach fluttered at the thought.

'Oh God,' she murmured, 'what have I done?'

The dress had exactly the effect that Cheska had hoped for. As she descended the wooden steps into the candlelit bar every head in the room turned to watch her. By the time she was at the bottom Bobby was waiting for her. He swung her round in his arms and kissed her on the cheek.

'Hey, baby. You look great!' His hands moved over her body. 'My little girl's growing up, isn't she?' he whispered, nuzzling her neck. 'C'mon, let's go and find you a drink.'

For the rest of the night Bobby was as attentive as he'd been that first week in Brighton. He didn't leave her side, holding her hand as they moved from one group of people to another. She drank every drink she was given and even tried to smoke a joint she was offered. She coughed and spluttered as Bobby laughed at her attempt.

'You'll get used to it.'

Cheska caught sight of the make-up girl he'd been talking to earlier watching Bobby and her gyrate together on the dance floor. It gave her a great feeling of satisfaction to see the disappointment in her eyes.

'I'm gonna miss you,' Bobby murmured as he swayed to the music, his body pressed close to hers.

'What do you mean?' she asked, pulling away.

'I mean, miss seeing you on the set every day.'

'And I will, too. But we can still see each other often, can't we, Bobby?'

'Of course we can. Though I've got to go away, sweetheart. Just for a few weeks.'

'Where to?'

'France. I'm doing a few gigs there. My record label wants to raise my profile on the Continent.'

'Oh.' There were tears in Cheska's eyes. 'When will you be back?'

'Before Christmas, I hope.'

'Could I come with you?'

'Not a good idea. I'm gonna be so busy, travelling from town to town. You'd be bored out of your mind.'

'I wouldn't mind, as long as I was with you.' Cheska put her head on his shoulder and smelt his familiar, spicy aftershave.

'Hey, baby, as we won't see each other for a while, how about a . . . quick goodbye present?' His hands traced the contours of her body.

'Where?' she asked, feeling light-headed from alcohol and excitement.

'Come with me.' Bobby pulled her off the dance floor, out of the room and along a dim corridor. He opened a door and led her into a small office, then locked the door behind him, grabbed Cheska and pinned her up against a wall. He kissed her, one hand rucking up her dress while the other cupped her breast.

'You are sensational,' he moaned, parting her legs and ramming himself into her.

'Bobby, shouldn't we use a—'

'All under control, baby, don't worry.' As Bobby lifted her up, Cheska's legs left the floor and curled round his hips.

'Doesn't that feel great?' Bobby crooned, moving rhythmically inside her.

Whether it was the alcohol, the danger of being caught or just Bobby, Cheska didn't know, but she'd never felt so happy, free and uninhibited. A great wave of exhilaration was building up inside her belly. She moaned in ecstasy, moving to meet his thrusts, her body begging for release. She screamed out in pleasure as it came for both of them.

Panting, they sank in a heap to the dusty floor.

'I love you, Bobby, I love you,' she whispered.

'Sorry about that. I lost control.' Bobby looked down at her and smoothed back her hair. 'It wasn't meant to work out like this, but, boy, you're one of the sexiest girls I've ever met.'

'What do you mean, "It wasn't meant to work out like this"?'

'Nothing, darlin'.' He stood up, tucked in his shirt and fastened his trousers. 'I only meant that I didn't expect to fall for my leading lady. C'mon.' He pulled her up from the floor and unlocked the door as she hastily straightened her dress.

'Bobby, you will call me when you get back from France, won't you?'

''Course I will.' He kissed her nose. 'I gotta go now. A friend's playing in a band at another club. Said I'd meet some people there and check out the scene. Goodbye, sweetheart. It's been a real pleasure.'

'But, Bobby, I haven't given you my telephone num—'

But he was off along the corridor and into the crowd before she could finish her sentence. Cheska's euphoria evaporated. She made her way to the lavatory, went into a cubicle, pulled down the toilet seat and sat with her head in her hands.

Tears fell down her cheeks as she contemplated the next few weeks without seeing Bobby. How could she possibly stand it?

# 29

Greta took far more time than usual to get ready to meet David at the Savoy. Over the past few weeks, as she'd watched Cheska moon miserably around the apartment pining over Bobby Cross, she had grown more and more certain how she felt about David.

She *did* love him, as she'd told Cheska, but now, since those first butterflies had circled her stomach, she knew she wanted him in another way, too.

'He's been right under my nose for years and I didn't see it,' she chastised her reflection in the mirror. 'Stupid, stupid woman!'

As she'd let her heart emerge from its prison, Greta had begun to tentatively imagine the life she could have had with David: how the easy, comfortable way they'd always been with each other could have given her the inner contentment that was so missing from her life. How full of love, companionship and physical closeness it would have been. Having David there to protect her, support her and enjoy the simple things in life together, rather than struggling defiantly through it all alone.

'Is it too late?' she asked her reflection.

She didn't know. All she could do was find a way to ask him.

David stood up as he saw Greta enter the Grill Room. He smiled as she walked over to him and kissed her warmly. 'How are you, Greta? It's lovely to see you. You look wonderful.'

'Oh, er . . . thank you. You too,' she said nervously.

'Did you have much trouble getting here? Most of London was brought to a standstill by the smog yesterday.'

'I walked. Getting a taxi was impossible. Mind you, I should never have worn these new shoes. My feet are killing me.' Greta indicated the Charles Jourdan alligator winkle-pickers Cheska had bought her on a shopping spree.

'They say it should have cleared by tomorrow morning,' David replied as the two of them sat down.

'Let's hope so.'

'Are you all right? You look a little harassed.'

'No, I'm, er, fine.' Greta knew she would need a couple of glasses of wine before she could pluck up the courage to speak to him about her recent revelations. 'I'm just having a bit of a time with Cheska.'

'She's not ill, is she?' He signalled to a waiter and ordered a bottle of Chablis.

'No, she's not ill, or at least, I don't think she is.'

'Would you like to order, sir?' asked the waiter politely. 'The soup of the day is tomato and basil.'

Greta glanced down at the menu. 'I'll have the soup and the Dover sole, please.'

'Good choice. I'll have the same, please.'

The waiter nodded and left them alone.

'So what exactly is the problem?'

'L-O-V-E.' Greta spelt out the letters. 'A particularly nasty case of the first-time type.'

'I see,' said David. 'I must admit I find it hard to think of Cheska experiencing adult emotions. I still think of her as a child.'

'Well, she's grown up very quickly in the past few months. Since the filming of *Please, Sir, I Love You* finished, she's hung around at home like a lost soul. She refuses to do anything except sit in her bedroom and listen to that stupid new song by Bobby Cross.'

'Oh, "The Madness of Love"? Good, isn't it?'

'Well, if you heard it fifty times a day like I have to, you might just go off it.' She raised her eyebrows and David chuckled as the waiter arrived with the wine. He opened it and poured two glasses. Greta took a large gulp from hers.

'Are the feelings reciprocated by the young man in question?'

'I don't know. He's been away for the past few weeks, which accounts for Cheska's behaviour. He might not be exactly what I had in mind as a first boyfriend but, to be honest, anything's better than seeing her so unhappy. She says she's certain he wants to marry her one day.'

'I see. And is he serious?'

'Who knows? Cheska believes so, but of course the whole idea is ridiculous. She's not yet sixteen, for goodness' sake. And he's a grown man.'

'And who exactly is he?'

'Oh, I'm sorry, I thought I'd said. It's her co-star, and crooner of that appalling song, Bobby Cross.'

Greta watched his forehead furrow. 'Oh dear, oh dear,' he sighed.

'David, I know it's hardly ideal, but why do you say it like that? Do you know the man?'

'Well, I wouldn't count him amongst my friends, but I have met him. He was a guest on my TV show a while back and he's been at a couple of Leon's parties. Leon looks after his fledging film career. I also happen to know he's married,' he said slowly.

'Oh my God.' Greta swallowed hard and wiped a hand across her forehead distractedly. 'Are you sure? I'm absolutely positive Cheska doesn't know.'

'I'm not surprised. It's a well-kept secret, as are Bobby's two young children.'

All thoughts of what she'd been so eager to tell him receded into the distance. Greta reached for her glass again and noticed her hands were shaking. 'David, I'm speechless—'

'I'm sorry, Greta, but it's better that you know. And so should Cheska. Bobby married very young, before he became a star. When his records started to sell his record company suggested that his wife and children never be mentioned in any publicity. They wanted his young female fans to think he was available.'

'But I've seen endless pictures in the papers of Bobby out with models and actresses! I just don't understand.'

'Well, as Leon puts it, Bobby and his wife have an "understanding". He's obviously become very rich and she loves a comfortable life out of the spotlight. She doesn't mind him seeing other women as long as he never divorces her. She's a devout Catholic, you see, and she's told him if he ever tries to do that, she'll blow the whistle and go public. It's what you might call a Faustian pact.'

'My God, David! If only I'd known, I could have—' Greta wrung her hands. 'So Leon knew all about Bobby?'

'Of course he did.'

'That bastard!' Greta rarely swore, but she was beside herself with fury. 'How could he?'

The waiter arrived to serve their soup. They sat in silence as he went about his business. Once he'd departed, Greta continued, 'Leon knew about Cheska's relationship with Bobby right from the start. In fact, he positively encouraged it. Cheska admitted she asked him to call me and lie to me about why she was staying in Brighton for the weekend. He must have known she was going to be with Bobby.'

'But why would Leon do that? He knows Cheska isn't even of age.'

'I don't know, David, unless it was to spite me. He's always resented the fact that Cheska listens to me rather than to him. I suppose he saw a way of coming between her and me. To become her confidant, her partner in crime. He disgusts me!'

'I don't know what to say, Greta. If it's true that he encouraged the liaison, then it's unforgivable of him. She's such an innocent, with absolutely no experience of dealing with men. And certainly not one as confident as Mr Cross. When will you tell Cheska?'

'As soon as possible. There's a producer in LA who wants her to go across to America for a screen test, but Cheska has refused even to contemplate it until she's heard from Bobby. She's obsessed, David. She really believes he's going to marry her. And that they'll live happily ever after.'

'I also know Bobby's had countless affairs, but that's all they ever amount to. He can't risk his wife spilling the beans. He'd be shown up as the charlatan he is.'

'Well, at least Cheska hasn't gone *that* far. I asked her whether she was sleeping with Bobby and she told me she wasn't.'

'And you believed her?'

'She swore to me it was the truth. Really, David, I think we're dealing with some kind of schoolgirl crush here. Or at least I hope so.'

'Tread carefully, Greta,' he advised her. 'As you've already said, Cheska has got it bad. And first love can override any moral code you've instilled in her. She's always been emotionally fragile and . . .'

'What do you mean, "emotionally fragile"?'

'Well, she's so young and therefore vulnerable – easy meat to an experienced Casanova like Mr Cross.'

'You said it,' murmured Greta. 'Look, Cheska's meeting me here early this evening for a drink before we go on to the theatre. I'll break the news to her, but I doubt she'll believe me. Could you by any chance join us? She's always been so fond of you. Maybe she'll listen if *you* tell her Bobby's married.'

'Of course, if you think it would help. I've got to go to Bush House after lunch to see the producer of my radio show, but it's very close and I can be back by about quarter to six.'

'Thank you so much. I don't think I can do this by myself.' Greta reached across the table and offered her hand to him. And despite years of trying to rid himself of his feelings for Greta – having realised it was a road to nowhere – the fact that she was again turning to him for help made him reach for her hand and squeeze it tightly.

Feeling the touch of his hand on hers reignited the thought of what she had come here to tell him. 'Actually, David, there's something else I wanted to . . . er . . . talk to you about.'

'Really? Fire away.'

'I—' Greta's courage failed her, and she sighed. 'Actually, with what you've just told me, it's not the moment, but could we meet up again for lunch early next week?'

'Of course. Is there anything wrong?'

'No, definitely not "wrong". It's just that—' Greta shrugged. 'I promise I'll explain next week after we've sorted out this Cheska problem. So' – she pulled herself together and gave him a weak smile – 'how's the television series going?'

Cheska sat nervously in the waiting room. She picked up a magazine from the pile on the scratched coffee table and flicked through it unseeingly.

The past few weeks had been dreadful. She hadn't heard from Bobby since the night of the party, nearly two months ago. She understood that he was busy in France, but the least he could have done was ring her to say hello. She'd been through hell and back, imagining all sorts of scenarios: Bobby with other girls, Bobby not loving her any more, Bobby dead . . . The only thing that comforted her was him singing to her on her gramophone, like he'd done that night in Brighton. And then she remembered and felt better. And Christmas was coming. Surely he'd be back in England for that?

But the voice had come back, tormenting her when she was awake and haunting her dreams when she managed to sleep.

*Bobby's gone . . . Bobby's gone . . . he doesn't love you any more . . .*

Cheska wondered whether it was because she hadn't taken her pills for a while that she was once more experiencing the terrible black headaches and hearing the voice, but she didn't think so. It was all because Bobby wasn't here.

Also, her monthlies had stopped coming. She'd ignored it the first time, but when nothing had happened again the previous week Cheska knew she had to see a doctor. She might be dying, and she'd need to tell Bobby if she was.

Four days ago she'd booked an appointment with a different doctor to her usual one. Dr Ferguson, a middle-aged woman, had taken Cheska into her consulting room and asked her a lot of questions, some of which had made Cheska blush. As the conversation had progressed, it began to dawn on her how little she really knew about the workings of her own body. Dr Ferguson had also given her a thorough physical examination, taken blood samples and suggested she take a pregnancy test. Cheska had gasped in horror but had agreed. Every night since then, she'd tossed and turned in bed at the thought of what might have happened to her.

And when she did sleep she had the nightmares and heard the voice. She knew the only thing that could take it all away was Bobby. He'd make her feel better.

After her mother had left for lunch with David this morning, Cheska had paced up and down her bedroom.

She was due at the doctor's to get her test results at half past two, but her mind was so confused she couldn't sit still for a second.

Then something dreadful had happened. She'd walked across to the mirror to brush her hair. But her reflection wasn't there.

She was invisible.

Choking back sobs, she'd rushed out of the flat and walked straight to the doctor's surgery, not daring to look for her image in any of the windows she passed.

'Cheska Hammond?' The receptionist eventually called her name and she stood up. Because she'd arrived so early, she'd been in the waiting room for almost an hour. 'Dr Ferguson will see you now.'

Heart beating hard, Cheska walked slowly down the corridor to the consulting room and knocked on the door.

'Hello, Dr Ferguson,' she said as she entered the room.

'Hello, Cheska. Please sit down. Now, I have the results of the tests we did a few days ago. You'll be pleased to know that you are not ill or at death's door. But the tests have confirmed what I originally thought. You are pregnant.'

Cheska burst into tears.

'There, there, it's all right.' Dr Ferguson handed Cheska a tissue. 'You said last week that you're not married, is that right?' she asked.

'Yes.'

'But you have a steady boyfriend?'

'Yes.'

'Do you think that when he hears the news he'll be prepared to do the right thing by you? It would obviously be far better for both you and the baby if he did.'

'I . . . do I have to have it?'

'Well, yes. Perhaps you don't know, dear, but abortion – which is how a woman ends an unwanted pregnancy – is illegal in Britain. So I'm afraid you have no choice.'

Cheska gulped back tears, unable to comprehend what the doctor was saying. But then . . . she began to imagine telling Bobby she was carrying his child. *Their* baby, made out of love. How could she doubt he'd marry her? Cheska felt a sudden calm descend on her. Her heartbeat slowed and she smiled at the doctor.

'Yes, I'm sure he'll stand by me and we'll get married,' she answered.

'Well, that's good news at least. Now, what I suggest is that you talk to him, and then come back and see me so we can book you into a local hospital for the birth. Do you have any other family?'

'I live with my mother.'

'Then I would tell her, too. It's best to have someone on your side in these circumstances. She might be shocked at first, but I'm sure she'll be supportive.'

'Yes, doctor, thank you.' Cheska rose from the chair. 'Goodbye.'

She left the surgery in a daze and walked out onto the busy street. The smog was still very bad and traffic was at a standstill. Dusk was beginning to descend and it was drizzling.

Cheska needed to go somewhere to think. She walked up Piccadilly, through the maze of Soho streets and went into the first coffee bar she found. Having ordered an espresso, she delved into her handbag, drew out a packet of Embassy and lit one up. It was the brand Bobby smoked and a habit she had begun recently. The smell of smoke evoked his memory and she found it comforting. She fumbled for her compact and drew it out. 'God, please let me be here, please,' she begged as she opened it. She breathed a sigh of relief as her features gazed back at her.

It was all right, all right. She wasn't invisible after all. It must have been the worry about her appointment with the doctor.

Her coffee arrived and as she sipped it, she reassured herself that the baby was the best thing that could have happened. Surely, now, Bobby would marry her and she would get her heart's desire? A blissful vision of the three of them – her, Bobby and their baby – appeared in her mind's eye, and she smiled. Then, tentatively, Cheska felt her stomach. In there was part of Bobby, a living, breathing reminder of the way he had loved her and would continue to love her in the future.

Cheska knew she had to think about the practicalities. She decided she would break the news to her mother over drinks at the Savoy this evening as she knew Greta wouldn't make a scene in a hotel. She would assure her that she and Bobby would marry as soon as possible. Her mother might be cross because she had lied a little, but she was sure Greta would forgive her when she knew she was going to be a grandmother and have a beautiful new baby to love. The screen test in Hollywood would have to be postponed indefinitely, but what was a silly film compared to her love for Bobby and their child?

The first thing she must do was ring Leon to get Bobby's telephone number in France. Draining her coffee cup, she walked to the back of the coffee shop in search of the telephone and dialled his number.

'Hello, Cheska, good to hear from you. Have you decided when you're going to America?'

'No, not exactly, Leon.'

'You really can't leave it too much longer. They won't wait forever, you know.'

'I know. Listen, Leon. I'm ringing because I need to get in touch with Bobby.'

'Bobby who?'

'Bobby Cross, of course,' Cheska said irritably. 'Do you have a telephone number for him in France?'

'In France?' Leon sounded surprised.

'Yes. That's where he is, isn't he?'

'Oh . . . er . . . yes. Of course it is.'

'It really is urgent I speak to him.'

'I see. I tell you what, why don't you leave it to me? He's . . . er . . . moving around a lot at the moment, but the next time he calls me I'll tell him to get in touch with you immediately.'

'All right, but please, Leon, tell him it's urgent.'

'I will. Everything's all right, isn't it, Cheska?'

'Oh yes, everything's fine. Goodbye.' She put the phone down then checked her watch. She had twenty minutes to get to the Savoy.

# 30

Greta was sitting in the American Bar drinking a gin and tonic and smoking a cigarette. She'd spent the past hour trying to think of exactly how she was going to break the dreadful news about Bobby Cross to Cheska.

She saw her daughter arrive and her heart skipped a beat. She watched as the men dotted around the bar followed Cheska's progress across the room. She really was maturing into a very beautiful young woman, and there was no reason why she couldn't move on from this and have any man she wanted. The thought gave Greta courage.

'Hello, Mummy.' Cheska sat down opposite her.

Greta noticed Cheska's eyes were a little too bright and there was heightened colour in her normally pale cheeks.

'Did you have a good lunch with Uncle David?' Cheska continued.

'Very pleasant. Actually, he's going to join us shortly for a drink.'

'Oh. It'll be lovely to see him.'

'Shall I get you something?'

'An orange juice, please.'

'Right.' Greta ordered from the waiter, then turned to

her daughter, at a loss to know how to begin, but then Cheska spoke.

'Mummy, I . . . have something to tell you. I know you're going to be a little upset, but I want you to know that everything is going to be fine in the end.'

'Really? What is it?'

'Well, this afternoon, I found out that Bobby and I are expecting a baby.' The words came out in a garbled rush and Cheska carried on quickly before Greta had a chance to reply. 'Please, Mummy, don't be angry with me. I know I lied to you about Bobby and me and the kind of relationship we have, but I knew you'd only worry if I told you the truth. The baby was a bit of a mistake, but now it's happened I'm so happy. It's really what I want and Bobby will be over the moon. I'm sure he'll want to marry me as soon as possible.'

Cheska saw her mother's face turn white with shock.

'I . . . Oh, Cheska.' A solitary tear appeared in her eye and trickled down her face.

'Mummy, please don't cry. Everything's going to be fine, really.'

'Excuse me, darling. I have to go to the powder room.' Greta stood up, walked briskly across the bar and down the steps to the sanctuary of the lavatories. She shut the cubicle door and nausea rose in her throat.

When she had finished being sick, she leant against the door, panting.

She had done everything – *everything* – to protect and nurture her child, to pave the way for her daughter to have the kind of love, financial security and career she had never achieved herself. And yet, after all her efforts, history was repeating itself. Cheska was pregnant by a man who didn't love her and would never marry her, even if he *were* free to do so.

'Why? Why?' Greta moaned.

'Mummy, Mummy? Are you in there? Are you okay?' It was Cheska.

'Yes, darling, I'm fine.' Greta heaved herself upright and pulled the chain. She took a deep breath, knowing she had to be strong for her daughter. The situation was just about salvageable, but she had to think fast. Putting a smile on her face, she unlocked the door. Cheska was standing, twisting her hands together, as she always did when she was nervous or upset. Greta went over to the basin, washed her hands and freshened her lipstick. Cheska watched her in silence.

'I'm sorry, darling. I think it must have been the shock of what you told me. I felt a little faint, but I'm all right now. Let's go and have our drinks, shall we? We have plenty of things to discuss.'

They walked out together and made their way back to the bar. Greta reached for her gin and took a large gulp, wishing David would hurry up.

'Mummy, please tell me you're not angry with me. I really don't want you to be upset. I'm not. I'm happy.'

Greta shook her head wearily. 'No, darling. I'm not angry, just very worried for you.'

'Well, don't be. As I said, everything's going to be fine.'

'Have you told Bobby the news?'

'Not yet, no. He's still in France, but I telephoned Leon earlier and Bobby will ring me as soon as he can. But

I know he'll be thrilled. And all it means is that we'll have to get married sooner than we planned.'

'So, Bobby has actually asked you to marry him, has he, Cheska?'

'Not in so many words, but I know it's what he wants. He loves me, Mummy, and I love him. Just think, you'll be a grandmother!'

Greta managed to keep her expression steady but, inside, her heart was breaking. She studied her daughter's earnest face and wondered if she really did have some kind of emotional problem. Or was it her own fault as a mother for shielding Cheska too fiercely from reality? Whatever the reason for it, her naivety was truly breathtaking. Cheska assumed – just as always happened in her films – that her life would have a happy ending.

Greta could wait for David no longer. She took a deep breath and reached for her daughter's hand. 'Darling, I have something to tell you. I know you may not believe me, so Uncle David is coming to confirm that I'm not lying to you. I was going to tell you anyway tonight, but with the news you've just given me it's even more important that you know the truth.'

Greta saw that Cheska's face had already hardened. Tension showed at the corners of her mouth. 'What "truth"?' she asked.

'Before I tell you, I want you to know that I love you more than anything else in the world and would never do anything to hurt you. I'd give anything to protect you from this, Cheska, but I can't. You've asked to be treated as a grown-up and now you must have the courage to behave like one. Do you understand what I'm saying?'

'Yes, Mummy. Just tell me what it is, please. Is it you? Are you ill?'

'In some ways, I wish it were that simple. Now, you're going to have to be very brave and remember that I'm on your side and will help you in any way I can.'

'Just tell me what it is, Mummy, please!'

'Cheska, darling, Bobby Cross is married. He has been for several years. He also has two small children.'

Cheska stared at her mother in silence, her face expressionless.

Greta continued. 'Uncle David told me today at lunch. Apparently it's one of the best-kept secrets in show business. A wife and children weren't good for his image as a heart-throb, so there's been nothing in the press about them. And even if he wanted to marry you, he wouldn't be able to, because his wife refuses to divorce him. What he's done to you is unforgivable, Cheska, but Uncle David says you're not the first and will certainly not be the last. I promise you, darling, it's the truth.' Greta paused and tried to gauge her daughter's reaction.

Cheska was no longer looking at her mother. She was staring off into space.

'Darling, please believe me when I say that, although the situation is difficult, it's not the end of the world. We can sort out your problem, Cheska. I'm sure you know there are ways and means. Afterwards, we could go off to America and do the screen test. Once your film opens there, every studio will be after you to sign with them. You'll soon forget Bobby and . . .'

'NO! NO! NO! I'm not listening to you, I'm not listening. You're lying! You're lying to me!' Cheska put her hands over her ears and began to shake her head from side to side.

People were starting to glance in their direction. 'Darling, please try to keep calm. I swear I'm telling you the truth. Why would I lie?'

Cheska removed her hands from her ears and stared at Greta. 'Because you can't bear the thought of losing me, that's why. Because you want me to stay your little girl forever and to keep me all to yourself. You don't ever want me to have my own life with Bobby, or with any man, for that matter. Well, it won't work, Mummy. I love Bobby and I'm going to marry him and have his baby. And if you can't handle that, then it's your problem, not mine!'

Greta shuddered as Cheska's face twisted into a hideous scowl, her rare beauty wiped away by her manic expression.

'Darling, listen to me. I understand that you're upset, but—'

'Upset? No! I'm not upset! I just feel sorry for *you*, that's all. Scared of being lonely for the rest of your life, are you?!'

'That's enough!' Greta's control shattered under the barrage of her daughter's bile. 'Let me tell you something about me and my "lonely" little life. I was eighteen when I got pregnant. Your father was an American officer who shipped out to the United States without so much as a goodbye, leaving me high and dry. I was penniless and homeless, but Uncle David saved me from destitution and sent me off to Wales. I met Owen Marchmont and married him so as to give my baby a father. When Owen began to drink, I took you to London and struggled to try and keep a roof over our heads. The only thing I've ever tried to do is to give you what I never had. Everything has been for you, Cheska. I don't want anything in return, but I do ask you to have the decency to believe what I'm telling you is true!'

Cheska smiled slowly, but her penetrating gaze was full of venom. 'Okay, Mummy. Can you tell me how you expect me to believe what you've told me about Bobby when you've obviously lied to me all these years about my real father?'

Greta crumpled. Her body sagged as all her energy left her. Slowly, she reached for her handbag, opened it and took out some money to pay the bill.

'I'm going to leave now. I suggest you wait here for Uncle David and have him confirm what I've just said. I can't do any more than tell you that I'll always be there for you if you want me, that I love you very much and have always tried to do what is best for you.' Greta stood up. 'Goodbye, Cheska.'

Cheska watched her mother walk out of the bar. And the voice began its insidious whispering.

*She's lying, she's lying . . . Bobby loves you . . . he loves you . . . She hates you, she hates you, she wants to destroy you . . .*

Cheska shook her head from side to side, closed her eyes, then opened them. Everything she saw was coloured misty shades of purple.

She stood up and followed her mother through the lobby and out of the hotel.

David was walking fast along the Strand from Bush House. The meeting had run over and he was late to meet Greta and Cheska. The smog was still dreadful, but at least patchier than it had been. As he headed towards the Savoy, he wondered if Greta had told Cheska about Bobby Cross. He stood on the pavement opposite the hotel, straining his eyes in the swirling, ice-cold mist, looking for a gap in the traffic so he could cross the road.

Before he could move, he heard the sound of tyres skidding on the wet road, a loud crash and then an ear-piercing scream. The traffic came to a standstill.

Dodging between the stationary cars, David began to cross. A small huddle of people had collected in front of a car on the other side of the road. They were looking down at someone lying there.

'Oh my God!'

'Is she dead?'

'Someone call an ambulance!'

'She must have tripped and fallen. One minute she was standing on the pavement, the next . . .'

'I couldn't see because of the smog and . . . !'

Just before he reached the circle of people David stumbled over an object lying in the road. He knelt down and picked it up.

He moaned as he cradled the dainty alligator shoe in his hand. 'No . . . *please*!' Pushing his way through the crowd, he knelt down next to the crumpled body that was lying so still. He tilted Greta's face up towards him and saw it was unmarked, just a patch of dirt and a slight graze on the cheek where she had fallen. He checked her pulse, and its weakness indicated her life was slowly draining away.

'Greta, darling Greta,' he whispered softly into her ear,

placing his cheek against hers. 'Please don't leave me. I love you, I love you . . .'

He didn't know how long it was before an ambulance pulled up beside him, lights flashing.

'Sorry, sir, could we take a look at her?' An ambulance-man was at his shoulder.

'She has a pulse, but . . . please be careful with her,' David cried.

'We'll take over from here, sir. Can you stand aside, please?'

Despairingly, David stood up, knowing he could be of little help. He watched from a distance as Greta was placed gently on a stretcher. Then he saw Cheska, standing alone under a street light a little way off. He walked over to her.

'Cheska,' he said quietly, but she didn't respond. 'Cheska.' He put an arm around her shoulders. 'It's all right. Uncle David's here.'

Cheska looked up at him, her eyes registering a glimmer of recognition.

'What happened? I—' She gave a small shake of her head and looked around her as if trying to remember where she was. 'Mummy? Where's Mummy?' Cheska's eyes searched the street in desperation.

'Cheska, I—' He pointed at the ambulance.

She pulled away from David and ran towards it. Greta was lying on the stretcher beside it whilst the ambulance crew prepared to put her inside. Her face had the colour and glassy appearance of white porcelain. Cheska let out a scream, hurled herself onto the stretcher and put her arms round Greta's limp body.

'Mummy! Mummy! I didn't mean it, I didn't mean it! Oh God! No!'

David stood behind Cheska, as he listened to her muttering into Greta's chest, then sobbing hysterically. He knelt down and tried to pull her away, but she clung on, her words muffled.

'Come on, Cheska. Come on, sweetheart. We have to let them take Mummy to the hospital.'

Cheska turned to David, a look of raw anguish on her face. Then she fainted in his arms.

# 31

In the days after the accident David shuttled between Greta in the intensive care unit and Cheska on a female medical ward at St Thomas's Hospital, in a hellish blur of anxiety.

After Cheska had fainted in the street that dreadful night, David had little choice but to stay with her, despite being frantic with worry about Greta. One of the ambulance crew had stayed behind to attend to Cheska but, as she was being examined, she came to and began screaming at the top of her lungs, then gabbling incoherently about ghosts and witches and coffins. She lashed out wildly at David when he tried to calm her. Eventually, the ambulanceman had no option but to sedate her whilst they waited for another ambulance to arrive.

Once he'd seen Cheska settled and sleeping on the ward, David had asked the nurse where he'd find Greta. Panic clutching at his heart, he took the lift to Intensive Care, not knowing whether she was alive or dead. He was informed that she was currently in a coma and that her condition was critical but stable. Visitors were out of the question.

For hours there had been nothing he could do but pace

up and down the corridor, anxiously questioning various medical personnel as they bustled in and out. They could tell him nothing, except to repeat that Greta was seriously ill.

It was two days – during which the doctors remained tight-lipped about her condition – before he was allowed in to see her. The first sight of her, rigged up to a bank of machines, tubes protruding from her mouth and nose, her face swollen and bruised, made him weep.

'Please be all right, my darling,' he whispered to her over and over again, as he sat at her bedside. 'Please, Greta, come back to me.'

'Ah, Mr Marchmont.' The consultant stood up and shook David by the hand. 'I'm Doctor Neville. Please, take a seat. I gather you're a relative of Greta's?'

'Yes, I am, I suppose, by marriage. She's also a very close friend.'

'Then I can tell you what we know so far. When she was hit by the car she suffered a badly fractured femur and severe trauma to her skull that has caused her to slip into a comatose state. It's obviously the head injury that's of the greatest concern, particularly as Greta has not yet regained consciousness, even fleetingly.'

'But surely she'll wake up eventually?'

'We're running tests, but I'm afraid there's nothing conclusive to report yet. If we don't find anything, we may transfer her to the brain injury unit at Addenbrooke's Hospital in Cambridge for further assessment.'

'So what's the prognosis at this stage, doctor?'

'As far as we can tell, we're in no danger of losing her,

if that's what you mean. Her vital signs are encouraging and we're now confident there's no internal bleeding. As to the coma, well . . . only time will tell. I'm sorry.'

David left the doctor's office with conflicting emotions. He was passionately relieved that Greta was out of danger but devastated by the possible ramifications the doctor had described. He didn't know which was worse – the thought that Greta might never wake up or that, if she did, her brain might be so damaged that her life would be untenable anyway.

Later that afternoon he made his way wearily upstairs for his daily visit to Cheska. As usual, she didn't acknowledge him but continued to lie motionless on the bed staring at a spot on the ceiling.

David tried everything to elicit some response from her, but there was none.

The glassy, staring eyes haunted him whenever he closed his own to snatch a few minutes' sleep in the visitors' waiting room. The hospital consultant had told him that Cheska was in a catatonic state, caused, he thought, by the emotional trauma she had suffered when she'd witnessed her mother's accident.

The following week a still-comatose Greta was transferred to Addenbrooke's Hospital. David was told it was best if the doctors spent a few days assessing her before he made the journey to see her. They would call him if there was any news.

Weak from lack of sleep and the sheer physical and emotional strain of tending to the two women he loved, David went home for the first time in days and slept for twenty-four hours. When he returned, refreshed, to see Cheska, her consultant called him into his office.

'Sit down, Mr Marchmont, please.'

'Thank you.'

'I wanted to talk to you about Cheska. We'd presumed when she was admitted that the shock of seeing her mother's accident would gradually lessen and she would improve. Sadly, so far, that's not been the case. Mr Marchmont, we are a medical ward and don't deal with cases such as this. I had our resident psychiatrist in to assess her, and he believes that she needs to be moved to a dedicated psychiatric unit. Especially under the circumstances.'

'And what are they?'

'Cheska's over two months pregnant.'

'Oh good God!' David groaned, wondering how much more he could take.

'I presumed you didn't know and, technically, I am breaking rules of patient privacy in telling you, but as Cheska is in no condition to tell you herself, and her mother is . . . incapacitated, you are the next of kin. I thought it was important for you to be aware of the whole picture.'

'Of course,' he answered weakly.

'Given the fact that Cheska is a famous face, I'd suggest a discreet private clinic.'

'Is that kind of institution really necessary?' asked David wearily.

'As Cheska is currently unlikely to respond if anything went wrong, she must be medically supervised during her pregnancy.'

'I understand.'

'Let me know which part of the country you'd prefer to send her to, and I'll ask our psychiatrist to make some calls to suitable establishments.'

'Thank you.' David left the doctor and walked slowly down the corridor, back to Cheska's bed.

She was sitting in her chair, staring out of the window. David knelt in front of her and took her hands.

'Cheska, you should have told me. You're having a baby.'

Nothing.

'Bobby's baby.' Instinct made him say the words.

Cheska inclined her head slightly towards him. She smiled suddenly.

'Bobby's baby,' she repeated.

David put his head in his hands and wept with relief.

'Is Leon in?' David asked the receptionist, as he walked purposefully towards the closed office door.

'Yes, but—'

Leon put down the telephone when David walked in without knocking. 'Hello David. Merry Christmas! How are Greta and Cheska?'

David went over to Leon and put his hands on his desk. He leant forward, using his height and powerful frame to the full.

'A little better, but no thanks to you. I want you to tell me whether you knew Cheska was having an affair with Bobby Cross and, if you did, why you didn't warn her about his marital status?'

Leon shrank back in his chair. David, usually so good-natured and gentle, seemed positively menacing.

'I . . . I . . .'

'So you *did* know?'

'Yes, I had a vague idea something was going on.'

'Oh come off it, Leon! Greta told me you called and said Cheska would have to stay down in Brighton for the weekend. Cheska admitted to her mother there was no filming then. You were covering for her, Leon. Why, for God's sake? You, of all people, know what Bobby's like!'

'Okay, okay! Sit down, David, please. You look like a hoodlum standing over me like this.'

David remained standing and folded his arms. 'I want to know why,' he repeated.

'Look, I swear I didn't actively encourage the relationship, although I know Charles Day wanted to because of the film. Cheska was having problems making the transition from the kind of little-girl parts she'd played, and Charles thought a pleasant romance with her co-star wouldn't do her any harm, in fact would help her mature a little. And it certainly helped her performance. You should see the rushes. Cheska's fantastic!'

David stared down at Leon in disgust. 'So you're telling me that for the sake of getting a couple of decent close-ups you helped Charles push an emotionally immature teenage girl – still legally underage, I might add – into the arms of a married man whose reputation stinks even more than your morals?! For Christ's sake, Leon! I knew business always comes first with you, but I didn't realise you were completely ruthless!'

Leon waved his hands in David's direction. 'Oh come on, it was a little fling, that's all. They probably had a kiss and a cuddle, nothing more. Sure, she's not quite of age, but what difference does a few months make? You've been in show business long enough to know that this kind of thing happens all the time. What could I have done? Forbid Cheska to see Bobby? It had started way before I arrived in Brighton. I'm sure there's no real harm done.'

'No harm done?' David shook his head in despair. 'How can you be so bloody naive? Apart from anything else, Cheska has fallen in love with Bobby.'

'She'll get over that. We all have to fall in love for the first time.'

'It's not quite as simple as that, Leon. I can only guess, but I think part of the reason Cheska is in hospital in a catatonic state is because her mother told her Bobby Cross is married.'

Leon leant forward. 'You know, that's always been the problem with Cheska. She's been so mollycoddled and protected by Greta that she's never had to face reality, or make her own decisions and—'

'Don't you *dare* speak about Greta like that!' David leant menacingly over the desk once more, his hands itching to grasp Leon by the throat and wipe the self-satisfied smile from his face.

'I'm sorry, David, really. That was thoughtless, given the circumstances. What I was trying to say was that Cheska is growing up. She's going to have to face experiences and learn to deal with them, like anyone else. She's had a bad time in the past few weeks. But she'll get over Bobby. I'm sure she will.'

'She might have done, of course, if she didn't happen to be pregnant by him.'

'Oh Jesus!'

David finally sat down. Silence filled the room as Leon took in the enormity of what he'd just been told.

'I'm sorry, David. I just . . . dammit! I never thought—'

'I'm sure you did, Leon. And chose to ignore the possible conclusions because it suited you to do so.'

'Is she going to keep it?'

'Cheska's in no fit state to make a rational decision at the moment. She's being moved in two days' time to a private nursing home near Monmouth where she can recover properly and in peace.'

'I see. I'll have a word with Charles Day and see if the studio will cover the costs of the place while Cheska recuperates. Under the circumstances, I think it's the least they can do.'

'I hardly care about that, but I want you to get in touch with that idiot of a client of yours and tell him the news. You do know he could be prosecuted for what he's done to my niece, don't you?'

'Christ, David! Surely you wouldn't take it that far? Apart from anything else, it would ruin Cheska's reputation as well as Bobby's.'

'Where is the slimy little shit?'

'Somewhere abroad, taking a private holiday with his . . . wife and kids.' Leon lowered his gaze in embarrassment. 'He never tells anyone where he's going. Not even me.'

'When is he back?'

'Sometime next month. He's due to record an album before he starts rehearsals for his season at the Palladium.'

'You wouldn't lie to me, would you, Leon?'

'Good God, David! Just remember that Cheska is my

client, too, and she happens to be worth far more to me than Bobby. Not to mention your good self, of course. When he gets back I swear I'll tell him straight away. I don't hold out much hope, though. Mind you, pregnant or not, Cheska's better off without him. She could have the baby adopted or something, couldn't she?'

'Thinking of business again, are we, Leon?' David spat scornfully.

'Look, I swear I'll do anything I can to help. I'm as horrified as you. And how's Greta?'

'Still the same.' David's eyes filled with sudden pain.

'Well, please send her my love.'

'She won't return it, Leon, as you know.'

'What are the doctors saying?'

'I hardly think you're interested, so I won't waste my breath telling you.' He stood up. 'But what I *will* tell you is that I'm dispensing with your services as my agent, with immediate effect.'

David turned and left the room before Leon could respond.

The day before Christmas Eve Cheska was transferred by ambulance to the Medlin Psychiatric Hospital just a few miles outside Monmouth. David followed by car and arrived to find LJ already waiting in reception. After a long phone conversation with his mother, who was desperate to support her son in any way she could, LJ had insisted that she would oversee the care of Cheska whilst David concentrated on being with Greta.

The Medlin Hospital could have been a hotel. It was a fine Georgian building, set in beautiful grounds, and the entrance hall and other communal rooms had the feel of a smart country house. The patients' rooms were small but tastefully furnished and homely. After ensuring Cheska was as comfortable as she could be, David and LJ left her in her room with a nurse and followed the receptionist to the chief psychiatrist's office.

'Good afternoon. I'm John Cox.' The grey-haired man smiled warmly as he shook hands with David and LJ. 'Do please sit down. Now, I have Cheska's case notes from the hospital but I do want to find out some background information to give me the bigger picture. Do you mind?'

'Not at all,' replied David, with a reassuring nod to his mother.

'Right, I'd like to go back to the beginning. Where was she born?'

David answered the questions as best he could, finding it painful to remember the past.

'So she went into films when she was four years old?' asked Dr Cox.

'Yes. I never approved of it, personally,' sniffed LJ.

'I rather agree. It's a lot of pressure for one so young. Tell me, has she had any problems of a similar nature before this that either of you know about?'

LJ bit her lip before answering. 'Well, there was one time . . .' She hesitated when she saw the quizzical look on David's face, but decided she must continue. 'It was when Cheska came to stay with me at Marchmont, when she was still very young. One evening I found her in the old nursery, mutilating a teddy bear.'

'Come now, Ma,' interjected David. 'Isn't "mutilating" a

bit strong? You've never mentioned this before and surely all children are sometimes careless with their toys?'

'You didn't see her face, David,' said LJ quietly. 'It was almost . . . maniacal.'

The psychiatrist nodded and made notes on his pad before continuing.

'So, from Cheska's hospital notes, I see she witnessed her mother's accident?'

'Yes, we believe so, anyway,' said David. 'At the very least, she arrived on the scene only moments after.'

'I see. Does she remember anything else about that night?'

'I honestly don't know,' said David. 'She didn't utter a word in the first few days after the accident, and since she started talking again she's never mentioned it. We haven't wanted to bring it up in case it upsets her. Her mother is still in a coma.'

'Well, often it's best to be honest with patients like Cheska. If the subject arises, there's no need to avoid talking about her mother, within reason of course.'

David and LJ nodded.

'Anything else you'd like to add that you think may be of help?'

'Well, you obviously know from her notes that she's pregnant. And very much in love with the father of the baby. But, unfortunately, he is never likely to shoulder the responsibility,' added David.

'Poor Cheska. No wonder she's having problems. Well, thank you very much, Mr Marchmont, Mrs Marchmont, for all this information. Cheska will be having an hour's therapy every day. I'll need to be able to judge her grasp of reality. Do you think she acknowledges that she is pregnant, for example?'

'Definitely,' confirmed David.

'Well, that's a step in the right direction. Leave it with me, and we'll see how we go.'

'Where are you going? You're not leaving me?' A look of horror crossed Cheska's face as David kissed her cheek. John Cox was standing discreetly a few feet behind David, keen to observe the exchange between the two of them.

'The doctors want you to stay here so they can keep an eye on you and the baby,' said David gently. 'It'll only be for a little while, I promise.'

'But I want to go home with you. It's Christmas, Uncle David!' Cheska's eyes filled with tears. 'Don't leave me, please don't leave me.'

'There, there. There's nothing to get upset about. LJ will be in to see you every day. I'll come to visit too, whenever I can.'

'Promise?'

'I promise, sweetheart.' He paused, weighing up in his mind the wisdom of what he was about to say. 'Cheska, before I go, if there's anything you want to ask me about your mother, you—' David stopped mid-sentence as he saw that Cheska's face hadn't even flickered at the mention of Greta. She merely stared at him blankly for a moment then turned to look out of the window. 'Well, goodbye, darling. I'll see you very soon.'

'Goodbye, Uncle David,' she replied over her shoulder.

David left the room, closely followed by Dr Cox.

'Don't worry, Mr Marchmont. While that little scene

may have been upsetting, it is, I believe, somewhat encouraging. The fact that she can express at least some emotion, such as being upset that you're leaving, is a positive step.'

'But I feel so cruel abandoning her here.'

'Please don't worry. I'm sure she'll adjust to it very quickly. Really, she's in the best place, and you must trust us. You go home and try to have a relaxing Christmas and we'll talk again afterwards.'

It was early evening when David and LJ arrived at Marchmont. Completely exhausted, emotionally and physically, he had succumbed to his mother's suggestion that he at least spend Christmas with her.

'Sit down, David, and I'll make us a strong drink.'

David watched as LJ poured them both a whisky. 'There.' She placed the drink in his hands then went to stir the fire.

'Cheers, and Merry Christmas. You look wonderful, as always, Ma. Younger than me, just now,' he joked.

'I think it's this place that keeps me going. I have so much to do, there's no time to get old.'

'Are you sure you can cope with visiting Cheska, Ma?'

'Of course, dear boy. And Mary said she will too.'

'But what about when she gives birth in a few months' time and she has to care for a tiny thing that's dependent on her for its every need? She's not capable of looking after herself, let alone taking on the responsibility of a child. And with Greta as she is, well . . .'

'Yes, that's been worrying me, too. But what can we do, other than pray she starts to recover? She has quite a time to go still.'

'She looks like a ghost. So pale, and with that awful glassy-eyed expression. She's so fragile, Ma. And she hasn't mentioned Greta once. She was completely blank when I made a reference to her mother just before we left.'

'Well, as I admitted to that psychiatrist this afternoon, I can't help wondering whether this is all part of a much larger mental problem, rather than just the shock of Greta's accident.'

'I don't think so. Cheska has always been very stable. She's coped with years of being in the limelight when other, much more mature people crack under the pressure.'

'Maybe, but don't you think that could be part of her problem? I mean, what *is* reality for her? And all that fame to handle at such a young age. You know I've never approved of her doing all those films. It seems to me that she missed out completely on being a child.'

'Yes, but Greta only wanted what was best for her, you know,' David said, as usual defensive of criticism on Greta's behalf.

'And what about the father of her baby? This Bobby Cross?'

'The evening of the accident Greta was going to tell Cheska he was married. Whether she did or not, at present, only Cheska knows. Leon is getting in touch with Bobby as soon as he's back in the country but, to be honest, it's a pointless exercise. I'm sure John Cox will broach the subject with her. Maybe we'll know more then.'

'What are your plans for the next few days?' LJ asked, changing the subject.

'I have to leave on Boxing Day and go to Cambridge to

see Greta,' he shrugged. 'Her consultant called to say they've found nothing in any of the tests they ran.'

'So, there's no change?'

'Apparently not.'

'Well, is it really necessary that you go? I don't wish to appear unkind, David, but the poor woman is in a coma. She's in good hands at Addenbrooke's and, besides, she's hardly in a state to miss you for a few days more. You need a break from all this, dear boy. It's too much for you.'

'No, Ma,' said David quietly, 'what I need is to be with the woman I love.'

# 32

'So, Cheska, how are you feeling today?' John Cox smiled at her across the desk.

'Fine,' she replied.

'Good, good. Are you settling down here all right?'

'I suppose so, but I'd prefer to go home.'

'To Marchmont?'

'Yes.'

'So you regard Marchmont as your home rather than the apartment you shared in London with your mother?'

Cheska stared at a figurine on a shelf and didn't reply.

'Would you like to tell me about your mother, Cheska?'

'I was once in a film where there was a psychiatrist.'

'Really?'

'Yes. He tried to get people to believe his brother was mad so he could lock him away and steal all his money.'

'But films aren't real, Cheska. They're make-believe. Nobody is trying to say you're mad. I'm trying to help you.'

'That's what the psychiatrist said in the film.'

'Let's talk about the baby, then. You do know you're having a baby, don't you?'

'Of course I do!' she snapped.

'How do you feel about that?'

'Very pleased.'

'You're sure?'

'Yes.' She fidgeted and looked out of the window.

'Well, you know then that you must take very good care of yourself. No skipping meals. Your baby is relying on you to help it grow.'

'Yes.'

'How do you feel about having the baby alone, without a father?' he asked gently.

'But my baby does have a father,' she replied confidently. 'We're to be married as soon as he comes back from France.'

'I see. What is your – er – boyfriend's name?'

'Bobby Cross. He's a very famous singer, you know.'

'How did your mother feel about the fact you were going to be married?'

Cheska again ignored the question.

'Okay. I think that's enough for today. I'll see you tomorrow. Oh, by the way, you have a visitor this afternoon. Your uncle is coming to see you.'

Her face lit up with a genuine smile. 'Oh, how lovely. Is he coming to take me back to Marchmont?'

'Not today, no. But very soon, I promise.'

He pressed a buzzer on his desk and a nurse appeared at the door.

Cheska stood up. 'Goodbye,' she said, and followed the nurse out of the room.

Later that afternoon David was ushered into John Cox's office.

'How is she?' he asked.

'As I told your mother, much better, I think. Certainly far more responsive than she was two weeks ago. She seems to be taking much more notice of the world around her. But she still refuses to talk about her mother. It's hard to gauge whether she believes Greta is alive or dead. Is she still in a coma?'

'Yes. At present, there's no sign of a change.'

'This must be so difficult for you, Mr Marchmont.'

'I'm coping,' David answered swiftly, not wishing to be subjected to a psychiatrist's analysis of his current state of mind. 'Perhaps under the circumstances it's best if Cheska isn't pressed any further about her mother. After all, even if she did admit to remembering the accident, seeing Greta as she is – on a life-support system – could hardly bring her daughter any comfort.'

'At this stage, I'm tempted to agree,' said Dr Cox with a sigh. 'Cheska also told me this morning that she and Bobby Cross are to be married as soon as he arrives back from France.'

'That could mean Greta didn't tell her about Bobby before the accident after all.'

'Who's to say? I suggest our next step is to get her through the birth and take it from there.'

David knocked on Cheska's door.

'Come in.'

He found her sitting in a chair next to the window.

'Hello, sweetheart, how are you?'

She turned towards him and smiled. 'Hello, Uncle David. Have you come to take me home?'

He went over and kissed her on the cheek. 'You look much more like your old self. It's nice to see you dressed.'

'Oh, I'm fine. I just want to know when I can come home, that's all. Bobby will be wondering where I am.' Cheska's face suddenly darkened. 'You know, I had this dream, Uncle David. It was terrible. Someone was telling me Bobby didn't love me any more, that he was married with children of his own, which meant he couldn't marry me. It was a dream, wasn't it, Uncle David?' Her eyes desperately searched his face for confirmation. 'Bobby loves me, doesn't he?'

David gulped, then nodded. 'How could he not love you? Now, give me a big hug.' He put his arms around her and felt how fragile she was. 'Hey, you're getting skinny, young lady. You're meant to be putting on weight, not losing it.'

'I know. I'm sorry. Tell Bobby I promise I'll eat from now on. What about the wedding, Uncle David? We really should be married before the baby arrives.'

'It's a very nice place this, isn't it?' David wandered to the window, desperate to change the subject because he didn't know how to answer. 'The grounds are beautiful. You should take a walk. Fresh air would do you both good.'

'Yes, I suppose it is pretty,' said Cheska, following David's glance. 'But some of the other people here are quite mad. At night, when I'm trying to sleep, I can hear people moaning. It's awful. I'd much prefer to be at Marchmont.'

'The more you look after yourself and do as Dr Cox tells you, the sooner I can take you home. Is there anything you'd like me to bring you while you're here?'

'I suppose a television would be nice. I get a bit bored with nothing to do.'

'I'll see what I can arrange.'

'Thank you. Uncle David? Am I ill? I don't feel ill.'

'No, you're not ill. You just had a . . . a nasty shock that has left you a bit weak, that's all.'

Cheska's face turned pale. 'I . . . I get so confused sometimes. I have all these awful nightmares and sometimes I can't remember what's real and what I dreamt. Sometimes I think I must be mad. I'm not mad, am I? Please tell me I'm not mad?' Her eyes glistened with tears.

David knelt down by her side and gently stroked her cheek. 'Of course you're not, sweetheart. You've been under a lot of stress for a long time, that's all. The reason you're here is to let you rest and have a little peace. You have nothing to worry about, apart from looking after yourself and the baby. Promise me you'll do that?'

'I'll try. I just get so frightened sometimes, that's all. I feel . . . I feel so alone.'

'But you're not alone, Cheska. You have the baby, living inside you.' He looked at the clock by her bed. 'I'm going to have to leave now, sweetheart. I'll come and visit next week.'

'All right. I love you, Uncle David.' She threw her arms around him. 'You don't think I'm a bad person, do you?'

'No, Cheska, I don't. See you soon.' David kissed her on the top of her blonde head and left the room.

On the drive back to London David mulled over their conversation. There was no doubt Cheska was better than she had been, and at moments she had seemed quite normal. But the Bobby fantasy made him feel sick to his stomach.

Four hours after leaving Cheska he was back at her mother's bedside.

David arrived home in Hampstead after his weekly vigil with Greta. Winter had turned to summer, but he'd hardly noticed the seasons changing. It was now almost six months since the accident and there was still no change. He'd cancelled most of his work commitments, only continuing his Friday-night radio show, so he could be with her for the rest of the week. The doctors at Addenbrooke's were baffled now that brain scans and further tests had showed no signs of permanent damage. All they could suggest was that David talk to Greta and read to her as much as possible, in the hope that it might prompt a response. This he had willingly done, but to no avail so far.

The telephone was ringing as he opened the front door and he ran to answer it.

'Hello?'

'Leon here, David. How's Cheska doing?'

'Better, no thanks to you,' replied David coldly.

'And Greta?'

'Still no change. What exactly do you want, Leon? You no longer represent me, and it's only because Cheska's been unwell that I haven't yet suggested that she sacks you as well.'

'Look, can't we let bygones be bygones? I thought you should know that I've spoken to Bobby and he sounded genuinely shocked. He says that yes, Cheska and he did have a little fling, but nothing intimate enough to produce a baby. He swears he can't possibly be the father. And that he had no idea how young she really was.'

'Do you believe him?'

'Do I hell! But what can we do? He's denying all knowledge or responsibility.'

David ground his teeth. 'I tell you something, if I ever come face to face with that bastard again I'll have his balls on a skewer! Did you ask him whether he would visit Cheska?'

'Yes, and he said no. He thought it might make matters worse than they already are. He says she's got the whole thing out of proportion, that what they shared was just a casual, short romance, with no strings attached.'

'I can't say I expected anything very different, but hearing his barefaced lies still comes as quite a shock.'

'The man has no morals, never has had. Listen, there is something we do need to discuss. I've had Charles Day on the telephone. He wanted to know if Cheska was well enough to attend the premiere of *Please, Sir, I Love You*.'

'And what did you tell him?'

'That I thought it was doubtful. Of course, I haven't gone into full details about her situation. Charles thinks she's had a breakdown due to the shock of her mother's accident. He knows nothing about the baby.'

'Well, Cheska's in no fit state to go anywhere. And even if she were, I presume Bobby Cross will be at the premiere? Leon, how can you even suggest it?!'

'Okay, okay. I'll tell Charles she's too poorly to attend and get him to tell the newspapers that she's got a bad bout of flu. It's a shame, though. They reckon the film is going to be huge on both sides of the Atlantic.'

'Yes, it *is* a shame, Leon. But then, if certain people hadn't manipulated Cheska, none of this would have happened, would it?'

'I know, David, what can I say? I'm sorry, I really am.'

'Well, next time you see Bobby, tell him to steer clear of me. I won't be held responsible for my actions.'

Slamming the receiver down, David knew that he was physically, mentally and emotionally at the end of his tether. Sitting by Greta's bedside day in, day out, doing as the doctors had asked and trying to jog her memory yet receiving no response was wearing his positivity away.

He was beginning to give up hope.

# 33

The months passed slowly for Cheska. Some days she would wake up feeling full of energy, thinking about Bobby and the baby, but on others she would sink into an abyss of gloom. LJ came to see her most days, but liked to talk about the weather and the lambs being born on the farm, when all she wanted to talk about was Bobby. Uncle David came sometimes, too, and she kept asking him why she couldn't leave Medlin, which she knew was a hospital for mad people. She had tried to talk to some of the other patients when they ate together in the dining room, but they either didn't reply or repeated themselves over and over.

David had promised her that, when the baby was born, he'd come and take her home, and she comforted herself with the thought that she didn't have long to go. She wrote Bobby long letters and gave them to David to post when he visited her. Bobby never replied, but she knew he was busy and she tried to understand. When they were married, she'd have to get used to him going away.

Sometimes, in the middle of the night, Cheska would have the old dreadful nightmares. She would wake up sobbing, and one of the nurses would come in, comfort her and give her a cup of cocoa and a sleeping pill.

Fragments of something terrible that she had done drifted back to her occasionally, but she shut the thoughts out. It was probably part of the nightmare.

In the last month of her pregnancy Cheska was confined to bed. Her blood pressure had risen and Dr Cox told her she must do nothing but rest. She spent most of the evenings watching the television that Uncle David had brought her.

One Sunday night she sat in bed watching the evening news.

'And now we go over to Minnie Rogers, who is in Leicester Square, reporting on the stars arriving for the premiere of *Please, Sir, I Love You*.'

Cheska jumped out of bed and turned up the sound.

'Hello, everyone.' The reporter smiled into the camera. Behind her Cheska could see a crowd of people standing behind barriers, like she'd seen them do countless times at her own premieres. 'We're just waiting for Bobby Cross, the star of the show, to arrive. Cheska Hammond, who plays the role of Ava, is in bed with flu, and unable to attend tonight. Oh!' The reporter turned round, the excitement showing on her face. 'And here he comes.'

A large black limousine pulled up in front of the cinema. Bobby appeared, smiling and waving at the screaming fans pushing towards him. Cheska's eyes filled with tears. She put one of her hands to the screen and caressed his face.

Bobby reached inside the car, and out stepped a beautiful, slim blonde wearing a sequinned mini-dress. He put his arm around her and kissed her on the cheek, then they walked towards the cinema entrance, turning to pose for the cameras.

'Bobby's fans are going wild! He's never been more popular, and is currently appearing at the Palladium in a sell-out season,' the reporter said breathlessly. 'And tonight, he's escorting Kelly Bright, Britain's most famous model. Bobby and Kelly are now going inside to join the rest of the cast. The film will be on general release tomorrow and, I can assure you, it's a must-see. Back to you in the studio, Mike!'

A low, animal groan emanated from somewhere deep inside Cheska. She dragged her nails repeatedly across her face and began to shake her head from side to side. 'No . . . no . . . no! He's mine . . . he's mine . . . *he's mine!*' Her words amplified to a scream as she stood up.

A passing nurse heard the commotion and rushed into her room.

'What on earth—' Cheska was now hitting the television with her fists.

'Stop it, Cheska!'

But she didn't pay any attention. The blows became increasingly fierce.

The nurse tried to pull her away. 'Come on now, let me lie you down. Think of the baby, Cheska, please!'

Cheska crumpled into a heap on the floor. The nurse knelt beside her, checked her pulse and then noticed the puddle of liquid on the floor. She leapt up and pressed the emergency button.

'Please God, please God,' David muttered under his breath as he drove into the hospital car park.

Running into the maternity wing, he was greeted by John Cox.

'Is everything . . . is Cheska—' He couldn't voice the words.

'She's fine. As soon as she went into labour we rushed her over here and she had a little girl about an hour ago, who weighed in at just over six pounds. Mother and baby are doing well.'

'Thank God.' David's voice cracked with the tension of the four-hour race from Cambridge.

'Your mother is with Cheska, who's being tidied up and made comfortable, but would you like to see her little one?'

'I'd love to.' He followed Dr Cox down a corridor to the nursery. A nurse stood up and smiled as they walked in.

'We've come to see baby Hammond,' Dr Cox announced.

'It's Marchmont, actually, Dr Cox,' David corrected him, feeling a sudden lump in his throat. Whatever the circumstances and the complexities of his familial ties to this child, a new life bearing his surname had just entered the world.

'Right you are.' She walked over to a bassinet, lifted out a tiny bundle and handed it carefully to David.

He looked down at the minute, screwed-up face. The baby's eyes opened and stared at him.

'She seems very alert,' he said.

'Yes, she's a strong little thing,' commented the nurse.

David kissed the baby on the cheek, his eyes wet with tears.

'I hope so. For her sake, I hope so,' he murmured.

# 34

Six weeks after the birth of Cheska's baby, John Cox called David into his office when he arrived for one of his fortnightly visits.

'I think Cheska's ready to go home.'

'That's wonderful news!' David was delighted.

'It seems that giving birth has cleared her mind. She's taken huge steps forward ever since and appears lucid, calm and relaxed. She seems to have developed a good rapport with the baby and her consultant from the hospital popped in yesterday to administer her six-week post-birth check-up and pronounced her physically fit. Obviously, it would be far more beneficial for both of them if Cheska was living in a more natural setting than a psychiatric hospital as she begins her journey into motherhood.'

'Absolutely. And you think she's mentally strong enough to cope?'

'All I can say is that she's hugely improved. She still refuses to talk about her mother, but we could keep her here for the rest of her life and she may never speak about what happened that night. The good news is that she hasn't mentioned Bobby Cross since the birth, which is a healthy sign. Of course, she'll need lots of support, but I do think that having her daughter to care for has given her a new purpose and someone else to think about other than herself.'

'Good. I sincerely hope you're right.'

'Only time will tell if I am, but take her home and see how she progresses. Any problems, you know where we are.' Dr Cox stood up. 'Let's go and tell Cheska the good news, shall we?'

Cheska was sitting in her room giving her daughter a bottle. She smiled as David and Dr Cox came in.

'Hello, Cheska, how are you and the baby? You both look very well,' said David, beaming down at the pair of them.

'We are. Oh, and we don't have to call her "baby" any more. You'll be pleased to know that, at long last, I've decided on a name. I'm going to call her Ava, after my character in *Please, Sir, I Love You*. I think it suits her, don't you?'

'It's a lovely name,' agreed David. 'And I have some good news for you: Dr Cox has said I can take you and Ava home.'

'Oh, that's wonderful! I can't wait to show her Marchmont.'

'I'll get a nurse to come and help you pack up your suitcase. We'll see you in my office in an hour to fill out the necessary paperwork,' said the doctor.

LJ stood in the nursery at Marchmont. After the phone call from David she and Mary had hurriedly set to work to make it welcoming.

'Well, everything's ready in here. Won't it be marvellous to have a baby around the place again?' she said to Mary, who was putting clean sheets on the mattress in the bassinet.

'Yes, Mrs Marchmont, it will now.'

Twenty minutes later, as the sun was setting, LJ spotted David's car coming up the drive. 'They're here!' She clapped her hands in delight. 'I'll go downstairs and greet them.' She flew down the stairs and hurried outside.

'Welcome, darlings. I'm so glad to have you both here,' she said warmly, helping Cheska and the baby out of the back seat.

'And I'm so happy to be back, Aunt LJ. Here, do you want to hold her?'

Cheska passed the bundle to LJ, who cooed at the baby as she carried her inside. 'She's even more beautiful than she was when I saw her last. I do believe she has your eyes, Cheska. Have you decided what to call her yet?' she asked, as they walked into the drawing room.

'Ava.'

'How lovely, like my favourite film star. Ms Gardner was quite stunning in *The Angel Wore Red*.' LJ sat down in a chair and cradled the infant in her arms. Ava's small features creased and she let out a yell.

'She's hungry,' said Cheska.

'Mary prepared some bottles earlier and put them in the fridge. Shall we go up to the nursery? I'll have Mary warm one up and bring it upstairs.'

LJ watched as Cheska sat in the nursery and fed her baby. She was impressed by the confident way she seemed to be handling her daughter, although she was little more than a child herself. Having winded her, Cheska stood up and gently placed a contented Ava in the bassinet.

'There, she'll probably sleep until midnight. She usually does.'

'Well, why don't you go to bed?' LJ suggested. 'I'll stay with her and do the midnight shift. You must be exhausted, my dear.'

'I am a bit tired. It's very kind of you to offer.'

'From now on, you'll be fighting me off. I adore tiny babies,' chuckled LJ.

'You know, when I was little, this room used to frighten me,' Cheska mused, as she gazed around it.

'Why, Cheska?'

'I don't know. Goodnight, LJ, and thank you.' Cheska kissed her lightly on the cheek and left.

The following morning Cheska left LJ and Mary to fuss over the baby and went out for a long walk. Her heart lifted at the sheer beauty of the Marchmont estate. The house lay basking against the hills in the glorious sunshine, its wide terraces filled with urns of scarlet geraniums. The woods below were a riot of green that seemed to tumble down the sides of the valley.

She arrived back just in time for lunch and joined LJ and David on the terrace.

'It's wonderful to have Mary's home cooking after all that disgusting food they gave me at Medlin,' she said to David.

'Well, you still look too skinny to me, *fach*,' announced Mary, serving her a large plateful of succulent lamb and tender new potatoes. 'What you need is lots of fresh air to put some colour in your cheeks. I remember saying as much to your mother when she first came here.'

LJ shot Mary a warning glance, but Cheska simply ignored the mention of Greta.

'I really feel I should go back to London quite soon. All my things are there, and I'd like to collect some of them.'

David eyed his mother, signalling caution.

'That's the spirit,' said LJ, taking no notice of him. 'Would you like me to look after the little one for a couple of days?'

'If you wouldn't mind. You see, I've decided Ava and I should make our home here for now, if you'll have us. I'm going to tell Leon that my film career's on hold whilst I bring up my little girl.'

'Well, well.' LJ shot a glance of triumph across the table at her son. 'Of course I will, darling. Nothing would please me more.'

'I have to go back to London on Monday, too, Cheska. You could drive down with me if you'd like,' said David, wondering why he felt so uneasy about the idea.

'Thank you. That sounds perfect.'

That afternoon David called Dr Cox to tell him of the planned trip.

'It sounds as if she really is facing up to reality at last. It's excellent news, Mr Marchmont.'

'So, I should let her go?'

'I can't see why not. You say you'll be going with her?'

'Yes. But what do I tell her about her mother?'

'Has there been any change?'

'No,' David confirmed.

'Then I should leave it to Cheska to lead the way towards the subject, if she wants to.'

'But she'll notice, surely, that Greta isn't at their apartment? Do I tell her the truth?'

'If she asks where she is, then yes. I would suggest that you don't leave her alone overnight, though.'

'Of course. I'll stay with her.'

'Well, give me a ring if you need my advice, but take your lead from her. It's important she's allowed to deal with this in the way she wants to.'

'Right. I'll let you know how we go.'

The night before Cheska was leaving with David for London she made her way along to the nursery and opened the door. The room still unsettled her, but tonight there were no ghosts to face, only a small baby sleeping peacefully in her cot.

Cheska reached over and caressed her daughter's cheek.

'I'm sorry I have to leave you, little one, but LJ will take good care of you,' she whispered. 'And one day, I'll come back for you, I promise. Goodbye, Ava.' Cheska bent over and kissed the baby on her forehead, then quietly left the room.

Cheska and David chatted amiably on the drive to London.

'It's wonderful to see you looking so much better, but you mustn't overdo it in London, sweetheart,' he said.

'I know. But I just feel I want to say goodbye to the past and start my new life with Ava at Marchmont.'

'You're being very brave, Cheska. Becoming a mother has certainly made you grow up.'

'I've had to, for Ava's sake. Uncle David, there are some things . . . some things I want to ask you,' she said slowly.

David prepared himself mentally. 'Fire away.'

'Was Owen my real father?'

David was taken aback by the question. It certainly wasn't what he'd expected her to ask, but there'd been enough lies in the past few months and Cheska seemed strong enough to take the truth.

'No. He wasn't.'

'Are you?'

David chuckled. 'No. Sadly not.'

'Then who was my father?'

'An American officer. Your mother and he fell in love just after the end of the war, then he left for America and was never seen or heard of again. Please try not to upset yourself, Cheska. Although there is no blood tie between the Marchmonts and yourself, both LJ and I regard you and Ava as family.'

'Thank you for telling me, Uncle David,' she said quietly. 'I needed to know.'

They arrived at the apartment in Mayfair at five o'clock that evening.

'Are you sure you wouldn't prefer to leave it until the morning, Cheska? We could go to my house in Hampstead instead and have an early night,' David said as they approached the entrance.

'No,' Cheska replied. She was already turning the key in the front door.

David followed her inside. 'I left everything pretty much as it was, though the cleaner's been coming in, as usual,' he remarked as she opened the door and switched on the lights. He tried to gauge her mood as she wandered into the sitting room.

'Would you like a drink, Uncle David? Mummy always kept some whisky for when you came around.'

'Yes, thank you.' It was the first time in all these months that Cheska had mentioned Greta.

She went to the drinks cabinet, took out a glass and poured the whisky.

'There you are.' She handed it to him and they both sat down on the sofa. 'I should like to stay here tonight, Uncle David. Would you stay with me?'

'Of course I will. Can I take you out for something to eat? I'm starving.'

'I'm not very hungry, to be honest.'

'Then why don't I pop round the corner to the shop, pick up some bread, cheese and ham, and we'll have an indoor picnic?'

'That would be lovely, Uncle David.'

When he had left, Cheska stood up and walked slowly into her mother's bedroom. She picked up the large, framed photograph of herself that sat on the bedside cabinet. She walked over to the wardrobe and opened the doors. The familiar smell of Greta's perfume hit her. She buried her face in the soft fur of a mink coat and wept.

What David had told her in the car had confirmed her deepest fears. The argument with her mother at the Savoy couldn't have been a dream. And if her mother hadn't lied to her about her real father, then in all probability she hadn't lied about Bobby being married either.

After the argument she had followed her mother from the hotel. And then . . .

'Oh God,' she moaned. 'I'm so sorry, Mummy, so sorry.'

Cheska lay on her mother's bed, her panicky breaths coming in short, sharp bursts. She ground her fists into the pillow, feeling a terrible, uncontrollable anger.

It was all Bobby's fault. And he would be punished.

Cheska heard the doorbell, hastily pulled herself together, and went to let her uncle in.

David prepared sandwiches in the kitchen as Cheska sat and watched him, then placed the plates of food on the table and sat down opposite her.

'It must feel strange coming back here,' he ventured, taking a bite of his sandwich.

'It does,' she agreed. 'Uncle David, Mummy's dead, isn't she? You can tell me, you know.'

David almost choked. He managed to swallow, took a sip of the disgusting wine he'd bought at the corner shop and looked at her. 'No, Cheska, she isn't.'

'Mummy's alive? Oh my goodness! I—' She looked about her as if Greta would appear through the kitchen door at any moment. 'Then where *is* she?'

'In a hospital, Cheska.'

'She's sick?'

'Yes, she is. She's in a coma and has been for the past few months. Do you know what a coma is?'

'Sort of, yes. In one of my films my brother fell out of a tree, bumped his head and was in a coma for ages afterwards. The director explained it was like Sleeping Beauty falling asleep for a hundred years.'

'That's a very good analogy,' David agreed. 'Yes, your

mother is “asleep” and, sadly, no one knows when she’ll wake up.’

‘Where is she?’

‘In Addenbrooke’s Hospital, in Cambridge. Would you like to go and see her? It’s only an hour and half away by car.’

‘I . . . don’t know.’ Cheska looked nervous.

‘Well, why don’t you think about it? I know Mummy’s doctors would be thrilled if you did. You never know, the sound of your voice might wake her up.’

Cheska yawned suddenly. ‘I’m awfully tired, Uncle David, I think I’ll go to bed.’ She stood up, then kissed him on the top of his head. ‘Night, night.’

‘Goodnight, Cheska.’

David drained his wine glass, then stood up to clear away the plates. He’d call Dr Cox tomorrow, tell him what had happened tonight and ask his advice. There was no doubt it was a breakthrough, not just for Cheska, but, just possibly, for his beloved Greta, too.

That night David sank into the guest-room bed full of renewed hope.

The following morning at ten o’clock, David went in to Cheska’s room and gently woke her.

‘How did you sleep?’

‘Very well. I must have been tired from the drive.’

‘And from having a baby six weeks ago. I’ve made you some tea and toast. And I insist you eat the lot, since you didn’t touch your sandwich last night.’ He placed the tray on her lap and sat down on the bed. ‘Now, I have to go to Shepperton Studios after lunch to discuss this year's Christmas special. Why don't you come with me?'

'No, thanks. I have a lot to do while I'm here.'

David frowned. 'I just don't like leaving you on your own.'

'Stop fussing, Uncle David, I'll be fine. Please try to remember that I'm a grown-up now, with a child of my own.'

'You're right,' he agreed reluctantly. 'But I won't be back until much later, so why don't I take you out to the Italian round the corner for supper tonight? And we can discuss whether you'd like to visit your mother before we drive back to Marchmont on Friday. Dr Cox said he thought it would be a very good idea.'

'Okay,' Cheska agreed, then threw her arms around his shoulders in a spontaneous hug. 'And thank you for everything.'

Later that afternoon, once Cheska had seen David drive off, she left the apartment. She visited her bank, then took a taxi to Leon's office.

'Darling! What a surprise! How are you?'

'Absolutely fine.'

'And how's the baby?'

'Oh, she's lovely.'

'Good. You look wonderful. Motherhood seems to suit you.'

'Ava's at Marchmont at the moment. Uncle David's staying here at the apartment with me.'

'You know, I've had countless calls from directors, both here and across the pond. You got such raves in *Please, Sir, I Love You* that everyone wants you. Maybe when the baby's a bit older you might consider coming back to work.'

'Well,' said Cheska, 'as a matter of fact, that's what I wanted to talk to you about. You say Hollywood is still interested?'

'Yes. Carousel Pictures want you to do a screen test.'

'The thing is, Leon, I feel I need a fresh start, what with everything that's happened. So, if they still want me, I'd be delighted to go and test for them.'

'They certainly do,' said Leon. 'Give me the nod and I'll set it up. It will only take a phone call.'

'How about I fly out tomorrow?'

'What?' Leon looked astonished. 'I thought you'd want to be with your baby for at least the next few months.'

'Well, there's no reason why I couldn't fly over, do the test and come back, is there? Then, if they like me, Ava and I could move over there permanently.'

'I see. And what does David have to say about this?' Leon asked cautiously, remembering his last conversation with Cheska's uncle.

'I think he's just pleased to see I'm better. And Aunt LJ is happy to look after Ava for a few days.'

'Right. Well, if you're sure, why don't you let me make that call? Hollywood wakes up in an hour's time. We'll see what we can organise.'

'Fine.' Cheska stood up. 'Remember what you've always said, Leon: "When you're hot, you're hot." I don't want to miss my chance.'

'Absolutely, Cheska. Leave it with me and I'll be back to you with an answer around six o'clock.'

*

The telephone in the apartment rang at twenty past six. Cheska picked up the receiver immediately.

'Leon here. It's all arranged. You'll fly out at five thirty tomorrow evening from Heathrow. I'll get Barbara, my secretary, to meet you by the BOAC desk with your visa and ticket – first class, of course. A representative from Carousel will meet you at the other end and take you to your hotel. You're booked into a suite at the Beverly Wilshire, all expenses paid. Talking of which, will you need some money?'

'No,' said Cheska. 'I went to the bank this morning and drew some out. I have plenty.'

'Good. I hope it goes well, darling. One thing, though, I haven't mentioned your daughter to the studio. They're quite old-fashioned over there, and I don't want your chances spoilt before you've done the test. Let's get you the contract and take it from there.'

'I understand, Leon.'

'Are you sure you're up to this? We could easily postpone it until you're a little stronger, you know.'

'I'm absolutely fine, Leon, I promise. I need to cash in on the success of *Please, Sir, I Love You* before they forget me.'

'That's all too true . . . Cheska, I just wanted to say how sorry I am about your mother. And, also, about Bobby,' he added.

'Why should you be sorry about *him*?'

'Because I knew about his marriage and his reputation and I didn't say anything to you. I let you down, Cheska, and I feel bad about it.'

'Well, I rather think it's he who's going to be sorry. Goodbye, Leon. I'll call you from the States.'

David arrived home an hour later and the two of them went out to the Italian restaurant.

'Have you had a good day?' he asked as they ordered.

'Yes. I've sorted out what I needed to,' she answered carefully. 'And it's made me realise that I've relied on Mummy for the whole of my life, and now she isn't . . . here, I have to learn to stand on my own two feet.'

'Yes.' David sighed. 'Sadly, you do, at least for now.'

'I also went to the bank, as I'd no idea how much money I have. As a matter of fact, Uncle David, I'm quite rich.' She gave a small laugh.

'Well, your mother always took great care to invest your earnings wisely and I'm sure the amount has grown over the years. At least that's one problem you don't have.'

'No. Actually, Uncle David, I've decided I want to go back to Marchmont tomorrow. I've done as much as I can here.'

'Of course. But if you could wait until Friday I could give you a lift, rather than you having to trek back on the train.'

'Thanks for the offer, but I'd prefer to go sooner. I'm missing Ava. I'll pack a suitcase with all the things I want to take back, so perhaps you could bring it up when you come?'

'Of course. And I understand completely about you wanting to get back to Ava. If you get the two o'clock train, I'll tell Ma to pick you up from Abergavenny Station at half past six. I've got meetings all day, so I'm afraid I can't take you to Paddington.'

'I'll be fine, Uncle David, really. I'll take a taxi.'

'I must say, I was rather hoping you might want to visit

your mother. I'm going up to Cambridge on Thursday. Are you sure you don't want to come with me?'

'I promise that, next time I'm in London, I will. I just . . . can't face it yet. Do you understand, Uncle David?'

'Of course, sweetheart. And I just want to say that I'm really impressed by the way you're handling things. It's been such a dreadful time for you, and to see you making such a fantastic recovery makes me very proud.'

'Thank you.'

'Just remember that Ma and I are always here for you and Ava, whatever happens.'

Cheska looked up at David. 'Whatever happens?'

'Yes.'

# 35

Cheska knew that time was short. As soon as her uncle left the apartment at nine o'clock the next morning, she zipped up her holdall and hailed a taxi to take her to Addenbrooke's Hospital. At first the cab driver baulked at going as far as Cambridge, but quickly agreed when Cheska offered him an enormous tip.

Having instructed the driver to wait, she introduced herself at reception and was directed to Ward Seven. She rang the bell outside it and a nurse came to open the door.

'I'm Cheska Hammond, Greta Marchmont's daughter,' she said. 'Can I see my mother?'

The Jamaican nurse stared at her in shock. 'Cheska Hammond! I saw *Please, Sir, I Love You* a few weeks ago.' She moved closer as if to double-check Cheska's features. 'Oh my God, it *is* you!'

'As I said, can I see my mother?'

'I . . . yes. I'm sorry. Come in, come in.' The nurse was clearly flustered. 'I had no idea Greta's daughter was *you*! I loved you in that film, Miss Hammond,' she said, dropping her voice to a whisper as they entered the ward.

'Thank you.'

All Cheska could hear was a low, irregular beeping emanating from the various machines and monitors that sat beside each bed.

'Welcome to the quietest ward in the hospital. I don't get much conversation out of my patients, I'm afraid. Right,' said the nurse, stopping at the end of a bed, 'here's your mother. She's doing well, aren't you?' she said, leaning over Greta. 'We did have a problem with some nasty bed-sores, but they've cleared up now. I'll leave you with her. Talk to her as much as you can and hold her hand. The patients respond to voices and physical contact. I reckon your mum is just being stubborn and she's *decided* she doesn't want to wake up, because her brain waves are functioning well. Call me if you need me.'

'Thank you.' Cheska sat in the chair next to the bed and stared down at her mother. Greta was ghostly white. The fragile skin of her thin arms was criss-crossed with surgical tape that held in place the needles and tubes that connected her to the drips that sustained her. A small pad with wires coming out of it was stuck to her temple, another to her chest. Tentatively, Cheska put her hand on her mother's and was surprised to find it was warmer than her own. She definitely felt alive, even if she looked dead.

'Mummy, it's me, Cheska.' She bit her lip, not knowing what to say. 'How are you feeling?'

She studied Greta's face for a reaction, but there was none.

'Mummy' – Cheska lowered her voice further – 'I just wanted to tell you that I'm so sorry about the awful row we had and . . . other things. I never meant to hurt you. I . . . I love you.'

Tears came to Cheska's eyes and she swallowed hard. 'But, Mummy, don't you worry, I'm going to make sure Bobby pays for what he's done to us. I'm doing it for both of us. I have to go now, but I want you to know I love you very, very much. Thank you for everything, and I promise I'm going to make you proud of me. Bye bye, Mummy. See you soon.'

Cheska kissed Greta tenderly on her forehead, then stood up and walked towards the exit. The nurse hurried towards her.

'Miss Hammond, can I please have your autograph for my son? He's a big fan and—'

But Cheska was already out of the door and walking away. She hurried out of the hospital and jumped into the waiting taxi. When they were back in London, she asked the driver to drop her outside the Palladium, then found a small supermarket just off Regent Street and purchased a small bottle of what she needed. At the florist's two doors down she bought a large bunch of red roses. Feeling for the bottle in her pocket, she turned back towards the Palladium.

She'd remembered that, one afternoon when they were filming *Please, Sir, I Love You*, Melody had taken her to the studio next door, where they were shooting a thriller, and that was what had given her the idea. It wouldn't take much. Making her way around the corner to the stage door, she peered inside. An old man was sitting in the doorkeeper's cubicle, smoking a cigarette.

''Scuse me, love. Hold the door open, will you?'

Cheska turned and saw a man behind her carrying a large box in his arms. She did as he asked and watched as he dumped the box on the floor in the cubicle. As both men bent down to survey its contents, she slipped past them, walking swiftly along the corridor. She knew exactly where she was going. She'd visited Uncle David in the Number One dressing room on more than one occasion. She opened the door, switched on the light and took a deep breath. The room smelt of *him*, of the musky aftershave he always wore.

Cheska made straight for the dressing table and put down the bunch of red roses. There, sitting on the surface, was a pot of Crowes Cremine, used to remove heavy stage make-up after the show. She opened the lid; it was only a quarter full. She reached for the bottle in her pocket, undid the top and poured some of the liquid inside it into the pot of cream. Then she used a nail file to stir it in.

The texture changed to something that resembled cottage cheese, but she doubted he'd notice. Switching off the lights, she walked back down the corridor. The two men were still bent over the box in the cubicle, emptying it of its contents.

Cheska walked past them unnoticed and back out on to the street.

Bobby Cross arrived in his dressing room and sniffed the air. He wrinkled his nose at the pungent smell and made a mental note to instruct the cleaners not to use so much bleach in future. Then his eyes lit on the large bunch of red roses on his dressing table. He read the card accompanying the roses. Usually, the doorman would remove the notes to be vetted before he saw them, but this one must have slipped through the net.

'You never understood the madness of love, so you won't sing of it again,' it said.

Bobby shuddered. He'd had notes like this from crazed fans before, and they always unsettled him. He tore up the card and dropped it into the wastepaper bin, along with the roses, and began to put on his make-up.

High on adrenalin, as he always was after a performance, Bobby sat down in front of the mirror in his dressing room and thought about the night ahead. He was having dinner with Kelly, and afterwards . . . well, afterwards they would go back to his hotel, where she'd help him relax. Smiling at his reflection in anticipation, he automatically dipped a wad of cotton wool into the pot of Crowes Cremine to begin removing his make-up.

He rubbed the cream in thoroughly, then wiped it across his eyelids to remove his eyeliner and mascara. A few seconds later he felt a strange burning sensation in his eyes, which spread out until he felt his entire face was on fire. He screamed out loud at the excruciating pain.

He caught a brief glimpse of his gruesome reflection in the mirror before he passed out cold.

LJ watched the last passengers make their way out of Abergavenny Station and saw the train pull out. She checked the platform again, but there was no sign of Cheska. Maybe she'd misheard David when he'd said she was arriving on the half past six. Anyway, there was no point in hanging around at the station. There were no more trains due that night.

When she arrived home she checked on Ava, who was

sleeping peacefully in the nursery, then walked into the library and dialled David's number.

'Hello, Ma. Cheska home safely?' he asked.

'No. She wasn't on the train.'

'How odd. Maybe she decided to stay another night in London. I'll give her a bell at the apartment.'

'Do that, then call me back and let me know she's there.'

'Will do.'

He rang back five minutes later.

'Well?' she asked.

'No reply. Maybe she's gone out.'

'Oh dear, David, she really shouldn't be wandering the streets of London alone at night. You . . . you don't think something's happened to her, do you?'

'Of course not, Ma. I'll drive round to the apartment now. I have a key so I can let myself in.'

'Get back to me with any news, won't you?'

'Of course I will.'

David awoke with a start when the telephone in Greta's sitting room rang.

'Any news, dear boy?'

'Hello, Ma.' David shook himself awake. 'What time is it? I must have fallen asleep on the sofa. I was waiting here to see if Cheska came back.'

'Half past eight in the morning.'

'Well, that means Cheska's been out all night.'

'Do you think you should call the police?'

'And say what? She's old enough to go where she pleases.'

'Yes, but she was only released from hospital a few days ago, David. Even though she seemed calm, I'm sure her psychiatrist wouldn't be happy if he knew nobody had seen her in the past twenty-four hours. Have you tried Leon? I know you've fallen out with him, but he is still Cheska's agent. Maybe he knows something.'

'I've already called him a couple of times at his office, and at home last night, but there was no answer. I'll try him again now. Let's not panic just yet, Ma.'

'I'll try not to. Let me know if you hear anything.'

David replaced the receiver, then dialled Leon's number again. This time, he answered.

'Leon, David here. I tried to call you last night.'

'I wasn't at home. I was at the hospital. Did you hear about what happened to Bobby Cross? He—'

'Never mind Bobby,' David said angrily. 'Have you heard from Cheska?'

'She came to see me a couple of days ago.'

'Did she indeed,' said David grimly. 'What about yesterday?'

'Hardly, David. Her plane will only just have touched down in Los Angeles.'

'I'm sorry? Los Angeles?'

'Yes.'

There was silence at the other end of the line.

'Oh God, David, don't tell me you didn't know? Cheska told me you were staying with her in Mayfair. She said you'd agreed it was a good idea. Even told me that your mother had volunteered to look after the baby until she came home.'

'I'd agreed *what* was a good idea?'

'The screen test at Carousel Studios in Los Angeles.'

'Leon, can you honestly imagine I would agree to Cheska flying off to America and leaving her baby behind just a few days after she's come out of a psychiatric hospital?!'

'David, I swear, Cheska told me you knew and—'

David crashed the receiver into its cradle then picked it up again to dial his mother. 'Ma, it's David.'

LJ greeted him at the front door of Marchmont four hours later.

'You poor darling, you look exhausted. Come in and I'll have Mary make us some tea.'

'A strong drink will suit me better, thanks, Ma.'

The two of them went into the drawing room and David sat down. LJ fetched a whisky for him.

'So, tell me everything, dear boy.'

After David had repeated what Leon had told him, LJ shook her head in disbelief. 'Why? I mean, why would Cheska lie to us?'

'Maybe she thought we wouldn't let her go to America.'

'Well, would we have done?'

'Probably not.' David swept an agitated hand through his hair.

'And Leon says she should be flying back in a matter of days?'

'Yes, that's what he said.'

'Well, David, I hope I'm wrong, but my gut instinct – which I've always found reliable – tells me Cheska has little intention of coming back.'

'Couldn't we just wait and see?' David said with a deep

sigh. 'There's no point in speculating, and I'm just too tired to think straight tonight.'

'Of course. At least we know where she is.'

'I'm going to have a bath and an early night. Could Mary make me something to eat, do you think?'

'I'm sure she can. But just before you go . . .' LJ handed him a newspaper. 'Did you see this morning's *Mail*? There's a big piece about Bobby Cross. Seems he met with an . . . accident yesterday.'

David glanced at the front-page photograph of Bobby and read the story underneath.

**POP STAR MAIMED IN CRAZED ATTACK**

Singer Bobby Cross was admitted to hospital last night with serious facial burns. He was found unconscious in his dressing room by theatre staff and rushed to Guy's Hospital, where doctors performed an emergency operation to try to save his left eye. A police spokesman said that bleach had been added to a pot of facial cream used by Mr Cross to remove his stage make-up. The attack was one of 'unrivalled viciousness', said the spokesman. It is suspected that it was carried out by a crazed fan. A bunch of red roses was found in his dressing room, accompanied by a sinister note.

David looked at his mother. He knew exactly what she was thinking.

'No, Ma. Cheska may have had a few problems, but this? Never. It's just a nasty coincidence.'

'You think so?'

'I know so. How's Ava?'

'Sleeping beautifully. She's such a dear little thing.'

'Well, let's just hope we hear from her mother soon. And that she comes back for her baby. Goodnight, Ma.'

LJ was silent as he left the room. For Ava's sake, she prayed Cheska would stay far away from her child for as long as possible.

The following day David left Marchmont at sunrise. He had meetings in London, but he planned to pop in and see Greta at Addenbrooke's Hospital first. One way and another, he hadn't visited her for over a month, even though he called the ward every day to check if there had been any change. There never was.

On the drive up to Cambridge he thought endlessly about Cheska. Bobby Cross's horrific maiming had been on the radio constantly and was splashed across every newspaper. He was not in any immediate danger, apparently, but from what was being reported, his eyes and face would not fully recover from the damage inflicted.

Bobby's talent as a musician had been limited but his sexual charisma had been undeniable. Now this had happened, cruel as it was, there was no doubt that his days as a teen idol and film star were over. David hoped that Bobby's wife would stand by him, because the man had never needed her more than he did now.

'What goes around, comes around,' he muttered to himself as he parked the car in front of the hospital. Still thinking about Bobby, he mused that his mother had always brought him up to live life honourably and truthfully. He'd watched as friends and colleagues had taken short-cuts to achieve what they wanted, but now, at the age of forty-three, he knew this was the best advice he'd ever been given. He had realised recently that everything came home to roost one day.

And yet Greta, who had done little in her life to hurt anyone, had suffered so terribly.

He got out of his car, locked it and walked towards the entrance to the hospital, wondering whether Cheska could have had anything to do with what had happened to Bobby Cross. His mother, he knew, thought she had. But surely, David rationalised, her imagination was working overtime and it was merely coincidence?

As he took the lift to Ward Seven, he remembered the sweet little girl Cheska had been. And still – as far as he was concerned – *was*. He had never witnessed anything in her behaviour to indicate she had the kind of violent, psychotic mind that could dream up such a thing. Yes, she'd been mad with grief in the moments after her mother's accident, but that had been natural, surely?

David pressed the bell and saw his favourite nurse, Jane, smile at him and walk towards the door.

'Hello, Mr Marchmont. I haven't seen you for a while,' she said as she led him into the ward, her blonde ponytail swinging under her nurse's cap. He knew she had a soft spot for him. She often brought him a cup of tea and biscuits when he was sitting with Greta, and her friendly banter provided relief from the thankless one-way conversation.

'I've been away.' It seemed the easiest explanation. 'Any change?'

'I'm afraid not, though the nurse on duty this morning

did notice a slight movement of her left hand. But, as you know, that's likely to be an automatic nerve reflex.'

'Thanks, Jane,' he said, as he sat down and stared at Greta – unchanged since he'd last seen her.

Jane nodded and walked away.

'Hello, my darling, how are you?' David took hold of Greta's hand. 'Sorry I've been away. I've been busy. I've got lots of news for you, mind you.' He looked down at her serene features, searching for any movement, perhaps a tiny flicker of an eyelid. But there was nothing.

'Greta, I told you last time – and it's ridiculous that this could be true, as you don't look old enough to have a daughter, let alone a granddaughter – Cheska has given birth to the most adorable baby girl. She's called her Ava. I really think that, when she's feeling stronger, she'll come and visit you. The baby is so beautiful. She looks a lot like her mummy and, considering she's only a few weeks old, is sleeping very well. Cheska's taken to motherhood like a duck to water. Even my old ma was impressed.'

David rambled on, as he always did, occasionally moving his gaze to a half-dead spider plant that sat on the windowsill above Greta's head and talking to that, just to have a break from her white, immobile features. While he talked, his brain flitted to other things he had to do.

'You said the baby has been named Ava. Is that after Ava Gardner, the film star?'

'No, I think it was after someone else,' David said automatically, still staring at the plant and thinking about possible sketches for his TV show. He'd been mulling over which famous faces he'd ask to come and join him on his

Christmas special and wondering if he could persuade Julie Andrews. 'I—'

It took a few seconds for his brain to compute what had just happened. He dragged his eyes away from the plant, dreading the thought that he'd just imagined her voice, and forced himself to look down at her.

'Oh my God!' he whispered as he gazed for the first time in nine months into her beautiful blue eyes. 'Greta . . . you're—'

He uttered no further words as he promptly burst into tears.

*December, 1985*

*Marchmont Hall,*
*Monmouthshire*

# 36

The sun had long since set by the time David finished talking. He pulled out his handkerchief and dried his eyes. He'd halted many times to look at Greta, who sat listening intently to every word he spoke, and asked her if she was sure she wanted him to continue. The answer had always been 'yes'.

He'd done his best to accurately recount the events that had taken place, as far as he knew or remembered them. But, in spite of her urging him to spare her nothing, he'd drawn the line at revealing his suspicions about Cheska's involvement in Greta's accident. The other detail he'd deliberately omitted was his marriage proposal. He'd felt that that, also, would be too much to burden Greta with at present, bearing in mind all the other revelations.

He looked at her now, staring off into space, and wondered what she was thinking. The story would be enough to shock a stranger to whom it was told, but this was Greta's *life*.

'Are you okay, Greta?'

'Yes. Or, at least, as okay, as I can be after what you've just told me. To tell you the truth, I'd remembered a lot of it, anyway. You've just clarified and made sense of it. What she did to Bobby—' Greta shuddered. 'She could have killed him.'

'You think it was her?'

'Almost certainly. The madness I saw in her eyes in the bar at the Savoy just before my accident when I told her Bobby was married . . . she was so disturbed, and I didn't see it,' she whispered. 'I refused to see it, David. I made so many mistakes. God forgive me. I should never have pushed her like I did.'

'Greta, you shouldn't be so hard on yourself. But right now, I'm in need of a very stiff drink. How about you?'

'Perhaps,' she agreed. 'Just a small one.'

'I'll make you a weak gin. Back in a moment.'

David left the room and walked to the kitchen. Tor was sitting at the table, reading the *Telegraph*. After hours of recounting the grim story, he felt now as if he'd entered into a world of calm and normality.

'How is she?' Tor asked.

'I really don't know, but after what I've just told her, pretty shell-shocked, I should think. Sorry I'm having to spend so much time with her,' he said, kissing her on the top of her head. 'I promise I'll make it up to you in Italy. It's only a few days away.'

Tor looked up at him and squeezed his hand. 'It can't be helped, and let's hope that, now Greta's remembered, she won't be so reliant on you in the future.'

'Yes, let's hope so. Can I get you a drink?' David asked, walking to the state-of-the-art fridge and putting a glass under the ice-maker.

'No, thanks,' Tor said, her head back in the newspaper.

David carried the drinks back to the drawing room and placed Greta's glass in front of her.

'Thank you.' She picked it up to take a sip and David saw that her hand was shaking.

'Anything I can do to help, Greta?' he asked, feeling that she must take the lead.

'David, it seems that *all* you've done for the past God knows how many years is to help me. And Cheska,' she added. 'I don't know how I can ever thank you. You were there for both of us all that time when I was in hospital. I don't know how you did it. I feel . . . so guilty, about so many things. How can I ever repay you?'

'You just have. You know, I always refused to give up hope, so it's very gratifying to be proved right. Anyway, it's the last thing you should be worrying about. You're family, Greta, and so is Cheska and at times of need, we stick together, don't we? That's what families do. And before you say you aren't related by blood, either of you, it's irrelevant.'

'LJ must have seen me as the instigator of Marchmont's destruction. And, in a way, her own. Although it's made me feel better to know that Owen used me as much as I used him. All those years, and he was in love with LJ. That was something I never knew. It's so sad, really, for both of them.'

'Well, they were both as stubborn as each other. Sometimes it happens that way.'

Greta shivered as a flashback of a moment came into her mind full throttle. She gasped involuntarily, it was so vivid.

'What is it?'

'Nothing. If you'll excuse me, David, I'm going to go upstairs and lie down for a while.' Greta stood up abruptly and walked from the room. David wondered what on earth it was she'd remembered. And realised it could be anything.

'Talk about a can of worms,' he muttered to himself, draining his gin, then went to join Tor in the kitchen.

Greta sat on her bed, wishing she could walk straight back downstairs and ask David if what she'd seen in her flash-back could really be true; that he'd once told her he loved her and asked her to marry him.

Greta closed her eyes again and saw them at a table . . . yes, yes! It had been in Monmouth at the Griffin Arms that he told her he loved her – she could see it in her mind's eye. And for some reason which seemed utterly unfathomable to her now, she had refused him. Greta searched the cob-webbed recesses of her mind, desperate to remember why.

*Patience, Greta, patience*, she told herself, having already learned that some things jumped into her brain involun-tarily whilst others she had to wait for. Because there was another memory; something that had happened after this which she knew might explain things more clearly.

She closed her eyes once more and, as if she were trying to net an elusive butterfly, attempted to relax and let her synapses reach out and try to catch it. Glimpses were there already . . . it was at the Savoy – she recognised the heavy silver cutlery and the immaculate white linen tablecloth – she and David were talking over lunch and she'd been very nervous because she had something to tell him. Then David had spoken to *her* and she'd been thrown off balance by it . . . What *was* it? Bad news, something that had shocked her . . .

Cheska and Bobby Cross.

Greta opened her eyes, knowing then the exact moment she had decided to tell David how stupid she'd been when she'd rejected his proposal all those years before. She had been about to tell him she loved him and ask him whether he still felt anything for her . . .

And then later that evening, they'd been due to meet for a drink, but Cheska had arrived before him, just as David had said. And they'd had that terrible argument. Greta now knew that she hadn't ever been able to say the words she'd needed to say to him because she'd walked into oblivion a few minutes later . . .

So he had never known over all these years what she had been planning to tell him.

Was it too late . . . ?

*Maybe not*, she thought, rerunning the memory of his declaration of love and his proposal over and over in her mind and hugging it to her. With a smile of pleasure, Greta eventually dozed off.

'Fancy some fresh air, darling?' David asked Tor after they'd eaten lunch the following day.

'Good idea. Greta's sleeping, is she?'

'Yes.'

The two of them set off, Tor sweetly asking questions about what he had told Greta. He answered most of them monosyllabically. He felt protective of Greta and what was happening to her but, equally, guilty that this Christmas had not quite been the one he'd envisaged. For him, or for

Tor. For months now he'd been working his way mentally towards asking Tor to marry him, understanding that he was too old to hang on to his dreams and visions of perfect love with Greta. He and Tor were happy together in a practical sort of way. And really, he should do the decent thing and put a ring on her finger.

All these intentions drifted through his mind as he answered her questions as best he could. At the same time, he pondered on what it was that Greta had just recalled – but did it really make any difference? Even if she had now remembered her past and the part he had played in it, she had never loved him. Or, at least, not in the way he wanted her to. Besides, despite his feelings for Greta, which he knew he would never lose, Tor had given him a sense of stability; such a refreshing contrast to the madness of the time he'd just recounted to Greta.

His current relationship might not contain the same passion, but was that relevant at this point in his life, given the pain he'd experienced in the past? That period of his life, running between Greta and Cheska when they were both so sick, had caused him so much stress he'd wondered at the time if he were half mad, too.

And he knew Tor was getting restless, feeling rightly that their relationship needed to be put on a firmer and more permanent footing. He'd even brought his mother's engagement ring with him to Marchmont – the very same one he'd had in his pocket that evening when he'd proposed to Greta. It was sitting in a drawer of their bedroom, ready for him to take out at the appropriate moment. Maybe, he thought, he should wait until they were away at his apartment in Italy for New Year. All this would be behind them then – but, at the same time, David was intuitive enough to know that Tor had been tense about Greta being here in the first place, let alone what had happened since.

'I think there'll be a thaw by tomorrow, judging by the heat of that sun.' Tor looked up at him and smiled.

'You're probably right,' David agreed. 'But it's been beautiful while it's lasted.'

'It certainly has.' Tor put her arm through his then leant up and kissed his cheek. 'We must decide what adventures we're going to plan for next year. Where do you fancy? I was thinking that we could either go back and do the Marco Polo route through China, given we didn't manage to get there last time, or maybe Machu Picchu. We could leave at the beginning of June and then travel through South America.'

David loved her for what she'd just said. It was the perfect antidote to the last few hours. She wasn't dwelling on or complaining about Christmas and his lack of attention to her, but propelling him forward into the future. David sighed inwardly. The past had gone. And Tor had been so patient about the Greta situation, unlike so many other women would have been. He owed her a lot for continuing to stand by him.

'Either sounds wonderful – whichever you prefer. Also,' David said, out of pure instinct, 'I want to ask you something.'

'Oh yes?'

'Well, I think that if we're going to be travelling abroad this year it would be a good idea to change the name on your passport sooner rather than later.'

'What do you mean?'

'I mean that I'd like you to be my wife, Tor. And excuse me if I can't go down on bended knee, because rheumatism might set in due to the snow and you'll never get me up again. But there it is.'

'Are you serious?'

'What kind of comment is that to make to a comedian?'

She smiled then, and gave an almost girlish giggle. 'Well, are you?'

'Tor, of course I am! I was going to wait until Italy but, just now, something came over me and I had to ask. So how about it?'

'I . . . are you sure?' Tor seemed surprised, almost dazed by his proposal.

'Yes. Are you?'

'I think so.'

'Goodness, darling, we've been together for years. Why is it that you're so shocked?'

She turned away from him for a while and he saw her taking a deep breath before turning back to him.

'Because I thought you'd never ask.'

Greta woke up feeling refreshed and exhilarated. Even though there were many things David had told her, and she had remembered many more herself that she must somehow deal with, the fact that David had loved her once filled her heart with happiness. And if he had loved her then, surely he could love her again . . . ?

Greta ran a bath then took extra care with her hair, make-up and clothes before joining everyone downstairs in the drawing room for drinks before dinner.

The moment she entered the room she could feel a buzz of excitement. A chilled bottle of champagne sat in an ice bucket on the coffee table.

'We were waiting for you,' said Ava, coming towards her and drawing her into the room. 'David has an announcement to make.'

'Although I think we all know what it is,' said Simon with a grin.

'Shh!' said Ava, digging him in the ribs. 'Uncle David, you've held us in suspense for nearly an hour.' She handed Greta a glass of champagne. 'Come on, then, spit it out.'

'Well, the thing is, Tor and I have decided to get married.'

Ava and Simon raised their glasses and cheered. 'Finally!' said Ava.

'Congratulations,' said Simon, going to kiss Tor on the cheek. 'Welcome to the family.'

Greta stood there, stunned, and as she did so, she saw that David was looking at her. They stared at each other for no longer than a few seconds before Greta recovered her equilibrium, pasted a bright smile on her face and went to congratulate the happy couple.

'What a Christmas this has been,' said Ava a little later as they sat at the dinner table. 'First you remembering, Granny, and now Uncle David and Tor. I didn't think there'd be a lot to celebrate with LJ gone, but I was wrong.'

'Yes,' said Tor. 'Let's raise our glasses to LJ.'

'To LJ.'

Greta, reaching the end of her ability to look as thrilled

as everyone else, excused herself on the pretext of a bad headache and went upstairs to bed.

Undressing and climbing under the duvet, she did her best to be happy for David. *And* Tor. Whatever David had once felt for her was obviously irrelevant, in the same way that, looking back, it was irrelevant how she'd felt about Max, Cheska's father. The moment was now, not then, and she couldn't expect anyone else to alter their plans just to suit her.

It was simply too late.

Greta woke up early the following morning, after a restless night. She went downstairs and found Tor alone in the kitchen, eating breakfast.

'Morning, Greta.'

'Morning.'

'There's some coffee on the go if you want it.'

'I'm afraid I'm a tea drinker at this time of the day,' Greta replied, switching on the kettle. 'It must be my Northern roots.'

'You disappeared early last night, but I wanted to apologise for the fact that the announcement wasn't exactly best timed, given what's been happening to you. Remembering everything so fast must be very difficult.'

'It is in some ways, yes, but in others it's very positive.'

'You're dealing with it okay, then?'

'I think so. How would I know?' Greta shrugged defensively.

'No, I suppose you wouldn't. Anyway, you get a bravo from me for being so stoic about it all. And it really is revelatory for you. Once you've got over the shock, I'm sure you'll be able to move on to a much more fulfilling and active life than you've had in the past few years.'

'Yes, I'm sure I will.'

'I think it was perhaps one of the reasons David felt that the moment was right to ask me to marry him. Knowing that, in time, you'd be much more able to be independent. I hope you don't mind me saying so.'

'Not at all.' Greta forced a smile. 'Now, I think I'll take my tea back upstairs. I have a couple of letters to write.'

Greta left Tor in the kitchen before she poured her cup of hot tea over the woman's head just to stop her well-meaning but subtly barbed comments. She didn't need anyone to remind her what a 'burden' she had been to David over the years. And although she couldn't blame Tor for resenting the fact, just now, Greta really couldn't handle her nose being rubbed in it.

She found Mary in her room, making her bed.

'Hello, *fach*, how are you?' Mary looked up at Greta, something like sympathy in her eyes. For what, Greta couldn't be sure.

'Coping, thank you, Mary,' she said, determined that everyone should stop feeling so damned sorry for her. 'What about David's news? Isn't it wonderful?'

'Yes, it is.' Mary's voice had a shallow ring to it and she gave Greta an odd look. 'Not what I was expecting, I must say.'

'Really? I thought it had been on the cards for years.'

'Well, now, that may be the thing. To my mind, *fach*, if you find someone you love you don't hang about for all that time before you make up your mind to marry them.

Especially not at Master David's age.' Her voice dropped to a whisper. 'Not that I don't like Tor, but . . . I've never felt his heart's been quite in it. Well now, it's none of my business, is it? I hope they'll be very happy, Miss Greta, and that you, too, will finally be able to find some happiness. You've been through a lot.'

'Thank you,' Greta said, feeling the difference between Mary's warm, genuine sympathy, and that of Tor.

'And I hope you won't be a stranger to Marchmont any longer after this. Young Ava's going to need as much support as she can get when the little one arrives. I remember you being a wonderful mother to your two.'

'Do you?' Greta glowed with pleasure. 'Well, yes, even if things weren't exactly perfect, what with Owen's problems, I've remembered now that I was very contented.'

'You were, and' – Mary blushed suddenly – 'can I let you into a secret? I always used to tell you everything. Do you remember Jack Wallace, the estate manager?'

'Yes, of course I do, Mary. He used to spend a lot of time in your kitchen, eating your home-made cakes.'

'Well, he's asked me to marry him, and I think I might say yes.'

'Oh Mary! That's lovely. You must have been very lonely since Huw died.'

'I have been, and so has he since his wife passed away. But do you think it's too soon? I've only been widowed three years, see. I wouldn't like people thinking I was a hussy!'

'I doubt anyone's going to think that.' Greta chuckled. 'And, honestly, Mary, having just wasted twenty-four years myself, if you've found happiness with someone, my advice is to go and grab it. Life's too short to worry what people think.'

'Thank you, Miss Greta,' Mary said gratefully. 'Now then, I've finished, and I'm off downstairs to prepare some lunch. I know Tor thinks she's helping, but I don't like anyone interfering in my kitchen.' She bustled out with a snort of irritation.

Greta sipped her tea, feeling comforted by Mary's words. They'd once been friends and Greta hoped they could be again. Finishing her tea, she went back downstairs in search of David; she didn't feel she had congratulated him appropriately the night before. Besides, before he and Tor left for Italy, Greta knew she had to ask for his help with the rest of the story.

He was in his usual chair by the fire, reading the *Telegraph*.

'Good morning, Greta. How are you today?'

'Well, thank you,' she said, as his eyes peered enquiringly at her over the newspaper. 'You?'

'Apart from the fact that I drank far more champagne than is good for me last night, yes.'

'I just wanted to tell you again, David, that I'm thrilled for you and Tor. I hope you'll be very happy. You certainly deserve it.'

'Thank you, Greta. And I hope you know it won't mean that I'll suddenly disappear in a puff of smoke from your life. Tor's still a few years from retirement, so it's very likely we'll keep everything as it is now, in terms of living arrangements.'

'David, honestly, you really mustn't worry about me,'

she replied, more brusquely than she meant to. 'But listen, have you any plans this morning?'

'No, not as far as I know. Why?'

'Well, obviously, there are a lot of things I now remember *before* the accident, but I was just wondering, given what I now know happened before, whether you've told me everything. Because I have a feeling you've probably – out of the best intentions, of course,' she added hurriedly, 'edited bits out. Would that be right?'

David folded the paper neatly and placed it on his lap. 'Yes. I didn't want to upset you. You've been so fragile, Greta.'

'Well, would it be all right if I went through what I know has happened since then and you fill in the blanks for me? It shouldn't take very long. I think it's important I know the full story. About Cheska,' she added pointedly.

'Okay.' David didn't sound too keen. 'If you begin, I'll do my best. I'm just concerned it's all going to be a bit too much for you.'

'It won't be,' she said firmly. 'So I came out of hospital after eighteen months. Ava was here at Marchmont, and Cheska was in Hollywood, yes?'

'Yes, and nothing of particular interest happened that you should know about over the next sixteen years. Sadly, it all turned into a bit of a nightmare – some of which you *do* know – just before Ava's eighteenth birthday . . .'

# Ava

## April 1980

# 37

Ava Marchmont walked up the lane and then down the long drive towards Marchmont. It was a trudge she hated in winter, especially if it was snowing. By the time she opened the kitchen door, her feet would be completely numb and she'd have to toast them by the Aga to thaw them out. But thankfully, winter was only a memory now and the ten-minute walk was one she relished during the spring. As she strolled along, she noticed the daffodils blooming at the base of the trees that lined the drive. The newborn lambs, some of which she had helped bring into the world, had begun to find their feet and gambolled happily in the nearby fields.

She gazed up at the clear blue sky and experienced a sudden burst of happiness. Dropping her heavy leather satchel onto the ground, she stretched her arms above her head, exhaling slowly. She felt the late-afternoon sun on her face, took off her glasses and let the world become a blurred mass of green, blue and gold, amazed at how her vision of life could be altered so completely. Eyes the colour of her mother's, LJ had always said. Ava only wished they worked the way most people's did. She'd worn glasses from the age of five, when her form teacher couldn't understand why such a bright little girl was struggling to learn to read and write. Chronic short-sightedness had been diagnosed.

She put her glasses back on, picked up her satchel and walked on. Spring term was over and for the three weeks of the Easter holidays she could relax and enjoy doing what she loved best.

Since she was a small child Ava had helped out on the farm, tending the animals. The sight of a creature suffering had always filled her with dismay and when the farmhands had shaken their heads Ava would refuse to give up on the animal and would nurse it back to health. As a consequence, she now had her own 'menagerie', as LJ called it.

A sick lamb, the runt of the litter, whom she'd bottle-fed until he was old enough to be weaned, had been the first. Henry was now a woolly, old-aged pensioner of a sheep and Ava doted on him. There was a fat, pink pig called Fred, numerous chickens and two bad-tempered geese. Then there were the leverets, covered in mites, which she'd saved from the claws of the farm cats, taking them to her bedroom in shoeboxes and tending their wounds as LJ shook her head and told her that there was little hope. Her great-aunt said small animals were more likely to die of fear than from their injuries, and looked on in surprise as Ava's gentle ministrations restored them to health. Her menagerie was housed in a large disused barn, and most of the animals in it became tame and greeted their saviour noisily whenever she appeared.

There was also a small burial ground in a quiet spot under an old oak tree at the back of the house. Each death was marked with a cross and copious tears on Ava's part.

As she grew older Ava became single-minded about what she wanted to do with her life. Her schoolwork was erratic, as she had little interest in subjects such as art or history, but when it came to anything to do with nature and biology, she shone. The past few months had been hard work, as she knew she must get excellent passes in her A-levels to get into veterinary college. However, over the next three weeks she could spend her time with her animals, which she was sure taught her a lot more than sitting in a classroom ever could.

Ava reached the bend in the drive where Marchmont itself came into view.

Watching the sun glinting off the slate roof, she thought how lucky she was to live here. It had such character and looked so warm and welcoming, she'd never wanted to live anywhere else. Her intention was to come back to Marchmont as soon as she was a qualified vet and, eventually, open a small practice of her own. Ava hoped her local reputation for helping animals would give the practice a good start.

She approached the house and was glad to see the dressmaker's car wasn't yet parked in the drive. She grimaced as she thought of the fitting she'd have later. She could only remember three occasions on which she'd worn a dress and, in the summer, there would be a fourth. Still, she thought, she'd have to grin and bear it. After all, it was going to be a very special day. Aunt LJ would be eighty-five. And she herself would turn eighteen just a few weeks before.

Ava opened the door that led into the kitchen. Jack Wallace, the farm manager, was sitting at the pine table drinking tea as Mary rolled out pastry.

'Hello, Ava, *fach*. How was your day?' asked Mary.

'Wonderful, because it was the last school day for three whole weeks!' Ava giggled and gave Mary an affectionate kiss on the cheek.

'Well, if you think you're going to have an easy time of it during the Easter holidays, you've got another think coming,' said Jack with a grin. 'I'll be wanting your help with the sheep dipping, now Mickey has moved to the town.'

'Fine by me,' said Ava, 'as long as you promise to take me to the cattle auction next week.'

'You got a deal, missy. Now, I've got to be going. Thanks for the tea, Mary. Goodbye, Ava.'

Ava waited until Jack had closed the door behind him.

'Jack's always in here these days, Mary. I think you might have an admirer.'

'Get along with you, I'm a married woman!' Mary dismissed the comment with a blush. 'I've known Jack Wallace since we were both babes in arms. I'm only a bit of company for him now his wife's passed away.'

'Well, I'd be careful if I were you,' Ava teased. 'Is Aunt LJ resting?'

'Yes. I had to threaten to lock her in her bedroom, mind. Your great-aunt is too strong-willed for her own good. She has to remember she's eighty-four now, and that nasty operation she had would have taken the strength away from a woman half her age.'

'I'll take her up a cup of tea.' Ava went to the Aga, lifted the kettle and took it over to the sink to fill it.

'Don't be too long. The dressmaker'll be here at five.

Indeed to goodness, I'll be glad when this birthday party is over!'

Ava listened to Mary complaining as she thumped the pastry into shape, knowing that she secretly enjoyed all the plans and activity. 'We're all going to help, Mary. Stop worrying. It's months away yet. If you carry on like this, you'll have a nervous breakdown. What's for supper tonight?'

'Steak and kidney pie, your great-aunt's favourite.'

'I'll just have a plate of vegetables again, then.'

'Now, don't you go blaming me for your silly vegetarian ideas, *fach*. Man's eaten meat for thousands of years, just as cats eat mice. It's natural, part of revolution.'

'I think you mean "evolution", Mary,' Ava corrected her with a grin, as she poured boiling water into the teapot and stirred it.

'Whatever. It's no wonder you're so pale. It's not right for a growing girl, and those tofu things you eat are no substitute for a good piece of red meat. I . . .'

Ava slipped out of the kitchen with the tea tray while Mary continued to chunter away obliviously, and made her way upstairs to LJ's room.

'Come in!' came the reply to her knock.

'Hello, darling, have you had a nice rest?' Ava asked as she placed the tea tray on her great-aunt's bed.

'I suppose so.' LJ's bright-green eyes twinkled at her. 'Can't be doing with all this napping in the afternoon. Makes me feel like a baby or a basket-case. I'm not sure which is worse.'

'You only had the hip replacement a month ago, remember? The doctor said you had to rest as much as you can.'

Ava poured the tea into LJ's favourite china cup and handed it to her.

'All this fuss! Never had a day's illness in my life until that damned cow sent me flying with her hoof!'

'Everything's under control, I promise. Mary's in the kitchen, grumbling and cursing, and the dressmaker will be here shortly. There's nothing for you to worry about,' soothed Ava.

'So you're saying I'm dispensable, are you, young lady?'

'No, LJ. I'm saying that the most important thing is for you to get your strength back.' Ava kissed her great-aunt's head fondly. 'You finish your tea and, when I've had my fitting, I'll come back and help you down the stairs.'

'Well, I'll tell you one thing, there's no way I'm arriving at my own party on that ridiculous Zimmer frame,' LJ said vehemently.

'Aunt LJ! You have weeks to recover, so stop panicking. And besides, think of poor me – I have to wear a dress!' Ava rolled her eyes in horror. 'Right, I have to go and practise being feminine.'

After Ava had left the room LJ put her cup down on the tray and sank back against her pillows. Ava was such a tomboy, always had been since she was small. And so shy, only comfortable with her close family. The only time her great-niece shone with confidence was when she was handling her precious animals. LJ adored her.

Nearly eighteen years ago, after several weeks of waiting for Cheska to return from LA, LJ had abandoned any plans to distance herself emotionally from the baby girl who'd been left behind. So, at a time when most women of her age were settling down in front of the fire with a tartan blanket wrapped round their legs, LJ was changing nappies, crawling on the floor after a toddling infant and joining anxious mothers almost young enough to be her grandchildren in the playground on Ava's first day at school.

But it had given her a new lease of life. Ava was the daughter she'd never had. Quite by coincidence, they shared the same love of the outdoors, of nature and animals. The age gap was wide, but it had never seemed to matter.

LJ had spent many hours since contemplating how a woman such as Cheska could have produced such a sensible, balanced child. When Cheska had left for LA all those years ago, she hadn't even had the decency to call to let David and LJ know she was all right. A few days later, David, having been caught up with Greta coming out of her coma, had been due to fly out and bring her home.

Then a letter had arrived, addressed to LJ at Marchmont, written in Cheska's childish script.

*The Beverly Wilshire Hotel*
*Beverly Hills*
*90212*

*18th September 1962*

*Dearest Aunt LJ,*

*I know you must think very badly of me for what you will see as me abandoning Ava. But I have spent a long time thinking about what to do, and I don't think I would make a very good mother for her just now. The only thing I'm good at is acting, and the studio has offered to place me under a five-year contract.*

*At least this way I will be paying for Ava's keep and her future, but I will be very busy making the films, which will mean I wouldn't have a lot of time to spend with her. I'd have to get a nanny and, besides, I don't think Hollywood is a very nice place for a baby to be brought up in.*

*I know it's a lot to ask you, but I'd like Ava to stay at Marchmont and have the kind of childhood in the beautiful countryside that I wish I'd had. Will you care for her, Aunt LJ? I always felt so safe and secure when I was with you there and I'm sure you will do a much better job of bringing up Ava than I would.*

*If you feel it's too much for you, I can send money for you to employ a nursemaid. Please let me know what you need.*

*Also, you will probably think I don't love or care about Ava. I swear I do, which is why I'm trying to do what's best for her, not me, for a change.*

*I will miss her terribly. Please tell her I love her, and I will come home to see her as soon as I can.*

*Please forgive me, Aunt LJ, and write back when you can.*

*Cheska*

LJ had read and reread the letter, trying to decide whether she thought the best or worst of her niece. It was only when she called David and read him the letter that he confirmed her worst fears.

'Ma, I hate to say it, but I'm afraid Cheska may be thinking of her career rather than Ava. The studio almost certainly doesn't know about the baby. They have a strict moral code for their actors and actresses and put all sorts of clauses in contracts so they have to adhere to them. If Cheska or her agent were to mention she was an unmarried mother at the age of sixteen, she'd be on the next flight home.'

'I see. Oh dear, David. I mean, of course I don't mind at all looking after Ava – she's such a dear little thing – but I'm no spring chicken and hardly a substitute for her real mother.'

There had been a pause at the other end of the line before David answered.

'You know, Ma, under the circumstances, I actually think it's the best thing for Ava. Cheska is . . . Cheska and, to be blunt, if Ava went to live with her in LA, we'd both be worried sick. The bigger question is can you cope?'

'Of course I can!' LJ had retorted. 'I have Mary to help me, and she adores her. I've managed to run the estate and the farm, so I doubt one little baby will make much difference.'

David was, as usual, in awe of his mother's self-belief. She was truly indomitable. 'Well then. I'll cancel my flight, and you should write back to Cheska saying you agree. Of course, Cheska must pay for Ava's upkeep. I'll write, too, and tell her that myself. To be honest, Ma, I'm relieved. What with Greta's slow rehabilitation, the last thing I needed was to get on a plane to Los Angeles.'

'How is Greta?'

'Currently having physiotherapy to strengthen her muscles. She'd been in bed so long, they'd practically wasted away. Yesterday, she managed to stand up for a few seconds.'

'And her memory?'

'Nothing much at the moment still, I'm afraid. There's been the odd mention of her childhood, but beyond that it seems to be a complete blank. Honestly, Ma, I'm not sure which is worse, talking to her for months and never getting a response, or now, when she stares at me as though I'm a complete stranger.'

'Dear boy, what a time you've had.' LJ swallowed her frustration. What she thought about her son's continuing devotion to Greta was best kept to herself. 'Let's hope she remembers soon.'

Since then – over seventeen years ago – Cheska had not returned. And, sadly, neither had Greta's memory.

The only contact from Cheska in the early years had been a monthly cheque and the occasional parcel for Ava containing large boxes of American candy and dolls with over-painted faces that Ava would discard in favour of her tatty teddy bear. The message was always the same: 'Tell Ava I love her and I'll see her soon.'

When Ava was old enough to understand, LJ explained that the parcels from America were from her mother. For a few weeks after that Ava had asked when her mummy would be coming back, as she had written it would be soon in the letters that accompanied the parcels. There was nothing LJ felt she could do but smile brightly and reassure her that her mother loved her.

Eventually, the parcels stopped coming and Ava stopped asking. LJ continued to talk about Cheska, when appropriate. She wanted the child to understand, just in case – though the thought appalled her – Cheska ever *did* come back for her daughter.

LJ had heard from David that Cheska was doing very well. She'd made a number of big films that had been shown in British cinemas – LJ had declined to watch them – and then, five years ago, she'd landed the lead in a new American soap opera. It had become internationally successful and Cheska was now a global television superstar.

Although LJ disapproved of television, she thought it unfair to stop Ava having a set, as all her friends at school did. One night, when Ava was thirteen, she'd walked into her bedroom and seen Cheska's face filling the screen. She'd sat down next to Ava on the bed and watched the programme with her.

'You know who that is, don't you, darling?' she'd asked her.

'Of course I do, Aunt LJ. It's Cheska Hammond, my mother.' She turned her attention calmly back to the screen. 'The show is called *The Oil Barons* and it's absolutely brilliant. The girls at school love it. Cheska is very beautiful, isn't she?'

'Yes, she is. Do you tell your friends that she's your mother?'

Ava had turned to her, an expression of astonishment on her face. 'Of course I don't! They'd think I was making it up, wouldn't they?'

LJ had wanted to laugh and weep at the same time. 'Yes, I suppose they would, dear girl.'

She had sat there for the rest of the episode, watching the woman she'd once known as a young girl strut around in an array of exquisite clothes, making her way through a stunning selection of apartments and houses, and, LJ noted, a number of beds.

When the programme had finished LJ turned to Ava. 'Is this really suitable for you, Ava? It looks a bit spicy.'

'Oh, Aunt LJ, don't be so old-fashioned. I know all about sex. They taught it to us at school when we were twelve. They even showed us a video.'

'Did they, indeed?' She'd raised an eyebrow and reached for Ava's hand. 'When you watch your mother, do you wish you were with her in Hollywood, leading that sort of glamorous life?'

'Goodness, no!' Ava had laughed. 'I know Cheska is my mother by birth, but I've never met her and I can't say I miss her at all. You're my mother and Marchmont is my home.' She'd thrown her arms round LJ. 'And I love you very, very much.'

Over the years Ava had become LJ's life, an intrinsic part of her being. The maternal instinct was as powerful as it had been with David. She sometimes chided herself for living through the child, just the way Greta had done with Cheska, but she couldn't help herself. Ava was such a darling and she'd do anything for her.

Now, LJ heard Ava's quick footsteps coming along the passage towards her bedroom and shook herself out of her reverie. Maybe it was to do with the operation, but recently, she'd experienced an impending feeling of doom. She'd tried to shake it off, but she'd trusted her instincts for eighty-four years. And they had rarely been wrong.

# 38

## *Los Angeles*

'Oh, it's you.' Cheska spoke tersely into the receiver, removed her satin eye mask and glanced at the clock by her bed. 'What the hell are you doing calling me at this hour of the morning, Bill? You know it's the only day I get to lie in.'

'Sorry, honey, but it's half past eleven and we need to talk. Urgently.'

'Does that mean they've agreed to the extra twenty grand per episode?'

'Look, Cheska, can we meet for lunch and I'll explain?'

'You know I rest on Sundays, Bill. If it's that urgent, you'd better come over. My masseuse is coming at two, so make it three.'

'Okay. See you then, honey.'

Cheska dropped the receiver back onto its ornate gilt-and-cream stand and sank into her pillows, feeling irritable. Saturday night was the only evening she could stay up into the early hours. The rest of the week she was awake with the birds at four thirty and the studio limousine collected her at five.

And last night had been . . . well, it had been . . .

Cheska patted the other side of the kingsize bed and felt only rumpled sheets. She looked across and saw a piece of paper on one of the pillows. She picked it up and read it: 'Last night was sweet. Hugs, Hank.'

Cheska stretched like a cat, remembering the night she and Hank had just shared. Hank was the lead singer with a great new band. He'd been guesting in the club she'd gone to last night with a couple of friends, and Cheska had known the minute she'd seen his lean body, blue eyes and dirty-blond hair that she had to have him.

Later that evening, as usual, Cheska got what she wanted.

Normally, the thrill of the chase was the thing that set her nerve endings tingling; the sex itself was a let-down. But last night had been fantastic. Maybe, just maybe, she'd agree to see him again. Cheska climbed out of bed and padded into the en suite marble bathroom to run a deep tub.

When she'd first moved into the house high up on Chalon Road in Bel Air, just after she'd won the part of Gigi in *The Oil Barons*, it hadn't had any security. Now, there was a ten-foot brick wall with twenty-four-hour cameras and alarms between her and the outside world. Even though the view from the upper storeys was spectacular – all Los Angeles spread out in the valley below – Cheska didn't open the blinds to let the glorious sunshine pour into the room. They were always kept firmly closed until she was fully dressed, because once, an enterprising photographer had climbed a ladder and snapped her wrapped only in a towel. He'd sold the shot to a couple of tabloid newspapers for a fortune. After all, she was now one of the best-known celebrities in America, and possibly the world.

Cheska turned off the taps, pressed the jacuzzi button and stepped into the tub. She sank down and the jets gently buffeted her body. She had no idea why it was so urgent that Bill saw her. Surely there wasn't a problem with the new contract? She shook her head, chasing away the thought. Of course there wasn't. Gigi was the most popular female character in *The Oil Barons*. Cheska got more fan mail than any other cast member, was asked to make more public appearances and stole more headlines than all the other actors put together.

Cheska knew it was partly due to her notorious private life. The studio had admonished her on various occasions when she was photographed with yet another young, blond lover, mumbling about the morals clause in her contract, but she took no notice. How could they possibly complain when it was more publicity for the show, anyway? And her private life was just that: private, and none of the studio's goddamned business.

Cheska gazed at her reflection in the mirror and noticed a couple of lines under her eyes. She was tired, worn out from nine months' non-stop filming. Thank God the summer sabbatical was only a few weeks away. She needed to take off, get some rest and relaxation. Maybe her messy and much-publicised divorce six months back had taken more of a toll than she realised. Under Californian law, the husband or wife was entitled to half of everything their spouse owned. As she owned a lot, and her rock-musician shit-of-an-ex-husband had had nothing, she hadn't come out of it well. She had lost the Malibu beach house and half her cash and other investments to Gene 'Bastard' Foley. He hadn't worked a day while they'd been married but spent his time hanging out at the beach house with his long-haired friends, smoking dope, drinking beer and using her hard-earned money to rage round seedy joints in LA. Cheska rued the day she'd decided to marry him, but they'd been high in Las Vegas and it had seemed like a gas to wake a minister at three in the morning and demand he marry them then and there. Gene had used a discarded ring-pull from a beer can to put on her finger. The publicity had been staggering. Their picture had been on the front of all the major newspapers across the world the following day.

The truth was, he'd reminded her of Bobby . . .

Because of one moment of madness, Cheska had lost a great deal financially. And she had always lived extravagantly. She bought expensive designer clothes and threw enormous parties, catered for by the best in the business, whenever the mood took her. Before the divorce, she'd had the money to pay for those things. Now she was running up what her accountant called a 'magnificent' overdraft.

He'd called to see her last week and suggested she start cutting down on her expenses. The bank was prepared to extend her overdraft by another fifty thousand dollars but only after they'd taken out a further charge on her house. She'd signed the papers he handed to her without even reading the small print.

All this was why she needed the raise on her new contract. As Gigi, she was indispensable to *The Oil Barons* and she'd wanted to negotiate aggressively. Bill, her American agent, had urged caution. He'd said the studios were volatile, that they didn't like actors feeling they were bigger than the show they starred in.

Cheska reached for a towel as she stepped out of the tub. She thought how ridiculous it was that the hottest TV star in Hollywood was having to penny-pinch. As she dressed, she comforted herself that the new contract should sort out all her financial problems.

'Come in, come in.' Cheska waved at Bill from the sofa, as her Mexican maid showed him into the large, comfortable sitting room overlooking the pool. 'I can't move, darling. I've just had a massage and my toes painted. Drink?'

'Iced tea would be swell,' Bill said to the maid.

'Make that two,' Cheska added as the maid left the room.

Bill walked over and planted a kiss on her cheek. 'How you doing, honey?'

Cheska smiled and stretched as he placed his briefcase on the glass coffee table and sat down. 'Fine, just fine. So, what's the news that's so urgent you had to leave your wife and kids on a Sunday?'

'It's about the show.'

'Well, I gathered it would be.' She studied Bill's face, and saw the tension written on it. 'Nothing's wrong, is it, Bill?'

'Look, the thing is, Cheska, I'm afraid the studio isn't going to renew your contract.'

Cheska drew in her breath. At that moment the maid returned with the iced tea and they sat silently as she put the two glasses on the table then left the room.

'You must have heard them wrong, Bill, surely?'

'Irving called me in to see him on Friday. They, well—' Bill paused, trying to think how to phrase it. 'The new head of the studio is a clean-living family man, and he wants his stars to set an example.'

'Hold on a moment, Bill. So you're telling me that even though the characters in *The Oil Barons* jump in and out of bed with each other on a regular basis, have illegitimate children, drug problems and violent husbands, its stars have to live like saints? Jesus!' Cheska shook her head then gave a bitter laugh. 'How hypocritical can you get?'

'I know, I know,' Bill soothed. 'But the show will be cleaned up in the next series. A bunch of those things you've just mentioned will be taken out.'

'Along with the high ratings,' she murmured. 'Why the hell does he think the great American public watches the show?'

'I agree, Cheska, and I can only say I'm real sorry you've been caught in the crossfire. But I've warned you time and again that the studio—'

'—the studio doesn't like its leading stars being seen in nightclubs, drinking, dancing or, in fact, having any kind of fun or life of their own,' finished Cheska angrily.

'Look, let's get real here, honey. During the past few months you've been late on set, you've forgotten your lines—'

'I was going through a divorce, for Chrissakes!' Cheska thumped a cushion hard and threw it on the floor. As she stared out of the window, those old, familiar feelings, the ones that she'd hoped were a distant memory, threatened to surface. She pushed them down inside her, swallowed hard and looked back at Bill.

'So, how does Gigi, I mean . . . ?'

It was the crucial question. If the studio had Gigi flying off into the sunset with a man, it meant there was room for a return. If not . . .

Bill took a deep breath. 'A car crash. Dead on arrival at the hospital.'

'I see.'

There was another long silence. Cheska struggled to keep herself under control. 'So,' she said eventually, 'that's it, then? Washed up, finished, at the age of just thirty-four.'

'Oh come on, you're exaggerating,' countered Bill. 'The studio thinks it best if they announce that you want to leave the series of your own accord to develop various projects. And there's no reason why you shouldn't move straight on to other things. I've already got a couple of ideas.'

Bill spoke with a confidence he didn't feel. Bad news travelled fast on the intimate inside track of Hollywood. And Cheska had picked up a reputation as being 'trouble'.

'They don't honestly expect me to let them fire me without fighting back?' Cheska shouted.

'Honey, really, there's nothing you can do.'

'I could call the *National Enquirer* and tell them what that bastard producer Irving is doing! He's never liked me, Bill, not since he tried it on and I kneed him in the balls. If my fans knew Gigi was being shelved by the studio, there'd be an outcry!'

Bill stifled a sigh. He'd seen this all before; stars who thought they were indispensable to both the studio and the public. In reality, both were fickle, and Gigi would soon be forgotten as another character caught the audience's imagination. Besides, Cheska was so difficult, always had been.

Up until now, for the sake of the ratings and a percentage of the profits, both he and the studio had been prepared to put up with her mood swings and volatility.

'Look, Cheska. I'm afraid making a stink about this is going to do no one any good, least of all you. Think about your career. We'll have to take it on the chin if you want any kind of future in this town.'

'I just can't believe this is happening, Bill.' Cheska rubbed her forehead, dazed with shock. 'I mean, the show's still high in the ratings, Gigi is the most popular character . . . I—' She wrung her hands. 'Why?'

'I've told you why. I understand how you feel, but we'll just have to put this behind us and look to the future. There isn't anything we can do about it.'

Cheska glanced at him, her eyes glinting malevolently. 'You mean you don't want me to do anything to hurt your cosy relationship with the studio?'

'Now, that's not nice, Cheska. I've done my best for you, you know that. I've gotten you some great deals in the past few years.'

'Well, if this is your best, I think maybe the time's come for a change. I'm calling ICM. You're fired, Bill. Please leave.'

'Come on now, Cheska, you don't mean that. We're gonna sort this out together and get you something real good.'

'Don't give me that baloney, Bill. You've got other, bigger fish to fry than me now; in your eyes, I'm a washed-up actress with a bad reputation.'

'Cheska, don't talk such shit!' Bill said.

She stood up. 'From now on I'll deal with you through

my accountant. Send all cheques to him, as usual. Goodbye, Bill.'

Bill looked at Cheska. Her chin was set at a defiant angle, her eyes were clouded with anger. He'd thought her one of the most beautiful young women he'd ever seen when she'd first walked into his office all those years ago. And she was probably even more lovely now she'd matured. Underneath that exterior, though, she was a real screwy broad, always had been. Paranoid about what people thought of her, believing everyone was out to get her, even when she was riding high. But then, the town was full of insecure women. Cheska was just the cream of the crop. Bill knew he was being let off the hook, and he wasn't sorry. He decided not to fight on.

'Okay, Cheska, if this is what you want.' He sighed, picked up his briefcase and walked towards the door.

'It is.'

'If you change your mind, let me know.'

'I won't. Goodbye, Bill.'

'Good luck.' He nodded at her and left the room.

Cheska waited until she heard the front door close. Then she sank to the floor and began screaming with rage.

# 39

Eight weeks later Cheska arrived home after her last day at the studio. There'd been champagne and a huge cake on the set afterwards, with the rest of the cast gushing about how much they'd miss her. She'd gritted her teeth and smiled her way through the party, pretending that leaving *The Oil Barons* was *her* decision. She realised that Bill had been right, it was the only way to salvage what was left of her pride and her career – even though she knew for certain they were all aware she'd been fired.

Whenever someone had asked her about her next project, Cheska had waved a hand nonchalantly, saying she was going to Europe for a much-needed vacation before she committed herself to anything. The truth was there was nothing in the pipeline. She'd called all the A-grade agents in town – ICM, William Morris and so on – operations that had been desperate to represent her a few years ago. Now, when she phoned, a secretary would take a message, but the agents never rang back.

Cheska asked her maid to bring her a glass of champagne and sank into an armchair in the sitting room. She'd begun to wonder whether she'd made a dreadful mistake when she'd told Bill to take a hike. Should she call him? Ask him to forgive her heat-of-the-moment decision and start scouting around town for suitable roles?

No, she decided. Her pride had taken a big enough battering and she couldn't go crawling back to him now. The only thing she could do was to set her sights a little lower, go for an up-and-coming agent who would be glad to add a big name like her to their list.

But was a second-rate agent worse than no agent at all? Probably.

'Shit!' Cheska closed a hand over her temples. She had a bad headache coming on.

The maid brought her the champagne and she took a large gulp, not caring if it made her headache worse.

And, of course, there was her financial problem. She was broke – in fact, worse than broke. She owed tens of thousands of dollars. Yesterday, she'd gone to Saks to buy a dress for her last-night party and her credit card had been refused. The assistant had rung through and returned to tell her that she was over her limit. So Cheska had written out a cheque which she knew would almost certainly bounce and walked out, red-cheeked and fuming. When she got home she'd called her accountant and asked him to send the next cheque he received from Bill direct to her, bypassing the bank. It would be for over twenty thousand dollars, which should see her through the next few weeks, if she was careful.

Cheska let out a wail of despair. She'd worked solidly from the age of four, and what did she have to show for it? A house that would have to be sold to pay off her debts and a wardrobe full of designer outfits that she now had no occasion to wear. Her friends in the business, so happy to accept her hospitality in the past, had deserted her in droves during the past few weeks.

She knew why: she was on her way down – they smelt it on her like cheap perfume. There was no room in their lives for a failure. It might brush off on them.

Cheska spent the rest of the night getting very drunk and awoke the following morning on the sofa, still fully clothed.

The following week was almost intolerable.

She cancelled her masseuse, her workout coach and her hairdresser. She fired the maid and her security company, knowing she couldn't afford to pay them at the end of the month. Her nails became chipped, her hair hung lank around her face and she stopped getting dressed in the morning.

Her financial problems, and the boredom, were bad enough, but those dreaded feelings, the ones she'd hoped and prayed had left her forever, were starting to bubble to the surface. Her dreams became overcrowded once more, and she woke up sweating and shaking.

Then a few days ago, she'd started hearing that familiar voice, the one that had made her do those terrible things. She hadn't heard it since she'd left England, nearly eighteen years ago. And other voices had joined in too. They weren't telling her about other people this time, they were telling her about *herself*.

*You're a failure, aren't you, Cheska? . . . A silly, no-talent little girl . . . you'll never work again . . . nobody wants you any more, nobody loves you . . .*

Cheska would move from room to room, trying to leave

the voices behind, but they always came with her, never giving her a moment's peace.

She tried banging her forehead with her fist to try and make them go away. She answered them back, shouting as loudly as they did, but the voices wouldn't stop . . . just wouldn't stop.

In desperation, she'd called the doctor a couple of days ago for some strong tranquillisers, but they did nothing to calm her or stop the voices.

Cheska knew she was going off the rails. She needed help, but she didn't know where to turn. If she told her doctor about the voices, he'd lock her away in a funny farm, like those other doctors had when she was pregnant.

After two weeks of living hell Cheska looked in the mirror one morning and saw that she was no longer there.

'*No! No!* Please!'

She sank to the floor. She was invisible again. Maybe she was dead already . . . she'd dreamed it often enough. What was reality? She didn't know any more. Her head was bursting, the voices drumming away, laughing at her.

She ran maniacally around the house, putting sheets over the mirrors that were too heavy to move and turning the rest around to face the walls. Then she sat down on the sitting-room floor, trying to still her breathing.

Cheska knew she could go on no longer. The voices were right when they told her she had no future.

'Somebody help me, help me, help me!' *There's no one to help you, Cheska . . . no one. Nobody loves you, no one wants you . . .*

'*Stop it! Stop it! Stop it!*' Cheska began banging her

head rhythmically against the wall, but still her tormentors continued.

A short while later, she sat up. There was no alternative. The peace she craved could only be achieved one way.

Cheska walked slowly to her bedroom and took out the bottle from her bedside drawer. She sat on the floor and gazed at the innocuous-looking yellow spheres peering at her from behind their glazed brown plastic screen. She wondered how many she'd have to take to make sure. She twisted the top and shook one of the pills into her palm.

The voices assailed her ears once more, but this time she laughed.

'I can stop you!' she cried triumphantly. 'It's easy, it's so easy . . .'

She put the pill to her lips, and her tongue tasted its burning, chalky texture. Taking a glass of water from the bedside table, she swallowed it. Tipping out three more, she looked up to the heavens, where she was sure Jonny was waiting for her.

'Can I come to you now, please? I don't want to go down there with them. If I say sorry and that I believe in God, will they let me?'

For once, there was silence in her head. No one answered and a single tear rolled down her cheek.

'I'm sorry, Mummy, so sorry. I didn't mean it, really.'

*And what about Ava? You abandoned your daughter . . . Who can forgive you for that?*

The voices were back again. 'Please! *Please!*' she begged them. She knocked back the pills in her palm and was about to tip out more when there was another noise . . . a bell chiming, as if at the gates of hell.

The chimes reverberated around her head. 'Stop! Stop! Please stop!' The noise was vaguely familiar, and gradually she realised it wasn't hell beckoning her in but the bell at the front gates. Somehow, she managed to walk into the hall, then sank to her knees.

'Go away, go away! Please!' she screamed.

'Cheska, it's me. Uncle David!'

Cheska looked up at the video screen. David? It couldn't be him. He lived in England. It was the voices again. They were trying to trick her.

'Cheska, please, let me in!'

She stood up and peered at his face on the screen, just to make sure. Older, heavier, with grey hair receding at the temples, but still with the same twinkling eyes.

'Okay, okay.' Cheska walked unsteadily down the hall to switch the alarm system off, then pressed the buzzer to let David in through the gates.

David did his best to hide his shock when Cheska opened the front door. Her hair was lank and greasy, her eyes glassy, with large black smudges beneath them. Her pupils darted from side to side, giving her the appearance of a hunted animal. In the centre of her forehead was a huge black bruise. A dirty sweatshirt hung from her thin shoulders and her once shapely legs looked like two sticks. She was swaying in front of him, as though she was drunk.

'Cheska, how lovely to see you.' He leant forward to kiss her and smelt an unwashed odour.

'Oh, David, David, I—' Her blue eyes looked up at him in anguish, then she burst into tears and sank to the floor once more.

He watched as she sat there, rocking herself backwards

and forwards, and knelt down to comfort her, but she screamed when he tried to touch her. Then he noticed the pill bottle clutched in her fist.

'That's it, I'm calling a doctor.'

She looked up at him. 'No! I . . . I'll be fine, really.'

'Cheska, look at you. You're not fine at all.' He wrenched the bottle from her grasp and looked at the label. 'How many of these have you taken?'

'Only three or four.'

'Do you absolutely swear?'

'I swear, David.'

'Right. Let's get you up off the floor.' He swiftly pocketed the pill bottle then helped her to her feet. She managed to make it into the sitting room, collapsing onto the sofa and holding out her arms to him.

'Please, come and hold me. Uncle David, just hold me.'

David did as she asked, and she buried her face in his lap. She lay there silently for a while, then stared up at him, studying his face. She lifted a hand and traced his eyes, nose and mouth.

'Are you real?'

He chuckled. 'Well, I should hope so! Why do you ask that?'

'Oh, because I've imagined so many things over the past few days. People, places . . .' A smile suddenly lit up her face. 'If you *are* real, then I'm so glad you're here.'

With that, Cheska closed her eyes and promptly fell asleep.

# 40

After a while, David gently moved Cheska's head onto the sofa and left her to sleep. He went into the kitchen, noting the filthy surfaces littered with used glasses and cups. Taking the bottle of pills from his pocket, he flushed the contents down the waste-disposal unit. He had little doubt what Cheska had been about to do, and thanked the fates that he'd decided to stop as he drove past her house on his way to stay with an old actor friend further up the hill.

He'd been working in Hollywood on and off over the past few years and had called in on Cheska occasionally for a drink, believing that, in spite of her abandonment of Ava, it was important to maintain some form of contact. But he had always found her company difficult to endure. There had normally been a man hanging around somewhere in the house and he doubted he'd had more than a few minutes alone with her over all his visits. He was aware that this was almost certainly done on purpose; no one in Hollywood knew that Cheska had a child and he was sure the last thing she wanted was him talking about Ava. She'd known he wouldn't in front of strangers.

He had dutifully written to tell her that her mother had

woken up from the coma soon after Cheska had left England, and had tried to keep her informed of Greta's progress over the years. But every time he'd seen her, Cheska had been singularly uninterested in talking about Greta. When David brought the subject up, it was a one-way conversation, with him offering short platitudes such as 'Your mother sends her love' – which was a lie, anyway, as Greta didn't even remember Cheska.

Whenever he visited he'd always leave her house feeling horribly depressed, as it was obvious Cheska's past in England no longer existed for her. As it didn't exist for Greta. It saddened and frustrated him, but his mother always said, 'Let sleeping dogs lie,' and, eventually, that was what he'd done.

David washed up a cup and made himself some tea, going over the situation in his mind. He had little or no idea what had driven Cheska to attempt suicide. He'd presumed that everything was going wonderfully for her.

He'd been in Hollywood for the past month shooting a cameo part in a big movie. Filming had ended yesterday and he was on his way home to England. Temporarily, at least. After attending his mother's eighty-fifth birthday party, he was going on a long-delayed 'gap year', as the teenagers these days called it. He was sixty-one years old, and his career – both here in the USA and in England – had reached the point where he felt he could take time off and return if he wished. He'd earned it, and knew if he didn't do it now, he might be too frail in the future to attempt it.

And, finally, he wasn't alone.

He smiled at the thought of her: her petite but shapely figure and her dark hair, swept up in a chignon, her brown eyes shining with warmth and intelligence. He'd liked her the first time he'd met her. It had been at a dinner party given by an old friend from his Oxford days. As a single man, he was usually seated next to a spare female on these occasions, most of whom left him cold. But Victoria, or Tor, as she liked to be called, was different. He had thought originally that she was in her mid-forties – though he found out later she was over fifty – and she had told him her husband had died ten years earlier and she had never felt the need to remarry. She was an Oxford don, specialising in ancient Chinese history, and her husband had been a classical scholar. Tor had spent her life closeted in the world of academia.

David had driven home thinking that such a cultured, well-read woman would have little or no interest in a light entertainer like him. Granted, he too had received an excellent formal education, but he'd lived in a very different world ever since.

However, a week after their first meeting, he received a note from her inviting him to Oxford for a recital he'd expressed interest in. He'd booked into a local hotel, wondering how he'd mix with Tor's intellectual friends. And he'd had a very enjoyable evening.

Later that night, over a quiet supper, Tor had chided him for his modesty. 'You entertain people, David. It's a great gift, far greater than writing a thesis on Confucius. Making people laugh and feel happy for a few seconds is a wonderful talent. Apart from that, you were at Oxford once, too. And this evening you held your own perfectly well with my friends.'

They had begun to see each other regularly and, eventually, he'd asked her if she'd like to go away with him for a weekend. He had taken her to Marchmont, where LJ had warmed to her instantly. Although, mused David, given his mother's thinly disguised frustration at his enduring devotion to Greta – 'For goodness' sakes, darling, she doesn't even remember who you are!' was her constant mantra – he was hardly surprised at her relief that at last he had a 'lady-friend', as she'd delicately put it.

'Ma, she really *is* a friend,' he'd insisted that first weekend.

Throughout the next few months David began to rediscover himself; his love for music and the arts, walking hand in hand down a country lane after a large Sunday lunch, books they'd both read which were discussed over a bottle of wine late into the night. He felt, above all, that he'd found a woman who appreciated and enjoyed his company as much as he enjoyed hers.

Then Tor announced that she'd decided to take a year's sabbatical from Oxford, visiting some of the distant places she'd taught and written endlessly about but never seen. She had asked him playfully if he wanted to go with her. And even though he'd laughed at the time, when he mulled the idea over, he'd started to think that perhaps it was exactly what he needed. Her eyes had been full of joy and disbelief when he'd said he wanted to join her.

'But what about your career? And Greta?'

Tor knew all about her, of course. She was a big part of his life. Most Sundays for the past seventeen years, Greta had come for lunch at his house in Hampstead or he had visited her – although, recently, David had guiltily cancelled a few times because he had arranged something with Tor. He was well aware how dependent Greta was on him. She rarely went out, finding crowds upsetting, had no visitors apart from himself and Leon, who paid the occasional duty call to her, and, even more rarely, LJ and Ava, when they visited him in London. Greta found the thought of spending even a night away from the sanctuary of her Mayfair apartment untenable. She lived as a virtual recluse.

That moment, when she'd opened her eyes after all those long months in a coma, was one he'd never forget. The joy he'd felt as all his love for her surged to the surface and he covered her face in kisses, his tears dripping unchecked onto her pale face, had quickly turned to horror when she'd batted him away with her thin arms and asked who on earth he was. Over the years, he'd begun to accept the way things were and might always be. He'd had little choice, as Greta's memory stubbornly refused to return.

David did not resent her dependency on him in the slightest; he loved her, after all. But as Greta had never given him a single indication of wanting anything other than his friendship and support, the situation had remained unresolved all these years.

Meeting Tor had crystallised their relationship further. David had finally begun to realise what his mother had been trying to tell him all along: it was hopeless pining for Greta.

Ma was right. He had to move on.

Once David had reassured Tor he was serious about joining her on her travels, they had begun to plan their route. They'd decided to visit India first and, from there, as Tor was a keen walker, they would fly up to Lhasa in Tibet before trekking for several weeks in the Himalayas. After that, they planned to travel through China by the Marco Polo route, a journey Tor had dreamed of making for years.

David poured the dregs of his tea into the sink. When he flew home, he knew he had to speak to Greta and tell her about his forthcoming trip. She was used to him coming to Hollywood for a few weeks at a time – he'd often asked her if she wanted to come, too, and perhaps visit Cheska – but she had always declined. However, six months was a long time. He'd have to ask LJ or Ava to visit her during his absence.

And now he was here, by complete chance, facing what he knew was going to be a difficult situation to extricate himself from quickly. He called Tony, his friend, and said something had come up and he wouldn't be able to make it today after all.

Putting down the receiver, he couldn't help but compare Cheska's current state as a wreck asleep on the sofa to the beautiful woman whose famous face filled television screens, newspapers and magazines across the world.

Something terrible must have happened recently to bring her to the brink of suicide. He wondered how he could find out what it was. He glanced at the names and numbers written on the pad next to the telephone in Cheska's childish looped writing. Bill Brinkley's was the third number. He was the agent she'd taken on after she'd moved here, having unceremoniously sacked Leon. Surely he'd know what had happened to her?

He dialled the number and asked to be put through.

'Bill, it's David Marchmont. I think we've met at a couple of parties here.'

'Yes, I remember. How're you doing, David?'

'I'm very well, thank you.'

'And what can I do for you? Looking for a new agent? I'd be happy to tender my credentials.'

'Thanks, but no thanks, Bill.'

'Okay. So if I can't represent you, what else can I do for you?'

'Have you seen Cheska recently? You know she's my niece.'

'Really? I didn't know that. And, as she fired me a couple of months back and made it clear she didn't want to hear from me again, the answer is no, I haven't seen her.'

'I see. Why did she fire you, if you don't mind me asking?'

'You don't know already? I thought it was all over town.'

'Maybe I know the wrong people, but the news hasn't crossed my bow-wave before now, no.'

'Well, it's certainly not in the public domain yet, so keep it to yourself. They're gonna announce Gigi's dramatic end a month or so before the show is aired again in October. Stir up interest to fever pitch. They're expecting record ratings when it's broadcast. So the reason Cheska fired me is that she blamed me for the studio writing her out.'

'I see. So who looks after her now?'

'No idea. Someone said she was going off to Europe to take a break before she decided what to do next.'

'Right. Do you mind me asking why they didn't renew her contract? It'll go no further, I promise you. I am her uncle, after all, and I'm just . . . concerned for her.'

'Well . . .' Bill paused. 'Okay, as you're related to her, I'll tell you. Cheska was becoming too hot to handle. Making big financial demands, turning up late at the studio and getting herself photographed alongside the wrong kind of guy. I'm afraid she brought it on herself, David. But if you do speak to her, don't tell her I said that.'

'Of course not. Well, good to talk to you, Bill, and thanks for being so honest.'

'No problem. Send my love to England and, if you see Cheska, give her my regards. She's one screwy dame, but I've got a soft spot for her. She was one of my first clients.'

'Will do, Bill. Thank you. Goodbye.'

He put down the receiver, walked back into the sitting room and saw that Cheska was still asleep. David sighed. He understood it all now. Playing nursemaid to his niece yet again was the last thing he'd anticipated when he'd flown into LA, but he could hardly walk away and leave her alone now.

David went out to his car to bring in his suitcase. Unpacking it in Cheska's spare room, he pondered why fate had propelled him back into the past, when, for the first time in years, he'd been so eagerly looking forward to the future.

# 41

Three hours later, Cheska woke up. Despite her protests, David insisted on calling her doctor and asking him to come and examine her. The doctor duly arrived and after a quick chat to let him know what had happened, David took him into the sitting room, expecting to find Cheska where he'd left her on the sofa. She wasn't there. He climbed the stairs and knocked on her bedroom door. He turned the handle, and discovered it was locked.

'Cheska, let me in. The doctor wants to take a look at you.'

'*No!*' Her voice was agitated. 'I'm fine. Tell him to go away!'

No amount of persuasion would make her open the door. Eventually, he retreated back downstairs.

'Well, there's not much we can do, is there?' said the doctor. 'Try and persuade her to come and see me tomorrow and, in the meantime, encourage her to eat something and let her sleep as much as possible. My guess is that she's suffering from depression.'

'I'll do my best,' David said, as he let the doctor out.

An hour later, Cheska appeared downstairs.

'It's all right. He's gone,' David said calmly, switching off the television. 'What on earth was all that about?'

Cheska slumped on the sofa. 'I hate doctors. I don't trust any of them. You and LJ put me in that mental hospital when I was pregnant and people used to scream and cry all night. No one's ever going to do that to me again.'

'It was the doctors who suggested that you went into hospital, Cheska. And we were only doing it for your own good. And Ava's, of course.'

Cheska stared off into the distance, as if she were listening to something. She turned to David, her eyes glazed and dull. 'Sorry?'

'Nothing. You're going to have to start eating and taking care of yourself, Cheska. You look dreadful. And your house is a pigsty.'

'I know.' She smiled suddenly and stretched out her arms to him. 'Oh Uncle David, I'm so glad you're here. You won't leave me alone, will you? I don't like being alone.'

'Well, if you want me to stay, you're going to have to start behaving yourself, young lady.' He stood up and went to embrace her.

Cheska snuggled into his arms, as she had when she was a small child. 'I will, Uncle David, I promise.'

The following few days were extremely difficult, as the whole sorry story began to come out. Cheska rarely slept and would appear in his bedroom at odd hours, shuddering with terror from another nightmare. He would hold her, comforting her as she talked.

'Oh Jesus, Uncle David. They fired me, they actually fired me! Me, Cheska Hammond, major star! It's all over.

I have no future now, no future at all. I'm all washed up, as they say here.'

'Come on now, sweetheart, don't be silly. There are heaps of actors who leave one show and make it big again in something else. Something will turn up, I know it will.'

'Yes, but it's got to turn up *now*, Uncle David, I haven't got a penny. I'm up to my neck in debt and the bank's bound to repossess the house—'

'But what happened to all the money your mother invested for you? And the money you've been earning since?'

'I spent it all. And what I didn't spend, my shit of an ex-husband took, or the taxman. There's nothing left, nothing. Oh, Uncle David, my life's such a goddamned mess.'

He put his arms around her thin frame and held her to him. 'Cheska, I'll help you sort things out.'

'Why would you want to help me, after the way I behaved all those years ago?' she cried.

'I watched you grow up, Cheska. You're the nearest thing to a child of my own I've ever known. And families stick together in times of crisis.'

Cheska looked up at him, her pale face streaked with tears. 'And you've always been like the father I never had. Thank you.'

A couple of days later David put in a call to Tor – who had been expecting him in Oxford for the coming weekend – and explained the situation.

'Never mind, darling. At least it's happened now and you can deal with it before we leave rather than when we're halfway up the Himalayas and uncontactable. You do think Cheska will be stable enough for you to leave her by then, don't you?'

David could hear the hint of anxiety in her voice. 'Yes. She'll have to be, because I'm not cancelling this trip for anyone. I'll let you know when I'm flying back.'

'Take care of yourself, David.'

'I will. And you.'

As David replaced the receiver, he hoped and prayed that his firm stance on the subject wouldn't be put to the test. This trip was for *him* and, for a change, he was going to put his own needs and wants first.

Fortunately, with each passing day, Cheska began to look a little better. The doctor had prescribed sleeping tablets and with their help, she began to sleep through the nights and the colour returned to her cheeks. David managed to get her to eat regularly and made sure she dressed in the mornings. There were still moments when she'd disappear off into her own private world, even when he was speaking to her, and her beautiful eyes would take on their strange, glassy expression. She never mentioned Greta or Ava. David followed her lead and didn't bring them up either. He also refrained from telling his mother the real reason he was delayed in Los Angeles. He knew how much any news of Cheska upset her.

One beautiful, balmy evening David had just put the phone down to Tor, after reassuring her that Cheska seemed much better and that he hoped to be able to fly home soon. He turned to see Cheska standing behind him.

'Who were you speaking to, Uncle David?'

'Tor . . . Victoria, my friend.'

'Are we talking "friend friend", or "girlfriend"?' she

asked, a hint of mischief in her voice. 'From the way you were speaking to her, I'd say the latter.'

'I suppose she's both,' David replied cautiously.

'I have some wine open on the terrace. Want to come out and watch the sunset and tell me about her?'

David followed her outside. The view from the terrace was incredible. In the valley below Cheska's exclusive hill-top perch the lights of downtown Los Angeles twinkled against the dark-blue sky, which was dramatically streaked with vermilion and gold clouds. He leant against the railings, taking in the spectacle.

'You are a dark horse, Uncle David.' Cheska smiled as she handed him a glass of wine. 'Come on then, tell me.'

So David found himself telling Cheska – who seemed hungry for even the tiniest detail – all about Tor and the trip they had planned together.

'She sounds lovely, and you sound a little in love,' she commented.

'Maybe I am. But when you get to my grand old age, things are different. We're taking it slowly. And the trip will tell us both a lot. We'll be thrown together for six months.'

'So when do you leave?'

'The middle of August, just after my mother's birthday party.'

'You know, I used to think you were in love with my mother,' Cheska mused. 'I even hoped that one day you'd get married.'

'I asked her once,' David confessed, 'but she refused me.'

'Then she was very stupid. Anyone could see she loved you, too.'

Surprised at her comment, David remained silent. He wanted to see if Cheska would ask how her mother was now, but she didn't, so after a few seconds he moved the conversation on. 'And Ava, of course, turns eighteen next month.'

'My little daughter, Ava, all grown up.' Cheska said the words as if she were reminding herself who Ava was. 'How is she?'

'Very well. Bright, pretty, and—'

'Does she look like me?'

'Yes, I think she does. She has the same colouring, but she wears her hair short, is much taller than you are and, well, to be frank, she couldn't be more different from you in personality.'

'That's a blessing,' she murmured to herself.

'Sorry?'

'Oh, nothing. Tell me about her, Uncle David: what she likes, what her ambitions are. Does she want to be an actress?'

He chuckled. 'No. Ava wants to be a vet. She has the most wonderful way with animals.'

'I see. Does she . . . does she know who I am?'

'Of course she does. LJ and I have made a point of talking about you. Ava is addicted to *The Oil Barons*. She watches you every week.'

Cheska shuddered and David kicked himself for his *faux pas*.

'And LJ? I suppose she hates me, doesn't she?'

'No, Cheska, she doesn't hate you.'

'You must both have found it difficult to understand why I came here and left Ava behind, but can't you see, I didn't have a choice? I knew if I told you, you wouldn't let me go. I had to make a clean break, get away from the past and try to start again.'

'Cheska, we both understand. But, to be frank, it's been very difficult for LJ in the past few years. She's become a surrogate mother to Ava and I think she's always worried that, one day, you might want your daughter back. My mother loves Ava like her own child, and any negative feelings she's had towards you have been completely forgotten for Ava's sake.'

Cheska sighed heavily. 'I've really screwed up my life, haven't I, Uncle David? My career's crumbled, I can't hold down a relationship and I abandoned my own daughter.'

'Cheska, you're only thirty-four. Most people's lives are only beginning to blossom at that age. You talk as if you're as old as I am.'

'I feel as old as you. I've been working my butt off for thirty of those years.'

'I know. And I wish I'd never introduced you to Leon all those years ago. You can blame me for beginning it all.'

'Of course I don't. It was what life had stored up for me. Uncle David, can I ask you something?'

'Fire away.'

'Do you . . . do you think I'm . . . normal?'

'It depends on how you define "normal", Cheska.'

'Well, let me put it like this: do you think I might be crazy?'

'You've had a very unusual life. Being under the kind of pressure you experienced from such a young age is bound to have had repercussions. If you're worried, you could always go and speak to someone about how you feel.'

'No way! Never again! Shrinks don't help, they just interfere where they're not wanted and make things worse. The thing is, Uncle David' – Cheska took a deep breath – 'sometimes I hear these . . . voices in my head. And they, well, they make me do things I . . . I—'

David could see that she was becoming agitated. 'When do you hear the voices?'

'When I'm angry or upset or—' She shivered. 'I can't talk about it any more. Please don't tell anyone, will you?' she begged.

'I won't, but I really do think you should talk to someone, Cheska. It might be something simple, like needing a complete rest.' David spoke with a confidence he didn't feel. 'When did you last hear them?'

Cheska seemed to be having an inner struggle with herself. 'I didn't hear them for years, and then . . . I said I can't talk about it anymore, *okay*?'

'All right, sweetheart, I understand.'

'What about . . . Ava's father? Does she know who he is?' she asked, abruptly changing the subject.

'No. Both LJ and I felt it was your job to tell her.'

'She's better off not knowing about him anyway!' Cheska's eyes darkened. 'I'll never tell her.'

'She may want to know some day.'

'Well, I . . .' Cheska stared out into space for a few seconds, her fingers playing with the tassels of the cushion on which she sat. Then she yawned. 'I'm sleepy. Would you mind if I went to bed?'

'Not at all. But I really think you should consider going to see someone about your . . . problem,' he said tactfully.

Cheska stood up. 'Okay. I'll think about it. Goodnight.'

She leant down and kissed him on top of his head before leaving the terrace.

The following morning David was woken from a restless night's sleep by Cheska placing a breakfast tray on his bed.

'There. A real cooked English breakfast, with all the trimmings. I remember how much you liked them when I was younger.'

David sat up, rubbing his eyes, and glanced at Cheska in astonishment. She was dressed in a smart silk shirt and jeans, her make-up and hair were perfect and her eyes were shining with life. She looked like a completely different person.

'Why, Cheska, you look wonderful!'

'Thank you,' she replied, blushing slightly. 'As a matter of fact, I feel great. Talking to you last night has taken a load off my mind.' She sat down on the bed and gazed at her hands. 'I've been stupid and self-indulgent. So I got up this morning, went for a swim in the pool and decided it's about time I pulled myself together.'

'Well, it's – if you don't mind me saying – a remarkable transformation, and one I most definitely approve of.'

'Hey, what about you and me going for lunch at the Ivy? I've not been out of the front door for what feels like weeks.'

'An excellent idea, if I have room after this huge breakfast.' David smiled.

'I'm sure you will.' Cheska stood up. 'I'll see you downstairs. I'm going to ring Bill, my agent, and apologise for firing him. See if he'll take me back.'

'That's my girl.'

'Oh, and I think it would be a good idea if I made an appointment to see a therapist. All my actor friends have one. It's *de rigueur*. No big deal, is it, Uncle David?'

'No, Cheska, it isn't, it really isn't.'

She left the room and David sank back on his pillows, a sigh of relief escaping his lips. Maybe now that Cheska had talked openly about her fears she would be able to deal with them. Of course, it was early days, but after the last week, when he couldn't see how he could possibly leave her, there was now a glimmer of hope.

Maybe his longed-for trip would take place after all.

# 42

'Have you got everything, Uncle David?' Cheska asked as he came downstairs carrying his suitcase.

'Yes, I think so.'

'Great. The cab's waiting.'

He put down his suitcase. 'Now, young lady, I want you to promise me you'll keep up the good work. Are you sure you'll be all right? I can always stay an extra day or two if—'

'Shush.' She put a finger to his lips. 'I'll be fine. Bill has already organised some stuff for me, so I'm going to be kept very busy. Who knows? Leaving *The Oil Barons* might be the best thing I ever did.'

'Just promise me you'll carry on seeing that therapist you've found. By the way, there's a cheque for you on the coffee table. It should see you through for a couple of months.'

'Thank you. I promise I'll pay you back as soon as I've got a job. Now, skedaddle, or you'll be late for your flight.'

Cheska accompanied David outside to the cab. Before he got in, she flung her arms round him.

'Thank you so much. For everything.'

'Don't be silly. Just look after yourself.'

'I will. Have a wonderful trip with Tor. Send me some postcards!'

'Goodbye, Cheska. I'll call you from England.'

David waved out of the window until she had disappeared from view.

On the long flight home David was unable to relax.

Was Cheska well enough to be left? Should he have stayed longer? There was no doubt her recent transformation had been remarkable and, outwardly, the woman with whom he'd spent the past few days had seemed balanced and calm.

But had the change been too immediate . . . too perfect? She'd fooled them all once before, when she'd returned to Marchmont from the hospital with Ava and then left so abruptly for LA. David only hoped Cheska would continue to see the therapist and prayed that she'd soon find an acting job to get her teeth into.

He also agonised over whether to tell his mother where he'd been for the past few days and the state he'd found Cheska in. After all, he was going away with Tor for months and it would be difficult to contact him in an emergency. That was the whole point of the holiday for him: to let the rest of the world slip away.

Eventually, he decided he couldn't tell her. It would only upset and worry her and, with her recent operation and her forthcoming birthday party, it just wasn't fair.

David was at least deeply thankful that Cheska had seemed to have no interest in seeing Ava. She was thousands of miles away from Marchmont and, he reflected, that was probably a good thing.

All he had to do now was tell Greta.

He closed his eyes and tried to sleep. He'd done all he could. Now it was *his* chance for happiness.

Cheska had watched David's cab depart with a mixture of relief and sadness. That night, after she'd tried to talk to him about how she felt and confided in him about the voices in her head, she had gone to sleep feeling calm and relaxed. But then the voices had woken her, telling her she'd let David get too close; if she talked any more, they would lock her away again.

She had sat up sweating and shaking. The voices were right. She'd been wrong to confide in him; so she'd had to make sure he went home. It had taken a great deal of effort to ignore them when they talked to her, but somehow she'd managed to appear normal for the past few days and now he was gone.

Her life wasn't over. The voices had told her what to do.

She was going to Marchmont, to see her daughter.

Greta, as she always did when David was coming to visit her, spent an hour in her local salon having her hair styled and set. Even though she was sure he didn't notice, it made her feel better. She then busied herself in the kitchen, baking a Victoria sponge and her special scones, which she knew David loved. She brought out her best china tea service from the cabinet and dusted it clean before laying it on the coffee table. Checking her watch – he was due here in under an hour – she went to her bedroom to change into the skirt and blouse she'd laid out earlier. Applying a little mascara, blusher and pale pink lipstick, she went into the sitting room to wait for the doorbell to ring.

She hadn't seen him for weeks, because he'd been in Hollywood making a film. Bless him, he always offered to take her with him, which she knew was just out of kindness. Besides, the thought of having to go to an airport, get on a plane, fly in a cramped cabin for twelve hours, then land at an unknown destination was simply too much for her. It took all her courage just to venture out to the local supermarket and the salon once a week. She'd hurry back home afterwards, sighing with relief when she was back in the sanctuary of her apartment.

David was very sweet when she tried to explain her fear of the outside world; he said it probably had something to do with the night of the accident. Apparently, there'd been a crowd waiting with her for the lights to change on the pavement outside the Savoy. Then someone had shoved her from behind and she'd fallen out into the road and in front of a car.

Greta thought this might partly account for her agoraphobia, coupled with the fact that she'd spent many months institutionalised in the quiet, calm atmosphere of a hospital. She'd remembered the day they said she could go home and how she'd put her hands over her ears in terror as David had led her out onto the noisy London street.

But it was also a feeling she couldn't explain to anyone. Everyone else out there in the world knew who they were, they carried their histories inside them everywhere they went; whereas she was just an empty husk of nothing masquerading as a human being. So, as much as she didn't like crowds or noise, the fact was that being with other, normal people only made her feel more desperate about what was lacking inside her.

The only exception to that rule was David, maybe because he was the first person she'd seen when she'd woken from the coma. He'd been there at the start of her miserable new existence and she trusted him absolutely. However, even though he was always patient with her, doing all he could to jog her memory, she could occasionally feel his frustration. He'd show her one of the endless photographs he used to remind her of her past, and when her memory remained as blank as ever, she could see it upset him.

Sometimes, when she looked down on the busy street from the safety of her third-floor window, Greta felt as though she was living in a twilight world. The doctors had suggested it was of her own making. They thought she *could* remember, because, apparently, no damage had ever shown up on any of the brain scans they'd done. This meant that her memory loss was somehow self-imposed; because of the trauma, they'd said.

'Your conscious mind has simply decided it doesn't *want* to remember,' one consultant had told her, 'but your subconscious knows everything.' He had suggested hypnosis, which she had tried for a good three months, to no avail. Then there had been a course of tablets – Greta reckoned they were antidepressants – which another consultant said might relax her and take away the fear of remembering. All they did was make her sleep until mid-morning and feel lethargic for the rest of the day. Then there had been the therapy sessions, where she sat in a room with a woman who asked her inane questions like how she was feeling, or what she'd had for supper the night before. This line of questioning had been something that had really irritated her; she might not be able to remember anything from before the accident, but her memory was as sharp as a tack on everything that had happened to her since she had woken up.

In the end, by mutual consent, they had all given up, closed the files and locked her unfathomable condition away into a steel cabinet.

Except for David. He never seemed to give up hope that, one day, she would remember. Even if she herself had lost hope long ago.

One of the most painful things was the fact that, because the doctors could find no reason for her condition, she was left with an endless sense of guilt that somehow this was her fault, a problem she could solve if she really wanted to. Sometimes, she saw a look in people's eyes – especially LJ's, on the few occasions she'd come up to town with Ava and they'd visited her for tea – that told Greta this was what other people believed, too. And out of everything, Greta thought this was the worst; that people actually thought she was pretending. Sometimes, during the endless, solitary evenings, her eyes would fill with tears of anger and frustration that anyone could think that she *wanted* to live like this. In her darkest hours she wished she had died in the accident, rather than having to suffer the incalculably lonely existence she'd endured since.

If it hadn't been for David, she might well have done something to put an end to this half life she led. No one would miss her: she wasn't needed or useful to anyone, simply a burden, which was why she made sure she never made too many demands on David – even though, when he stood up to leave, she wanted to throw herself into his arms, tell him she loved him more than she could ever say and ask him to stay forever.

The words had been on the tip of her tongue often enough but she'd always stopped herself just in time. What kind of a life would she be subjecting him to? A woman who jumped at the sound of the telephone ringing, would rather die than have to go out and be sociable with David's many friends, could never in a million years see herself travelling further than her local high street, let alone to America or David's newly purchased apartment in Italy.

*All I can give him is scones.* She sighed to herself as the doorbell rang.

'Hello, Greta, you look very nice today,' David said, kissing her on both cheeks and handing her a bunch of tulips. 'They're so gorgeous, I had to buy them.'

'Thank you,' Greta said, touched by the gesture.

'You used to love tulips,' he said as he made himself comfortable in the sitting room and surveyed the scones. 'My favourite. I'm meant to be on a diet, but how can I resist?'

'I'll just put the kettle on to boil.' Greta hurried into the kitchen. She'd switched it on only a few minutes ago, knowing it would take less time to boil a second time, because she didn't want to waste a single second with David.

Carrying the teapot through, she placed it on the table and sat down opposite him. 'So, how was Hollywood? You were away a little longer than you said.'

'Yes, filming overran, as it often does. I'm glad to be

back. That town is not a place I'd ever choose to be for long, as you know.'

'Well, at least you got a tan,' she said brightly, pouring out the tea.

'You look as though you could do with some sun, Greta. I know I'm always saying it, but it might do you good to take a walk and get some fresh air. Green Park is looking very beautiful at the moment, with all the summer flowers out.'

'That sounds like a good idea. Maybe I will.'

They both knew she was lying.

'So, are you busy in the next few weeks?'

'Very,' David said. 'Apart from anything else, I'm going to Marchmont this weekend for Ava's eighteenth, and then of course, it's my mother's eighty-fifth birthday party in August. I presume you got the invitations to both?'

'Yes, and I've written back to them, and put some money in a card for Ava. I'm sorry, David. I just . . . can't.'

'I know, but it's a great pity. We'd all have loved you to be there.'

Greta swallowed hard, knowing that she was letting him down again.

'Maybe another time?' David said, understanding her discomfort all too well. 'Anyway, Greta, I have some news.'

'Really? What's that?'

'Well, I've decided to take a sabbatical.'

'You're going to stop work?'

'Yes, for a while anyway.'

'Goodness, that *is* news. And what will you do instead?'

'I've decided to go off and see a bit of the world. I have a friend – Victoria, or Tor as everyone calls her – and we're off on an adventure. India, the Himalayas, Tibet, and then on to do the Marco Polo route through China – which is why I shouldn't be reaching for another of your delicious scones.' David chuckled as he did so. 'I'm meant to be getting myself fit for the trip.'

'Well . . . that sounds interesting,' Greta managed, determined not to let David know a dagger had just sliced through her heart.

'I'm going to be away for six months, perhaps longer. And you understand, Greta, that it means we won't be seeing each other for a while, but I really feel it's now or never. I'm getting old.'

'Of course!' Greta feigned enthusiasm. 'You deserve a holiday.'

'Well, I'm not quite sure I'd call it that, but it will certainly do me good to take a break from the treadmill. Are you going to be all right without me?'

'Of course I am. As a matter of fact, I'm working my way through all of Charles Dickens's books, so that's keeping me occupied. After him, I'm moving on to Jane Austen. One of the few good things about my memory loss is that I can read all the great classics again, but for the first time!' Greta smiled brightly. 'Please don't worry about me. I'll be fine.'

David's heart went out to Greta, knowing she was putting on a show for him so that he wouldn't feel guilty. He was her lifeline, and they both knew it. Yet again, he wavered in his determination to make this trip with Tor, and Greta saw it immediately.

'Really, David. Six months isn't that long, you know. And it will be so interesting to hear all about it when you get back. Just don't catch some nasty foreign bug or fall off a mountain, will you?'

'I'll do my best, I promise.'

After that, they sat and made small talk about LJ, and Ava's plans to go to veterinary college, both of them feeling uncomfortable and upset.

Finally, Greta found the courage to ask the question that had been burning on her tongue ever since David had mentioned his 'friend'. 'Are you and this lady – Tor – an item these days?'

'Well, I suppose you could say we were,' said David, realising that honesty really was the best policy. 'We've been seeing a lot of each other recently. She's very nice. I think you'd like her.'

'I'm sure I would.'

'Anyway' – he looked at his watch – 'I'm afraid I'll have to make a move. I've got a meeting at the BBC in half an hour.'

'Of course.'

David stood, and Greta followed suit. They walked in silence to the front door.

'I'll try and pop in before I leave,' he said, kissing her on both cheeks. 'Take care, won't you?'

'Yes. Goodbye, David.'

The door closed behind him and Greta walked slowly back into the sitting room. Mechanically, she put the cups and plates onto a tray and took them into the kitchen to wash them up. She looked at the cake, untouched, and threw it in the bin. Having done the washing up and put it all away, she went back to the sitting room and sat down on the sofa. She stared into the distance and wondered how on earth she could continue her life while David was gone.

Even though LJ had done her best to persuade Ava to throw a party for her eighteenth birthday, Ava had staunchly refused.

'Really, I'd much prefer a family dinner at home,' she'd entreated.

LJ had raised her eyebrows. 'Surely, dear girl, it should be the other way round? You having a big bash and me having the dinner. I hope I haven't stolen your thunder. We could have used the marquee for both events and got twice the use out of it.'

'No, LJ, from what everyone tells me, uni will be one long party. A dinner is what I'd prefer, honestly.'

So, on a beautiful night in July, David, Tor, Mary and LJ sat on the terrace for dinner and toasted Ava's health and happiness. They had all chipped in to buy her a beautiful sapphire pendant that matched her eyes. Ava had gone to bed that night feeling very loved indeed.

# 43

Ava smiled as she drew back her curtains a month later and the August sun streamed in. It was going to be a hot day. The house was already awake and she could hear the faint sound of footsteps downstairs. She scowled at her dress, which was hanging on the wardrobe door, and padded along the corridor to take a shower.

Twenty minutes later, she was downstairs making tea for LJ. Mary was cutting an enormous salmon into slices, her hair in tight curlers and her language robust.

'I know your aunt said this would be easy, but has she ever tried preparing enough for over fifty people?! I'll still be stinking of fish when the guests arrive.'

'Relax,' Ava soothed her. 'You're nearly done.'

'I just want everything to be perfect, see. I only hope those two nieces of mine don't drop the peas over the guests when they serve them.'

'Of course they won't, Mary. Here, have a cup of tea and sit down for a second.' Ava pulled out a chair and put a mug on the table. 'I'm taking this one up to LJ.'

*

Later that morning, Ava stood in front of the mirror in her dress. She studied her reflection and supposed she didn't look too bad. The dress was made of cornflower-blue chiffon and hung in soft folds to just below her knees. Tor, David's girlfriend, had said the colour would match her eyes, which, at the moment, were red and itchy as she had just put in her contact lenses. She picked up her shoes and went along the corridor to knock on Tor's bedroom door.

'Hello, it's only me,' she said, as she entered. 'God, I feel ridiculous!' She sat down on Tor's bed and watched her putting on her make-up in the mirror.

'Enough of that rubbish, Ava!' chided Tor. 'I simply don't understand why you put yourself down all the time. You're lovely and slim, you've got beautiful blonde hair and the most exquisite blue eyes. It's a pity you don't wear your contact lenses more often.'

'But they're so uncomfortable. Do you like wearing all that stuff on your face?' Ava asked as she watched Tor apply her lipstick. 'I don't think LJ's ever worn make-up in her life.'

'Well, I see nothing wrong in giving nature a little help, Ava, as long as you're not hiding behind it, as some women do. Come here,' Tor beckoned her over, stood up from the stool in front of the mirror and pushed Ava gently down onto it. 'Let me show you.'

Ten minutes later, Ava gazed at her reflection. Tor had put a little mascara on her lashes, blusher on her cheeks and added a pale pink colour to her lips.

'Wow! Is that me?' She put her face close to the mirror and studied it disbelievingly.

'Yes, dear. It is you. So, from now on, let's have no more nonsense about being a plain Jane.'

'It's the thought of all those poor animals used for testing cosmetics, just because of women's vanity,' remarked Ava, still staring at her reflection. 'I look like . . . I look like—'

'Yes, Ava, you look like your mother, widely regarded as one of the most beautiful women in the world. Shall we go and see if LJ needs any help?'

Ava smiled. 'Yes, let's.'

Contrary to her expectations, Ava enjoyed the party. It was a glorious day and the guests drank champagne on the terrace, before entering the marquee on the lawn for lunch. Ava was seated next to LJ – with David on the other side of her – and revelled in her great-aunt's joy at seeing all her old friends gathered from far and wide.

'It may be the last chance I get to see many of them outside their coffin,' LJ had muttered at one point. 'Good God! Most of them look half dead already. Can I really be that old?'

After lunch, as everyone gathered back on the terrace, a bright-eyed, elderly gentleman with a deep tan and a walking stick made his way towards LJ.

'Laura-Jane! Goodness, can it really be over sixty years since we last saw each other? I believe it was at young David's christening.'

'Lawrence!' LJ blushed in pleasure as he kissed her on the cheek. 'You've been in Africa ever since, so it's hardly surprising.'

'I'm home now, though. Didn't want my bones resting abroad.'

'No, I'm sure. Now, let me introduce you to my great-niece, Ava.'

'A pleasure,' said Lawrence, taking Ava's hand and kissing it. 'And this is my grandson, Simon.'

Ava stared at the tall young man who stepped forward from behind his grandfather to be introduced. She'd noticed him earlier, mostly because he was one of the few members of the lunch party under seventy. He was broad-shouldered with thick blond hair and brown eyes fringed by dark lashes.

She glanced up at him shyly. 'Hello,' she said. It was her turn to blush.

'Ava dear, would you mind if Lawrence took your place so we can sit in comfort and catch up?' requested LJ.

'Of course not,' Ava said, as she stood back to let Lawrence manoeuvre himself into the chair, which left Ava standing awkwardly and tongue-tied with Simon.

'Do you fancy a cold drink?' he asked her. 'I'm absolutely boiling in this suit. Grandpa made me wear it,' he confided.

'My great aunt insisted I wore this,' Ava said, indicating her dress.

'Well, she made a good choice with the colour. It matches your eyes. Now, where can we get some water?'

Searching the terrace for Megan and Martha, Mary's nieces – who were meant to be on hand with jugs of elderflower water and juice – and not finding them, Ava led Simon through the house and into the kitchen. Whilst she filled two glasses with ice and the pure, clean spring water that flowed from the tap, Simon sat down at the table in relief.

'It's lovely and cool in here. Thank you,' he added, as Ava placed the water in front of him.

'Yes, so cool in the winter that Mary, our housekeeper, calls it our freezer.'

'Would you mind if I took off my tie and jacket? I feel like a trussed turkey.'

'Please, feel free.' Ava sipped her water, not sure whether she should sit down opposite him or not. Even though she often worked alongside the men on the farm, they were all years older than she was, and she attended an all-girls school, so she couldn't remember ever having been alone with a younger man.

'Are you needed elsewhere?' he asked her.

'No. Not for the moment anyway.'

'Well then, can we stay in here and talk for a while before we go back outside and I have to put my tie on again?'

'Of course,' she said, glad he had taken the initiative.

'Where do you live?'

'Here at Marchmont, with my Aunt LJ.'

'So you're a country girl through and through.'

'Yes.'

'You're so lucky. I was born and bred in London but I've spent the past twenty-three years wanting to live in the country. I suppose we always want what we can't have.'

'Well, I'm very happy here. I don't think I could bear to live permanently in a city.'

'It's pretty insufferable, I agree. Waking up here and

opening the curtains must be like getting a present every morning. It's so beautiful.'

'It rains a lot, though.'

'It rains a lot in London, too. What do you do here?' Simon asked.

'I've just finished my final year of school. I'm hoping to get into the Royal Veterinary College in London, so, if I do, I'll be in the city, too,' Ava replied with an ironic smile. 'You?'

'I'm in my last year at the Royal College of Music. Then I'll be turfed out into the great unwashed world of wannabe musicians.'

'What do you play?'

'The piano and the guitar but, really, I want to be a songwriter. More Paul Weller than Wagner. But, as my family says, a good, solid grounding in classical music is important. And even if I have yawned my way through most of my lectures, they're probably right.'

'Well, I admire you – I don't have a musical bone in my body.'

'I'm sure you do, Ava. I haven't met a person yet that doesn't, even if it's just humming along to the radio. Have you always lived here?'

'Yes.'

'Your parents, too?'

'I . . . it's a bit of a complicated story, but I regard LJ as my mum.'

'Right. Sorry to ask.' Simon gave her an apologetic smile.

'That's okay.'

'If you're just finishing school, you must be eighteen. I thought you were older. You seem very mature.'

Ava felt his eyes upon her, appraising her, and shifted in her seat.

'God, that must have sounded patronising coming from someone of the lofty age of twenty-three!' He chuckled. 'It was meant as a compliment, by the way.'

Ava smiled at him. 'Thank you. But I'd better be getting back to LJ now. The day must have worn her out.'

'Of course. It's been very nice to meet and talk to you, Ava. And if you do come to London, I'd be happy to show you around.'

'Thanks, Simon.'

Ava walked from the kitchen, feeling light-headed. She wondered if it was the champagne she had drunk earlier, or talking to Simon, who was without a doubt the most handsome young man she'd ever met.

The guests had begun to depart and Ava saw LJ looked grey with exhaustion.

'Do you want to go up and have a rest, darling?' Ava asked her.

'Absolutely not. Today I will be the last man standing. Metaphorically, at least,' she answered stoically.

Ava left her in the capable hands of David and Tor and went off into the kitchen to help Mary begin the huge task of washing up.

'Did you have a good day, *fach*?'

'Lovely,' said Ava, rolling up her sleeves. 'And the salmon and Eton Mess went down a treat.'

'It did my heart good to see your aunt surrounded by so many of her friends. And who was that young man you were talking to earlier? I saw him giving you the eye during the speeches,' Mary said, nudging her and winking as they stood together over the sink.

'He's called Simon, and he's the grandson of Lawrence somebody, one of LJ's friends. He's a music student, but he's far older than me.'

'How much older?'

'Five years.'

'Look you, that's perfect! You, of all young women, couldn't be doing with a young-un, having grown up the way you have.'

'Honestly, Mary, he was just being polite. It was nothing like . . . that.'

'And what is "that"?' Mary nudged her again.

'You know. *That*. Anyway, stop teasing me. I'm never going to see him again.'

'Where does he live?'

'London.'

'Where you're about to go to college.'

'If I get *in*—'

'We all know you will. Mark my words' – Mary nodded, her hands submerged in the suds – 'you'll see him again.'

Later, as the sun set spectacularly over the valley below Marchmont, Ava joined LJ, David and Tor on the terrace. The last guests had left and they were chatting about the day.

'I can't thank you all enough for making this possible.' LJ put a hand out towards her son. 'Now I feel I can die in peace.'

'For goodness' sake, do shut up, Ma,' said David. 'You've got a lot of life left in you yet.'

'Let's hope I shall be here to see the two of you return from your trip,' she said, unusually maudlin.

'Of course you will,' said Tor, 'we're only going for six months. I'm sure nothing untoward will happen in that time.'

'And I'll be here for the first few weeks of it,' commented Ava, seeing the look of concern on David's face.

'You'll have our itinerary anyway, Ma. You can always leave a message at the hotels we'll be staying at from time to time,' he said.

'David, I'm sure there'll be no need. I'm just being a silly old woman. Must be all the champagne. Right, bed for me. I may be past my sell-by date, but it really has been the most wonderful day.'

'I'll take you up,' said Tor firmly, as the three of them rose. 'David, darling, you stay here and relax with Ava.'

Once LJ and Tor had left, David turned to his niece. 'Ma's worried about us going away, isn't she?'

'A little, perhaps. But I suppose, when you're eighty-five, maybe you do worry whether you'll live to see another summer.' She shrugged.

'Goodness, Ava, you're so mature. Older than your years.'

'Well, I've been brought up by a very wise lady.'

'I saw your grandmother in London, by the way. I told her that I won't be around for the next six months.'

'Don't worry, Uncle David, I'll keep tabs on her.'

'And I saw your mother when I was in Los Angeles.'

'Really?' replied Ava, obviously not especially interested. 'How was she?'

'Okay, but going through a difficult patch.'

'Has she mislaid another husband?'

'Ava, really! She *is* your mother.'

'I only know of her from the gossip columns, the same as everybody else. Sorry, Uncle David.'

'I understand. And I suppose the good news is that you've been far better off growing up here with Ma than you would ever have been with Cheska. Not that that makes it right, of course,' he added hastily.

'Anyway, Uncle David, I just want you to know that Aunt LJ and Granny will be fine. I want you to be able to go away and not worry about anything. Now' – Ava yawned – 'I'm going to go upstairs and kiss LJ goodnight, and then I'm going to bed, too.'

'Oh, before I forget.' David dug in his jacket pocket and handed her a folded piece of paper. 'That young man – the grandson of Ma's old friend – asked me to give you this.'

'Thank you,' she replied, taking the folded piece of paper from him.

David saw the flush rise to her cheeks and was glad of it. 'So, what's his name?'

'Simon.'

'He really reminded me of someone, but I can't think who just now. Anyway, he said to tell you to give him a call if you end up in London. Goodnight, sweetheart.'

Ava kissed him warmly on the cheek. As she wandered into the house, David wished he could shake off the sense of anxiety he felt. Holding the fort while he was gone was a lot to ask of an eighteen-year-old girl who needed to concentrate on her own future. But, as Tor said, he'd been there for all of them for years, and it was only six months, after all . . .

Two days later, David and Tor boarded the plane to Delhi. As it left the runway and he looked below him at the fast-disappearing landscape of England, Tor took his hand and squeezed it.

'Are you ready for our big adventure?'

David tore his gaze away from the window and turned to kiss her. 'Yes, I am.'

# 44

Two weeks after the party LJ was enjoying her ritual afternoon cup of tea on the terrace. Although she had never travelled out of Great Britain, she doubted that, if she had, she would ever have seen a view to compare with the one in front of her. However many years she had left – and the doctor seemed to think it was a good few, if she were careful – LJ knew she could die happy tomorrow at her beloved Marchmont. As the late August sun beat down she closed her eyes and dozed, enjoying the warmth and the soothing sound of the stream below her. Very soon it would be September, and autumn, her favourite time of year.

'Hello, Aunt Laura-Jane.'

The voice was familiar, but LJ didn't open her eyes. She thought she must be daydreaming.

'LJ.' A hand shook her gently. 'It's me, I'm back.'

LJ blinked against the sunlight when she opened her eyes, and as the woman standing in front of her came into focus, her face drained of colour.

The woman came closer, and cold hands covered her own. 'Darling LJ, it's me, Cheska.'

'I know who you are, dear. I'm not senile yet,' she replied as steadily as she could.

'Oh, it's so wonderful to be back.' The hands moved upwards from her hands and wrapped themselves tightly around her shoulders, almost squeezing the breath from her.

'What . . . why are you here?'

The grip unlocked and Cheska knelt in front of LJ, a look of hurt crossing her features. 'Because this is my home, my daughter lives here and I wanted to come and see my dear Aunt LJ.' She paused. 'You don't seem very pleased to see me.'

'Well . . . I . . .' LJ swallowed hard. 'Of course I'm pleased to see you. I'm just . . . a little shocked, that's all. Why didn't you write and let us know you were coming?'

'Because I wanted to surprise you.' Cheska stood up. 'Oh! Just look at that view! I'd forgotten how beautiful it is here. Any chance of a cool drink? I got in a taxi at Heathrow and came straight here. I was so excited about seeing you all.'

'I'm sure Mary could find you something.'

'Mary! Goodness, is she still here? Nothing's changed, has it? I'll run along to the kitchen, find a drink and say hi to her. Back in a second.'

As Cheska disappeared into the house LJ found tears in her eyes. Not of joy, but of fear. Why now, when David was away with Tor . . . ?

Cheska returned after a while, holding a tall glass of iced water. 'I have so many gifts for you – they're in the hall. Where is . . . is Ava here?'

'She's out on the estate somewhere.'

'Do you think she'll be surprised to see me? Will she know who I am, do you think?'

'Of course she will, in answer to both of your questions.'

Cheska started to pace up and down. 'She won't hate me, will she? For leaving her, I mean. It was impossible to send for her at the beginning. And then, as time went by, I thought it was unfair to unsettle her when she was obviously so happy here. You do understand, don't you?'

LJ nodded slowly. She felt too numb to begin a fight.

'But do *you* hate me, LJ?'

'No, Cheska,' she replied wearily. 'I don't hate you.'

'Good, because now I'm back I promise I'm going to make up to Ava for all the years I've been away. Wow, it's hot! If you don't mind, I'm going to go and change into something cooler. I feel horribly sticky. Can I use my old bedroom?'

'That's Ava's room now. Use the old nursery. It's been turned into a guest room,' LJ said coldly.

'Okay. If Ava comes back while I'm upstairs, don't tell her I'm here, will you? I want to surprise her.'

Ava returned exhausted after her day out on the farm. She felt exhilarated as, a week ago, she'd received her A-level grades, and they'd been more than good enough to secure her place at the Royal Veterinary College in London. And, yesterday, she'd passed her driving test, which meant she could finally drive LJ's old Land Rover.

LJ had been as thrilled as she had, although Ava had initially been concerned about how much the course and her living in London would cost. They'd discussed it over a celebration dinner that night.

'Darling girl, you've helped me on the farm since you were small and never asked for a penny. Besides, there is a legacy, Ava, from your grandfather. It's quite a lot of money, and will comfortably cover the cost of your board and lodging in London. I know it's what your grandfather would have wanted. I'm so very proud of you, darling. You've achieved your dream.'

Ava swung open the kitchen door and saw Mary was preparing a rack of lamb.

'Hello, Mary. I thought LJ and I were just going to have a salad for supper tonight?'

Mary looked up and shook her head. 'There's been a change of plan, *fach*. You have a guest, see. They're out on the terrace. I think you'd better go and say hello.'

'Who is it?'

Mary shrugged noncommittally. 'Go and see for yourself.'

As Ava walked into the drawing room she could hear the sound of LJ's voice, and another vaguely familiar one, with the faintest twang of an American accent. She took the steps down to the terrace and saw the back of a woman with a mane of blonde hair sitting in a chair next to LJ.

Ava stood stock-still, unable to move. The woman must have heard her footsteps, for she turned around.

The two of them stared at each other for a long time.

Then Ava heard LJ's voice. It sounded strained and unnatural.

'Ava, dear. Come here and meet your mother.'

*

LJ watched the two of them together, her heart a churning cauldron of emotions. When Ava had first appeared on the terrace, LJ had seen the apprehension in her eyes. Cheska had stood up and flung her arms round her daughter, and Ava had stood numbly, unable to respond. Then they'd sat down and talked like the strangers they were. Slowly, as the evening had worn on and they'd drunk the champagne Cheska had brought with her and insisted they open, Ava had lost a little of her shyness.

During the supper that followed, LJ saw that Cheska was working hard to bring her daughter under her spell. She told stories of her life in Hollywood, the people she'd met and anecdotes about other cast members of *The Oil Barons*.

LJ thought she knew Ava inside out, but it was hard to know how she was feeling tonight. Outwardly, she certainly seemed to be listening in delight to her mother's stories.

Eventually, after coffee, Cheska yawned. 'Pardon me, but I'm exhausted. I'm going to turn in now. I was in the air all last night and didn't sleep a wink.' She stood up and kissed LJ on the cheek. 'Thank you for supper. It was delicious.' Then she moved to Ava and put her arms round her. 'Goodnight, honey. I do hope you don't have much planned for the next few days. I want us to spend as much time together as possible. We have a lot of lost time to make up for, don't we?'

'Yes. Goodnight, Cheska.' Ava nodded calmly. 'Sleep well.'

As Cheska's footsteps retreated inside the house, LJ stretched across the table and placed a hand on Ava's arm. 'Are you all right, darling? I'm so sorry I couldn't warn you, I had no idea she was coming. It must have been a shock.'

Ava turned, her face shadowy in the dim light. 'It wasn't your fault. She's very beautiful, isn't she?'

'Yes, but not as beautiful as her daughter.'

Ava chuckled. 'Some of the stories she had to tell. Can you imagine living that kind of life?'

'No, dear, I can't.'

'Do you think she's staying long?'

'I have no idea.'

'Oh.' Ava stared at a moth that was flickering near the night light on the table, then gently steered it away and off into the dark.

'Are you sure you're all right?' repeated LJ.

'Yes. I mean, she's very nice and everything, and seems like fun, but it doesn't feel like she's anything to do with me. I've always wondered how it'd be if I ever met her, and what I felt was . . . nothing, really. I feel a bit guilty.'

'Well, you mustn't. It'll take time to get to know her. You do want to, don't you?'

'I . . . think so. The only problem is, I don't think I can ever regard her as my mother – I mean, not in the proper sense. You're my mother, and that will never change. Never. Darling LJ, you must be exhausted. Shall I help you up to bed?'

When LJ was settled, Ava went and sat in her usual spot on the edge of the bed. She kissed her great-aunt tenderly on the forehead. 'Don't worry about me, LJ. I'm fine. I love you. Goodnight.' She left the room and closed the door softly behind her.

LJ lay staring into the darkness. She felt confused,

concerned and, for the first time, every one of her eighty-five years. There were things she wanted to tell Ava about her mother; she wanted to warn her that Cheska was not all she seemed. But she couldn't. It would sound like sour grapes, and LJ didn't want Ava to feel any guilt about getting to know her mother if she wanted to. And David had telephoned from Delhi only yesterday to say that he and Tor were setting off to Tibet and would be incommunicado for the next few weeks. She felt insecure and vulnerable without him.

She eventually drifted into a restless sleep. At some point, she woke with a start, a strange noise disturbing her. She switched on her bedside light and saw she'd been asleep for less than an hour. Yes, she could definitely hear someone, or something, moaning softly. Then she heard a high-pitched laugh. Just as she was about to reach for her walking stick and haul herself out of bed, the moaning stopped. She lay listening intently, but the noise was not repeated.

She switched off the light and tried to relax.

She'd heard that laugh once before, a long time ago, and wracked her brain as to where and when.

Then she remembered.

It had been the night she'd found Cheska in the nursery, tearing apart the poor, defenceless teddy bear.

# 45

On Saturday evening, a week after Cheska's arrival, Ava sat on the terrace with LJ, drinking lemonade and enjoying the sunset.

'Where did you go today, dear?' asked LJ.

'Shopping in Monmouth. Cheska seems to have a lot of money and keeps buying me clothes she thinks will suit me. The only problem is, people keep recognising Cheska and asking for her autograph. It was okay at first, but now I'm finding it a real pain. She's very patient with her fans. I know I wouldn't be.'

'And do you feel you're getting to know her?'

'She's very good company, and we laugh a lot, but I can't get it to sink in that she's my mother. She doesn't really act like one, in the way you do. She's more like a sister, I suppose. Sometimes she seems terribly young.'

'Has she said when she's leaving?' LJ asked tentatively.

'No. But I suppose it'll be soon. She has all her commitments in Hollywood. To be honest, I'll be glad when she's gone. I've got a million things to do before I leave for London. The village children are coming over next weekend and I'm taking them on a nature tour of the estate. I can't imagine Cheska donning a pair of jeans and helping out with the barbecue afterwards.' Ava chuckled.

'No. She's not cut out for the country.'

An hour later Cheska joined them with a bottle of champagne she'd bought on their shopping trip and poured out three glasses.

'To celebrate us being together after all this time. Cheers, as you say over here.'

'Yes, cheers,' said LJ weakly. Cheska always seemed to find a reason to open another bottle, and she was getting rather bored of pretending to drink it. Fizz didn't suit her stomach at all.

'Oh, I thought you might have put on that pretty dress I bought you today, Ava,' Cheska pouted.

'As a matter of fact, I live in these jeans,' Ava replied. 'I'll save it for a special occasion. You've bought me so much, I don't know what to choose.'

'Well, it won't hurt to stock up your wardrobe, will it? And what about some new glasses? Those really aren't very flattering, you know. You have such lovely eyes – my colour, I reckon. It seems a shame to hide them behind those heavy frames.'

'I have contact lenses, but these are much more comfortable.'

'I think glasses give Ava's face character, Cheska,' said LJ.

'Yes, of course they do. Anyway' – Cheska smiled – 'I have something to tell you both. I've enjoyed this week so much that I've decided to forget about going home and stay on here for a while longer. That is, if you'll have me.'

'But surely you have filming commitments for your

television show and, besides, won't you be bored? Marchmont is hardly Hollywood,' LJ said slowly.

'We don't start shooting until the end of September, and of course I won't be bored, LJ,' replied Cheska, the annoyance plain in her voice. 'The peace here is just what I need after LA. Besides, this is where my family is,' she added, reaching for Ava's hand and squeezing it. 'I'm just sorry dear Uncle David isn't here, too.'

*So am I*, thought LJ.

'Cheska, I hope you won't mind, but I have some things planned over the next few days, so I won't be able to come out with you as often I have been,' said Ava.

'Of course I don't mind. I'll be happy just to enjoy the scenery and relax.' She stretched, then sighed. 'Oh, I'm so glad I came home!'

Cheska had insisted on taking Ava out to lunch at an expensive local hotel the following day, even though Ava had promised to help Jack on the farm. To keep the peace, Ava agreed to go, hoping it would let her off the hook for the rest of the time her mother stayed at Marchmont.

'I can't believe you want to be a vet, honey.' Cheska shuddered, putting a dainty morsel of beef onto her fork. 'I don't know how you could contemplate it. The sight of blood makes me faint.'

'Well, the sight of you eating a piece of that poor cow makes me feel faint,' retorted Ava with a smile.

Cheska raised an eyebrow in irritation, then continued. 'By the way, you told me yesterday that LJ is paying for your expenses whilst you're studying. How will she find the money? Living in London can be very expensive. I feel it's my job to pay.'

'Apparently, my grandfather – your father – left me a legacy. She says it's quite a lot and will easily cover everything, so really, don't worry, Cheska.'

'Oh, but your grandfather didn't—' She stopped herself. She had been about to say that Owen had died before she herself was ten, so how could he possibly have left money to a child who hadn't yet been born?

Ava was oblivious to the sudden steely look in her mother's eyes. She was chattering away about her dream of eventually starting up her own veterinary practice locally.

'Well, you do have your life planned out, don't you, Ava? Unfortunately, the future isn't always as predictable as we'd like to think, but I'm sure you'll learn that as you get older.'

'You may be right, but I know what I want. And if I plan it carefully, I don't think anything can really go wrong, can it?' But her mother was now staring blankly out of the window. 'Are you okay?'

Eventually Cheska looked back at her daughter and smiled slowly. 'I heard you, honey. I'm sure everything will turn out just fine.'

A gentle September mist, which hung lethargically over the valley, greeted Ava every morning when she opened her bedroom curtains. She soaked in every second of the beautiful view, storing it up for when she was in London and unable to see it. As she'd told Cheska she would, she'd been spending most of her time out on the estate, helping the farmers bale the hay for winter. She only saw her mother at supper, as she was long gone by the time Cheska rose at mid-morning. Occasionally, returning to the house through the woods, Ava would see a small figure in the clearing, standing by Jonny's grave. She supposed that Cheska was paying her respects to her twin brother, who had died when he was tiny. She could hardly believe how quickly the holiday had flown and wondered when her mother would be flying back to Hollywood. Any time now, she supposed.

A week before Ava was due to leave for London, Mary rushed up the drive to greet her on her way back from the estate farm.

'What is it, Mary?' Ava's heart began to pound.

'It's your great-aunt, *fach*. She took a fall this afternoon. Cheska saw it and said she stumbled on the staircase.'

'Oh God! Is she all right?'

'I think so, yes. Just badly shaken. Dr Stone's with her now.'

Ava dashed into the house and ran upstairs. She opened the door to LJ's room, panting hard. Cheska was standing at the bottom of the bed, her arms folded, watching as the young doctor took LJ's blood pressure.

'Oh LJ!' She rushed to the side of the bed and knelt down, taking in her great-aunt's ashen complexion. 'What have you been doing? I told you to leave those hurdles alone while I wasn't here to watch you!'

LJ managed a weak smile at the joke she and Ava had shared since her hip operation.

'How is she, doctor?'

'Well, nothing broken, just some nasty bruising,' he replied. 'But I'm afraid your blood pressure has shot up,

Mrs Marchmont. I'm going to increase your medication and I want you to promise me you'll remain in bed for the rest of the week.' He turned to Ava and Cheska. 'Absolutely no excitement, please. We want Mrs Marchmont to remain calm and rested and see if we can get her blood pressure down. And if you don't behave' – he wagged a finger at LJ – 'I'll have no choice but to put you in hospital.'

'Honestly, doctor, I'll make sure she doesn't move a muscle.' Ava gripped LJ's hand tightly. 'I can always delay going to London.'

'No, you can't, Ava. I can look after her.'

It was the first time Cheska had spoken. Ava glanced up at her mother and thought that she looked odd, somehow. 'But I thought you had to get back to Hollywood?'

'I do, but I can't leave you to cope alone. I'm going to call my agent and tell him to let the studios know. They can film around me for a while, or write me out of the first few episodes. After all,' Cheska added, 'family is much more important, isn't it? You mustn't miss out on the start of your course, must she, LJ?'

'Of course not.' LJ shook her head wearily. 'But remember: I do have Mary here, too. Please, Cheska, don't stay on my account. You should go back to Los Angeles as planned.'

'I wouldn't dream of it, darling LJ, so you'll just have to put up with me being your nurse.'

'Do you want to see me out, Ava?' asked Dr Stone.

'Of course. I'll be back in a moment, LJ.'

'And do try and behave yourself for five minutes, Mrs Marchmont.'

'I'll see that she does.' Cheska smiled at him. 'Goodbye, doctor, and thank you.'

The doctor blushed and mumbled a goodbye.

Ava accompanied him down the stairs. 'Are you sure she's going to be all right?'

'As long as she rests, I would hope so. The problem with high blood pressure is that it can lead to strokes. Your great-aunt's had a nasty shock and, although she's very fit for her age, the hip operation has taken it out of her.' The doctor turned to Ava at the front door. 'By the way, was that really Gigi from *The Oil Barons*?'

'Yes.'

'A relation?'

'My mother, actually.'

He raised an eyebrow. 'I had no idea. Anyway, I'm sure she'll take good care of your great-aunt. Rather convenient she's here, with your uncle being away and you off to London. I'll pop in tomorrow. Goodbye.'

The doctor left and Ava closed the front door. She turned and saw Cheska standing on the stairs behind her.

'I thought I'd get LJ a cup of tea,' Cheska said.

'Good idea. I'll go and sit with her for a bit.' Then she noticed the tears in her mother's eyes. 'What is it?' she asked, climbing the stairs towards her.

'Oh Ava, I feel so goddamn guilty. I mean . . . I was right behind her and then . . . she tripped and fell.' She crumpled onto the stairs and began to sob.

Ava sat next to her and put an arm round her shoulders. 'Don't cry, Cheska. Of course it wasn't your fault.'

Cheska looked at Ava and grasped her hand. 'Ava, whatever LJ tells you, I love you very much. Very much.' Her eyes looked huge, like steel saucers. 'You do know that, don't you?'

'Why, I . . . yes, Cheska,' Ava said, bemused.

Cheska was staring off into the distance again. 'There are so many things we do . . . things that—'

Ava saw her mother shudder, then visibly pull herself together.

'I'm sorry, I'm just upset, that's all. And I do wish you'd call me Mother, not Cheska.'

'I . . . of course. You go and sit in the kitchen for a bit . . . Mother. I'll go up to LJ.'

'Thank you.' Cheska got up, then walked sadly through the hall towards the back of the house.

Flummoxed by her mother's strange behaviour, Ava bounded up the stairs and went to sit by LJ, who, although pale, seemed to be a little brighter.

'How are you?' she asked gently.

'Better, I think. Is your mother downstairs?'

'Yes.'

'Ava, I . . .'

'What is it?'

'Well, I know it's horrid to discuss it, but I really feel we must.'

'Discuss what?'

'What happens to you if I die.'

Tears sprang into Ava's eyes. 'Oh, please, LJ. Not now.'

'Listen to me.' LJ gripped her hand tightly. 'If it happens, Marchmont goes to your Uncle David, but the will also says you can continue to live here. David has told me definitively that he doesn't want to. And when David dies, we've both agreed that Marchmont will go to you. It's in his will too. There's also some money, as you know, bequeathed from your grandfather. It's yours, Ava, and . . . and no one else's.'

'But what about my mother? Shouldn't Marchmont and the money go to her if Uncle David dies?'

LJ sighed heavily. 'Ava, there are so many things you don't know about your past and about your mother.'

'Then tell me,' she urged. 'I mean, I don't even know who my father is.'

'One day, maybe. But the most important thing of all is . . . please be wary of Cheska.'

'Why?'

LJ released Ava's hand suddenly and fell back onto her pillows, exhausted.

'Ask your uncle, he'll explain.'

'But, LJ, I . . .'

'Sorry, Ava, I'm being overdramatic. Ignore me. I've had a shock, that's all.'

'Well, I'm not leaving until you're better. Really, I'm sure the veterinary college will understand if I have to delay going for a few days.'

'I will get better,' LJ replied firmly. 'And over my dead body will I allow you to ruin your future. There's a few days left before you leave.'

'Yes, and we'll see how you are then,' Ava countered, equally firmly.

'Here we go. A nice hot cup of tea.' Cheska came into the room with a tray. 'Well, this is a new role for me, playing nursemaid,' she said, handing the cup to LJ.

That night Ava tossed and turned, remembering what LJ had said. And only wished Uncle David were here to explain what she had meant.

*

LJ made very good progress over the next few days. Her blood pressure came down, and the doctor – who had been extremely attentive, visiting LJ every day and staying on to have a cup of coffee with Cheska to reassure her afterwards – told Ava he was happy with her recovery to date.

'I think you can go to London tomorrow with a clear conscience. And your mother really is taking excellent care of her – with Mary's help, of course.'

Ava closed her suitcase that night with a heavy heart.

She'd be leaving early tomorrow morning and, as well as feeling nervous about her new life and how she would cope living in a city and away from everything she knew, she felt deeply uneasy about LJ.

She took up her great-aunt's nightly cocoa, knocking on the bedroom door before she went in.

'Hello, darling girl. All packed and ready to go?' LJ smiled at her.

'Yes.' Ava put the cocoa down on the nightstand and sat on the bed, surveying her great-aunt, and noting with relief that the grey tinge had left her skin and her eyes were bright. 'Are you sure you don't want me to stay? It's only Freshers' Week, no lectures or anything. I—'

'Ava, how many times do you want me to tell you that I am absolutely fine and completely on the mend? Besides, university life isn't just about lectures – Freshers' Week is all about making new friends and having fun. I want you to enjoy yourself too.'

'I will, I'm sure, but . . .' Ava swallowed hard as tears came to her eyes. 'I'll miss you terribly.'

'And I you, my darling, but I hope you'll find the odd five minutes to write me a letter telling me what you're up to.'

'Of course I will. And here.' Ava dug into her jeans pocket and drew out a piece of paper. 'This is the telephone number of the hall of residence I'm in. If there's any problem, please call and they'll get a message to me. I've given it to Mary, too. I'll put it in your bedside drawer. And I'll telephone every Sunday at about six o'clock.'

'Well, don't worry if you can't. Darling Ava' – LJ lifted a hand to her great-niece's cheek and stroked it gently – 'you have been an absolute joy to me, from the first minute I saw you. I'm so very proud of you.'

They hugged then, for a long time, neither of them wishing the other to see their tears.

'Now, you have a very early start, so off to bed with you. Take care, darling girl,' she added, as Ava stood up and kissed her goodnight.

'I will. And *you*. I love you.'

Even Cheska roused herself at eight o'clock the following morning to say goodbye to Ava.

'Now, you're not to worry about a thing. I promise I'll take the best care of LJ. Dr Stone says I was born to be a nurse.' She giggled girlishly. 'So, off you go and have a wonderful time at college. I'm so sad I never got the chance to go myself.' Cheska threw her arms around Ava's shoulders. 'I love you, honey. Don't forget that, will you?'

'I won't,' said Ava as she climbed into the taxi. 'Let me know how LJ is, won't you? I'll call tonight. Bye!'

The taxi sped down the drive and away from Marchmont.

# 46

Ava was glad to be swept up in the whirlwind of newness – good and bad – that first week away from LJ and Marchmont. There was so much to learn, like how the underground and London buses worked, and the way her peer group seemed to think it was huge fun to have drinking competitions, even to the point of passing out. And, above all, getting used to the incessant hum of traffic outside her airless shoebox of a room. On the plus side, everyone on her course that she'd met so far seemed nice, and already a camaraderie had built up between them. Unused to crowds, or being with other people all the time, Ava was still shy about joining in. But the merry-go-round of events organised for the new intake left her feeling far more relaxed by the end of the week.

And the best news was that a letter from Simon had been waiting for her when she'd arrived. He told her that he was keeping true to his promise in the summer and would love to meet up with her and show her around London.

At moments during the first few long, airless nights, when every atom of her being longed to be back in the fresh, open space of Marchmont, Ava thought of him. She'd written back to him after he'd left the note with Uncle David, giving him her new London address, but had tried since to push down any ideas that he might actually have liked her. The fact he'd written to her again sent a tingle of pleasure up her spine.

It had taken her until Thursday to pluck up the courage to use the student payphone at the end of her corridor and call him to set up a meeting. And this Sunday he was coming to take her out, as he put it, to show her the sights.

On Sunday morning, having got to bed at gone three after the Freshers' Ball, she staggered out of bed.

'I really must learn not to drink whatever's put in front of me,' she told herself, her head pounding. She swallowed two paracetamol and stared at the contents of her wardrobe. For the first time in her life, Ava thought carefully about what she might wear. She chose a pair of bright-pink trousers and an expensive cashmere jumper that Cheska had bought for her, put them on, then decided she looked far too like her mother, so discarded them in favour of a pair of jeans and a T-shirt. Her eyes were far too sore for contact lenses this morning – they would just turn red and water if she put them in – so she put on her glasses.

At eleven o'clock she arrived uncertainly in the entrance hall of her building, which, for a change, was deserted. Everyone else must be sleeping off their hangovers from the night before. Simon was already waiting outside; she could see him through the glass doors. Her heart beating hard, and telling herself firmly that he had only got in touch because of the connection between their families, she pulled open the front door and went to greet him.

'Hi, Ava. Goodness you look different!' said Simon, kissing her on both cheeks.

'Do I?'

'Better different, like you're the real you. And I love you in your glasses,' he added. 'You look rather like a very pretty young teacher I had when I was seven. I had a huge crush on her for years, and I've had a thing about glasses ever since!'

'Thank you – I think.' Ava smiled shyly, taking in his similar attire of jeans and a sweatshirt.

'Now, I thought on the way here that there was no point taking you to the usual tourist attractions – you can easily go yourself – so I'm going to show you the London that *I* love. Okay?'

'Great.'

He offered her an elbow, which she took, and the two of them walked off together along the sleepy Sunday-morning street.

When she arrived home at seven o'clock that evening Ava felt completely exhausted. Simon might be a city boy but, ironically, everything they'd done had involved a great deal of walking. They had strolled through Hyde Park and paused at Speakers' Corner to listen to the would-be orators extolling their radical political views; some of which were so bizarre that the two of them had to leave as hysteria got the better of them. Then they'd walked along the Thames on the towpath from Westminster to Hammersmith, where they'd stopped at a riverside pub for lunch.

Ava had loved every second of it, because they hadn't been studying ancient monuments or jostling with tourists to get the better view of a painting in a gallery, they had just talked about anything and everything. And, in the wide-open spaces Simon had chosen as the backdrop to their day, Ava had stopped feeling claustrophobic – both physically and mentally – and relaxed.

The day had been warm enough for them to sit outside the pub and, while they ate, Simon told her more about the job he'd just landed in a musical in the West End.

'It's not really my chosen career path, as you know, I want to be a songwriter,' he'd admitted, seeming embarrassed by the whole thing. 'But they needed real musicians who could sing and play a couple of instruments, and someone I know suggested I audition. I went along and got the job. No one was more surprised than me, I can tell you, but on the other hand, it pays the bills. And once the show's up and running, it leaves me all day to concentrate on writing my own stuff. I even have a theatrical agent now, too.' He'd rolled his eyes at this.

'What's the musical about?'

'Oh, four very famous singers from the fifties and sixties. It's full of their hits, so it's a sure-fire crowd-pleaser for thirty and forty-somethings.'

'When does it open?'

'In three weeks or so. You can come to the opening night if you like.'

'I'd love to.'

'Mind you, I don't think I'm much of an actor to be honest.'

'But it might make you famous, Simon.'

'Famous is the last thing I want to be, I promise you. I'm aiming to open my own recording studio one day, where I'll write and produce songs for other people. I'd prefer to remain firmly in the background.'

'Me too,' Ava had agreed fervently.

At the end of their day, Simon had escorted her back to her hall in Camden and kissed her on the cheek. 'Good luck this week, Ava. Try not to fall asleep in too many lectures,' he'd added with a grin.

'I won't. And thank you so much for today. I really enjoyed it.' She'd turned to walk inside, but he'd caught her arm and pulled her back to him.

'Look, I know what the first few weeks can be like but, if you could spare the time, I'd love to see you again.'

'Really?'

'Yes! Why do you look so surprised?'

'Because I thought you were probably doing this as a favour to your grandfather, that he ordered you to take me out because he's friends with my great-aunt.'

'Then you're assuming I'm a much less selfish person than I really am. Seriously, I've really enjoyed today. So how about this Friday evening? Pick you up at seven?'

'If you're sure?'

'Ava, I'm perfectly sure.'

Ava lay on her bed and daydreamed about Simon. She must have dozed off, because when she woke up it was already dark. She turned over and checked the clock by her bed. It was past ten o'clock.

'Damn!' she swore to herself. It was far too late to call Marchmont, as she'd promised LJ she would.

She went to make herself a cup of tea in the communal kitchen along the corridor, then took it back to her room and sipped it while she prepared what she needed for her first lecture in the morning. Then she sank back into bed, making a mental note to call LJ tomorrow.

After she had taken LJ's cocoa up to her, Cheska went back downstairs into the library. After days of searching, she had finally found the key to the desk drawer that afternoon, secreted under a plant pot. The fact that it had been hidden confirmed her suspicions that it was in this drawer that LJ kept her private documents.

She sat down at the desk, put the key in the lock and turned it. She slid the drawer open and pulled out a bulging green folder. There were numerous documents inside. Cheska leafed through them until she found what she was looking for. Putting the folder aside to look through later, she opened the thick vellum envelope and unfolded the piece of paper within. On it was written: 'The Last Will and Testament of Laura-Jane Edith Marchmont'.

Cheska began to read.

> The Marchmont estate is being left to my son, David Robin Marchmont. And on his death my wish is that the estate in its entirety passes to my great-niece, Ava Marchmont, in tandem with my son's current will.

Cheska could feel the rage bubbling up inside her, but she did her best to control it and read on. It was only in a codicil that she finally found her own name.

A few minutes later, she was incandescent with fury. Slamming her fist down on the desk, she read the codicil again, just to make sure.

> As executor for the trust of Cheska Marchmont (known as Hammond), left to her by her father, Owen Jonathan Marchmont, it is my duty to revoke this trust. It is stated in Owen Marchmont's will (attached) that 'the sum bequeathed in trust to Cheska Marchmont be given only on the condition that she visits Marchmont at least once a year until she is twenty-one years of age'. I confirm that Cheska has not been to Marchmont once since she was sixteen therefore this condition has not been fulfilled. Not only that, but she has left her daughter in my care and not seen fit to contact either of us for a number of years. Therefore, I feel I have no alternative but to follow Owen Marchmont's stipulation and pass the proceeds of the trust to Cheska Marchmont's daughter, Ava, who has lived at Marchmont all her life. This money, I believe, is rightfully hers.

It was signed by LJ and witnessed.

'Bitch!' Cheska screamed, then rifled maniacally through the folder until she found what she wanted. It was an interim statement from a firm of stockbrokers, revealing the amount accrued in what should be *her* trust: it was over one hundred thousand pounds.

She looked at a number of other bank statements. The most recent showed that there was over two hundred thousand pounds in the Marchmont estate account.

Cheska broke down completely. 'I'm his daughter!' she sobbed. 'It should all be mine. Why didn't he love me . . . ? Why? Why?'

*Remember, Cheska, remember* . . . said the voices.

'No!' She put her hands over her ears, refusing to listen to them.

On a damp October morning, a few days after Ava had left, LJ woke to see Cheska sitting in the chair by the window.

'God, I feel groggy. What time is it?' she asked.

'Past eleven.'

'Eleven o'clock in the morning? Good grief! I've never slept that long in my life.'

'It'll do you good. How are you feeling?'

'Dreadful today, actually. Ancient and sick. Don't get old, Cheska. It's not a pleasant experience.'

Cheska stood up, crossed the room and sat beside her on the bed. 'I hope you don't mind me asking you, but I feel I have to. What's happened to the money my father left in trust for me?'

'Well, I—' LJ winced as a sharp pain darted up her left arm.

'I mean, it is still there, isn't it? The thing is, I need it rather urgently.'

LJ could hardly believe that Cheska was asking her about this now, standing over her like some beautiful avenging angel, as she lay weak, sick and defenceless. The pain intensified, and she experienced a strange tingling sensation on the left side of her head. She felt breathless and struggled to reply to Cheska's question.

'There was a clause in your father's will. It said that you had to come back and visit Marchmont at least once a year. You haven't done that, have you?'

Cheska's face hardened. 'No, but you wouldn't stop me

having my rightful inheritance because of some goddamn silly clause, would you?'

'I . . . Cheska, can we discuss this another time? I really don't feel too well.'

'*No!*' Cheska's eyes glittered with anger. 'That money's mine!'

'I'm giving it to Ava. Don't you think she deserves it? After all, I thought you had lots of money. I—' LJ caught her breath as the pain ripped up her neck and into her head.

Cheska seemed oblivious to LJ's agonised expression. 'And what about Marchmont? I'm the direct heir, being my father's daughter. Surely it must come to me? Not Uncle David?'

'Cheska, I am the legal owner of Marchmont and I can leave it to whomever I wish. And, of course, the rightful heir, the true blood relative of your father, is David, my son—'

'*No!* I'm Owen's daughter! I even have a birth certificate to prove it. Not only have you given the money in my trust fund to my daughter, but my home to my uncle. What about me?! When will anyone ever care about me?!' she shouted.

LJ watched Cheska through a veil of red mist. Brightly coloured patterns were dancing in front of her eyes. She wanted to answer . . . to explain, but when she opened her mouth to do so, it refused to form the words.

'You've always hated me, haven't you? Well, you won't win, dearest Aunt, because—'

LJ jerked forward, let out a small moan, then fell back onto her pillows. She lay still and was deathly pale.

'LJ?' Cheska shook her aunt harshly. 'Wake up and listen to me! I know you're only pretending so you won't have to talk about it! LJ! LJ?'

As her aunt lay motionless, the expression on Cheska's face turned from one of fury to horror.

'LJ! For Chrissakes, wake up! I'm sorry, I didn't mean to upset you. Please! Please! I'm sorry! I'm sorry!' She threw her arms round LJ's limp shoulders, sobbing hysterically.

And that was how Mary found them, after hearing Cheska's cries from downstairs. She called an ambulance and went with both LJ and Cheska to Abergavenny Hospital.

# 47

Ava found the first few days of lectures both terrifying and exhausting as she embarked on a whole new way of learning. Sitting in a lecture theatre with eighty other students straining to catch every word that dropped from her professors' mouths, she'd scribble everything down as fast as she could, then she'd scurry home to write up her notes neatly and in context. She was also loving every second of it, starting to make friends and settling down into university life.

For the past three days, she'd rung Marchmont in the evening and received no reply. This hadn't worried her unduly, as there were only two telephones in the house, one in the study, the other in the kitchen. And if everyone was outside or upstairs, they wouldn't hear it. However, when there was no reply on the fourth night, Ava began to worry. On Friday evening, when again no one picked up, she found Mary's home number in her address book and dialled it. The broad accent of Mary's husband, Huw, greeted her at the end of the line.

'Sorry to bother you, Huw, but I'm a bit worried. No one's answering the phone at Marchmont,' she explained. 'Is everything all right?'

There was a silence before Huw said, 'I thought they would've told you, Miss Ava. I'm afraid your great-aunt had a stroke three or four days ago and your mother has been at the hospital with her. Mary's been visiting her, too, every evening, which is why I reckon you haven't had a reply from the house.'

'Oh my God! How bad is it? Is she in danger? I—'

'Now, don't you go upsetting yourself, *fach*. I don't know all the details, except for the fact that your aunt's stable and in the best place. Why don't you give me the number you're calling from and I'll get Mary to call you back as soon as she gets home?'

'Yes, and in the meantime, can you tell me which hospital my aunt is in? I'll call them straight away.'

'Abergavenny Hospital, it is. So, you'll wait right there, will you? Mary should be back in fifteen minutes or so.'

Shocked and puzzled that no one had told her sooner that LJ was in hospital, Ava dialled Directory Enquiries to get the number. She got through to the hospital switchboard and, after what seemed like an age, to the ward LJ was on. But then all her change ran out and the beeps went just as the ward sister finally came to the phone. Ava slammed down the receiver in frustration, then looked at her watch and saw it was ten past seven. She had been supposed to meet Simon outside her halls at seven o'clock. Not wanting to leave the payphone in case Mary called back, she asked one of the girls along her corridor to go and tell Simon where she was. He appeared through the double doors just as the payphone rang.

'Hello? Mary? What's happened? How is she? Why did

no one tell me? I—' Ava burst into tears of fear and frustration.

'Calm down, *fach*,' Mary soothed her. 'Your mother insisted that we didn't tell you and disturb your studies, she said it was better to wait until we had good news so as not to worry you. Although I did tell Cheska that I personally thought you'd want to be told what had happened straight away . . . anyway, as you know from Huw, your great-aunt has had a stroke. She's been in intensive care for the past few days, but you'll be happy to know she's just this evening been moved onto a medical ward and they say she's out of danger. There, there, my pet.' Ava was sobbing down the line.

'I knew I shouldn't have left her. Are you absolutely sure she's going to be okay?'

'The doctors have said she should be, yes.'

'I'm going to get on the train and come home now. I'll get a taxi from the station and go straight to the hospital.'

'There's no point in doing that – they won't let you see her. Visiting hours are over now and she's tucked up in bed for the night. Come to Marchmont, and I'll let your mother know you're on your way.'

'Okay,' said Ava, trying to pull herself together. She could see Simon standing watching her out of the corner of her eye. 'Warn her it won't be until after midnight.'

'I will, *fach*. Now you take care of yourself on that long journey and I'll see you at the house tomorrow.'

'Thanks, Mary.'

Ava hung up, wiped her tears away roughly and turned to Simon.

'Your great-aunt is in hospital?'

'Yes, and I can't believe my mother didn't tell me. I'm so sorry, Simon, but I have to go home straight away.'

'Of course you do. Look, Ava, why don't I drive you? It's a hell of a way by train.'

'That's really kind of you, Simon, but I'm sure I'll be fine. I must go and pack.'

'Ava' – Simon grabbed her arm as she turned to walk along the corridor – 'I *want* to take you. I'll nip back home and get my car and I'll see you outside the front door in half an hour, okay?'

'Okay,' she said gratefully.

'But I'm warning you, it's not exactly a Rolls Royce,' he added as he turned and headed for the exit.

Five hours later Simon was steering his ancient Mini along the bumpy lane that led to Marchmont. The heating had broken down on the way and Ava's teeth were chattering, whether from cold or tension, she didn't know.

Mary had left them soup and bread in the kitchen and Simon ate his hungrily whilst she played with hers, feeling nauseous. There was no sign of Cheska as Ava led Simon upstairs to a spare room.

'Thank you so much for driving me here,' she said.

'No problem at all.' Simon reached for her and hugged her tightly. 'Try to get some sleep, won't you?'

'Yes. Goodnight.'

The following morning, Ava found Mary in the kitchen.

'How are you, *fach*? Come and give me a cuddle,' she said, wiping her hands on her apron.

'Oh Mary, why didn't anyone tell me? My God, if she'd died, I—'

'I know, I know. But she's out of danger now and I'm sure seeing you will cheer her up no end.'

'Do you think we should contact Uncle David?'

'I did ask your mother that and she said we shouldn't be bothering him on holiday. Now your great-aunt's on the mend, I think we can leave him be; otherwise, we both know he'd be home like a shot. Look you, I'm just taking up your mum's breakfast – you know she always has it in bed – so why don't you come up with me and say hello?'

'I'll just make myself and Simon a cup of tea,' Ava said, switching on the kettle.

'Simon, is it?'

'Yes, he kindly gave me a lift here last night.'

'And that would be the same Simon that was here for your great-aunt's eighty-fifth birthday?'

'It would.'

'Well, that was very good of him, now, wasn't it? Told you that you'd see him again,' she said, a twinkle in her eyes. 'Look you, I'll see you upstairs.'

Having taken the tea in to a still-sleeping Simon and left it by the side of his bed, Ava walked down the corridor to her mother's bedroom. Taking a deep breath, she knocked and entered. Cheska was sitting up in bed eating her breakfast.

'Ava, honey! Come and give your mother a kiss.'

Ava did so and Cheska patted the bed, indicating she should sit down.

'I feel exhausted this morning. Since poor LJ's stroke I've been at the hospital night and day. It really was touch and go whether she'd make it.' Cheska gave a dramatic yawn.

'Why didn't you tell me she'd had a stroke?'

'Because I didn't want to worry you, honey. And, besides, I was here to take care of her so there was really no point you interrupting your studies.'

'If anything ever happens again, Mother, please contact me straight away. LJ is everything to me, you know that.'

'Yes I do – you've said it often enough! Anyway, she's recovering now. And it's me who feels dreadful.'

'Well, you mustn't worry about visiting her today. I'll go.'

'If you wouldn't mind, that would be kind of you.' Cheska yawned again. 'I think I'll stay right here and catch up on some sleep. Can you take the tray down to Mary and tell her I'm not to be disturbed?'

'Of course. I'll see you later.'

Simon insisted on driving Ava to Abergavenny Hospital and told her he'd wait for her outside and not to worry how long she was. Up on the ward, she introduced herself to the nurse on the desk and asked if she could see her great-aunt.

'It's not visiting hours just yet, but as you've come so far I can make an exception,' she said kindly.

'How is she? My mother says she's out of danger now.'

'Yes, she is. Mr Simmonds, the consultant, is on the ward somewhere. I'll just pop and get him so he can have a word with you before you see her.'

Ava waited anxiously. The doctor arrived and shook her hand.

'I'm Mr Simmonds, Miss Marchmont. Why don't you come with me, and we can have a chat in private.'

Ava followed him to a small office. Mr Simmonds closed the door behind her and offered her a chair. She sank into it gratefully, her legs feeling like cotton wool.

'Miss Marchmont – or may I call you Ava? As your mother has no doubt told you, your great-aunt has had a stroke. She's pulled through, but she's going to need an awful lot of rehabilitation. She'll be in hospital for another week or so but, after that, might I suggest a nursing home? They could provide the kind of intensive physiotherapy that Mrs Marchmont is going to need, and in less sterile surroundings than here. I'm hopeful that, with the right care, she should regain her speech. It's more doubtful that she'll regain full use of her left arm, but who knows? Your great-aunt is a formidable lady, Ava, with an iron will.'

'Yes, she is.' Ava was horrified by what she'd just heard. 'You say she can't speak?'

'Not at present, no. I'm afraid it's quite a common symptom with a stroke. Now, I've already given your mother a list of some very good places not far from here which I think you both should take a look at.'

'Okay. Thanks for talking to me. Now, I must go and see her.'

'Of course. I'll take you.'

LJ was sleeping. Ava stood quietly by her bed, studying her. She looked so frail, so old.

'Spend as long as you like with her,' Mr Simmonds said as he walked away.

Ava went to sit by the bed and took her great-aunt's

hand. 'Darling LJ. I've just seen the doctor, and he says you're doing so well. He even said he thought you'd be ready to leave hospital quite soon and go to somewhere a little more comfortable while you recover. Isn't that wonderful?'

Ava felt a slight pressure on her hand and saw that LJ's eyes were open – and filled with joy at seeing her beloved great-niece.

'I'm so sorry I didn't come sooner, but nobody told me you were ill. But I'm here now, and I promise I won't leave you until you're out of here.'

Ava watched LJ trying to form her mouth into words that just wouldn't come. She noticed that the left-hand side of her aunt's face seemed to sag downwards, as if one side of her mouth were in a permanent grimace. 'The consultant said that, in time, you should be able to speak, but don't worry about it now. Instead, why don't I tell you all about London and university?'

For twenty minutes Ava spoke as cheerfully as she could about her new life, clasping LJ's limp left hand tightly in her own and steeling herself not to be upset when she saw LJ struggle to respond. Eventually, she ran out of things to say, and noticed that LJ was gesticulating weakly with her right hand.

'Are you conducting an orchestra?' Ava teased her gently. LJ shook her head in frustration and mimed again until Ava finally understood what she meant.

'You want a pen?'

LJ nodded, and indicated the drawer by the bed.

When she'd written what she wanted, LJ handed Ava

the piece of notepaper. In spidery writing, it said, '*I love you.*'

'How was it?' asked Simon as Ava got into the car.

'Dreadful. She can't speak at the moment and she's paralysed down her left arm. But the consultant did warn me that she looks far worse than she actually is. I—' Ava's bravado faltered for a moment. 'And I must hang on to that,' she managed.

'Yes.' Simon's hand reached for hers and squeezed it tightly. 'You must, sweetheart.'

When they arrived back at Marchmont, Mary was just on her way home. 'There's beef stew and dumplings in the Aga for your guest and a cheese salad in the fridge for you. I'll be back in tomorrow to make you both a nice lunch. How was your aunt?' she asked, seeing Ava's pale face.

Ava could only shrug.

'I know, *fach*, I know. But she'll get better. You must believe that.'

'Have you seen my mother today?' Ava asked, to change the subject.

'I did about an hour ago. She was about to take a bath. 'Bye now, and I'll see you tomorrow. You take care of Ava now, won't you, Simon? She's had an awful shock.'

'Of course I will.'

When Mary had left, Ava served out their meal and set it on the table.

'Does your mother always take a bath at two o'clock in the afternoon?' Simon asked as he began to eat.

'Probably. She was very tired this morning, because she's been with LJ at the hospital all week. Simon, I'll have to stay on here for now. I can't leave LJ until she's at least out of hospital. And I know you have to get back for rehearsals.'

'Well, I don't have to leave until tomorrow, so why don't we take a walk this afternoon? It might do you some good to get some fresh air, and I'd love to see the estate.'

Ava was just about to reply when Cheska came into the kitchen.

'There you are! I thought I heard a car but . . .' Cheska's voice trailed off as her gaze fell on Simon.

'Mother, this is my friend, Simon Hardy. Simon, my mother, Cheska Hammond.' Ava watched as Simon's jaw dropped.

'You mean, *the* Cheska Hammond? Gigi in *The Oil Barons* Cheska Hammond?'

Cheska was staring at him with the oddest look in her eyes, but then she seemed to recover her equilibrium, and her lovely face broke into a broad smile. 'Yes, it is me. And it's so wonderful to see you! I'm sure we've met before. I—' Cheska looked at him again. 'Don't you think?'

'No. I would certainly remember.' Simon smiled, rising from his chair and offering his hand politely. Instead of taking it, Cheska kissed him warmly on both cheeks.

'Well, it's great to meet you, Bobby.'

'It's Simon, Miss Hammond.'

'Please, call me Cheska. So,' – Cheska swept across the kitchen towards the fridge – 'I think this calls for champagne.'

'Not for me, Mother.'

'Or me,' Simon added.

'Really?' Cheska, bottle in hand, pouted at them. 'But it's so wonderful to have you here. We should celebrate.'

'Maybe later. It's only three o'clock in the afternoon,' Ava said, completely taken aback by her mother's behaviour in the light of what had happened to LJ.

'Oh, don't be such a spoilsport, Ava. But okay, we'll save it for later. So what are we doing this afternoon?'

'Well, Ava was going to take me out for a walk and show me the estate,' said Simon.

'Wonderful idea! Just what we all need, a nice breath of fresh air. I just love walking at this time of year. Autumn is so pretty, don't you think? Let me go and change into something more sensible, and I'll see you back here in ten minutes.'

Ava watched, confused, as Cheska practically skipped out of the room. To the best of her knowledge, her mother had never set foot on a walk any further away than the nearby woods, and she hated the cold.

'My goodness, Cheska Hammond is your mother,' Simon murmured, shaking his head. 'Why on earth didn't you tell me?'

'Is it important?' Ava snapped and then apologised immediately.

'No, of course it isn't important. But when a full-blown international superstar walks into a kitchen in the middle of nowhere completely unannounced, it's understandable to be shocked, isn't it?'

'Well, there you are. That's my mother.'

'As a matter of fact, it explains why you looked familiar the moment I saw you. And you're every bit as beautiful as she is,' Simon said gently.

'Well, we'd better get ready for this walk.' Ava stood up abruptly. 'I'll find you some wellingtons.'

Ten minutes later the three of them were walking down the steps from the terrace, her mother looking faintly ridiculous in an old Barbour and a pair of wellington boots that were far too big for her.

'So, where shall we start?' asked Cheska, linking her arm through Simon's. 'The woods are beautiful, especially at this time of year, and then we can take a walk by the stream.'

'Sounds good to me,' Simon agreed.

Ava trailed behind them, amazed that Cheska hadn't yet asked her how LJ had been that morning, and also unsettled by the territorial way her mother was behaving with Simon. Ava could see he was entranced not only by meeting Cheska, but by the attention she was lavishing upon him.

Even though Simon had never declared his intentions to Ava, and had certainly never done more than give her a peck on the cheek and a cuddle, she felt a sharp twinge of envy as she watched the two of them laughing together as they walked on ahead. Surely Cheska couldn't be thinking of Simon in *that* way? She was old enough to be *his* mother.

But then, Ava calculated that if Cheska had only been sixteen when she gave birth, it meant she was actually only eleven years Simon's senior. And besides, she looked ten years younger than she was. Ava shuddered with distaste at the way her mother had suddenly changed from her exhaustion of this morning into a sparkling . . . *girl* the moment she'd seen Simon.

'Let them at it,' she murmured to herself.

*

When they came back from the walk, Ava said she was returning to the hospital for evening visiting hours.

'I'll drive you there,' offered Simon immediately.

'Oh goodness, you don't need to do that, Simon. You've done enough today already,' announced Cheska. 'Ava can take the Land Rover and drive herself, can't you, honey? And don't worry, I'll keep Simon company. I might even treat him to my scrambled eggs and smoked salmon. Everyone in Hollywood comes to me on a Sunday for brunch. My secret recipe is famous!'

'Really, it's no problem—'

'It's okay, Simon.' Ava had already taken the keys to the Land Rover from the hook. 'I'll see you later.'

Ava sat in the chair next to LJ, trying not to think of Simon and Cheska at Marchmont together and glad that LJ seemed far brighter and more alert than earlier. Ava had come armed with a couple of notepads and pens, and also her great-aunt's favourite Austen novel. LJ scribbled short words of reply to Ava's questions:

'*Yes, feeling better.*'

'*Doc says I can sit in chair tomorrow.*'

'*And they will give me a shower!*'

When Ava saw that LJ was tiring, she opened *Emma* and began to read to her. When the bell rang to indicate the end of visiting hours, Ava looked up from the book and saw that LJ had dozed off. Kissing her gently on the cheek, she left the hospital, dreading returning home.

When she arrived, she found Simon and Cheska sitting in the kitchen chuckling at something. There was an empty champagne bottle on the table.

'Hello, darling. Simon and I have had a lovely evening, haven't we? He's been telling me all about his West End debut and he's invited me to the first night. Sixties music is my era, of course,' said Cheska.

'Maybe the two of you could come together?' Simon's deep brown eyes turned to Ava.

'If LJ's out of hospital by then,' she answered abruptly.

'Want a drink, darling?' Cheska asked, proffering a newly-opened bottle of wine.

'No, thanks. If you'll excuse me, I'm going to bed. Goodnight.' Ava walked to the kitchen door and left them to it.

# *48*

At lunchtime the following day, despite Cheska's protests that Simon must stay for lunch, he said he had to leave and head back to London.

'We're teching the show in the theatre from tomorrow, so it's going to be a long week.'

'Well, I can't wait to see it,' said Cheska, following Simon out to the car with Ava. 'Perhaps we can go out to supper afterwards?'

'I think I'll be expected at the first-night party, Cheska. But thanks for your hospitality. Ava' – he beckoned her towards him though Cheska was still hovering close by – 'will you let me know when you're heading back to London?'

'Yes.' She nodded.

'I—' he looked at her, then at Cheska, and shrugged. 'Send my love to your great-aunt, and take care of yourself.'

'I will.'

'Well, wasn't he charming?' Cheska said as they walked back inside together.

'Yes.'

'So mature for such a young man.'

'I'm off to the hospital now, Mother,' Ava said briskly, not wishing to hear her extolling Simon's virtues. 'Will you come with me?'

'Maybe not today. Simon and I had a pretty late night. And you said earlier that LJ was a lot better yesterday evening. I'm going to catch up on some rest after lunch.'

Ava spent as much time as she could with LJ at the hospital over the following few days and was delighted by the improvement in her. At the end of the week, the consultant called Ava into his office and said that he thought LJ would soon be ready to leave the hospital.

'Have you looked into any of the nursing homes I suggested?'

'No, but we will now that you think she's ready to leave. Thank you, doctor.' Ava stood up. 'I'm very grateful for all you've done.'

'Just doing my job, Miss Marchmont,' he said, showing her to the door. 'By the way, how is that charming mother of yours? I haven't seen her this week.'

'She's been very tired after being here all last week with my great-aunt, so I've taken over.'

'Well, do send her my regards, won't you?'

'Of course.'

'And let me know how you get on with the nursing homes. I'd book her in provisionally from next Wednesday.'

When she got home Ava dialled the numbers of the three establishments the doctor had suggested. One of them was full, but the other two said they could take LJ from the date Mr Simmonds had suggested. Having assiduously avoided her mother as much as possible over the last few days, bored now with the never-ending monologues on how marvellous Simon was, Ava went in search of her. She found her in the library looking through some papers.

'Would you like to come with me this afternoon to visit the nursing homes the doctor has suggested? LJ is going to be allowed out on Wednesday.'

'I . . . is it necessary, Ava? I'm sure I can trust your opinion on where will be suitable, darling. Obviously, the one nearest to here, as, once you're back at college, I'll be the one visiting her all the time.'

Ava could see that her mother was distracted. 'Okay. I'll go and see them and report back.'

'Thank you, Ava. Anything else?'

'No. Isn't it good news that LJ is getting better?'

'Wonderful.' Cheska nodded, her eyes back on her paperwork.

On Wednesday Ava travelled with LJ in an ambulance to the nursing home she had chosen. Cheska had said she would drive LJ's Land Rover and meet them there. True to her word, she was standing in the car park when they arrived.

The nursing home was set in well-kept parkland. The staff were friendly, LJ's room was bright and had a lovely view over the gardens. When she'd first visited, Ava had been happy to see that there were just as many young patients as there were old.

'We cater for all sorts here, dear,' the matron had

explained. 'We're not a dumping ground for the elderly but a recovery unit for the sick of any age.'

Ava helped unpack LJ's case and arranged her things as she liked them. Cheska just sat in a chair, seeming distracted. Ava and LJ had developed a form of communication: LJ would squeeze Ava's hand, or raise an eyebrow, pointing shakily with her good arm at whatever she wanted. If she couldn't make herself understood, she would write down what she wanted.

'Honey, I think we should go now, give LJ a chance to get settled in.' Cheska was staring out of the window, her fingers twisting nervously.

'Oh, I was hoping I could stay on for a bit, Mother. Don't worry, you go home and I'll call Tom the Taxi to come and pick me up.'

'It's okay. I'll wait,' Cheska said firmly.

LJ squeezed Ava's hand and shook her head slightly, indicating the door.

'Are you sure you'll be okay?'

She nodded.

'I'll be back tomorrow. Anything you need, write it down and hand it to the matron. When I call her later, she can tell me what to bring in for you.'

LJ was looking irritated.

'I know, I know, I'm fussing,' said Ava, then kissed her great-aunt's forehead. 'I just can't wait until you're back home. I love you.'

LJ smiled her lopsided smile and waved so pathetically it brought fresh tears to Ava's eyes.

Outside, she bit her lip as Cheska unlocked the car. 'Oh dear. I do hate leaving her here.'

'Don't be silly, Ava. She's in good hands, as you can see. It's costing the earth as well, so the place should be good.'

'I know. I'm sorry. I suppose it's because I know I have to go back to London soon.'

'Well, I'll be here, won't I?'

Cheska started the engine and put the car hard into reverse.

Ava visited LJ every afternoon for the next three days, reassuring herself that her great-aunt was happy and settled. The staff seemed kind, and the physiotherapy was helping enormously. Even though her speech hadn't yet returned, LJ was now able to take short walks around the garden with the aid of a walking stick.

*'You must go back to London. I am better.'*

Ava read the note and saw LJ looking at her and nodding. She wrote another note and handed it to her niece.

*'Tomorrow!'*

'But, LJ, I don't want to go until you're home.'

*'You must. Don't disobey me.'*

'I'm not, but—'

*'I am still your aunt.'*

'All right, if you insist. But I'll be back next weekend.'

*'We'll see about that.'*

Later that evening, when Ava told her mother she felt that LJ was well enough for her to leave for London, Cheska announced she, too, would be visiting the capital.

'And I have Bobby's . . . I mean, Simon's show to see. I thought I'd also stop by and see my old agent. While I'm in England, it seems a pity not to explore opportunities.'

'But what about LJ? I thought you'd be here to visit her while I was away?'

'For goodness' sake, Ava. I was only thinking of coming to London for a night! Mary's here, and I'm sure LJ can survive for twenty-four hours without both of us. We can meet at the theatre for a drink before the show. I have to find something to wear beforehand, of course. It is a premiere, after all. I'm so excited!'

Cheska said goodbye to Ava the following morning with a kiss and a smile.

'See you on Wednesday night. And don't worry about LJ. I'm going straight off to see her now.'

'Okay. Send her my love.'

'I will.'

The next morning Cheska put on a fitted silk blouse that matched her eyes and showed just a hint of cleavage. Then she went downstairs to greet Dr Stone, whose car had just pulled up outside.

When he'd left, Cheska drove into Monmouth and walked into the reception of Glenwilliam, Whittaker and Storey, the solicitors for the Marchmont estate.

'Hi, my name is Cheska Hammond. I have an appointment with Mr Glenwilliam.'

'Er, yes . . . Miss Hammond . . .' The receptionist stumbled slightly over her words. 'Do sit down, and I'll let Mr Glenwilliam know you're here.'

'Thank you.' Cheska sat. A minute later, the door opened and a man in his early thirties came out. She stood up.

'Miss Hammond, it's a pleasure. Do come through to my office.'

'Thank you. I thought you were going to be crusty and old.' Cheska giggled coquettishly.

'Er, no. You would be thinking of my father. He retired a couple of years ago and I took over the practice.'

'I see,' she said, following Mr Glenwilliam into his office.

'Please sit down, Miss Hammond.'

'Thank you.'

'Now, what can I do for you?'

'Well, the problem is, my uncle is abroad on an extended holiday and at present uncontactable.' Cheska crossed her legs slowly and watched the solicitor's eyes follow their movements. 'And now that LJ, my aunt, is so sick, I—' Her eyes filled with tears and she reached into her handbag for a handkerchief.

'Please try not to distress yourself, Miss Hammond.'

'Well, it's all been left up to me to sort out, and I really need some advice.'

'I will try to help in any way I can,' Mr Glenwilliam reassured her, staring into those famed blue eyes.

'I'm grateful for that, Mr Glenwilliam. As I'm sure you know, running the Marchmont estate is a full-time job. My aunt has managed it well for so many years but, recently, her illness has meant that all sorts of things haven't been attended to. There's a pile of bills that haven't been paid, fences in need of immediate repair. Jack Wallace, the farm manager, came to see me yesterday. Something has to be done.'

'Really?' Mr Glenwilliam raised an eyebrow. 'You surprise me, Miss Hammond. I was there not long ago to see your aunt and I thought things were running like clockwork, as always.'

'Well, let us say that appearances can sometimes be deceptive. Anyway, the immediate difficulty is that I need some money to pay the wages and some general bills.'

'That won't be a problem. We've dealt with the affairs of the Marchmont estate for many years. If you let me have the bills, I'm authorised to write out cheques using the estate account. There's plenty of money in it. Then, once your aunt is better, she—'

'But that's the trouble, Mr Glenwilliam.' Cheska let the tears flow once more. 'I don't think my aunt is ever going to fully recover. At least not enough to manage the estate. And with my uncle out of the country, I am the next of kin, and I want to do what I can, at least until he returns.'

'I see. As you say, Marchmont is a full-time job. What about your acting career?'

'Family comes first, doesn't it? I shall just have to take a sabbatical until my uncle gets back.'

'Well, I think that may be a bit drastic, Miss Hammond. As I've said, this practice has run the Marchmont estate on numerous occasions and will happily do so again, temporarily, of course.'

'No, I don't think that's going to be the answer, Mr Glenwilliam. Pardon me for seeming rude, but I really don't want to have to run to you every time I need a cheque for some hay or animal feed, however enjoyable the interlude might be.'

'I understand, Miss Hammond.' Mr Glenwilliam straightened his tie. 'So what you really want is a temporary power of attorney?'

'Do I? Could you explain what that means?'

'Well, when someone is deemed unfit by the doctor to manage their own financial affairs or businesses, power of attorney can be granted either to a close member of the family or a legal body. This gives them access to finances and enables them to act on the person's behalf.'

'I see. So you could do that for me?'

'In theory. Although I do think I should attempt to contact your uncle before we undertake such a measure.'

'Unfortunately he's trekking in the Himalayas, then in China. It could be weeks if not months before you're able to get hold of him. I've tried myself, of course, with no luck so far.' Cheska recrossed her legs and again saw Glenwilliam's eyes flicker in their direction.

'I can see that makes matters difficult, Miss Hammond. But are you sure this is even what you want? Marchmont is a huge responsibility, especially for someone with – pardon me for saying it – little experience of this kind of thing.'

'Yes, at least for the foreseeable future. When my uncle gets home, we can take things from there.'

'Well, I'd have to have some papers drawn up, and your aunt would have to sign them.'

'That might be a problem. At the moment, my aunt cannot lift a cup to her mouth, let alone sign her name. She has also lost the power of speech.'

'Well, then, we'd have to ask her doctor to write a letter confirming that, at present, Mrs Marchmont is unable to conduct her own affairs.'

'I have it here, actually. Dr Stone has seen my aunt and confirms in the letter what I have just said.'

'I see.' Mr Glenwilliam opened the letter and read its contents. 'I stress it would be *temporary* power of attorney, until your aunt recovers or . . . well, then her will would come into operation, anyway.'

'Of course,' Cheska whispered, lowering her eyes. 'And the estate passes to my Uncle David, doesn't it?'

'Exactly,' Mr Glenwilliam confirmed. 'I must repeat, it really is a lot of responsibility, Miss Hammond.'

'I know. But I want to do whatever I can to help my aunt. If she knows Marchmont is in safe hands, it'll be a huge weight off her shoulders. I have Jack Wallace, and you'll be here to advise me, won't you, Mr Glenwilliam?' She gave him the benefit of her most beguiling smile.

'Of course. Any time you need any help or advice, just pick up the telephone. In the meantime, I'll have the papers drawn up.'

When she arrived home, Cheska made a phone call.

'No, she isn't incontinent, but she can't talk at present. Do you think you might have room for her? Great. Well, I'd like to bring her across on Monday afternoon, if that's okay with you. Yes, I will. Goodbye.'

That night, Cheska didn't sleep. She was afraid of the dreams she knew she would have.

On Monday morning she drove into Monmouth with Tom the Taxi. Telling him she'd find her own way back home, she went to Mr Glenwilliam's office and picked up the envelope containing the temporary power of attorney, then walked around the corner to the bank. There, she arranged for the transfer of a large sum of money from the Marchmont estate account to be credited to her own. Having enquired where she could rent a car, she followed the bank clerk's instructions and found the garage.

She paid the rental for the car, climbed in and drove off in the direction of LJ's nursing home.

Later that day, she was back at Marchmont. She went up to her bedroom and began to pack. Then she went downstairs to see Mary.

'As you know, I'm off to London tomorrow, Mary, and I was thinking that you should leave early today and take tomorrow off as well. Spend time with that husband of yours. You've been working so hard recently. In fact' – Cheska dug into her handbag and pulled out her purse – 'why don't the two of you go out for dinner tonight? It would be a "thank you" from me.' Cheska proffered two twenty-pound notes.

Mary looked at her in surprise. 'But, surely, if you're not here for a couple of days, I should come up to the house to check on it anyway?'

'There's no need, Mary. I promise that I'm fully capable of locking up before I leave. Really, I insist.'

'If that's what you want, it's very generous of you, Miss Cheska. And you're right, it will be nice to spend some time with Huw. I'll go and see Mrs Marchmont whilst you're away, of course.'

'Actually, when I saw her earlier today the matron told me that, tomorrow, she's going to Abergavenny Hospital for a couple of days so her consultant can run some tests and assess her progress. It's probably best if you leave visiting her until later in the week. For once in your life, forget about Marchmont and all of us' – Cheska smiled kindly – 'then you can come back feeling refreshed.'

'Okay,' Mary agreed doubtfully. 'I'll be off now. Your supper is in the Aga,' she said, removing her apron. 'Have a lovely time in London and send a kiss to my Ava, won't you?'

'Of course.'

As Mary left for her cottage, she couldn't help feeling uneasy. Miss Cheska had always been a strange one and no mistake, but as she was Mrs Marchmont's niece, she felt it wasn't her place to question her instructions.

That night, Cheska roamed the deserted corridors of Marchmont. The voices in her head – and one in particular – were very insistent tonight.

*It should be yours, you have to fight for it . . . She hates you, she always has . . .*

Cheska sank onto the bed in her old nursery, the room where Jonny and she had once lain sleeping peacefully together in their cribs. She'd adored him. And then he'd gone away.

'But you *didn't* go, did you, Jonny? And you never will!' she wept, her legs crossed in the way she'd always sat as a child, but now with fists in her eyes to stop the tears and the voices.

'They'll never stop, will they? You'll never stop!' she screamed in anguish. 'Leave me alone, leave me alone . . .'

As the voices reached an unbearable pitch in her head, Cheska suddenly realised what she had to do to stop them.

Destroy the memories and they couldn't haunt you any longer.

Yes, yes, that was it!

She closed the large case she had packed in preparation to leave for London the following morning, picked it up and took it downstairs with her to the front door. Then she entered the drawing room, went to the fireplace and collected the box of firelighters and matches, and headed back upstairs. Calmly, she pulled the wastepaper basket towards her and set it underneath the old wooden rocking horse her aunt had once told her had been David's. Taking an old picture book she had once loved as a child, she tore out its pages and screwed them up into balls, putting them one by one into the basket.

Kneeling down, she lit some matches and dropped them onto the paper. It leapt into flames immediately and she sat down on the edge of the bed, watching as they licked at the peeling painted flank of the wooden horse. Satisfied, she stood up to leave.

'Goodbye, Jonny,' she whispered.

By the time she left the room, the rocking horse was a bright, burning mass of fire.

# 49

When Ava returned to her room after her last lecture, she jumped hurriedly into the shower, climbed into a clinging black dress Cheska had bought her in Monmouth, put on a dab of lipstick and ran back out again to catch the bus to Shaftesbury Avenue.

The theatre foyer was already crowded, and she weaved her way through it up to the dress-circle bar, where her mother had said they should meet.

'Honey!' A radiant Cheska flung her arms around Ava and kissed her on both cheeks. 'Come and sit down. Dorian has ordered champagne.'

'Who's Dorian?'

'Dorian, my darling, is my new agent. Well, he's not really new. He's just taken over from Leon Bronowski, who used to look after me when I was an actress in London years ago. He's just dying to meet you. Look, there he is now.'

'Oh.' Ava watched as a balding, middle-aged man dressed flamboyantly in a scarlet velvet evening jacket and gold cravat approached their table.

'Miss Marchmont . . . Ava.' The man took her hand and kissed it. 'I'm Dorian Hedley, agent extraordinaire and about to be responsible for your mother's already glittering career. Good God, Cheska, she could be your double! Champagne, Ava?'

'Just a small glass, thanks.' She turned to Cheska, who was looking fabulous in a sparkling midnight-blue evening dress. Seeing her in it made her feel plain and dull in comparison. 'But I thought you already had an agent in Hollywood?'

'Yes, honey, I do. But . . . oh, I've been feeling for a while that it was time for a change. Dorian here has convinced me that I'm right, haven't you, Dorian?'

'Yes. We Brits seem to lose all our best products to the States, so I'm happy I just might have lured one back.'

'So . . . Mother, you're going to stay here in the UK permanently?'

'Well, I'm going to give it a try. I walked into Dorian's office late this afternoon just to say hello, and the two of us began chatting and found we saw eye to eye about so many things. Dorian was coming to the first night tonight as he has a client in the show, so we went out for a drink and he's convinced me that my future lies here in England.' She reached for Ava's hand. 'Isn't it wonderful? I mean, now we can be together in London.'

Ava frowned, thinking of LJ. 'Of course.' She sat quietly, listening to Cheska and Dorian dissect various television programmes, giggle at gossip and bitch nastily about a particularly well-known actress. She wished she hadn't come. She felt completely out of place.

Eventually, the two-minute bell rang and Dorian led them into a box on the left-hand side of the stage. Ava looked down into the stalls and saw people whispering and pointing up towards her mother.

The lights went down and soon the auditorium was full of the sound of fifties rock and roll. Simon made his entrance and Ava's eyes never left him as he and the other actors impersonated some of the best-known pop stars from the era.

After the interval, the show moved into the sixties. The lights dimmed and Simon came forward to stand at the microphone, dressed in a pair of jeans and a cardigan.

Ava was enraptured by his lovely, mellow voice as he sang a ballad. She noticed that her mother was straining forward, breathing hard, her eyes focused on Simon too.

'Yes, that's the madness, the madness of love . . .'

Mother and daughter sat side by side, lost in their memories. For Cheska, the terrible thing she had done yesterday was wiped from her mind. That had been a dream. *This* was reality. He'd come back to her, and this time it would be forever.

Ava remembered when Simon and she had walked along the Thames together and how comfortable she'd felt with him. But at the same time she realised that Simon was a talented, handsome man who, after tonight, would have a horde of girls after him. He was obviously way out of her league.

The cast got a standing ovation at the end of the show, and Cheska cheered louder than anyone.

'You don't mind popping backstage with us, do you, Ava?' Cheska said to her as they left the theatre. 'I must go and tell Bobby how wonderful he was.'

'You mean Simon, Mother,' Ava corrected her.

Once inside the stage door, Dorian went to see his client and Cheska strutted off towards Simon's dressing room. Without knocking, she marched inside to find a throng of well-wishers already there. Elbowing her way through them, Cheska went up to Simon, who was talking to someone, and threw her arms round his shoulders, kissing him on both cheeks.

'Honey, you were wonderful! What a debut! You'll be the toast of the town tomorrow, I promise you.'

'Er, thanks, Cheska.'

Ava, who had stayed near the door because of the crush, saw that he was taken aback by her mother's extravagant praise. Then he spotted her and smiled, moving past Cheska towards her. 'Hello, how are you?' he asked softly.

She smiled shyly. 'Fine, thanks. You were great.'

'Thank you. I—'

Cheska broke the moment, her voice unusually shrill. 'I'll see you at the party, Simon.'

'Er, it's ticket only, Cheska, I'm afraid.'

'I'm coming as the guest of Dorian, my agent, actually. Come on, Ava, let's give Simon some time to talk to other people.' Cheska almost pushed Ava out of the dressing room and towards the stage door, where they found Dorian waiting for them. 'Ava, darling, I'm afraid Dorian doesn't have a spare ticket for you. Why don't you come to the Savoy tomorrow for breakfast with me?'

'I have a lecture, Mother.'

'Well, lunch then, or dinner. We'll speak tomorrow. 'Night, honey.'

Ava watched as Cheska linked arms with Dorian, who

mouthed goodnight to her as she pulled him away along the street. Feeling depressed and deflated, Ava walked along the road to catch a bus back to her halls.

When she arrived in her room, she saw a note that had been pushed under her door.

'*Sorry,*' it said. '*Forgot to tell you earlier that someone called Mary rang for you at lunchtime. She says can you call her back urgently. Helen from the room next door.*'

Ava's mouth turned dry and her heart began to beat against her chest. LJ . . .

Grabbing some change, she went to the payphone. It was past eleven at night now, so she just hoped Mary was still up and would answer the phone. Thankfully, she did.

'Mary, it's Ava. I've only just got your message. What's wrong?'

'Oh thank God, Ava!'

'Please, just tell me! Is it LJ?'

Ava heard a sob from the other end of the line. 'No, it's not LJ.'

'Thank God! Oh, thank God. Then what is it?'

'Ava, it's Marchmont.'

'What about it?'

'There's been a dreadful fire. Oh, Ava, Marchmont has burnt down.' Mary began to cry in earnest now.

'Was anyone . . . hurt?'

'They can't find your mother and, as the fire started at night, they don't know—'

'Mary, my mother is fine. I've just seen her here in London.'

'Well, look you, what a relief! I knew she was coming there, but I thought she was leaving this morning, and . . .'

Mary's voice trailed off. 'Well, it's good news she wasn't at the house last night.'

'She told me she's staying at the Savoy. I'll call now and leave a message for her. She's at a party now, though, and I've no idea what time she'll be back.'

'Ava, I really think we have to try and contact your Uncle David. Do you have the list of numbers he left for emergencies?'

'Yes. I'll work out where he's likely to be and leave a message *poste restante*. Although how long it'll take for it to reach him is anyone's guess. I think he's still in Tibet. Listen, Mary, I'm going to get on the first train home to Marchmont tomorrow.'

'No, Ava! You've missed too much of your first term already, your great-aunt would say the same I'm sure. And besides, there's nothing you can do for the moment, really there isn't.'

The beeps on the phone went. 'Mary, I'm sorry, I have to ring off now, as I don't have much change and I need to call my mother. I'll speak to you tomorrow morning.'

Replacing the receiver then picking it up again, Ava got the number of the Savoy from Directory Enquiries and left a message for Cheska to call both Mary and her immediately. As she walked shakily back down the corridor, Ava's eyes filled with tears as she thought of her beloved Marchmont, burnt to the ground.

Wondering how on earth she could sleep, she curled up in bed and lay there shivering, thinking how everything seemed to have gone so terribly wrong since Cheska had arrived at Marchmont.

*

Ava knocked on the door of Cheska's suite at the Savoy at ten o'clock the next day. Having tried calling and been told that Miss Hammond's number was blocked, she'd decided to skip yet another lecture and go in person.

'Mother, it's me, Ava.'

After a moment, the door opened and Cheska, mascara streaked down her face, hair awry, threw herself into Ava's arms.

'Oh God! Oh God! I've just spoken to Mary. LJ will never forgive me, never! Why did it have to happen while I was in charge? They'll both blame me, you know, oh yes they will!'

Ava saw the expression in her mother's eyes. She looked quite mad.

'Of course they won't. Come on, Mother. It was an accident, surely?'

'I . . . I don't know. I don't know . . .'

'Mother, you must calm down. *Please*. This will do no one any good, least of all you.'

'But I . . . oh God . . .'

'Look, I . . . I think I ought to call a doctor. I—'

'*No!*'

The vehemence of Cheska's response startled Ava. She watched as Cheska wiped her eyes and blew her nose on a sodden handkerchief. 'There's no need to get a doctor. I'll be fine now that you're here, really.'

'Okay, well, what about a brandy or something? It's good for shock, I think. Shall I send down for some?'

Cheska pointed to a cabinet in the corner of the exquisitely furnished sitting room. 'Try in there.'

'Right. Why don't you go and tidy yourself up a little.

I'll pour you a glass of brandy, then we can discuss where we go from here.'

Cheska stared at her daughter. 'How did I ever manage to give birth to someone like you?' she said, and took herself off to the bathroom.

Ava poured out the brandy and sat on the sofa until her mother returned looking pale, but immaculate. 'Now, all I know is there was a fire. Could you please try to tell me exactly what happened?'

'Well, I left Marchmont on Monday at about eight o'clock in the evening. Mary said Jack Wallace called her when he saw great clouds of smoke billowing out of the upstairs windows in the early hours. He called the fire brigade, but I think by that time it must have got a really good hold.'

'So how bad is the damage?'

'Pretty bad, Mary told me. The roof has gone and most of the inside, but apparently the outer walls are still intact. Jack told Mary they were saved by torrential rain. I suppose we must be grateful for that, at least.'

'Do they know how it started?'

'Mary said it might have been an electrical fault. Some of the wiring was very, very old. But, oh Ava' – she shuddered – 'the worst thing is that I could have been in there. I only decided to leave for London earlier that evening on the spur of the moment. I'd originally planned to go the next day.'

'What about the animals? Are they all right?'

'I'm sure they are and that Jack's making sure they're looked after. The fire only affected the house.' Cheska covered her face with her hands. 'I don't want to see it. I just can't bear the thought of that beautiful house blackened and smouldering.'

'We have to go up to Wales. In fact, we ought to leave immediately.'

Cheska removed her hands from her face and looked at Ava in horror. 'You don't mean you want me to drive to Marchmont now, do you? No, no, I couldn't face it.' She began to cry again.

'Well, I'll go then.'

'*No!* Please, Ava.' Cheska grabbed her hand. 'I need you here with me. You can't leave me alone, *please*. Just give me some time to recover from the shock. I can't go yet, I just can't.'

Ava could see that Cheska was becoming hysterical again. She moved closer to her and put an arm round her. 'Okay,' she sighed. 'I won't leave you.'

'Jack Wallace said there's nothing we can do, anyway. He's taking care of the farm as usual, and Mr Glenwilliam is dealing with the insurance company.'

'Well, when you're calmer, we must go as soon as possible. Mary said the police will want to talk to you, to see if you noticed anything strange before you left Marchmont.'

'Surely they can come here? I'm far too distressed to drive. Besides, I've got a big meeting on Friday morning. I met a director at the after-show party last night who is desperate for me to be in his new television series.'

'Can't you reschedule it?' Ava was aghast that her mother could even think about her career at a moment like this.

Cheska caught the look on Ava's face. 'If necessary, of

course I will. And I called the nursing home this morning. LJ is doing very well. Obviously, we mustn't tell her anything until she's strong enough to cope, so I think it's best we don't visit for a day or two. None of us would be able to hide it from her if we saw her now.'

'I suppose you're right, although she'll need to be told soon. I just thank my lucky stars she was in the nursing home, otherwise . . .' Ava shivered. 'And poor Uncle David. What is he going to say when he discovers his mother is recovering from a stroke and Marchmont has burnt down? I've left him a message, but I don't know when he'll get it.'

'Have you? Well, you and I are going to have to deal with this ourselves until he's home. We can get through if we stick together, can't we? Give each other support and try and sort things out.'

'Yes. Mother, listen, if we're not going to Marchmont today, I have a lecture this afternoon. Is it okay if I go? I'm horribly behind as it is.'

'You will come back afterwards, won't you? Promise me?'

'If you need me to.' Ava rose, kissed her mother and left the hotel, glad to be out in the biting October air and on the streets, where everything seemed to be going on as normal.

Ava returned dutifully to the hotel after her lecture to find that her mother had ordered room service and copious champagne.

'I thought we could watch a movie together,' Cheska suggested as she poured the drinks and lifted the silver lids from an array of different dishes. 'I didn't know what you wanted, so I ordered a selection.'

'I have an essay to write, Mother, and an early lecture tomorrow. I'll eat, and then I must go home.'

'*No!* Please, Ava, I don't want to be alone tonight. The police have contacted me and they're coming to see me tomorrow afternoon. I'm frightened, really frightened. Maybe they'll say it's my fault.'

'I'm sure they won't. They just want information.'

'Please, I beg you, stay over with me. I just know I'm going to have the most terrible dreams.'

'Okay,' Ava agreed reluctantly, seeing the desperation in her mother's eyes.

They ate, then watched a movie and Ava yawned. 'Time for bed,' she said. 'I'll sleep on the sofa.'

'Would you mind . . . would you mind sleeping with me?' Cheska asked her. 'It's a kingsize. I just don't want to be by myself tonight. I just know I'll have bad dreams. Come and see.'

Ava followed her out of the sitting room and into the palatial bedroom. Cheska disappeared and came back in a satin nightgown.

'Won't you get changed, Ava?'

'I haven't got anything with me.'

'You can borrow one of my nightdresses, honey. I've got several. Go and take a look.'

Ava went into the dressing room and gasped in astonishment. Hanging on the rail were a number of suits and dresses. Blouses, underwear and nightclothes were neatly folded on shelves. Even for someone as excessive as her mother, this was a lot to bring for a twenty-four-hour stay.

Unless Cheska had been planning not to return to Marchmont at all . . .

Too exhausted, drained and confused even to begin to think about it, Ava chose one of her mother's less revealing nightgowns and slipped it on.

When she walked back into the bedroom, Cheska was sitting up in bed. She patted it. 'Jump in.'

'Can I turn off the light?' she asked as she did so.

'I'd rather you didn't. Talk to me, Ava.'

'What about?'

'Oh, anything nice.'

'I—' Ava couldn't think of a thing to say.

'Okay then, I guess I'll tell *you* a story, as long as you come and give me a cuddle. This is fun, isn't it? Like being in a dorm,' said Cheska, settled into Ava's arms.

Ava thought with anguish of her lovely bedroom at Marchmont, now blackened and open to the night sky, all her cherished possessions gone. No, this wasn't fun, not fun at all.

'Well now, once upon a time . . .'

Ava half listened to the fairy story her mother was telling her, something about a pixie called Shuni who lived in the Welsh mountains. Dreadful images flashed in front of her eyes: Marchmont on fire, LJ in a nursing home, David out of reach . . .

Eventually, she dozed off. Vaguely, she heard her mother's voice and felt a hand stroking her forehead.

'Maybe it's for the best, honey, and, anyway, Bobby's coming for brunch tomorrow. Won't that be lovely?'

Ava knew she must be dreaming.

# *50*

Ava woke to find Cheska's side of the bed empty. She sat up and rubbed her eyes. She'd drunk too much champagne last night and had a headache. She looked at her watch; it was almost twenty to eleven. With a groan, she realised she'd missed her lecture.

'Hi, sleepyhead.' Cheska smiled as she emerged from the dressing room looking as if she'd just walked off the set of *The Oil Barons*. Her hair and make-up were perfect and she was wearing one of her smartest suits. 'My guests are arriving in fifteen minutes. Do you want to take a shower?'

Ava stared at Cheska in confusion. 'But, Mother, surely you're not having people to brunch? You said the police were coming later, and we really have to think about going home as soon as possible.'

Cheska sat on the edge of the bed. 'Honey, I told you, there's nothing we can do at Marchmont. I called Jack Wallace an hour ago and he told me that everything is under control. He thinks, as I do, that it's better to stay here for the moment. I've also called the nursing home and asked them to tell LJ that we've come down with a stomach bug and we don't want to pass it on. It's a white lie, I know, but at least now she won't worry about us not visiting. Let me speak to the police this afternoon and we'll take it from there.' There was a knock at the door of the suite and Cheska jumped off the bed. 'That'll be room service. I asked for six bottles of champagne. I guess that will be enough, won't it?'

'I've no idea, Mother,' Ava said helplessly.

'Well, we can always order some more, can't we?' With that, Cheska flitted out of the bedroom, closing the door behind her.

Ava sighed in despair at her mother's mercurial mood swings, then heaved herself from the bed. Her usual energy seemed to have deserted her, and every muscle in her body ached as she walked into the luxurious bathroom to shower.

As the water revitalised her, she tried to make sense of her mother's behaviour, but she struggled. Last night Cheska had been distraught; this morning it was as if nothing out of the ordinary had happened.

Dressing, she heard laughter from the room next door. She sat on the bed and shook her head. She couldn't face going in. A tear trickled down her cheek and she sent up a prayer that David would get her message soon.

There was a sudden knock on the door. 'Hello?' she said.

'Hey, sweetheart, it's me. What's wrong?' asked Simon, as he entered and walked towards her.

Ava looked up in surprise, wondering why he was here. 'Didn't Cheska tell you?'

'Tell me what?'

'That Marchmont has burnt down? That my beautiful home is a pile of cinders?!'

There was a short pause as Simon digested this information. 'No, she didn't. I did hear her mention to Dorian a few minutes ago that there'd been a problem, but that was all. Jesus!' He ran a hand through his thick blond hair. 'You say Marchmont is destroyed?'

Ava wiped her eyes and nose with her hand. 'Yes. And she doesn't even seem to care! How could she have a party this morning? How could she?!'

Simon sat down on the bed next to her. 'God, Ava, I'm so sorry. Was anyone hurt?'

'No. The house was empty.'

'Well, that's something, at least. I'm sure it'll be rebuilt in no time. There'll be insurance money and—'

'But that isn't the point! Everything has gone! My great-aunt's in a nursing home, my uncle's God knows where and my mother is behaving like it's Christmas next door! I just . . . don't know what to do.'

'Ava, I promise you, I'll help in any way I can. Now—'

'Honey! Whatever's the matter?' Cheska was at the door, watching them.

'Ava is upset about the fire at Marchmont,' answered Simon. 'Understandably.'

'Of course she is.' Cheska came and sat next to him on the bed. 'I know it's been an awful shock for you, honey, but I'm sure Bobby doesn't want to be bored by your tears, do you, Bobby?'

'My name's Simon, and I really don't mind at all,' he said firmly.

'Come with me, Simon,' Cheska cajoled. 'I want to discuss something with you.'

'I will in a bit, when Ava's calmer, okay?'

'Well, don't leave it too long. There's someone I want you to meet.'

Cheska left them alone, and Simon turned to Ava.

'Sorry I couldn't talk to you much on opening night.'

'That's okay.' She shrugged. 'You were busy.'

'Your mother is certainly a monopolising force. She seems to want to turn me into a star.'

'She probably can,' Ava said miserably. 'She usually seems to get everything she wants.'

'Maybe, but look, Ava, I've missed you. Can I take you out to dinner one evening after the show?'

'I'd like that, but with what's happening at the moment, it may be a while before I'm able to take you up on the offer. I'm planning to head up to Wales in the next couple of days.'

'Of course. I know you've got other things on your mind at the moment.' Simon tipped her chin up towards him and gave her a light peck on the lips. 'But when you get the chance, we can—'

They both heard Cheska calling his name from the sitting room.

'You'd better go,' Ava said.

Simon sighed and nodded. 'She's got some record producer in there she wants me to meet before he leaves. Come with me?'

'No thanks. I can't face it, sorry.'

'Okay. I understand. Anything I can do in the meantime, just call, promise?'

'Promise.'

'Bye, sweetheart. Please take care.'

'I'll try.'

Ava watched him go, then went to the bathroom, locked the door and ran all the taps at full pelt to drown out the sound of laughter emanating from the sitting room.

Despite her misgivings about the bizarreness of the situation, Ava had felt guilty about not emerging for the brunch party, so she'd pacified her mother as she left by saying that she was free to come and see her the next day. She'd attended her morning lecture, but knew her concentration was shot to pieces, and returned reluctantly to the Savoy afterwards.

Cheska was full of her meeting that morning at the BBC. 'They're writing me in especially. It's so exciting, and I want to take you shopping to celebrate. And, if I'm staying here in London, I need some new clothes.'

'Did the police come yesterday afternoon?' Ava asked.

'I rang to cancel,' Cheska said airily. 'They're coming tomorrow instead. Now, let's go shopping.'

This was not a pastime Ava enjoyed at the best of times, and it seemed ridiculously frivolous in the light of what had happened, but, as usual, Cheska wouldn't take no for an answer. So, Ava trailed after her mother around Harrods as she flitted through the racks of clothes like a bird in search of a worm.

'Here, honey, can you hold this?' Cheska lifted yet another expensive dress off the rail and into Ava's already overflowing arms.

'But, Mother, what about all those clothes you have at the hotel?'

'They're old. This is a fresh start and I want to look my best. Here, why don't you try this on?' Cheska had plucked a short red jacket and matching skirt off the rails.

'I have lots of clothes. I really don't need any more.'

'That isn't the point. You don't buy these kinds of clothes to be practical. Besides, most of your stuff is at Marchmont, probably destroyed. I'm sure you're going to need far smarter things now you're living in London.'

Ava glanced at the price tag on the red jacket when she tried it on. It was almost eight hundred pounds.

'What do you think?' Cheska entered Ava's cubicle in a fashionable black-and-cream suit, sharply cut, with large shoulder pads. 'I think it's too officey, don't you?' Cheska twirled in front of the mirror.

'I think you look lovely, Mother.'

'Thanks. Well, there's a heap of others to try on before I decide.' She glanced at Ava in her red jacket and skirt. 'That looks great. We'll take it.'

After what felt like hours later they left Harrods and hailed a taxi. Cheska had been unable to decide which outfit she preferred, so she'd bought all five, along with matching shoes and a couple of handbags. Everything was being delivered to the suite at the Savoy later.

'Beauchamp Place, San Lorenzo, please,' Cheska said to the taxi driver.

'Where are we going?' Ava asked.

'To meet Dorian for an early supper.'

'Do you really want me to come with you? I desperately need to finish an essay.'

'Of course I want you to come, honey. Dorian wants to talk to you.'

Dorian was already waiting at a table. He stood up and kissed them both, then poured some white wine into their glasses. After a preliminary round of small talk, Dorian turned to Ava. 'Darling, myself and your mother need your help.'

'Really? How?'

'Well, it looks as if Cheska has landed herself a great part – especially written for her – in a big new TV soap that airs on the BBC next spring. The thing is, we need to build up her profile here in the British media. Announce she's come home to stay and put a positive spin on why.'

'And what does that have to do with me?'

'Well, although her character in *The Oil Barons* is a household name, Cheska's almost one hundred per cent associated with that role. And we have to wean the British public away from that association, start people thinking about Cheska herself and who she is. I have a very good friend from the *Daily Mail* to whom I drop titbits. She's salivating over the thought of getting the story on you and Cheska.'

'What story?'

'As I'm sure you know, Ava, at the moment, no one knows you even exist. But, mark my words, they'll find out once Cheska is on TV every Sunday night. Therefore, it's far better for you to tell the story in your own words: a well-known actress gives birth to a daughter when she's little more than a child herself, but has to leave her behind while she goes to forge her career in Hollywood. Mother comes back to England and is reunited with her. It's front-page stuff, I guarantee you. What do you think?'

'It sounds ghastly to me.' Ava shuddered. 'I don't want the world to know about my private life.'

Cheska took her hand. 'I know, darling. But the problem is that if I want to stay with you here in England I've got to earn some money. The only way I can do that is to work as an actress. And the press will have a field day if they find out about you themselves. They'll destroy me, I swear.'

Ava wanted to say that the cost of the suite at the Savoy and the huge bill at Harrods would have kept her quite happily for a while.

'Well, I won't tell anyone I'm your daughter, I promise. I'd really, really prefer not to, Mother.'

'I understand, Ava,' Dorian interceded, 'but we must handle this very carefully, for your mother's sake. The journalist I have in mind would be . . . sympathetic. And you'd have copy approval, of course.'

'You wouldn't mind, would you, honey? Just one little article and a picture. Please? I need you to do this for me. My whole future career depends on it.'

'I don't want to, sorry,' Ava said firmly.

'But surely you want to help your mother as much as you can?' said Dorian.

'Yes, of course I do, but . . . I'm frightened. I've never met a journalist in my life!'

'I'll be there with you, Ava. You leave it to me to do the talking,' said Cheska.

Ava knew she was being steam-rollered. The sulks and cajoling she knew would ensue if she refused were too much for her to contemplate just now. She felt exhausted. 'Fine,' she said, but it wasn't.

'Thank you, darling,' Dorian said with relief. 'That's settled then. I'll ring Jodie tonight and organise a time for her to come to the Savoy. Now, shall we order? I'm famished.'

After supper, which Ava only picked at, as her stomach was churning at the thought of what she'd been manipulated into, Dorian paid the bill and said he had to leave to see a client in a show. Ava sat uncomfortably at the table, waiting for Cheska to finish her coffee so she could leave.

'Are you busy tomorrow?' Cheska asked her.

'Yes. All day.'

'Really?' Cheska said as they walked out onto the chilly Knightsbridge street. 'I was assuming you'd want to be there when I see the police. They're coming some time in the afternoon.'

'Well, I can't be there. I have a lot of work to catch up on, and I must make arrangements to go up and see LJ sometime this weekend. I don't want to put it off any longer.' Ava caught a glimpse of her mother's stricken face. 'But I'll come to the Savoy to see you around five.'

'Thank you, honey.' Cheska hailed a passing cab. 'You take this one,' she said, pressing a twenty-pound note into Ava's palm.

'Really. I can get the bus.'

'And really, I want you to take a cab. You know I love you, don't you?'

Ava lowered her eyes and nodded. What else could she do?

'You know, Ava, you weren't there back then when I found out I was having you. I was fifteen, and so scared. I had no one to turn to. You have to remember that abortions were still illegal. Not that I'd have thought about it,' Cheska checked herself quickly, 'because I wanted to have you. But your grandmother had just had her accident and was in a coma, and I had no idea how to bring up a baby.

When I went to Hollywood for a screen test and got myself a contract, I was told by my agent not to mention you to anyone. I know I should have refused, but can you try to understand how naive and vulnerable I was? I was younger than you are now, Ava.'

Ava felt the eyes of the waiting cabbie upon them both. 'Let's talk about it another time,' she said quickly.

'See you tomorrow, darling.' Cheska waved brightly at her as the cab pulled away. Ava sank onto the seat, her head spinning with the awful knowledge that she had been out manoeuvred by her mother yet again.

Back in her room, she tried to write her essay but found her thoughts drifting back to her mother. Everything Cheska was – or, at least, seemed to be – was beyond comprehension. Ava put down her pen and rested her head on her half-finished essay, thinking who on earth she could turn to for advice.

She didn't want to worry Mary and, for the moment, LJ wasn't an option as a confidante. And Simon? Ava just didn't know.

'Uncle David,' she sighed, sinking into bed exhausted, 'please, please get my message soon.'

The door to the suite opened and Cheska greeted Ava, smiling. 'Inspector Crosby is just leaving. Come in and say hello.'

Ava followed her mother through to the sitting room. The inspector looked relaxed and was putting a file into his briefcase.

'This is Ava, my daughter, Inspector.'

Ava shook the inspector's hand. 'Have you found out what caused the fire yet?'

'The investigators are still working on it, but they're pretty sure it was deliberate. They think it started in one of the bedrooms. Don't you worry, miss, we're taking this case very seriously indeed. Marchmont Hall is an important piece of national heritage, as well as being your family home, and—'

'I was shocked, as you can imagine,' Cheska interrupted. 'As I said to Inspector Crosby, it might have been an intruder who wanted to kill me. Celebrities such as myself often attract stalkers, as you know. To think I could have burnt to death in my bed!'

'There are certainly some very strange people out there, Miss Hammond,' agreed Inspector Crosby. 'And Marchmont is hardly protected security-wise. Obviously, I asked your mother if she smoked, or had lit a candle and may have accidentally dropped a match,' he added.

'Did you, Mother?'

'Ava! You know I don't smoke, and I think I might have remembered if I'd done anything to start a fire.'

'You certainly had a very lucky escape, Miss Hammond,' the inspector confirmed. 'Now, would it be possible to have a couple of autographed photographs to take back for the boys?'

'Of course, let me go and get some.'

Ava was left standing uncomfortably with the inspector.

'I didn't know Cheska Hammond had a daughter. You look just like her,' he said.

'Thanks. So, what happens from here with Marchmont?'

'The investigators have nearly finished. They'll put in their report sometime next week. I have a few more loose ends to tie up and we'll see where it takes us.'

'But you think it was an intruder who started the fire deliberately?'

'At present, there seems to be no other explanation – unless your mother wanted to burn her own house down,' he quipped.

'It's not my mother's house, Inspector, it's my aunt's.'

'Here you are.' Cheska appeared, brandishing the photographs.

'Thank you. The boys will be very happy.' He placed them carefully in his briefcase and held out his hand. 'It was a pleasure to meet you, Miss Hammond. And your daughter,' he added, glancing at Ava. 'I'll be in touch.'

'I feel like I've been on trial for the past hour!' Cheska wailed as the door closed behind him. She slumped onto the sofa. Then her eyes filled with fear. 'You don't think . . . you don't think he suspected me of anything, do you, Ava?'

'No, Mother.'

'It was just, some of the questions he asked, it made me feel like a . . . a criminal.'

'I wouldn't worry. By the time he left he'd obviously become one of your biggest fans.'

'Do you think so?'

'Yes. Now, I'm afraid I have to go.'

'Go where?'

'Home, to do some work.'

'But you can't! Jodie will be here in fifteen minutes.'

'Who's Jodie?'

'The journalist. I promise it won't take long. I'll order you something from room service.'

'I'm not hungry.'

'Champagne, then? I'll get some sent up.'

'No, thanks.'

'Look, honey, I know you don't want to do this, but you did promise me and Dorian you would. Let me do all the talking. I'm used to it. Okay?'

An hour and a half later, Ava left the Savoy, feeling sick to the stomach. Cheska had insisted on sitting next to her whilst Jodie interviewed them, holding her hand, putting her arm round her shoulder and acting the role of devoted mother to perfection. Ava had said very little, answering the questions put to her monosyllabically. A photographer had arrived, and after the pictures had been taken, Ava had stood up, kissed her mother and left. As she was leaving, Cheska had muttered something about seeing Simon the next day, and that she'd have some good news for Ava afterwards.

As Ava sat down on the bus, she forced herself to acknowledge that Cheska was in love with Simon. And maybe he with her. When she arrived back in her room, Ava lay on her bed for a few minutes with tears in her eyes but decided that there was no point brooding over it now. She made up her mind that she would leave for Wales tomorrow and go and see LJ. Even though she knew she couldn't tell LJ about the tragedy that had struck Marchmont, she felt she needed to be in her aunt's secure, solid presence. As she closed her eyes, desperately tired and willing sleep to come, she thought about where the investigators had said the fire had started. And suddenly, with every fibre in her body, she knew her mother was lying.

# 51

'Hello, Mr Glenwilliam, I have a call for you from David Marchmont.'

'Thank you, Sheila.'

'Glenwilliam?'

'David, I'm awfully glad you've called.'

'We've only just arrived back at our hotel in Lhasa from a trek in the Himalayas. There were messages asking me to contact both you and Ava urgently. I couldn't reach Ava at the number she gave me in London, so you were my next port of call. What's happened? Is it my mother?'

'No. She's all right, as far as I know. At least, she's in a nursing home—'

'A nursing home?!'

'Yes, but in the circumstances, we can all be relieved she was. One of the reasons I was trying to get hold of you is because Marchmont was badly damaged in a fire a few days ago.'

'Oh God! Was anybody hurt?'

'No.'

'Thank heavens. I'm grateful to you for contacting me, Glenwilliam.'

'Well, Miss Hammond did advise me that I wouldn't be able to reach you, but I thought it best that I—'

'Cheska?! She's back in the UK?'

'Yes, although, apparently, she's in London now. And, of course, Ava's there, too, at college.'

'Jesus Christ! It sounds as if all hell has broken loose! My mother's in a nursing home, Marchmont has gone up in smoke and Cheska's back in England. Is she with Ava now?'

'Miss Hammond is staying at the Savoy, so your housekeeper tells me. I've rung the hotel a number of times, but she's yet to return my calls. I really must speak to her. Now she has temporary power of attorney for Marchmont, I can't do anything without her say-so. Plus—'

'Power of attorney? Cheska? Why?'

'I'm sorry, David, allow me to back-track a little. The reason your mother is in a nursing home is because she had a stroke in September. It was thought best by the doctors and myself for Miss Hammond to handle Marchmont's financial affairs whilst she recovers.'

'A stroke? How bad was it?'

'From what I've gathered, she's recovering well. However, there is another problem you need to be aware of, which is' – Glenwilliam paused nervously for a moment before imparting the news – 'that a substantial amount of money has been withdrawn from the Marchmont estate account, and I wanted to check that this was done on Miss Hammond's instruction and obviously, why she's transferred it.'

'What? Why in God's name did you allow Cheska to

have power of attorney?!' David exploded. 'Surely you could have waited until you had spoken to me?'

'Forgive me, David, but I didn't know how long it might take to contact you, and Miss Hammond was most insistent. Of course, I offered to run the estate for her in your absence, but she seemed determined to take on the responsibility herself. There was little I could do to stop her. Your mother's doctor had written a statement that she was unfit to continue running the estate.'

'And both your heads were turned by her famous face and legendary charm, no doubt. Did she also ask who would inherit the estate on my mother's death?'

There was another pause. 'I believe she did, yes.'

'And you told her?'

'She seemed to know already, David. I merely clarified the situation.'

'Look, I'll fly home as soon as possible. I'll go to London first, speak to Cheska and find out what the hell is going on. I'll be in touch when I land. Goodbye.'

David slammed down the receiver and lay back on the bed with a groan.

Tor had just emerged from the shower. 'My goodness! It's nice to have a few luxuries after weeks of washing with buckets and sleeping on those dreadful mats! David, what on earth is it? You're as white as a sheet!'

'I knew we shouldn't have been out of contact for such a long time. It's complete mayhem in England!'

'But, darling, that was the whole point. To get away from things, be by ourselves for a while.'

'If anything's happened to her . . . I'll . . .' David's shoulders began to heave.

Tor sat next to him and put her arms around him. 'Happened to who? What? Tell me!'

'My mother's had a stroke. Glenwilliam says she's in a nursing home. And Cheska's come home.'

'Cheska? She's at Marchmont?'

'No, Tor. On top of that, there's been a fire. The house has burnt down. I don't know how bad it is, but Glenwilliam gave Cheska power of attorney and now she's gone to London, having removed what Glenwilliam called a "substantial amount of money" from the Marchmont estate account.'

'Good Lord! It sounds as if we'd better see if we can get a flight back to London immediately. I'll ring the concierge while you go and make yourself a stiff drink. And one for me, too,' Tor added.

David stood up and wandered over to the minibar. He poured himself a large gin, added some tonic and ice and took a healthy gulp.

Twenty minutes later Tor was off the phone and was starting to stuff clothes into David's overnight bag. 'You're booked on a flight tonight. You'll have to go via Beijing, then transfer to London. It's rather a long wait in Beijing, but it's the best I could do at short notice. You should get into Heathrow early evening on Sunday, local time.'

'What about you?'

'Only one seat left on the plane, I'm afraid, darling. They're making enquiries for me now, and I'll follow on as soon as I can.'

'This is all my fault.' David sighed in despair. 'If I hadn't been so fixated on taking this trip, I might have realised Cheska was up to something.'

Tor sat him down on the bed and gently took his hands in hers. 'Dear David, you've spent your life trying to look after Greta, Cheska and Ava. None of them is even a blood relation to you. The fact that you allowed yourself some time for you doesn't make you guilty of anything. You must remember that.'

'Thank you, darling. I'll try to.'

'Now, you'd better jump into the shower. You've only got twenty minutes before you need to leave for the airport.'

Ava was sitting at her desk, desperately trying to finish her essay so that she could leave it in her tutor's pigeonhole before she left for Marchmont, when she heard a knock on the door.

'Phone call for you, Ava.'

Ava walked to the payphone.

'Hello?'

'It's me, Mary. I'm sorry to bother you, but I don't know what else to do. I tried last night and nobody picked up the telephone.'

'Is it LJ?' Ava's heart yet again missed a beat.

'Ava, don't panic, she's not dead, or at least not that I know. She's just . . . missing.'

'Missing? What on earth do you mean?'

'I went to visit her last night at the nursing home. The matron was surprised to see me. She thought I would know that Mrs Marchmont had been removed by her niece a few days ago, but she doesn't know where to.'

'What?! You're saying Cheska has taken her out of the nursing home and didn't tell us?'

'Yes. On Monday, before she left for London. She told me not to visit for a couple of days as your great-aunt was being taken to Abergavenny Hospital for an assessment.'

'Then, surely, that's where she is?'

'No, I telephoned them and they say that Mrs Marchmont isn't due for any assessment until next week.' Ava heard Mary stifle a sob.

'Well it's very simple, I'll call my mother now and find out where and *why* she's moved her.'

'I tried her last night at the Savoy, but the receptionist said that she'd blocked her line until further notice. Oh Ava, what has your mother done with her?'

'I don't know, but I promise you I'm going to find out. Try not to panic, Mary. I'm sure she's all right. Any word from Uncle David? According to his itinerary, he should be at his hotel in Lhasa about now.'

'No word yet, but I'm sure he'll call as soon as he gets the message.'

'We need him home urgently, Mary, he's the only one who can make sense of what's happened. I was planning to come up to Wales this evening, but obviously I need to see my mother first. I'll be in touch as soon as I've seen her and found out where she's taken LJ.'

'Thank you, *fach*. But please take care when you go and ask her, won't you?'

'What do you mean?' Ava asked her.

'I . . . just that, perhaps your mother isn't quite what she seems.'

Ava thought grimly that she'd begun to work that out for herself.

Simon knocked on the door of Cheska's suite.

'Come in!'

He tried the handle and discovered it was unlocked.

'Hello?' he said as he walked inside.

'In here, darling,' said a voice from the bedroom. 'Come through.'

'Okay.' He opened the door. 'Sorry I'm a bit late, Cheska, I . . .'

The sight that met his eyes rendered him silent. Cheska was lying on the bed clad only in a black bra, briefs and sheer stockings held up by a lace suspender belt. She had a glass of champagne in her hand.

'Hello, honey.' She smiled at him.

'Where's the record producer you wanted me to meet?' Simon asked, trying to look anywhere other than at Cheska.

'He's arriving later. Come here, darling. We have so much to celebrate.' She held out her arms to him.

Simon sank into a chair.

'Bobby, there's no need to be shy. You never used to be shy, did you?'

'I don't know what you're talking about, Cheska. And, for the umpteenth time, my name is Simon.'

'Sure it is. Here, have some champagne. It'll relax you.'

'No, thanks. Look, Cheska, I'm afraid there's been a bit of a mistake.'

'What "mistake"?'

'I think, I—' Simon struggled for the right words. 'I think you want things from me that I just can't give you.'

'Such as?' Cheska smiled seductively. 'If you mean your body and your heart and your soul, then yes, you're right. I want them. I love you, Bobby. I always have. I know you're angry with me for what I did to you, but I'll make it up to you, I swear. And, besides, your face is all healed up now.' She stood up and advanced towards him. As he sat there frozen with shock, she climbed on top of him, straddling his legs with hers. 'Please, Bobby, forgive me, forgive me.' She leant forward to kiss his neck.

'*No!*' Recovering his senses, Simon jumped up, throwing her off and almost toppling her backwards.

Cheska regained her balance and looked up at him from under her eyelashes. 'I know you're playing hard to get. You always did tease me. Give in now, Bobby, let's forget about the past and make a fresh start. Life is going to be so wonderful. I'm moving to London so we can be together. I've seen a fabulous apartment in Knightsbridge I'm going to rent for us. I've got a great part in a television series and you'll have a recording deal and—'

'*Stop it! Stop it!*' Simon took her by the shoulders and shook her.

Cheska continued to smile at him in her dreamy way. 'I remember you did like to hurt me sometimes. I don't mind. Anything you want, darling, anything.'

Simon felt her foot rubbing up and down his leg. 'Shut up!' His hand whipped across her face, not hard enough to hurt, but the shock silenced her. She looked up at him, a wounded expression in her eyes.

'Bobby, what have I done? Please tell me.'

Simon steered her to the chair and sat her down. 'Cheska, for the last time, my name is not Bobby. It's Simon Hardy. I only met you a few weeks ago. We have had no past, and we have no future either.'

'I . . . oh, you always were cruel, Bobby. Don't you like me any more? Tell me what it is I've done.'

'You haven't done anything, Cheska. It just wouldn't work out, that's all.'

'Please give me a chance to show you how happy I can make you.'

'No. You have to understand that any relationship is impossible.'

'Why?'

'Because I'm in love with someone else, that's why.'

Cheska stared into the distance, then turned back to him, her face full of hate.

'You're doing it again, aren't you?'

'No, Cheska. I've never done this before. To you, or anyone else.'

'Don't lie to me! All those nights we spent together. You used to say you loved me, would always love me, and then, and then . . .' Cheska's voice trailed off.

'Look, I have no idea what you're talking about, but I'm going to leave now.' Simon moved towards the door.

'Who is she?! Is it that wife you hid away for years, or that little whore of a make-up girl you were screwing at the same time as me?'

'I have no idea what or who you're talking about. I'm sorry things have turned out like this.'

'If you walk out now, I swear I'll come after you and punish you like I did before.'

Simon turned round and saw the darkness in her glassy eyes.

'I think you need help, Cheska. Goodbye.'

As Ava sat on the bus to the Savoy, her thoughts seemed to crowd in on her. There had been plenty of moments in the past few weeks when she had watched Cheska's mood change in an instant, but she'd always put her mother's odd behaviour down to her having lived in such a rarefied world and being so famous. Everyone that met her felt honoured and in awe of her; they all adored her. Ava knew that she, too, had initially fallen under Cheska's spell.

But she now knew that her mother had lied to both her and Mary about removing LJ from the nursing home. And, as for the fire – Ava sighed as she stepped off the bus and waited for the traffic lights to change so she could cross the road to the Savoy – did the inspector really believe that Cheska could have had nothing to do with it? Had he been taken in like the rest of them?

The problem was, whether he had or he hadn't, there was little she could do about it. Cheska was her mother, and she could hardly call him and tell him she suspected her.

Walking down the short road that led to the Savoy and shivering in the misty evening air, Ava tried to work out what she would say to her. Accusing Cheska of anything always led to tears on her mother's part, and guilt and apologies on her own. Just as she was thinking these things, she saw a familiar figure appear out of the revolving doors of the hotel entrance.

She slid back into the shadows of the building, but Simon had already spotted her and walked towards her.

'Ava, hello.'

She could see he looked anxious and was breathing heavily. 'Are you okay?' she asked.

'Yes. Sort of, anyway.'

'Don't tell me, you've just been to see my mother,' she said, turning her eyes from him and trying to act as if she didn't care.

'I have. She said there was somebody I had to meet. A record producer.'

'Great. I hope it went well.'

'He wasn't there.'

'I'm sorry.'

'Ava, look, can you stop treating me like a stranger? I promise you, it's not as it seems.'

'You're the second person to say something like that to me today.'

'Well, I'm sorry to be repetitive, but I think, given what happened upstairs just now, your mother got completely the wrong idea about me.'

'So, what did happen?'

'Look, I've got to get to the theatre now, there's a charity performance tonight and it's starting early. And what I've got to tell you is quite difficult to explain.'

'Why don't you have a go?' Ava was looking at her feet. Anywhere but at him.

'I think your mother . . . fancies me.'

'Really? Is that the first time you've realised it?'

'Yes, I mean, no. I knew she was being very friendly. But I presumed it was because of you.'

'Why because of me?'

'Well, it's not unusual for mothers to try to be welcoming to their daughter's boyfriend, is it?'

'But you're not my boyfriend, Simon. We've never even kissed.'

'I . . .' Simon grabbed her softly by her upper arms and pulled her to him. 'Look at me, Ava, please.'

'Simon, if you want to go out with my mother, that's your business, but don't expect me to like it.'

'I *don't* want to – of course I don't, you silly thing! I was just being nice for *our* sake. Paving the way, if you like.'

'For what?'

'For us! Look, Ava, you're younger than me and I didn't want to push anything. I thought we could get to know each other slowly without pressure, but it must have at least been obvious to you that I was interested.'

'I don't know.' Ava shook her head miserably. 'I'm so confused just now, about lots of things.'

'Of course you are,' he said gently. 'Please, let me give you a hug. Please?'

Ava still stood rigidly as he put his arms around her.

'Why are you here, anyway?' he asked.

'Because, apparently, Cheska has moved my great-aunt from her nursing home and no one knows where she is. Why would she do something like that?'

'I don't know but, after what I saw upstairs, something isn't right with her.'

'No, it isn't.' Ava choked back a sob and Simon pulled her closer. 'If she's hurt LJ, I swear I'll—'

'Listen, Ava, I don't want you to see your mother without me. Meet me at the theatre after the show, around nine thirty. Then we can come back to the Savoy together and confront her. Promise?'

'If you really think it's important,' she said.

'It is.'

When Bobby had left, Cheska had dressed in an instant and was soon on her way downstairs to follow him to the theatre. It wasn't his fault he held a grudge against her. She needed to explain again, to make things right and show him how the future would be. She came out of the lift, walked across the foyer and went through the revolving doors that led into the street. As she stood waiting for the doorman to hail her a cab, she saw Bobby out of the corner of her eye, standing a few yards further along. He was embracing a woman, but she couldn't see clearly who it was. He tipped the girl's chin up towards him, and she saw it was Ava, her daughter.

'Traitor!' she gasped under her breath, feeling a dreadful rage consume her. She watched as the two of them turned away from her and began to walk towards the Strand. Bobby had his arm protectively around Ava's shoulders. Cheska waved away the doorman and the waiting cab and began to follow them. On the main road, she saw them pause. He kissed Ava's forehead, gave her a last hug and turned away to walk out of sight along the street. Ava stood on the pavement, waiting for the lights to change so she could cross the road.

A memory came to Cheska then. She'd been here before.

The voices told her what to do, as they had done last time, so many years before.

Cheska walked swiftly towards her daughter.

# 52

David arrived at Heathrow completely exhausted, his nerves in shreds. Once he had cleared Customs, he walked swiftly to the taxi rank.

'The Savoy Hotel, please.'

The taxi made good progress until it reached the top of the Strand, where the traffic became heavy. David sat in the cab, trying to clear his brain, wondering what exactly he was going to say when he came face to face with Cheska.

'All right if I drop you here, guv? Something's happened up ahead. You can walk the next few yards. It'll be faster than waiting here.'

'Yes, fine.'

David climbed out with his overnight bag and began to walk up towards the Savoy. He dodged in and out of the bumper-to-bumper cars and made his way to the other side of the street. There'd been an accident of some kind, at the traffic lights near the entrance.

A crowd had gathered around someone lying in the road, just by the pavement. Taking a deep breath, as it brought back the most dreadful memories, David walked past the crowd, making sure to look away, but once he was on the pavement something made him stop and turn round. The stretcher was being lifted up into the ambulance, and David caught a glimpse of blonde hair and an all too familiar profile lying on it.

'God, no!' he cried, pushing his way through the crowd. He climbed onto the footplate of the ambulance, and explained who he was to the paramedic.

'We're leaving now, sir. Got to get the traffic moving. You coming with us?'

'Yes. How badly is she hurt?' David asked.

'Go and talk to her yourself. She's awake and coherent. We're taking her to A and E to check for any broken bones. The car hit her shoulder and she took a bump on the head but, apart from that, she seems to be in one piece. The traffic was moving so slowly the impact was minimal. Ava,' the paramedic called to her above the wail of the siren, 'look who's come to see you.'

David went to sit beside his niece and took her hand. 'Ava, it's me, Uncle David.'

Ava's eyes fluttered open. She focused on him and, as she registered who he was, her expression turned to amazement. 'Uncle David, is it really you, or am I hallucinating because of the accident?'

'No, it really *is* me, darling.'

'Thank God you're home! Thank God!'

'I am, and I'm going to sort everything out from here. I don't want you to worry about a thing. Do you know where your mother is?'

'No, not really,' said Ava. 'I was going to see her at the Savoy to ask what she'd done with LJ, but Simon stopped me outside.'

'What do you mean, "done with LJ"?'

'She's moved her out of her nursing home and not told us where. Sorry, Uncle David, I—'

Ava had said nothing else by the time they arrived at St Thomas's Hospital. 'I wouldn't worry unduly, sir,' said the paramedic as they took the stretcher from the ambulance. 'She seems very lucid. Good luck.'

As Ava was wheeled off, David filled in the necessary paperwork. Sitting anxiously in the waiting room, he went over in his head what Ava had said about LJ having been moved from the nursing home, and half wondered whether she had been dreaming out loud. He bent down and took his address book out of his overnight bag. Then he went to the payphone to dial Mary's number. Even though he had only enough coins to speak to her briefly, she confirmed what Ava had said, and his heart missed a beat. He told Mary to start ringing round local hospitals and other nursing homes in the area to see if she could find LJ. Surely, even Cheska couldn't have done away with her, could she? His mother had to be somewhere and, whatever it took, he would find her. As soon as he'd made sure Ava was okay, he'd go to the Savoy and see his niece tonight, even if he had to batter down her door to do it. Of course, the other burning question was whether Ava's accident was simply that? Or had Cheska – for whatever warped reason her confused mind had invented – been involved?

*Why had he ever left?* He should have known that Cheska might think about coming home to England. She was broke, her career in Hollywood all but finished. Poor, innocent Ava, who knew nothing about the dark side of her mother, had borne the brunt. Not to mention his mother . . .

Eventually, the doctor came to find him.

'How is she?' asked David.

'The good news is, there's no sign of a break or a fracture in her shoulder, but she does seem to have a mild concussion from the bang on her head. We'll keep her in for observation overnight. I've just rung up for a bed on the ward. If all goes well, she should be fine to come out tomorrow morning. Come and see her. She's sitting up and drinking a cup of tea.'

The doctor led him along the corridor and pulled open the curtain. 'I'll leave you to it. I have other patients to see,' he said apologetically.

David went to sit next to Ava. She looked a lot better than she had earlier. 'How are you feeling, darling?'

'Apart from a seriously bad headache, not too awful, considering. The doctor said I had a lucky escape.'

'You did indeed.'

'Uncle David, you know when Granny had her accident, wasn't that outside the Savoy, too?'

'Yes, it was.'

Ava shuddered. 'What an awful coincidence, isn't it?'

'Yes, it is, but please, that's *all* it is.' David wasn't at all sure that he believed what he'd just said.

'What time is it?'

'Just after nine.'

'Oh no! I told Simon I'd meet him after his performance. We have to find out where LJ is. I'm so worried about her. Could you go and meet Simon at the Queen's Theatre and explain what happened? Then perhaps you could go and see my mother.'

'Simon?' David scratched his head. 'Who's he?'

'You met him at LJ's eighty-fifth birthday party. You said at the time he looked like someone you knew.'

'Yes, I finally remembered that he looks like someone called Bobby Cross.' David sighed.

'Bobby?' Ava frowned. 'That's funny. Cheska keeps calling him that.'

'Does she?'

'Yes, and the reason Simon was there today was because Cheska had said that she wanted to introduce him to a record producer. I met him coming out of the Savoy, and he more or less said that she had jumped on him.'

David had been wondering if things could get any worse, and realised they just had.

'Would you go and see Simon for me, Uncle David? It's not far from here.'

'Ava, I really think I should stay here with you.'

'No, I'm feeling much better. And I'd be far happier knowing that LJ was all right. But please be careful with Cheska. Simon was really shaken up by the way she was behaving.'

'Don't worry about me, Ava. I've known your mother since she was a little girl. But yes, I would like to speak to Simon to find out just what's been going on. Although I have a pretty good idea.'

The nurse drew back the curtain and told them that Ava's bed upstairs was ready. 'Are you able to get into the wheelchair, or shall we take you up on the trolley?'

'Definitely the wheelchair,' said Ava, climbing out of the bed and standing up. 'See? I'm fine, Uncle David. Please go and find out where LJ is.'

'I'm afraid you won't be allowed up on the ward at this

time of night anyway, sir,' clarified the nurse. 'It's lights out in twenty minutes.'

'Okay, but can I take the number of the ward so I can telephone later to see how Ava is?'

'Of course. They'll give it to you at reception. Now, here's your carriage, madam,' the nurse joked, as a porter arrived with the wheelchair. Ava climbed into it and David kissed her on the cheek.

'Any problems at all, you have my contact numbers,' David said to the nurse as they walked down the corridor with Ava.

'Goodbye, Uncle David. Please come and see me tomorrow morning and let me know what you found out.'

'I will, I promise,' he said, blowing her a kiss as Ava was wheeled into the lift and the doors closed. Hailing a taxi outside the hospital, David gave the address of the Queen's Theatre on Shaftesbury Avenue and tried to make sense of what Ava had just told him.

Simon hurriedly made his way back to his dressing room after the charity performance. He had hoped to be changed and ready to meet Ava by now, but there had been a couple of young royals – patrons of the charity – in the audience, so the cast had been kept behind to be introduced to them. He glanced at his watch and realised he'd better step on it. He was already unbuttoning the shirt of his costume as he opened the door, so it took him a few seconds to notice that he had a very unwelcome guest.

'Hello, honey. I came to tell you that I understand why you're so cross with me. It was a bad thing to do to you, but you'd hurt me so much, you see, I—'

'Cheska, I'm sorry, but, as I said earlier, I have no idea what you're talking about. And I'd really prefer it if you would leave.' Simon sat down at the dressing table and turned his back to her.

'Come on now, Bobby,' she wheedled, standing up so that her reflection appeared in the mirror behind him. 'You must remember what a good time we had?' Her hands went to his shoulders and she started massaging them.

'For the last time, Cheska,' he said, shaking them off then standing up himself to face her, 'I have no idea who this Bobby is. My name is Simon. And if you don't leave of your own accord, I'm afraid I'm going to call Security.'

The expression on Cheska's face changed. 'You're throwing me out? After all we've shared together? After what you did to me? I saw you earlier with Ava. It's disgusting!'

'What? How on earth can you call it disgusting? I'm in love with her! There's a very good chance I want to spend my life with her. And I'm afraid, if you don't like it, that's tough.'

Cheska threw back her head and laughed. 'Come now, Bobby. You know you can never be with Ava.'

'You'd better tell me why not.'

'Because' – Cheska's eyes flashed victoriously – 'she's your daughter! What do you have to say to that?'

Simon stared at her, aghast. 'You really are insane, aren't you?'

'Insane? Hardly. It's you who's the bastard here. You got me pregnant and then abandoned me. Yes, *abandoned* me! And I was only fifteen years old.'

'Cheska, I'm going to say it again: I really think you're confusing me with someone else.' Simon tried to keep his voice calm. Cheska's was rising to fever pitch, and he could see the madness in her eyes. He edged towards the door as she advanced on him.

'You always were a no-good lying cheat!' She reached out suddenly and slapped him hard across the face. And again, and again, until Simon, reeling with shock, managed to grab her by the wrists.

'Stop it!' he said, as he held her fast. Her head dived down and she bit him on his hand. With a howl, Simon let her go and, at once, she was on him, attacking him like a wild animal, clawing at his face with her long, red nails. She kneed him hard in the groin and he cried out in agony, the pain rendering him helpless. As he doubled over to catch his breath he felt her hands grasp his neck and begin to squeeze.

'You don't deserve to live,' he heard her say. Spots appeared in front of his eyes as her iron grip strengthened and she harangued him with expletives. Too dazed by now to defend himself, he fell to the floor, taking her with him.

*Oh my God,* he thought, *she's going to kill me. I'm going to die here . . .*

As he began to lose consciousness he saw a figure come through the door and grab Cheska from behind. Suddenly, the grip on his neck was released. Coughing and spluttering as he sucked in as much air as he could, he saw someone he recognised but couldn't quite place holding Cheska firmly by her shoulders as she struggled and kicked against him.

'Cheska! Stop it! Enough! Uncle David's here now, and everything is going to be all right.'

Cheska went limp in the man's arms and she crumpled against him like a rag doll. 'Sorry, Uncle David, I didn't mean to hurt anyone, really I didn't. Bobby just wasn't being very nice to me, you see. Please don't punish me, will you?'

'Of course I won't,' he said. 'I'll look after you, just like I always have.' Simon sat up, the dizziness beginning to recede, and saw the man fold Cheska into his arms and stroke her hair. 'I think I should take you home and put you to bed, don't you? You're exhausted, Cheska.'

'I am,' she agreed.

The man looked at Simon as he led Cheska to a chair and sat her down. She was almost catatonic now, staring into space, all her aggression gone.

Simon realised his saviour was David Marchmont, Ava's uncle, known to his many fans as Taffy.

'Are you okay?' David mouthed over the top of Cheska's head.

'I think so. No harm done,' Simon said, reaching for a tissue to stem the blood on his hand from Cheska's bite. 'She caught me by surprise, but I'm okay.'

David left Cheska in the chair and moved to give Simon a hand up. 'Ava met with a bit of an accident tonight. She's fine, but perhaps you'd like to telephone St Thomas's Hospital and find out how she is for me,' he whispered. 'We'll need to speak tomorrow, so I'll meet you at the hospital at ten in the morning. And now,' he said, raising his voice and turning to Cheska, 'I'm going to take—'

But Cheska had already got up and was at the door, turning the handle. Before either of them could react fast enough to stop her, she was through it and gone. Running after her along the corridor, David saw her disappearing out of the stage door and into the night. Outside in the busy street a few seconds later David looked left and right but could see no sign of her.

'Damn it!' he berated himself. He should never have let her go. He'd just have to hope she returned to the Savoy. Deciding he'd take a taxi there straight away in case Cheska tried to pack and leave in a hurry, he hailed one and climbed inside.

When the cab arrived at the hotel, David climbed out and tipped the doorman. As an afterthought, he turned back to him. 'I was just wondering if you saw my niece, Cheska Hammond, leave the hotel earlier tonight? And whether she's returned yet?'

The doorman knew David of old. 'As a matter of fact, sir, she came out of the hotel at about half past six and asked me to hail her a cab. I got it for her, but then she must have changed her mind, because I saw her walking up towards the Strand. I presumed she'd seen somebody she knew. I remember, because it was just before that nasty accident at the traffic lights. The cabbie I'd hailed was very put out, as he was stuck here with no fare for a good half an hour before the road was unblocked. And I haven't seen her come back yet, sir.'

'Thanks,' David said, pressing another note into his hand. Inside, he walked over to reception and explained he was meant to be meeting his niece, Miss Hammond, in her suite, but that she hadn't yet returned. 'Would you kindly let me in so that I can wait for her in comfort? She might be some time.'

'We wouldn't usually, sir, but seeing as it's you, I'm sure it will be all right. Let me just check with the manager.'

David waited by the desk impatiently, reeling at what the doorman had just told him. He definitely needed to speak to both Ava and Simon tomorrow, but if Cheska had seen them together outside the hotel . . .

He managed a smile of gratitude when the receptionist confirmed that the manager would allow him into Cheska's suite.

He wandered through the exquisitely furnished rooms, noticing the many carrier bags from Harrods and various designer stores sitting unopened in the dressing room. God only knew how much the suite was costing and what Cheska had spent so far. He was all too painfully aware of how she was funding her excesses.

Longing for a shower but not wanting to be taken unawares by a returning Cheska, David poured himself a stiff whisky and sat down to wait.

# 53

Greta was fast asleep when she heard the doorbell ring. Switching on the light, she saw it was almost midnight. When it rang again, fear coursed through her. Who on earth could it be at this time of night? The bell rang again, and again, and then whoever it was began hammering loudly on the door. Putting on her robe, she tiptoed nervously towards the front door.

'Mother, it's me, Cheska! Let me in! Please let me in.'

Greta froze in shock. This was the daughter David had told her about, who she hadn't seen for many years, because she was off in Hollywood being a star on the television.

'Please, Mummy, open the door. I—' Greta heard a loud sob. 'I've come back home.'

A tremor of sudden terror made its way up Greta's spine.

'Mummy, *please*, I beg you. It's your little girl here, and I need you. I need you, Mummy . . .' There were more sobs, and Greta stood paralysed, torn between the irrational fear she felt, the horror of her neighbours being disturbed and her fascination that this daughter she'd been told she had was now outside her front door.

As the sobbing got louder, the neighbours won. Greta walked towards the door and undid every lock except for the chain that would hold it fast, checking through the opening that this really was Cheska.

'Hello? Cheska?' Greta peered through the gap in the door, but could see nobody.

'I'm down here, Mummy, sitting on the floor. I'm too tired to get up. Please let me in.'

She peered round then and saw a blonde woman who she recognised immediately from the television. Taking a deep breath, Greta unlocked the chain and opened the door slowly. Cheska, who'd been leaning against it, almost fell into the apartment.

'Mummy! Oh Mummy, I love you. Come and give me a big hug like you used to. Please.' Cheska held out her arms and Greta caught them. She almost dragged her inside, then closed the door behind them and relocked it. The good news was that Cheska didn't look scary at all. In fact, she looked the opposite: like a sad, frightened little girl.

'*Please* hug me, Mummy. Nobody loves Cheska, you see, nobody loves me.'

Greta stood awkwardly above her, wanting to feel or hear or see *some* memory of this daughter she had apparently brought into the world. And, according to David, had brought up and loved until Cheska went off to Hollywood whilst she was in hospital after her accident.

She'd often wondered why her daughter had never come to visit her or contacted her. As she stared down at the woman, she only wished that the feelings which had once been there for Cheska would suddenly reignite now she was here in front of her. But just as with David when she'd first opened her eyes and seen him, looking at Cheska was like seeing a stranger. She did as she was asked anyway, and knelt down to take Cheska in her arms.

'Mummy, oh Mummy . . . I need you. You'll keep me safe, won't you? Don't let them take me away, please.'

All Greta could do was listen as Cheska babbled on. It was odd to have a grown woman the same size as she was sitting on her knee behaving like a child. But then, Greta supposed, maybe this was what motherhood was like.

After a while, she quietly suggested that they move from the floor in the hall to the sitting room.

'Maybe you need something to eat? Or a cup of Horlicks? I like that at night.'

'Mummy, I know you do. We used to have one together, remember?' said Cheska, as Greta settled her on the sofa.

'Of course I do,' Greta lied, and, seeing Cheska was shivering, she fetched a blanket from a cupboard and put it around her.

'And what about those sandwiches you used to make me when I came home late from a night shoot? What was it . . . ? Yes! Marmite. I used to love those.'

'Did you?' Greta asked her uncertainly. 'Well, I'll make some for you now if you like.'

Greta went into the kitchen, amazed that Cheska didn't seem to know she couldn't remember anything. Well, she'd just have to pretend. As she switched the kettle on, another shudder of fear crept up on her, but she dismissed it. This woman was her daughter, and no threat to her whatsoever.

Cheska ate the Marmite sandwiches and drank the

Horlicks, and then Greta suggested it was time for them both to go to bed, as it was one o'clock in the morning.

'Can I sleep with you, Mummy, like we used to? I don't want to be alone. I have bad dreams . . .'

'Everyone does, but if you want to sleep with me, that's fine. I'll get you something to wear, as you haven't brought anything with you.'

Greta went to her wardrobe and pulled out a nightgown, wishing she could tell David that Cheska was finally here with her. She thought how strange it would be to sleep in a bed with a grown-up female stranger, but it was nice to have someone to look after, someone who seemed to need her.

Once Cheska had changed, they both climbed into bed.

'This is so wonderful. I feel safe here. I think I can sleep.'

'Good. You look very tired, so you probably need to.'

'Yes. Goodnight, Mummy.' Cheska reached over and planted a kiss on Greta's cheek. 'Sleep tight.'

Greta switched off the light and lay in the darkness, listening to her daughter's steady breathing. She touched her cheek where Cheska had kissed it and tears sprang to her eyes.

Simon was already at Ava's bedside when David arrived at the hospital the following morning.

'Hello, Uncle David. The doctor says I'm fine and I can go home,' Ava said, giving him a kiss. 'You two have met before, haven't you?'

'Yes,' said Simon, exchanging an ironic glance with David.

'At LJ's party, and last night at the theatre?' she prompted.

'Yes,' confirmed David.

'So where's LJ?' Ava looked at both of them.

'Unfortunately, we didn't manage to ask your mother,' said David. 'She didn't go back to the Savoy last night.'

'Oh God.' Ava put her head in her hands. 'So now we have two missing people.'

'David, have you seen this?' Simon said, handing him a copy of the *Daily Mail*.

David looked at the front cover and was stunned to see a big photograph of Cheska looking particularly glamorous, her arms folded around an uncomfortable-looking Ava.

> Gigi's Lost Daughter: The heartbreaking story of how world-famous soap star Cheska Hammond came back to England after eighteen years in search of the baby she'd left behind. FULL STORY ON PAGE 3.

David turned to page three.

> Cheska Hammond, once the biggest box-office draw in England, and more recently achieving worldwide fame as Gigi in *The Oil Barons*, has returned to England to stay. And the story behind why she has come back is more poignant than any film she has ever starred in.
>
> I met Cheska in her suite at the Savoy. As stunning in the flesh as on screen, yet with a delicacy and vulnerability that make her seem little older than the child she has come home to care for, Cheska told me her compelling story.

'I was fifteen when I discovered I was pregnant. I guess I was very naive and was taken advantage of by an older man [she still refuses to name the father]. Of course, my career at the time was going really well. I'd just made *Please, Sir, I Love You*, and Hollywood was beckoning. I could have done what a lot of girls in my position did and had an abortion, even though it was illegal at the time.'

Cheska's lips tremble at the memory and tears come into her eyes. 'I just couldn't do it. I couldn't kill my baby. I'd made a terrible mistake, but it was my responsibility and I couldn't murder a tiny, innocent thing because of a stupid error I'd made. Then my mother was horribly injured in a road accident and I suppose that made me even more determined to have my baby. So I went into hiding while I was pregnant and it was arranged after she was born that my aunt should care for Ava. If the studio in Hollywood had found out about her, my career would have been ruined and I would have been unable to support my child.' Cheska pauses for breath, choking back the tears. 'I left her in Wales in a beautiful house in the countryside, knowing she was in good hands. Of course, I sent every penny I could to help towards her upkeep . . .'

Ava had already read it, so she sat quietly, watching David's face for his reaction.

'. . . I was always writing to my aunt, asking if she wanted to send Ava out to Los Angeles on a holiday to see how she'd like it, but my aunt was never very keen.

Of course, I understood why. It would have been very unsettling for a small child. So, even though it broke my heart, I decided Ava was better off where she was. That was until I heard my aunt was seriously ill. I dropped everything and came back to care for both her and my baby. And this is where I intend to stay.'

I watch Cheska put a hand gently on her daughter's shoulder. Eighteen-year-old Ava, the image of her mother, smiles up at her. The bond between them is obvious. I ask Ava how she feels about her mother returning.

'Wonderful. It's wonderful that she's back.'

I ask her if she feels any bitterness towards her mother for leaving her for so long. Ava shakes her head. 'No, not at all. I always knew she was there. She sent me some lovely presents and wrote me letters. I understand why she did what she did.'

Then Cheska and I discuss her plans for the future. She shrugs. 'Well, I hope to start working again as soon as I can. There may be a television series in the pipeline and I'd like to try my hand at theatre. That would be quite a challenge.'

I ask her about the men in her life, and she looks shy and giggles. 'Yes, there is someone, but I'd prefer not to talk about it just yet.'

I say goodbye to the actress who was as famed in Hollywood for her high-spirited performances off the screen as those on it. From the calm, contented look of the woman who gazes at her daughter with obvious adoration, there is no doubt that motherhood has now matured and mellowed her. Welcome home, Cheska. We, like Ava, are glad to have you back.

David finished reading and folded the newspaper firmly shut. He looked at Ava to gauge her feelings.

'I nearly vomited all over the page when I read it. But I couldn't, because then the doctor might have thought I was still sick and kept me here longer.' She laughed weakly, doing her best to make light of it. 'More importantly, where has Cheska gone? She wasn't with you, was she, Simon?'

'Of course not!'

'I can confirm that,' said David. 'And I'm furious with Cheska for putting you through *that*.' He pointed at the newspaper.

'I begged her not to make me, but she's very hard to refuse. I can't tell you how weird she's been these past few weeks.' Ava shook her head in despair. 'It seemed to get worse after she met you, Simon.'

'Oh great, thanks.' Simon gave her a smile, then turned to David. 'But Ava's right. Last night, when she was attacking me in my dressing room – sorry, Ava – I'm sure she said something about me being your father. Christ, how insane is that?'

'Not quite as mad as it sounds, if Cheska believed you were her first love, Bobby Cross,' David explained. 'You do look very like him.'

'Bobby Cross . . . Simon's impersonating him in the musical he's in at the moment, aren't you?' Ava added.

'The plot thickens,' muttered David. 'Did Cheska come and see you in it?'

'She was there on the opening night with Ava. I invited

her when I met her at Marchmont. I'd given Ava a lift to Wales to see her great-aunt after she had the stroke. I was just being polite to Cheska, David, nothing more,' he said pointedly.

'Of course. And you weren't to know about her past.'

'Uncle David' – Ava had been listening quietly – 'was this Bobby Cross my father?'

David paused before answering. 'Yes, Ava, he was. I'm so sorry it's me telling you and not your mother but, under the circumstances, it's best you know, because it explains quite a lot. Poor Simon's been the victim of a very confused and troubled mind. I'll never forgive myself for leaving you. What a mess. I'm so sorry.'

'Don't be silly, Uncle David. The most important thing now is to find my mother.' Ava was reeling from what he'd said but decided she would give herself time to think about it once Cheska and LJ had been found. 'When did you last see her?'

'In Simon's dressing room. I managed to calm her down and was sorting Simon out when she bolted for the door and ran off before I could catch her. Have you any idea where she might have gone?'

'No, but . . . I've been very upset in the past few weeks. And all I've wanted to do is run to LJ. Where would my mother's safe place be?'

'I have absolutely no idea. You?' David looked at Simon.

'I barely know the woman. She can't go back to Marchmont, so where would home be for her if it wasn't there?'

'Doesn't Granny still live in the same Mayfair apartment Cheska grew up in?' asked Ava.

'Greta? But Cheska hasn't been near her mother since the accident,' said David.

'Still, where else would she run?' Ava shrugged.

'Ava, do you know, you might just be right. Simon, can I leave you here to take care of Ava?'

'Of course.'

'Where will you two go?' David asked as he rose to leave.

'I'm taking Ava to *my* place of safety, in other words my unsanitary bedsit in Swiss Cottage.' He smiled. 'Let me write down my telephone number for you.'

David thanked him, kissed Ava and left, saying he'd be in touch with any news.

'Simon?' Ava said quietly.

'Yes?'

'You know you just said you were taking me to your home when I left here?'

'Yes.'

'Well, actually, I need to go to mine. Can you possibly drive me to Marchmont later on, after your performance?'

'Of course, if you're sure you're up to it.'

'I am. I have to be. Oh God.' All Ava's reserve cracked suddenly and tears filled her eyes. 'It's all so dreadful! Sorry,' she muttered, embarrassed.

'Ava, you don't need to be sorry. You've had a terrible time,' said Simon, taking her in his arms and holding her as she sobbed.

'I just . . . promise me that I never have to go anywhere near Cheska again. She's completely mad, Simon. And I've been so frightened because I haven't known what to do.'

'I promise. Your uncle's back now, and he'll sort everything out, I'm sure. And later, as long as you're well enough, I'll drive you to Wales and we'll find LJ, I swear.'

'Thank you, Simon. You've been wonderful.'

'So have you. You're amazing, Ava, really,' he murmured in admiration, and stroked her soft blonde hair.

# 54

David knocked on the door of Greta's apartment. As usual, Greta peered out from behind the chain, saw who it was and gave him a big smile of welcome as she undid it and opened the door.

'David, what a surprise! I thought you weren't home for a couple of months yet.'

'Well, circumstances have changed. How are you?'

'I'm fine,' she said, as she always did. 'As a matter of fact, I'm rather glad you're here. I have a guest. She arrived last night in the early hours and we need to be quiet' – Greta lowered her voice as she led him into the sitting room – 'because she's still sleeping.'

'Cheska?' David's heart flooded with relief.

'How did you know?'

'I just did. Or, at least, Ava thought she might come to you. How did she seem?'

'Well, to be quite honest,' said Greta, shutting the door behind them, 'I wouldn't really know. She was a little upset when she arrived and told me she'd just wanted to come home.'

'You said she's still sleeping?'

'Yes. In fact, she hasn't stirred since the moment she closed her eyes next to me last night. She must be very tired, poor thing.'

'She hasn't said anything to you, has she?'

'About what?'

'How she was feeling? Or what it is that's upset her?'

'Not really, no. Goodness, David, you sound almost like a police officer.' She chuckled nervously. 'Is everything all right?'

'Yes, fine.'

'Well, it's awfully nice to see you. How was your holiday?'

'It was . . . incredible, fantastic. But that's not what I'm here to talk about. Greta, do you think Cheska trusts you?'

'Well, she seems to. She came to me last night, after all. As you've told me, I am her mother,' she said proprietorially.

'Do you remember her?'

'No, sadly, I don't. But she seems nice enough. And, really, it's no problem at all for her to stay here with me if necessary. I rather enjoyed looking after her last night. It made me feel useful.'

'Listen, Greta, I have something I need you to ask her when she wakes up.'

'Oh yes? What is it?'

'It seems' – David thought how he could explain it – 'it seems she may have taken my mother out of her nursing home and moved her somewhere else. And, just now, we don't know where.'

'Well, surely you can simply ask her, David?'

'I can, yes. But if she trusts you, she's more likely to tell you.'

Greta frowned. 'David, what is this all about?'

'It's complicated, Greta, and I promise I'll explain more another time. But, for now, I'm concerned that, if Cheska sees me, she may get scared and run away again.'

'Honestly, you talk about her as though she were a child, rather than a grown woman of – what must she be?' Greta worked it out. 'Thirty-four? She's not in any trouble, is she?'

'Not really, no, although, between you and me, she's not very well at the moment.'

'What's wrong with her?'

'The best way to put it is that she's a little confused,' David said tactfully. 'I think she may be having some form of nervous breakdown.'

'I see. Poor thing. She did say that she felt as if nobody loved her, that she was all alone.'

'Well, obviously, I want to get her the help she needs. But first, could you perhaps take her in a cup of tea and gently ask her if she remembers the name of the nursing home she's put my mother in.'

'Well, of course I can. It's hardly a question she'll find threatening, is it?'

'No,' David reassured her.

'Do you want me to go and wake her up now?'

'Yes. It's nearly midday, after all.'

'Okay.'

'And, Greta, don't say that I'm here.'

As she walked away from him to make the tea in the kitchen, David crept to the front door, turned the key in the lock and put it in his pocket. If Cheska tried to make a run for it, she wouldn't be able to get out. He wondered if it would be better to tell Greta the truth. But given she couldn't remember anything about Cheska, how would she cope with what her daughter had become, and what her part in it had been?

David heard Greta knock gently on the bedroom door and step inside. In an agony of tension, he waited for her to come back. Ten minutes later, she did.

'How is she?' he asked, turning from the window. He'd been pacing up and down the sitting room like a caged animal.

'A little tearful.'

'Did you ask her where LJ was?'

'Yes. And she said that of course she knew where she was,' Greta said, a little defensively. 'She said that she put her in a nice nursing home called The Laurels, just outside Abergavenny. Although she also said that LJ and you hadn't been very nice to her recently.'

'Thank you, Greta.' David felt a huge sense of relief. 'What's she doing now?'

'I suggested she got up and took a bath.' Greta narrowed her eyes. 'What's going on, David?'

'Nothing. Cheska just needs some help, that's all. She's a little . . . depressed just now.'

'Well, I know how that feels. Now, she did ask me if she could stay here with me for a bit, and I told her that yes, of course she could. And she can, David. It's nice having the company. And she is my daughter.'

'Greta, please, you have to trust me on this. Cheska

can't stay here with you. I have to take her with me now, get her the help she needs.'

'I'm not going anywhere.'

Greta and David looked up. Cheska was standing at the door in a borrowed pair of her mother's trousers and a blouse.

'Hello, Cheska. Your mother tells me you've had a good night's sleep.'

'I have, and I'm feeling a lot better. And I'm staying here, with Mummy, Uncle David. You can't make me go, and I won't.'

'Listen, Cheska, darling, we only want what's best for you. At the very least, let me take you to see a doctor.'

'*No doctors!*' Cheska screamed, startling Greta. 'You can't make me! You're not my father!'

'No, you're right. But if you refuse to come with me, I'm afraid I'll have to speak to the police and tell them it was you who started the fire at Marchmont. It was you, wasn't it, Cheska?'

'What?! Uncle David, how could you say such a thing!'

David tried another tack. 'Cheska, darling, if I was expecting to inherit a house and some money because I was the only surviving child of the previous owner, I might get a little upset when I found out I wasn't going to. And maybe even angry enough to want to do something silly on the spur of the moment.'

Cheska eyed him suspiciously. 'Would you?'

'I understand that you were probably very upset because you felt you were being cheated out of your inheritance. And if you had only asked me I would have given Marchmont to you. Really, I would.'

Cheska looked at him, seeming disoriented. She wavered for a moment before nodding in what appeared to him to be relief. 'Yes, I was upset, Uncle David, because it should have been mine. And I was fed up with people leaving me out. It just wasn't fair. But it wasn't just that . . .'

'What was it, Cheska?'

'It was . . . the voices, Uncle David. You know about them because I told you in LA. They wouldn't stop, you see, and I needed to make them. So I decided it was the best thing to do. Are you going to tell the police? Please don't. They might put me in prison.'

David saw the terror in her eyes. 'No, I won't, I promise, as long as you come with me now quietly.'

'I don't know, I . . .'

David approached her slowly. 'Come with me, sweetheart, and let's try and help you feel better.' He put out his hand towards her, and Cheska began to offer hers in return. Then, suddenly, she screamed again.

'*No!* I've trusted you before, Uncle David, and you always tell! You'll put me in one of those terrible places again, and they'll lock me up forever.'

'Of course they won't, Cheska. I'd never do that to you, you know I wouldn't. Let's just go and get you some help. I'll make sure you're safe, I promise.'

'Liar! You think I don't know what you'll do if I take your hand. I don't trust you! I don't trust anyone! Mummy' – she moved towards Greta – 'please say I can stay here with you?'

Greta was looking at David, shocked by what she had just heard and witnessed. 'Well, perhaps, if Uncle David thinks you should go with him, dear, it's for the best.'

'Traitor!' Cheska shouted, then spat at her mother. 'Well, you can't make me go! I won't go!' She bolted to the door and ran out into the corridor towards the front door.

Greta went to follow her, but David held her back. 'I locked it earlier, so she can't get out. But better that you stay in here and I'll deal with her,' he said.

They heard Cheska trying desperately to open the front door. When she failed, she banged on it, again and again.

'I'm sorry, Greta, but could you please call an ambulance? I think we're going to need some back-up,' said David, leaving the sitting room and locking Greta inside it with the key.

'Cheska,' he begged as he walked towards her, 'please try and calm down. Don't you understand I want to get you better?'

'No, you don't! You've always hated me, all of you! You can't make me go, you can't! Let me out now!'

'Come on, darling. It's not doing anybody any good, least of all your poor mother.'

'My mother! And where has she been for these past few years, I'd like to know?!'

'Cheska, surely you remember? She was badly hurt in a car crash years ago outside the Savoy. Like Ava was last night. You'll be pleased to know that Ava's okay, at least. Now, can you stop thumping that door before one of the neighbours calls the police, let alone me?'

At his words Cheska turned and fled back along the corridor. She dived into the bathroom and locked the door. 'I'm staying in here! You can't get me! Nobody can! Nobody!'

'All right, sweetheart, you stay in there and I'll wait outside for you.'

'Go away! Leave me alone!'

'David?' came Greta's voice from the sitting room. 'Why have you locked me in? What on earth is going on?'

'Greta, did you make the phone call?' he asked, as the sound of hysterical sobbing from the bathroom got louder.

'Yes, they should be here any minute, but—'

'You're in there for your own safety, Greta. Please trust me.'

The paramedics arrived five minutes later. David briefly explained the situation, and they nodded calmly, as if they dealt with these kinds of circumstances every day. Which, David thought, they probably did.

'Leave her to us,' said one of them. 'Steve, you run down to the van and get a straitjacket, just in case.'

'I doubt you'll be able to get her out of there of her own volition,' sighed David.

'We'll see. Now, why don't you go and sit in the other room with the woman's mother, sir?'

David unlocked the door to the sitting room and went to Greta, who was sitting on the sofa, pale and shaking. He sat beside her and gave her a hug. 'I'm so sorry, Greta. I know it's hard for you to understand, but, really, this is the best thing for Cheska.'

'Is she mad? She certainly sounds it.'

'She's what I'd call . . . disturbed. But I'm sure that, with time and help, she'll recover.'

'Was she always like this? Is it my fault?'

'It's no one's fault. I think Cheska has always had problems. You mustn't blame yourself. Some of us are born that way.'

'I was so happy this morning when I woke up,' she

whispered. 'It was nice to have some company. I get so lonely here by myself.'

'I know you do. At least I'm back now, so that's something, isn't it?'

Greta looked up at him and smiled wanly. 'Yes, it is.'

In the end, having tried every tactic to coax Cheska out, the paramedics had to break down the bathroom door. Greta and David winced at her shrieks as they restrained her. There was a brief knock on the sitting-room door and a paramedic put his head around it.

'We'll be leaving now, sir. Probably better you don't come in the ambulance with her. We've given her something to calm her down and we'll be taking her to the psychiatric unit at Maudsley Hospital in Southwark, where she'll be assessed. Perhaps you or her mother would like to phone later on today.'

'Of course. Should I come and say goodbye to her?'

'I wouldn't if I were you, sir. She's not a pretty sight.'

Having left Greta half an hour later, promising to contact her with any news, David went back to the Savoy and explained to the girl on reception that Cheska had been called away to an emergency and wouldn't be returning. He said that he would take the suite for the night and pack up her belongings.

Once upstairs, he called Directory Enquiries, only to discover that there were four nursing homes called The Laurels within a ten-mile radius of Abergavenny. Taking down all the numbers, he called each of them in turn. He finally found her when he called the last number. A woman had answered.

'Good afternoon,' said David. 'I was wondering if you have a resident called Laura-Jane Marchmont staying with you?'

'Who are you?' The woman asked rudely.

'Her son. So, do you?

'Yes, she came in last week.'

'And how is she?'

'She's all right. Not very talkative, but you know that anyway.' David grimaced at her tactlessness.

'I'm coming to visit her. Can you give me the address?'

'How should I know if you are who you say? It was a female relative who brought her in. You could be anyone.'

'I've said that I'm her son,' David replied, his temper rising. 'Surely you have relatives visit your residents all the time?'

David realised he was talking to thin air. The woman had hung up.

He called Mary, asking her to look up the address in the local telephone directory and get there as soon as possible. In turn, she told him that Simon was driving Ava up tonight after his performance and that they'd be staying at her cottage.

'I'll get the address, and Simon and Ava will go first thing tomorrow,' Mary promised. 'Where's Cheska?'

'In hospital. She ran to Greta here in London and had to be forcibly restrained and taken away in an ambulance. It was . . . awful.'

'There, there, Master David. Really, hospital's the best place for her. Will you be coming this way yourself soon? The police inspector called yesterday. I told him you were back and he'd like to speak to you. I think they want to question Cheska again. It was her that set fire to Marchmont, wasn't it?'

'Yes, Mary, I think it was.'

'God forgive me, because I love her, but honest to goodness, I hope they don't let her out of hospital for a very long time. Poor Ava, she didn't know where she was with her mother.'

'I know, and this time I promise I'll make sure she can't ever hurt anyone again. Send my love to Ava when you see her and tell her I'll be there tomorrow. Let's just pray my old ma is still in the land of the living. From the sound of the woman I spoke to, something's not right. Thank you for everything, Mary, really.'

'No need to thank me, David. Oh, there was me nearly forgetting to tell you. Tor called me at home this evening. She's in Beijing and will be landing at Heathrow at eight o'clock tomorrow morning.'

'Then I'll go and meet her, and we'll drive on to Marchmont. We can stay at Lark Cottage.'

'I'll put the heating on for you. Goodbye, Master David. Take care of yourself, now, won't you?'

David put down the receiver and walked over to the chair. He sat down, put his head in his hands and sobbed.

Simon drew his car up in front of the dismal terraced house off a narrow side road in a down-at-heel suburb of Abergavenny.

'Are you sure this is the right place? Surely Cheska wouldn't have left her here?' Ava bit her lip.

'Yes.' He reached across the gear stick and squeezed her hand. 'Right, let's go in and get her.'

They walked up to the front door. Ava noticed there were bags of rotting rubbish piled up to one side of it. Simon tried the bell, which didn't work, so he knocked loudly on the door. It was opened by a fat, middle-aged woman wearing a dirty overall.

'Yes?'

'We're here to see my friend's great-aunt, Mrs Laura-Jane Marchmont.'

'I wasn't expecting you, and everything's in a tip. My cleaner's just walked out on me. Can you come back tomorrow?'

'No. We want to see her now.'

'That's not possible, I'm afraid.' The woman folded her arms. 'Go away.'

'Right, then I'll have to call the police and they'll visit instead, as Laura-Jane Marchmont is currently listed as a missing person. So, it's them or us,' Simon added menacingly. Ava looked up at him gratefully, thanking God he'd come with her.

At this, the woman shrugged and let them in.

Simon and Ava walked behind her down the narrow corridor, the smell of urine and boiled cabbage making them both feel sick.

'That's the residents' lounge,' announced the woman as they passed a small room full of ancient chairs placed round an old black-and-white television. Four elderly patients were asleep in front of *Tom and Jerry*.

Ava's eyes darted round the faces and she shook her head. 'She's not in there.'

'No, she's upstairs in her bed.'

Simon and Ava trudged up the stairs behind her.

'Here we go.' The woman led them into a dim room. There were four beds jammed into it and the smell of unwashed human flesh made Simon and Ava want to gag. 'Your aunt's in that one over there.'

Ava choked back a sob as she saw LJ lying motionless on the bed, her skin grey, her hair unkempt.

'Oh LJ, what have they done to you? LJ, it's me, Ava.'

Her great-aunt's eyes opened, and Ava saw they were dull, blank, hopeless.

'Do you recognise me? Please tell me you do.' Tears streamed down Ava's face, as she watched LJ attempt to move her mouth. A hand appeared from under the covers and reached out to her.

'What's she saying, Ava?' asked Simon.

Ava leaned closer and studied LJ's lips.

'She's saying, "home", Simon. She's saying "home".'

December, 1985

Marchmont Hall,
Monmouthshire

# 55

David and Greta sat silently for a while, lost in their own thoughts. 'So, there we are,' sighed David, as he drained his whisky. 'Did I ever tell you Ava put in a complaint to the authorities about the dreadful place Cheska had dumped poor Ma in? Shortly afterwards, it was closed down and the owner prosecuted.'

'I don't think so, no. I'm not surprised it took some time for poor LJ to recover,' said Greta. 'And even though Cheska deserved it, I'm grateful the police didn't press charges against her when they found out she'd caused the fire. I think that would have destroyed her completely.'

'Actually, Greta, they wanted to prosecute. And advised my mother, as the legal owner of Marchmont, to do the same. The inspector discovered that Cheska lied about the time she arrived at the Savoy that night. When he checked with reception, they told him it was well past four in the morning when she checked in. Then Mary told him Cheska had told her to take a couple of days off whilst she was away, which was suspicious in itself.'

'I see. So how did you stop the police taking it any further?'

'It was Ma, mostly. The publicity would have been a nightmare and she was concerned about Ava – who'd been through enough. But what finally clinched it with the police was that Cheska was in a psychiatric unit and would have been deemed unfit to plead anyway. Of course, it meant we lost the insurance money, but that was hardly the point.'

'David,' Greta said tentatively, knowing she had to voice the suspicion that had been burning in her mind ever since he'd told her about Ava's accident outside the Savoy, 'do you think it was Cheska who pushed me off the pavement that awful night?'

'I—' David sighed, not sure what answer to give. He decided on the truth. It was what she had asked for, after all. 'In retrospect, I think there was a good chance that she might have done, yes. Especially after what I've just told you happened to Ava, it would be the most outrageous coincidence if Cheska hadn't been involved. But, of course, there's no proof, Greta, and there never will be. I'm so sorry, it must be dreadful for you to think it could even be a possibility.'

'It's difficult to believe, yes, but I have to accept that Cheska was very sick indeed. God, David' – Greta put her fingers to her temple – 'you can't imagine how awful I feel that all this was going on and you never told me. I've been living in a world of my own all these years and you've had to pretend that Cheska had simply had a breakdown and decided to give up her career and live a quiet life in Switzerland.' She looked at him. 'Is that the truth?'

'More or less, yes. Although, sadly, she can't leave of her own free will. She's in a small, secure psychiatric unit at a sanatorium near Geneva. I had to commit her, for her own sake as much as everyone else's.'

'Do you . . . do you think that I'm to blame for her . . . problems? I should never have pushed her so much as a child, I know. After what I've remembered, I fear I created a monster!'

'If I'm blunt, I doubt her strange childhood was the best thing for her flawed personality. But you must remember there was already something wrong with her. Part of Cheska's condition is that she suffers from delusions and paranoia. She lived in a make-believe world when she was a child actress, although you weren't to know that she'd always found it difficult to distinguish between fantasy and reality. Look at Shirley Temple. She was in a similar situation to Cheska – a huge star very young – yet she's grown up to have successful relationships and become a force for good in her adult life. So, no, Greta, really, you mustn't blame yourself. You did what you thought was right at the time.'

'I let her down, David. I should have seen the effect it was having on her. The truth is, she was living the dream I'd once wanted for myself.'

'We all let her down, one way or another,' David replied quietly. 'And being so beautiful and so famous meant that people around her who should have seen what she was were blind to it. She was a brilliant actress. Every moment of her life. And her powers of manipulation were sublime. She could twist any situation to her benefit and have us all believe her. She certainly took me in time and time again. The only person who was never completely fooled was dear old Ma. God, I miss her.'

'I'm sure you do. She was an incredible woman. I wish I could have thanked her for all she did for me, Cheska and Ava before she died.'

'I think she was ready to go,' David said. 'And at least there were no hospitals at the end. When my time comes, I hope I follow Ma's way out and simply drift away in my sleep.'

'Don't even talk about it, David.' Greta shuddered. 'I can't bear to think of you not being here. At least there's new life coming to Marchmont. The next generation.'

'Yes, I'm grateful for that, too.'

'What havoc Cheska's caused us all.' Greta shook her head. 'And we're not even your blood relatives. Just think how different your life would have been if you hadn't taken pity on me all those years ago and packed me off to Marchmont.'

'And how dull! I promise, I don't regret a second of it.' David put a hand on Greta's and squeezed it.

Tor walked in then. 'How are you, Greta?' she asked.

'Very shaken, to be honest. There's plenty I don't want to remember.'

'I'm sure,' agreed Tor. 'Anyone for a cup of tea or a hot chocolate before bed?'

'No thanks, darling,' said David.

'Well, I'm going up. It must be all this country air that's knocking me for six.'

'I'll join you in a while.'

'Okay.' Tor said goodnight to both of them and left the room.

'But at least you've found happiness now.' Greta managed to smile.

'Yes. Tor's been an absolute brick. And what about you, Greta? I hope that, now you're back with us, you'll make up for lost time.'

'So many wasted years, but it's going to take me a while to get over what's happened in the past few days,' she admitted. 'It's as if the floodgates have opened, and I'm finding it very difficult to sleep. The memories keep appearing in my mind – like a familiar film, seen a long time ago.'

'It's been very traumatic for you, and I think you've coped admirably so far, really. Although I do think you should go and see your doctor when you get back to London. You might need some help, just for a while. Right,' David stood up then bent to kiss Greta goodnight. 'I'm for my bed. You?'

'I think I'll just sit here a little longer, but you go up. Goodnight, David, and thank you again for . . . everything you've done for me and my troublesome family.'

David left the room and Greta stared out into the blackness of the night. David mentioning London and the end of the holiday here had filled her with fear. Walking back into the emptiness of her existence – even *with* the memories she'd now found – was utterly depressing. She would have to deal with the guilt, not to mention the fact that her own daughter had almost certainly tried to murder her and had rendered her an empty, useless husk for the past twenty-four years. But dealing with it at home, and alone again once more, was an awful thought.

'Come on now, Greta, you've coped before and you'll cope again,' she told herself. And perhaps, she mused, trying desperately to be positive, now that she had her memory back the world wouldn't seem quite such a frightening place and she wouldn't feel like an alien wandering around in it. Maybe David was right and this was the start of a whole new life. She smiled as she thought of him, and the precious history they had shared and had recently found again. He'd loved her once . . . but now it was too late.

Greta stood up and switched off the lights. She must *not* be selfish or think of herself. David was happy now with Tor. And he deserved that happiness more than anyone.

'Telephone call for you, Master David,' said Mary, popping her head round the drawing-room door the following morning. David was reading the *Telegraph* by the fire. 'It's from Switzerland.'

David's stomach turned over as he went into the library to take it. He'd called the sanatorium the night before he'd arrived here at Marchmont, asking after Cheska and passing on his Christmas greetings to her. He'd been told that she had a bout of bronchitis – something she'd been prone to over the past few years – but was calm and on antibiotics.

He had visited her sporadically since flying over in the air ambulance with her five years ago. He'd thought it best to get Cheska out of the country and have her disappear rather than endure the humiliating press interference that would ensue if it was discovered she'd been committed. The place cost a fortune – it was more luxury hotel than hospital – but at least he knew she was well cared for.

He picked up the receiver. 'David Marchmont here.'

'Hello Monsieur Marchmont, it's Dr Fournier here. I'm sorry to trouble you at this time of year, but I have to inform you that your niece is in intensive care in Geneva.

We had to transfer her there in the early hours of this morning. Sadly, her bronchitis worsened and has now turned to pneumonia. Monsieur, I think you should come.'

'She's in danger?'

There was a pause before the doctor answered. 'I think you should come. Immediately.'

David's looked up to the heavens and railed at them. Then, feeling selfish because his initial thoughts had been about having his New Year plans with Tor disrupted rather than Cheska's obviously critical condition, he said, 'Of course. I'll get on a flight as soon as I can.'

'I am sorry, Monsieur. You know I would not suggest it unless—'

'I understand.'

David took down the details of the hospital Cheska was in, then rang the local travel agent and asked her to find him the next available flight. Mounting the stairs to throw some things into a holdall, and dreading telling Tor, he met Greta coming down them.

'Morning,' she said.

'Morning.'

She looked at him. 'David, is everything all right?'

'No, Greta. Forgive me for sharing more bad news with you, but it's Cheska. She's got pneumonia and is in intensive care in Geneva. I've just called the travel agent and I'm flying over immediately. I'm just going to pack.'

'Hold on a minute, David. You say Cheska is seriously ill?'

'From what the doctor said, yes. To be honest, I don't understand it. When I called a few days ago they said she had a touch of bronchitis. Now it seems she's deteriorated dramatically.'

Greta stared at him, then nodded. 'Sadly, it can happen, David. The same happened to her twin, Jonny. Remember?'

'Yes. Well, let's hope she pulls through.'

'I'll go.'

'What?'

'I'll go. Cheska is my daughter, after all. And I think you've done enough for her. And for me.'

'But you've been through a lot in the past few days, Greta, to say nothing of the fact that you've barely left your apartment for the past twenty-four years—'

'David, stop treating me like a child! I'm a grown woman. And it's not in spite of but *because* of the past few days that I'm going. You have plans with Tor and I have none. And, besides anything else, I *want* to. Despite everything Cheska is and has been, I love her. I love her—' Greta's voice broke, but she pulled herself together. 'And I just want to be with her. Okay?'

'If that's what you really want, I'll call the travel agent back and book the ticket in your name. You'd better go up and pack.'

'I will.'

An hour later Greta was ready to go. She went along the corridor to knock on Ava's bedroom door.

Ava was lying on her bed, reading a book. 'Hello,' she said. 'Simon's told me I'm not allowed to get up. I had a very restless night. This little one seems to have multiple arms and legs. Goodness, I'll be glad when it's born.'

Greta remembered how uncomfortable she'd been in

her last weeks of pregnancy, and a thought crossed her mind. 'You're very big, Ava, even for thirty-four weeks. The doctor hasn't mentioned twins, has she?'

'No, not so far, but to be fair, I haven't had a scan since I was twelve weeks and – and you mustn't tell Simon, or he'd kill me – I've missed my last couple of appointments. I just had too much on at the practice to make it in to Monmouth.'

'Well, you must go and have a check-up, darling. It's very important. The baby must come first.'

'I know.' Ava sighed. 'The problem is that we weren't exactly making plans to start a family so soon. Both of us are so busy with our careers just now.'

'Well, I can certainly sympathise with that. I was eighteen and horrified.'

'Really? Well, I'll let you into a secret, I was horrified, too! But it seemed so selfish, I didn't want to tell anyone. Thanks, Granny, you saying that actually makes me feel a lot better. Did you love your babies when they arrived?'

'I adored them.' Greta smiled: the wonderful memory was back within her grasp. 'Those first two years I now remember as some of the happiest of my life. Now, I don't know whether word has filtered through to you, but I'm flying to Geneva tonight. I'm afraid your mother is ill.'

Ava's face darkened. 'No, it hadn't. Is she very sick?'

'I won't know until I get there, but I think we should all face the fact that the doctor wouldn't have called and suggested that someone come if it wasn't critical.'

'I see. I'm not quite sure how I'll feel if she—'

'I'm sure, after what she put you through. Ava, now the past has started to come back, I just wanted to tell you how sorry I am about what happened to you. And that I haven't been there more for you as a grandmother.'

'You couldn't help it, Granny. Cheska is the one to blame, for almost killing you. You've had a horrible time ever since. I can't imagine what it must have been like to have your memory wiped away.'

'Dreadful,' Greta admitted. 'Anyway, I want you to know before I leave that I'm happy to do anything I can to help once the baby arrives. Just give me a call and I'll be there.'

'Thank you, that's so sweet of you.'

'Now, I have to go. Take care of both of you, won't you?' Greta leant over to kiss her granddaughter.

'And you. Send my love to Cheska,' Ava added as Greta left the room.

'Well then, I'd better be off.' Greta stood by the front door, about to get into the taxi that would take her to Heathrow. She hugged David, Tor, Simon and Mary goodbye and thanked them all for having her. 'I'll call as soon as I'm there.'

David carried Greta's bag to the car for her, and took her hand as she opened the passenger door. 'Are you sure you don't want me to come with you?' he asked.

'Positive.' She reached up and kissed him on the cheek. Instinctively, he put his arms around her.

'What a journey we've been on, Greta,' he whispered. 'Please take care of yourself. I'm so proud of you.'

'Thanks, and I will. Bye.'

Greta climbed into the taxi before David could see the tears that had appeared in her eyes.

*

The first thing Greta noticed when she walked into the hospital was the smell. It didn't matter what country the hospital was in, how expensive and upmarket it was, it was always the same, and always reminded her of her own long stay after her accident. She introduced herself at reception, and was taken up in a lift by a woman in a smart suit and handed over to the night sister in ICU.

'How is she?' Greta asked. The dreadful hush, broken only by the sound of machines, was something she also remembered vividly.

'I'm afraid she's in a critical condition. Her lungs have filled with fluid from the pneumonia and, even though we have done all we can to remedy it, so far the treatment has not been effective. I'm sorry,' she said in her brisk Swiss accent. 'I wish I could give you better news. Here she is.'

All kinds of machinery surrounded the frail figure in the bed. Cheska had on an oxygen mask, which seemed far too big for her delicately sculpted, heart-shaped face. Greta wondered if it was her imagination, but her daughter seemed to have shrunk. Her tiny wrist bones were painfully visible through her thin white skin.

'The doctor is checking on her every fifteen minutes. He'll be in soon.'

'Thank you.'

The nurse left, and Greta watched her daughter for a while. She seemed to be sleeping peacefully.

'My precious little girl, how can I ever tell you how much I've loved you? You must know that none of it was your fault. I should have seen, I should have known,' she whispered. 'I'm sorry, I'm so, so sorry . . .'

She reached out a hand and stroked Cheska's cheek. She

looked as innocent and vulnerable as she had when she was a small child. 'You were such a good baby, never gave me a moment's trouble, you know. I adored you. You were so very beautiful. And you still are.'

Cheska didn't stir, so Greta continued.

'The thing is, Cheska, I've remembered now. I've remembered everything that happened and how many mistakes I made. I didn't put you first, you see. I thought then that money and fame were more important, and I pushed you, because I didn't understand what it was doing to you. I didn't see that you were suffering . . . please forgive me. For everything I got wrong.'

Cheska shuddered suddenly and then coughed – a deep, viscous noise which Greta remembered so well from those final agonising days with Jonny.

'My darling, I can't bear it if you leave me now, because I really think it's the first time I'm able to be the mother you've always needed. You've lost so much. First Jonny, your beloved twin. I remember you used to follow him everywhere. And then your father . . .'

'Jonny . . .'

A strange, guttural sound came from inside the oxygen mask and Greta saw Cheska's eyes were wide open.

'Yes, darling, Jonny. He was your brother and—'

Cheska was moving her arm weakly up to her face. She tapped the oxygen mask and shook her head.

'Darling, I don't think I can remove it. The doctors said—'

Cheska struggled to pull it off.

'Let me do it.' Greta leant over her and pulled it away from Cheska's mouth. 'What is it you wanted to say?'

'Jonny, my brother. He loved me?' she rasped, panting with the effort.

'Yes, he absolutely adored you.'

'He's waiting for me. He'll be there.' Cheska's breathing became even more laboured and Greta put the oxygen mask back into place.

'Yes, he is, but please remember that I love you and need you too—'

The doctor came in then, and checked on Cheska. She seemed to have drifted back to sleep.

'Can I have a word, Mrs Hammond?'

'It's Mrs Marchmont, actually, but of course.'

The doctor indicated she should leave the room.

'Goodbye, my darling little girl,' she said. She stood up, kissed Cheska on the forehead and left the room.

'Goodbye, Mummy,' came a whisper from behind the mask. 'I love you.'

# 56

It was Mary who answered the telephone when it rang at lunchtime on New Year's Eve.

'Hello?'

'Mary, it's Greta. Cheska died at three o'clock this morning.'

'Oh, I'm so, so sorry.'

There was silence for quite a while.

'Is David there?' Greta said eventually.

'I'm afraid he and Tor left earlier this morning for his apartment in Italy. I'm sure you can contact him there. Shall I give you his number?'

'No. Let him have his holiday. Is Ava around?'

'She's resting. Simon's downstairs somewhere, though.'

'Could I speak to him, please?'

Mary went to find Simon. He listened to what Greta had to say and agreed that he would tell Ava gently when she woke up.

'I'm sorry, Greta. Really.' He put the phone down and sighed.

'End of an era, isn't it?' said Mary.

'Yes. But there's a new one coming very soon, and we must all try not to forget that.'

Mary watched him as he walked off, his hands deep in his pockets, and knew he was right.

David and Tor were watching the magnificent New Year fireworks light up the harbour in Santa Margherita.

'Happy New Year, darling,' David said, hugging Tor to him.

'Happy New Year, David.' After a few seconds she pulled away from him and went to sit down on the tiny balcony.

'What is it, Tor?' David frowned. 'Something's wrong. You've been a bit distant ever since we arrived here. Tell me,' he said, sitting down opposite her.

'Really, David, I—' Tor rubbed her forehead. 'This isn't the moment.'

'If it's bad news, it's never the moment. So please, just tell me.'

'Well . . . it's about us.' She took a gulp of champagne. 'We've been together almost six years now.'

'Yes, we have. And I'm finally going to make an honest woman of you.'

'And I was truly honoured and happy that you asked me . . . at first. I love you, David, very much. I hope you know that.'

'Of course I do.' David was puzzled. Tor would never usually instigate a conversation like this. 'But what do you mean, "initially"?'

'Over Christmas, I realised something, even after you asked me to marry you.'

'Tell me.'

'Well, the thing is, I know you tell me you love me, and in one way I believe you, but the truth is, David, I think you're in love with somebody else. And that you always have been.'

'With whom?'

'Darling, don't patronise either yourself or me. Greta, of course.'

'Greta?'

'Yes, Greta. And, more to the point, I know she loves you, too.'

'Oh for goodness' sake! How much champagne have you had, Tor?' David chuckled. 'Greta has never loved me. I told you I asked her to marry me once and she refused.'

'Yes, but that was then and this is now. I'm telling you, David, she loves you. Trust me. I saw it over Christmas. I saw the two of you together.'

'Really, Tor, I think you're exaggerating.'

'I'm not. Your whole family can see it, not just me. And if two people love each other, then the obvious thing is for them to be together. David' – Tor reached out her hand and squeezed his – 'I really think you should admit it to yourself: there's only ever been one woman for you. I'm not trying to make you feel guilty, but I think we should both face up to it. We've had a fantastic six years together, not a moment of which I regret, but I think it's run its course. And Christmas showed me that very clearly. Frankly, I don't want to be second best and I'm afraid that's how I feel.'

'Tor, please, you're wrong! I—'

'David, we'd already decided that, even after we marry,

nothing will change, at least for a while. I have my life in Oxford and you have yours in London and at Marchmont. We've kept each other company and it's been wonderful. And I'm terribly fond of you, but—'

'Are you saying you're leaving me?'

'Oh David, please don't be so dramatic. No, I'm not leaving you. I hope we'll always be friends. And if either you or Greta ever plucks up the courage to admit your feelings to each other, I really hope I'm invited to the wedding.' Tor slid the engagement ring from her finger and handed it to him. 'Right, I've said it. Now, let's go into town and celebrate the New Year.'

Greta arrived back at Heathrow on a miserable grey day in early January. She had decided not to hold a formal funeral for Cheska. It would have meant asking the family to come to Geneva, and there was also the possibility that the media would get wind of it. Instead, in her suitcase, she carried Cheska's ashes, which she would take to Marchmont and bury beside Jonny's grave when she next returned.

Her apartment was freezing cold, as it had been empty for almost two weeks. After switching on the water and the central heating, Greta made a cup of tea and went to sit on the sofa, warming her hands on the mug. She wasn't sure when David was back from Italy, and had told everyone at Marchmont to wait until he had returned before telling him the news.

The clock ticked. And she heard the dull thud of pipes filling with water.

Apart from that, silence.

Greta sipped the tea and it burnt her tongue. She

thought how much had changed since she had left for Marchmont two weeks ago. Before, she had been empty, devoid of feeling. And now she felt so full of emotion she wondered how she would contain it.

She'd been desperate to speak to David after Cheska's death, knowing he'd be the only one who would understand how devastated she felt. She'd lost both her babies now, and even if it was perhaps the best thing for her poor, tormented daughter to be released from her tortured mind, the loss of the beautiful child she'd once adored so soon after her memories had returned ate into her.

But Greta was determined that the one thing she mustn't do any longer was rely on David. It was only since she'd regained her past that she could truly see what he had done for her and been to her over the years. Now, even if she had never needed him more, she had to let him go.

The following week passed achingly slowly. To while away a bit of time over the bleak post-Christmas period, Greta wrote a letter to David, thanking him profusely for all his help over the years and explaining that Cheska had died peacefully. She also wrote to Ava, wanting to explain to her, too, that her mother hadn't suffered at the end and that she'd sent her love to her.

'I have never been of much use to you but, as I said to you before I left Marchmont, if you need me when the baby is born, I'd be very happy to help in any way I can,' she wrote.

David rang immediately after reading his letter, asking her how she was and telling her she had been right: Ava was having twins. It took Greta every bit of strength she had to tell him that she was doing well, and yes, she'd taken his advice and was forging a new and busy life for herself. He asked her out to lunch at the Savoy in a couple of days' time, but she declined, saying she'd already made plans for a holiday but would be back by the second week in February and could see him then. Ava wrote back, complaining that she'd been confined to the house by the doctor and that she hoped Greta would visit after the birth.

Greta scrubbed the apartment until it shone, baked cakes that no one was going to eat and signed up for yoga and art classes at the local adult education centre. She set to knitting matinee jackets, bootees and hats, just as she had done all those years ago for her own babies and to pass the time at Marchmont. She also crocheted two shawls, and posted everything off in a big box to Ava.

She could do this, she kept telling herself. It would just take time.

January finally became February, and the news came from Simon that she was a great-grandmother. Ava had given birth to a boy, Jonathan, and a girl, Laura.

'Can you please tell her how delighted I am, Simon? And, of course, anything I can do, I'd be happy to help. I know how exhausting it can be with two,' she said. Then she replaced the receiver and wept with joy – and equally with grief that Cheska couldn't be there to see her grandchildren.

A few days later, as she settled down in front of a soap opera, her supper on her knee, the telephone rang.

'Granny?'

'Yes. Hello, Ava, how are you? Congratulations, darling!'

'Thanks. I think you know how I am, because you've been through it. Sleepless, exhilarated and feeling like a milk machine.' Ava sighed. 'But happier than I've ever been in my life.'

'I'm so glad, darling. As you know, I loved having my little babies.'

'So Mary said. She told me you were a wonderful mother.'

'Did she?'

'Yes. By the way, thank you for the gorgeous shawls, and everything else. You've no idea how useful they all are. It's freezing here, and both Laura and Jonathan seem to vomit over everything. You're so clever. I wish I could knit like that.'

Greta smiled. 'I can teach you one day if you want, just like LJ once taught me. It's easy.'

'Well, that's the thing . . . To be honest, I'm really struggling at the moment and it will be even harder when I go back to work, which is what I want to do in a couple of months or so. I was just wondering, Granny, how do you feel about coming here for a bit and helping me? I know David says you just got back from a holiday and are quite busy in London, so please say if you can't. It's just that I really don't want to employ a stranger so I thought I'd ask you. I really am desperate just now,' she added, with a catch in her voice that smacked of the bone-aching exhaustion Greta remembered all too well.

'Of course. I'd be delighted to come and help you, darling. When would you like me?'

'As soon as possible. Simon's up to his eyes in the barn producing an album and, even though Mary's doing her best, she has so much to do in the house and I don't want to put upon her.'

'Why don't I come up at the weekend? That'll give me a chance to sort out a few bits and pieces here.'

'That would be wonderful. Thank you so much, Granny. Let me know what time your train arrives in Abergavenny and I'll send someone to come and get you.'

Greta put down the telephone and gave a small whoop of joy.

The following day, Greta went to the hairdresser in preparation for having lunch with David. She'd spend the rest of the afternoon and evening packing. At least now, she felt she could cope with seeing David and hearing about Tor. For a change, she had plans too.

They met at their usual table in the Grill Room and Greta immediately saw that David had lost weight.

'Have you been on a diet?' she asked.

'No, I think it's genetic. As old age approaches, some people put it on and some lose it. You're looking extremely well, Greta, I must say. Champagne?'

'Yes, why not? Isn't it wonderful news about Ava?'

'Absolutely. Have you seen the twins yet?'

'No, but I'm going up to Marchmont tomorrow to help out. Ava sounds exhausted.'

'I'm amazed you can find the time in your busy new life.' David smiled.

'Well, she is my granddaughter, and she needs me. How have you been?'

'Oh, all right. I've been working on my book and contemplating my retirement.'

'How's Tor?' she asked lightly.

'Fine, as far as I know. We haven't seen each other for a while.'

'Is she busy in Oxford?'

'I presume so. Actually, Greta, we're no longer together.'

'Really? Why?'

'It was Tor's decision. She said the relationship wasn't going anywhere and, to be honest, she was probably right.'

'I'm astonished,' Greta said, as the champagne arrived. 'I was expecting to hear all about your wedding plans.'

'Well, better that it happened now, before we tied the knot. Anyway' – he clinked his glass on hers – 'here's to the new arrivals . . . And to you, Greta. I'm really proud of you.'

'Are you? That's sweet of you, David.'

'Yes. You've been through so much, especially since Christmas, and by the looks of things you've handled it terrifically.'

'I wouldn't say that. There have been times when I've seriously wondered what it's all about, but one has to do one's best and just get on with it, doesn't one?'

'Yes, that's true. And I'll admit that I've been very low since Cheska's death, especially coming so soon after my mother's.'

'It's a bit like running a marathon, isn't it? It's only when you reach the finish line that you have time to collapse. Perhaps that's what's happening to you, David.'

'Maybe.' He shrugged, unconvinced. 'And I doubt writing my autobiography has helped. It means I spend the whole of my time having to think about the past.'

'Am I in it?' Greta teased.

'As I promised you, I've left you, Cheska and Ava out of it. Which mean it's pretty thin. You've all been such a big part of my life. Anyway, shall we order?'

Greta ate her lunch hungrily whilst David only picked at his.

'Are you sure you're all right, David?' Greta frowned. 'You really don't seem yourself. It's probably because of Tor. You must miss her terribly.'

'No, it's not that.' David concentrated on folding his napkin into a small triangle.

'Then what is it?'

'It's what she said when she told me she thought it best to end our relationship.'

'And what was that?'

'I—'

'Spit it out, David. Nothing you could say will shock me. I've known you for far too long.'

'The thing is' – he paused for a second – 'she said that it was pointless us continuing because I'd always been in love with someone else.'

'Really? And who is that?'

David rolled his eyes. 'You, of course.'

'*Me?* Why on earth would she think that?'

'Because it's true. And she was right.'

'Well, I was wrong when I said that nothing you could say to me would shock me,' Greta said quietly after a long pause.

'Well, you did ask. Anyway, there we are. I told her that you've never felt the same about me—'

'David! Of course I feel the same about you! I've felt it for years and years. In fact, on that dreadful day when

Cheska almost certainly pushed me off the pavement after I'd told her that Bobby Cross was married, I was going to tell you! And then, of course, I couldn't remember anything at all, so I simply fell in love with you all over again.'

'Are you serious?' David looked at her with such a terrified expression that Greta wanted to chuckle.

'No, I'm joking! Of course I'm serious, you silly old thing. I've stayed away from you for the past two months because I didn't want to be a burden to you any longer.'

'I thought it was because, now you'd remembered everything, you didn't need me any more.'

'As we both know all too well, I've always needed you. I love you, David.'

He saw the happiness on her face and, as what she'd said began to sink in, he grinned back.

'Well then,' he said.

'Well then.'

'Here we are.'

'Yes, here we are.'

'Better late than never, I suppose. It's only taken forty years for this moment to happen. Worth waiting for, though.'

'Yes. And, David, it's me who's been so stupid. I didn't see what was right under my nose.'

'People often don't.'

'Oh Taffy,' she said, suddenly reverting to his pet name, 'if only I had, how different things would have been.'

'Well, we do have the rest of our lives ahead of us, don't we?'

'Yes.' For the first time in years, Greta felt she did.

'And how about we begin it by me driving you up to

Marchmont tomorrow? We can greet the new arrivals together.'

David put out his hand to her across the table and she took it.

'Yes.' She smiled. 'That would be a perfect beginning.'

# Acknowledgements

Claudia Negele at Goldmann Verlag, Jez Trevathan and Catherine Richards at Pan Macmillan, Knut Gørvell, Jorid Mathiassen and Pip Hallén at Cappelen Damm, Donatella Minuto and Annalisa Lottini at Giunti Editore, and Nana Vaz de Castro and Fernando Mercante at Editora Arqueiro.

'Team Lulu' – my band of 'sisters' – Olivia Riley, Susan Moss, Ella Micheler, Jacquelyn Heslop, my lovely 'blood' sister Georgia Edmonds, to whom this book is dedicated, and my mother, Janet.

Special thanks to Samantha and Robert Gurney for allowing me to use their fabulous house and their two beautiful daughters, Amelia and Tabitha, in my film.

Stephen, my husband and agent, and my 'fantastic four': Harry, Isabella, Leonora and Kit.

And to my wonderful readers around the world – without your support, this book would never have had a second chance.

# Author's Note

It was Christmas 2013 when I was asked if I would like to republish *Not Quite an Angel*, which was first published in 1995 under my old pen name, Lucinda Edmonds.

I had enjoyed revisiting *The Italian Girl* (previously *Aria*) the year before, and amidst our family's yule-tide celebrations, a picture began to form in my mind of a snowy Welsh landscape and a beautiful house with an enormous Christmas tree standing in the front hall . . .

I dusted off my one dog-eared copy of the book, read it for the first time in eighteen years, and was pleasantly surprised by what a compelling tale it was. However, my writing style has evolved over the years and I knew I could make it even better (I understand now why some novels are several years in the writing – sometimes it's only distance that truly gives an author perspective on a manuscript). So I set to work, little knowing what I was letting myself in for, and became so engrossed that I ended up writing a virtually completely new novel – *The Angel Tree*.

While many elements of the original remain, key characters have had their roles and dialogue rewritten, settings have been enhanced, and several chapters and plotlines are entirely new. I even resurrected one character I'd always regretted killing off in the original novel. I feel privileged to have had the opportunity to breathe new life into this story. I hope that you enjoy it.

Lucinda Riley, 2015

OUT NOW

# The Seven Sisters

A MAJOR NEW SERIES FROM LUCINDA RILEY

***Maia's Story***

Maia D'Aplièse and her five sisters gather together at their childhood home, 'Atlantis' – a fabulous, secluded castle situated on the shores of Lake Geneva – having been told that their beloved father, the elusive billionaire they call Pa Salt, has died. Maia and her sisters were all adopted by him as babies and, discovering he has already been buried at sea, each of them is handed a tantalising clue to their true heritage – a clue that takes Maia across the world to a crumbling mansion in Rio de Janeiro in Brazil. Once there, she begins to put together the pieces of where her story began . . .

Eighty years earlier, in the Belle Epoque of Rio, 1927, Izabela Bonifacio's father has aspirations for his daughter to marry into aristocracy. Meanwhile, architect Heitor da Silva Costa is working on a statue, to be called Christ the Redeemer, and will soon travel to Paris to find the right sculptor to complete his vision. Izabela – passionate and longing to see the world – convinces her father to allow her to accompany him and his family to Europe before she is married. There, at Paul Landowski's studio and in the heady, vibrant cafés of Montparnasse, she meets ambitious young sculptor Laurent Brouilly, and knows at once that her life will never be the same again.

In this sweeping, epic tale of love and loss – the first in a unique series of seven books, based on the legends of the Seven Sisters star constellation – Lucinda Riley showcases her storytelling talent like never before.

*Turn the page to read the first spellbinding chapter now.*

# 1

I will always remember exactly where I was and what I was doing when I heard that my father had died.

I was sitting in the pretty garden of my old schoolfriend's townhouse in London, a copy of *The Penelopiad* open but unread in my lap, enjoying the June sun while Jenny collected her little boy from nursery.

I felt calm and appreciated what a good idea it had been to get away. I was studying the burgeoning clematis, encouraged by its sunny midwife to give birth to a riot of colour, when my mobile phone rang. I glanced at the screen and saw it was Marina.

'Hello, Ma, how are you?' I said, hoping she could hear the warmth in my voice too.

'Maia, I . . .'

Marina paused, and in that instant I knew something was dreadfully wrong. 'What is it?'

'Maia, there's no easy way to tell you this, but your father had a heart attack here at home yesterday afternoon, and in the early hours of this morning, he . . . passed away.'

I remained silent, as a million different and ridiculous thoughts raced through my mind. The first one being that

Marina, for some unknown reason, had decided to play some form of tasteless joke on me.

'You're the first of the sisters I've told, Maia, as you're the eldest. And I wanted to ask you whether you would prefer to tell the rest of your sisters yourself, or leave it to me.'

'I . . .'

Still no words would form coherently on my lips, as I began to realise that Marina, dear, beloved Marina, the woman who had been the closest thing to a mother I'd ever known, would never tell me this if it *wasn't* true. So it had to be. And at that moment, my entire world shifted on its axis.

'Maia, please, tell me you're all right. This really is the most dreadful call I've ever had to make, but what else could I do? God only knows how the other girls are going to take it.'

It was then that I heard the suffering in *her* voice and understood she'd needed to tell me as much for her own sake as mine. So I switched into my normal comfort zone, which was to comfort others.

'Of course I'll tell my sisters if you'd prefer, Ma, although I'm not positive where they all are. Isn't Ally away training for a regatta?'

And as we continued to discuss where each of my younger sisters was, as though we needed to get them together for a birthday party rather than to mourn the death of our father, the entire conversation took on a sense of the surreal.

'When should we plan on having the funeral, do you think? What with Electra being in Los Angeles and Ally somewhere on the high seas, surely we can't think about it until next week at the earliest?' I said.

'Well . . .' I heard the hesitation in Marina's voice. 'Perhaps the best thing is for you and I to discuss it when you arrive back home. There really is no rush now, Maia, so if you'd prefer to continue the last couple of days of your holiday in London, that would be fine. There's nothing more to be done for him here . . .' Her voice trailed off miserably.

'Ma, of *course* I'll be on the next flight to Geneva I can get! I'll call the airline immediately, and then I'll do my best to get in touch with everyone.'

'I'm so terribly sorry, *chérie*,' Marina said sadly. 'I know how you adored him.'

'Yes,' I said, the strange calm that I had felt while we discussed arrangements suddenly deserting me like the stillness before a violent thunderstorm. 'I'll call you later, when I know what time I'll be arriving.'

'Please take care of yourself, Maia. You've had a terrible shock.'

I pressed the button to end the call, and before the storm clouds in my heart opened up and drowned me, I went upstairs to my bedroom to retrieve my flight documents and contact the airline. As I waited in the calling queue, I glanced at the bed where I'd woken up this morning to Simply Another Day. And I thanked God that human beings don't have the power to see into the future.

The officious woman who eventually answered wasn't helpful and I knew, as she spoke of full flights, financial penalties and credit card details, that my emotional dam was ready to burst. Finally, once I'd grudgingly been granted a seat on the four o'clock flight to Geneva, which would mean throwing everything into my holdall immediately and taking a taxi to Heathrow, I sat down on the bed and stared for so long at the sprigged wallpaper that the pattern began to dance in front of my eyes.

'He's gone,' I whispered, 'gone forever. I'll never see him again.'

Expecting the spoken words to provoke a raging torrent of tears, I was surprised that nothing actually happened. Instead, I sat there numbly, my head still full of practicalities. The thought of telling my sisters – all five of them – was horrendous, and I searched through my emotional filing system for the one I would call first. Inevitably, it was Tiggy, the second youngest of the six of us girls and the sibling to whom I'd always felt closest.

With trembling fingers, I scrolled down to find her number and dialled it. When her voicemail answered, I didn't know what to say, other than a few garbled words asking her to call me back urgently. She was currently somewhere in the Scottish Highlands working at a centre for orphaned and sick wild deer.

As for the other sisters . . . I knew their reactions would vary, outwardly at least, from indifference to a dramatic outpouring of emotion.

Given that I wasn't currently sure quite which way *I* would go on the scale of grief when I did speak to any of them, I decided to take the coward's way out and texted them all, asking them to call me as soon as they could. Then I hurriedly packed my holdall and walked down the narrow stairs to the kitchen to write a note for Jenny explaining why I'd had to leave in such a hurry.

Deciding to take my chances hailing a black cab on the London streets, I left the house, walking briskly around the leafy Chelsea crescent just as any normal person would do on any normal day. I believe I actually said hello to someone walking a dog when I passed him in the street and managed a smile.

No one would know what had just happened to me, I thought, as I managed to find a taxi on the busy King's Road and climbed inside, directing the driver to Heathrow.

No one would know.

Five hours later, just as the sun was making its leisurely descent over Lake Geneva, I arrived at our private pontoon on the shore, from where I would make the last leg of my journey home.

Christian was already waiting for me in our sleek Riva motor launch. And from the look on his face, I could see he'd heard the news.

'How are you, Mademoiselle Maia?' he asked, sympathy in his blue eyes as he helped me aboard.

'I'm . . . glad I'm here,' I answered neutrally as I walked to the back of the boat and sat down on the cushioned cream leather bench that curved around the stern. Usually, I would sit with Christian in the passenger seat at the front as we sped across the calm waters on the twenty-minute journey home. But today, I felt a need for privacy. As Christian started the powerful engine, the sun glinted off the windows of the fabulous houses that lined Lake Geneva's shores. I'd often felt when I made this journey that it was the entrance to an ethereal world disconnected from reality.

The world of Pa Salt.

I noticed the first vague evidence of tears pricking at my

eyes as I thought of my father's pet name, which I'd coined when I was young. He'd always loved sailing and often when he returned to me at our lakeside home, he had smelt of fresh air and of the sea. Somehow, the name had stuck, and as my younger siblings had joined me, they'd called him that too.

As the launch picked up speed, the warm wind streaming through my hair, I thought of the hundreds of previous journeys I'd made to Atlantis, Pa Salt's fairy-tale castle. Inaccessible by land, due to its position on a private promontory with a crescent of mountainous terrain rising up steeply behind it, the only method of reaching it was by boat. The nearest neighbours were miles away along the lake, so Atlantis was our own private kingdom, set apart from the rest of the world. Everything it contained was magical . . . as if Pa Salt and we – his daughters – had lived there under an enchantment.

Each one of us had been chosen by Pa Salt as a baby, adopted from the four corners of the globe and brought home to live under his protection. And each one of us, as Pa always liked to say, was special, different . . . we were *his* girls. He'd named us all after The Seven Sisters, his favourite star cluster. Maia being the first and eldest.

When I was young, he'd take me up to his glass-domed observatory perched on top of the house, lift me up with his big, strong hands and have me look through his telescope at the night sky.

'There it is,' he'd say as he aligned the lens. 'Look, Maia, that's the beautiful shining star you're named after.'

And I *would* see. As he explained the legends that were the source of my own and my sisters' names, I'd hardly listen, but simply enjoy his arms tight around me, fully aware of this rare, special moment when I had him all to myself.

I'd realised eventually that Marina, who I'd presumed as I grew up was my mother – I'd even shortened her name to 'Ma' – was a glorified nursemaid, employed by Pa to take care of me because he was away such a lot. But of course, Marina was so much more than that to all of us girls. She was the one who had wiped our tears, berated us for sloppy table manners and steered us calmly through the difficult transition from childhood to womanhood.

She had always been there, and I could not have loved Ma any more if she had given birth to me.

During the first three years of my childhood, Marina and I had lived alone together in our magical castle on the shores of Lake Geneva as Pa Salt travelled the seven seas to conduct his business. And then, one by one, my sisters began to arrive.

Usually, Pa would bring me a present when he returned home. I'd hear the motor launch arriving, run across the sweeping lawns and through the trees to the jetty to greet him. Like any child, I'd want to see what he had hidden inside his magical pockets to delight me. On one particular occasion, however, after he'd presented me with an exquisitely carved wooden reindeer, which he assured me came from St Nicholas's workshop at the North Pole itself, a uniformed woman had stepped out from behind him, and in her arms was a bundle wrapped in a shawl. And the bundle was moving.

'This time, Maia, I've brought you back the most special gift. You have a new sister.' He'd smiled at me as he lifted me into his arms. 'Now you'll no longer be lonely when I have to go away.'

After that, life had changed. The maternity nurse that Pa had brought with him disappeared after a few weeks and Marina took over the care of my baby sister. I couldn't understand how the red, squalling thing which often smelt and diverted attention from me could possibly be a gift. Until one morning, when Alcyone – named after the second star of The Seven Sisters – smiled at me from her high chair over breakfast.

'She knows who I am,' I said in wonder to Marina, who was feeding her.

'Of course she does, Maia, dear. You're her big sister, the one she'll look up to. It'll be up to you to teach her lots of things that you know and she doesn't.'

And as she grew, she became my shadow, following me everywhere, which pleased and irritated me in equal measure.

'Maia, wait me!' she'd demand loudly as she tottered along behind me.

Even though Ally – as I'd nicknamed her – had originally been an unwanted addition to my dreamlike existence at Atlantis, I could not have asked for a sweeter, more loveable companion. She rarely, if ever, cried and there were none of the temper-tantrums associated with toddlers of her age. With her tumbling red-gold curls and her big blue eyes, Ally had a natural charm that drew people to her, including our father. On the occasions Pa Salt was home from one of his long trips abroad, I'd watch how his eyes lit up when he saw her, in a way I was sure they didn't for me. And whereas I was shy and reticent with strangers, Ally had an openness and a readiness to trust that endeared her to everyone.

She was also one of those children who seemed to excel at everything – particularly music, and any sport to do with water. I remember Pa teaching her to swim in our vast pool and, whereas I had struggled to stay afloat and hated being underwater, my little sister took to it like a mermaid. And while I couldn't find my sea legs even on the *Titan*, Pa's huge and beautiful ocean-going yacht, when we were at home Ally would beg him to take her out in the small Laser he kept moored on our private lakeside jetty. I'd crouch in the cramped stern of the boat while Pa and Ally took control as we sped across the glassy waters. Their joint passion for sailing bonded them in a way I felt I could never replicate.

Although Ally had studied music at the Conservatoire de Musique de Genève and was a highly talented flautist who could have pursued a career with a professional orchestra, since leaving music school she had chosen the life of a full-time sailor. She now competed regularly in regattas, and had represented Switzerland on a number of occasions.

When Ally was almost three, Pa arrived home with our next sibling, whom he named Asterope, after the third of The Seven Sisters.

'But we will call her Star,' Pa had said, smiling at Marina, Ally and me as we studied the newest addition to the family lying in the bassinet.

By now I was attending lessons every morning with a private tutor, so my newest sister's arrival affected me less than Ally's had. Then, only six months later, another baby joined us, a twelve-week-old girl named Celaeno, whose name Ally immediately shortened to CeCe.

There was only three months' age difference between Star and CeCe, and from as far back as I can remember, the two of them forged a close bond. They were akin to twins, talking in their own private baby language, some of which the two of them still used to communicate to this day. They inhabited their own private world, to the exclusion of us other sisters. And even now in their twenties, nothing had changed. CeCe, the younger of the two, was always the boss, her stocky body and nut-brown skin in direct contrast to the pale, whippet-thin Star.

The following year, another baby arrived – Taygete, whom I nicknamed 'Tiggy' because her short dark hair sprouted out at strange angles on her tiny head and reminded me of the hedgehog in Beatrix Potter's famous story.

I was by now seven years old, and I'd bonded with Tiggy from the first moment I set eyes on her. She was the most delicate of us all, suffering one childhood illness after another, but even as an infant, she was stoic and undemanding. When yet another baby girl, named Electra, was brought home by Pa a few months later, an exhausted Marina would often ask me if I would mind sitting with Tiggy, who continually had a fever or croup. Eventually diagnosed as asthmatic, she rarely left the nursery to be wheeled outside in the pram, in case the cold air and heavy fog of a Geneva winter affected her chest.

Electra was the youngest of my siblings and her name suited her perfectly. By now, I was used to little babies and their demands, but my youngest sister was without doubt the most challenging of them all. Everything about her *was* electric; her innate ability to switch in an instant from dark to light and vice versa meant that our previously calm home rang daily with high-pitched screams. Her temper-tantrums resonated through my childhood consciousness and as she grew older, her fiery personality did not mellow.

Privately, Ally, Tiggy and I had our own nickname for her; she was known among the three of us as 'Tricky'. We all walked on eggshells around her, wishing to do nothing to set off a lightning change of mood. I can honestly say there were moments when I loathed her for the disruption she brought to Atlantis.

And yet, when Electra knew one of us was in trouble, she was the first to offer help and support. Just as she was capable of huge selfishness, her generosity on other occasions was equally pronounced.

After Electra, the entire household was expecting the arrival of the Seventh Sister. After all, we'd been named after Pa Salt's favourite star cluster and we wouldn't be complete without her. We even knew her name – Merope – and wondered who she would be. But a year went past, and then another, and another, and no more babies arrived home with our father.

I remember vividly standing with him once in his observatory. I was fourteen years old and just on the brink of womanhood. We were waiting for an eclipse, which he'd told me was a seminal moment for humankind and usually brought change with it.

'Pa,' I said, 'will you ever bring home our seventh sister?'

At this, his strong, protective bulk had seemed to freeze for a few seconds. He'd looked suddenly as though he carried the weight of the world on his shoulders. Although he didn't turn around, for he was still concentrating on training the telescope on the coming eclipse, I knew instinctively that what I'd said had distressed him.

'No, Maia, I won't. Because I have never found her.'

As the familiar thick hedge of spruce trees, which shielded our waterside home from prying eyes, came into view, I saw Marina standing on the jetty and the dreadful truth of losing Pa finally began to sink in.

And I realised that the man who had created the kingdom in which we had all been his princesses was no longer present to hold the enchantment in place.

*The Seven Sisters*

is out now

THE STORY WILL CONTINUE IN

*The Storm Sister*

Out Now

## *A personal message from Lucinda*

I hope you enjoyed *The Angel Tree*. I would like to tell you about Olivia, the youngest child of my oldest friends, Kate and Jeremy Pickering. Olivia has Angelman Syndrome, a rare genetic condition and chromosome disorder, which causes severe learning difficulties. She is now eighteen, with a lovely smiling demeanour, but requires full-time care for the rest of her life. And she, like all sufferers, will have a normal life expectancy.

If you would like to find out more about this often misdiagnosed condition, and donate to the charity Assert – which is run entirely by volunteers, all of whom are parents of children with Angelman Syndrome – please go to their website:

Assert

www.angelmanuk.org